PERFECTLY TOXIC

BY
KRISTINE MASON

Print Edition

ISBN 10: 0986161721
ISBN 13: 978-0-9861617-2-8

Dedication

For Stanley.

Acknowledgements

I'd like to begin by acknowledging my husband and kids. I know I give them credit in each book, but if they aren't supportive, I don't get to play with my characters. I especially want to thank my husband for taking a tremendous amount of stress off my shoulders as I wrote this book. I love knowing you have my back. And, Jack, my oldest boy…thanks for helping me come up with a few key ideas for this story. I doubt I'll ever let you read it—not even when you're an adult—but I appreciate the help! Jamie Denton…what can I say that hasn't been said before? You're fabulous, darling! Thank you Tessa Shapcott for your editing skills, Elle Rossi, from EJR Digital Art for working with me on my covers, and Sherry Fundin for proofreading Perfectly Toxic. Finally, I'd like to acknowledge/admit one last thing…my name is Kristine Mason and I have imaginary friends—be glad they aren't real.

PART I

"You know, a long time ago being crazy
meant something. Nowadays
everybody's crazy.
—*Charles Manson*

Welcome to the House of Archer

The House of Archer, Bower, Georgia
Monday, 5:26 p.m. Eastern Daylight Saving Time

"I THINK I broke her."

Fear sickened Rodney Archer as he stared at the small bundle swaddled in the white afghan Gramma had crocheted. No movement. No sound. He looked to the baby's mother who sat on the wooden porch step. "What did you do?" He took a jerky step away from his car and approached her.

Adeline lifted her shoulders and shook her head. Her mess of long dark curls hid her face, her eyes. He needed to look into her eyes, to know if whatever she'd done had been an accident or if Adeline had...slipped again.

The screen door behind Adeline groaned. He glanced up, and met Gramma's gaze. The old woman stepped onto the weathered porch. "I think we should bury her in the family plot. No reason to call anyone about this." She sniffed and glared at the back of Adeline's head. "Lord knows we don't need a minister. After all, how would we explain...this?"

"Shut up, old woman." Adeline let the bundle dangle over her knees. "I don't need to hear your senile nonsense right now."

Rodney rushed to the porch and took the baby from Adeline. "Gramma's right. We'll bury her in the plot. No marking."

Adeline stared up at him, squinting against the late afternoon sun. "You're a doctor. Maybe you can fix her," she said, her tone holding no apology, no remorse. "You can fix anything."

His throat tightened. Rigor mortis had already set in, meaning the child had been dead for at least two to six hours. Sadness and rage settled on his filthy soul. The baby had been doomed from conception. She'd been created by the wicked, born of the depraved and had never had a chance. Even if she had survived, the child would never have left the House of Archer. No one but him, Adeline and Gramma knew of her existence. No one could ever know…especially now. Adeline's sickness was misunderstood. It scared those who looked at anything abnormal as bad, frightening.

Lately, Adeline frightened him. She hadn't been able to take her medication during the pregnancy. During the three weeks since the baby's birth, she'd gone back to the pills—or so she'd said. If she was still taking her pills, he suspected that she needed a stronger dose to combat the high level of extra hormones running through her body. Whatever she needed would have to happen fast before she did something that would send her to prison.

Adeline stood, brushed the dust from the back of her pale-pink cotton nightgown, then poked at the bundle. "Well, aren't you going to even look at her and see if I really did break her?" The corner of her mouth turned up in the tiniest smile. Her green eyes glittered with challenge and—damn her—amusement.

"I checked the baby," Gramma said, her voice strong and filled with outrage. "She's gone. Rodney, you need to change your clothes and start digging. We can't have her lying about, not in this heat."

"Put her in the cellar. It's cool there. Right, Rod?" Adeline licked her lips. "Unless you're down there doing *vigorous* activities."

How could he hate someone he loved so damned much? Rodney stared at her, remembered the night he'd discovered her in the cellar. Oh, God, how he'd had no willpower, no fight against her wicked seduction.

"Enough," he said, then looked to Gramma. The old woman scowled at him, her narrowed eyes accusing. As if this was his fault. Which it was. If he hadn't planted his seed, the pregnancy wouldn't have happened. Guilt weighed on his chest like an anvil. He hadn't murdered his daughter, but he knew what her mother was—a fucking psychopath.

Ignoring Adeline, he carried the child up the steps, then handed her to Gramma. "I'll come for her when I'm finished digging the grave."

"Need any help?" Adeline asked.

"Haven't you done enough?" Gramma's voice shook with outrage. "Go to your room and don't come out until you've been called."

Adeline sauntered across the porch. The sun shone through the sheer fabric of her nightgown exposing her sexy curves. "Don't tell me what to do, you old bitch." She grinned. "Or I just might break you, too."

Gramma clutched the baby to her chest and gasped. "After all I've done for you? For both of you?"

Rodney touched the woman's arm. "Go inside."

Gramma raised her chin and narrowed her eyes at Adeline. "Don't ever threaten me again, or I'll force you to leave," she said, the threat falling flat due to the fear in her eyes and voice.

Once the old woman entered the house, he turned to Adeline. "Why don't you go lie down?"

"You know, that's a great idea." Her hips swayed as she neared him. "It's been an emotionally exhausting day." She reached down and rubbed her hand along his crotch. "I could use some comforting. Why don't you nap with me?"

He grabbed her wrist. "Because I have to *bury* our daughter." Rodney shoved her away, then went inside. Twenty minutes later, now dressed in old jeans, t-shirt and boots, and standing at the edge of the family plot, Rodney plunged the shovel into the ground. He'd wanted to bury the baby closer to the oak tree, but knew the roots would give him an issue. Instead, he chose the vacant spot next to his mother. Matilda Archer had been a patient, nurturing woman who'd had the misfortune of loving a cold, ruthless son of a bitch. How could his mother have ever loved his father? After the first strike, she should have left Dean Archer, and Gramma should have protected her. But the old woman hadn't. Either out of love, loyalty or fear of her son, or hatred for his mother, the woman had never once admonished Dean.

Rodney grunted as he thrust the shovel into the earth. He should hate Gramma. He certainly didn't love her, but since she had been the victim of an abusive husband, he supposed Gramma assumed abuse was part of life.

He tossed dirt onto the growing pile. No matter how many times Adeline had angered him, he hadn't and wouldn't raise a hand to her. He'd never bought into that *the apple doesn't fall far from the tree* nonsense. He was a strong believer in nature versus nurture, and would bet anything that his grandfather's father had also had no problem hitting a woman.

The strong scents of dirt, grass and tobacco tickled his nose. He stopped digging for a moment, expecting a sneeze that never came, and stared at the bright blue lobelia bush his mother had planted after his father had died. She had chosen the flower when she'd learned the beautiful plant symbolized hate and spite. His mother had wanted the plant's roots to travel deep into the ground, stretch until they'd reached his father's casket, then burrowed inside the wooden box. Matilda Archer had wanted her husband to know, even in death, how much she had hated him. That had been ten years ago and the plant, despite never being cared for through frosts and droughts, still thrived, his mother's hatred keeping it alive.

Rodney wiped his sweaty palms on his jeans, and picked up the shovel. Would he come to hate Adeline just as much? They were born for each other, meant to be together through good times and in bad. She was his second half, the one person who truly understood him. He loved her deeply, the bond they shared, the secrets…oh, God, the passion. He slammed the shovel into the dirt, then tossed a chunk to the side. That couldn't happen again, no matter how much she tempted him. He refused to take advantage of Adeline's mental state or risk impregnating her again.

She killed our daughter.

He should weep for the tiny soul, but he couldn't, not when she should have never been brought into the world. The baby hadn't been right. He wasn't a pediatrician, but he was an M.D., and suspected lack of oxygen right after birth had done something to the baby's brain. It hadn't helped that the baby had been born one month early and without proper neonatal care. But he hadn't been able to take Adeline to a hospital in time for the child's delivery, and instead had delivered her himself during a violent storm.

His throat tightened and he stabbed the earth again. He should have taken the baby to the hospital instead of listening to Gramma. He should have taken her there and left her, let another family have her. She could have had a chance. Or she could have ended up like her mother.

Sick. Diseased.

Psychopathic.

"You're going to have to do something about Adeline," Gramma said.

He tossed more dirt on the pile. "I *am* doing something."

"That's right. You're digging your child's grave because her crazy mother is a murderer." Gramma grabbed his arm, stopping him. "Rodney, I sleep with my door locked and a gun under my pillow. When you're not home, I carry a bat with me wherever I go. I don't trust Adeline. She hates me. The only one she loves and will listen to is you. Lord knows I've tried to talk sense into that girl, but she won't have it." Gramma drew in a deep breath. "She belongs in an insane asylum."

"We've been over this before," he said, his patience with the old woman waning. "If she's taken to a mental health institute, they'll misdiagnose her and she won't get the help she needs."

"I don't think anyone can help her." Gramma gripped him tighter, her nails digging into his skin. "Please, Rodney. I'm tired of living in constant fear. Every Sunday I go to church and pray Adeline will die, or run away and never come back. What kind of woman does that make me? I hate what she's done to me, how she's taken my morals and has warped them. If you're not careful, she'll do the same to you."

Rodney knocked his grandmother's hand away. "No, she won't. Not after I finish developing the proper medication to balance her and make her normal."

Gramma folded her arms over her chest. "That girl doesn't know the meaning of the word. I know damned well she killed that college girl."

The police had accused Adeline of stabbing her college room-mate, but they'd had no evidence to prove it. Nothing. Not a hair or minutest fiber, and the detectives had been forced to let Adeline go. The police had investigated him, too. Fortunately, he'd helped Adeline dispose of the evidence the detectives had desperately needed before they'd searched his apartment. Eight years later, the case remained unsolved, the girl's family forced to live without closure and justice for their daughter.

"You don't know what you're talking about," Rodney said.

"I absolutely do. And don't even get me started on your cousin."

There had been times over the years when he regretted not turning Adeline over to the police. One of those times had been four years ago when his fifteen-year-old cousin, Geoffrey, had gone missing. The last person seen with him had been Adeline. Since Geoffrey had been a troubled kid, taking the divorce of his parents hard and dealing with bullying at school, local police assumed the boy had run away.

"No one knows what happened to Geoff," he lied.

During a hot, summer day the year after Geoffrey's disappear-ance, Adeline had taken him for a long walk on the vast fifteen hundred acres that now made up the Archer property. Over two hundred years ago, the acreage had quadrupled in size, and the Archers had been one of the wealthiest families in the state. Al-though land had been lost, the house his ancestors had built had survived the Civil War, the Great Depression, storms, droughts and murder. Natural bogs, forests and tall grasses now covered the once thriving plantation. Adeline had walked him through the pine forests they'd at one time explored together, until they'd reached a small pond. She'd stopped him there and had pointed to the pond, which was an abnormal shade of blue, as if someone had scooped buckets of the Caribbean Sea and filled the chasm with its turquoise waters. He'd been so mesmerized by the odd, yet beautiful shade of the water, he hadn't noticed the stark white bones lying near the bank until Adeline had pointed to them.

"I guess Geoffrey didn't run away after all," Adeline had said with a tsk.

Terrified, petrified, he'd stared at the skull of his aunt's son, at the large gaping hole at the temple, and had fallen to his knees. He'd asked her why, and she'd simply answered, "Why not?"

"Why do you continue to defend and protect her?" Gramma asked. "She is evil. From the moment I laid eyes on her, I knew she wasn't right. Just like the baby she killed today. Don't get me wrong, my heart goes out to the child, but in a way, Adeline has done the world a favor by taking the baby's life and—"

"Stop it," Rodney shouted. He threw the shovel to the ground and gripped his grandmother by the upper arms. Through the haze of his grief and rage, the thinness of her skin, her boniness, registered, but it hadn't erased the urge to snap her arms, then her neck. "Adeline was right. You are a stupid old bitch. And you need to mind your place. I *will* fix this." The shock and fear in Gramma's eyes had him loosening his grip and regretting his outburst. "Just stay away from Adeline." He patted her arms. "I'll take care of everything." He stepped away, then bent for the shovel.

"How? With your experiments?" Gramma moved toward his daughter's grave. "You tried and failed. Your drug killed people and your reputation."

He clenched the shovel. "Those people killed themselves."

"After they murdered others." She clutched her neck. "Your drug turned crazy people crazier.

"The tests were inconclusive," he argued. But deep down he

knew Gramma and anyone else who had pointed fingers at him were right. Something had gone wrong. The drug had worked during the final testing phase. The chemical combination he'd created had proved to deaden certain urges—lust, the need to hurt, to dominate. The drug had made the test subjects empathetic toward others, not violent, and the pharmaceutical company who had backed him and paid him handsomely for his concoction had been thrilled. Medizen Pharma would, thanks to Dr. Rodney Archer, help rid the world of violence, one psychopath at a time.

When certain members of the U.S. government had heard about Rodney and his findings, they'd become interested in the drug, and testing had been permitted at a federal prison. Five convicts, who were known to have psychopathic tendencies, were chosen. These men would have taken Rodney from the unknown, unobtrusive M.D. and pharmacologist that he was, and had him featured on the cover of *Time* magazine. He'd been featured all right, but not because the masses had praised him for his brilliance, or for helping those who couldn't stop the need for violence eating at their brains. No. Reporters had trashed his reputation. They'd called him Frankenstein or compared him to Joseph Mengele, the Nazi doctor who'd famously performed horrific experiments on Jewish prisoners. It hadn't helped that Medizen Pharma was a German-based company.

After the convicts who'd taken the drug had murdered fellow inmates and guards before killing themselves, Medizen Pharma had been sued by the prison. Rodney had been immediately dismissed without severance. He'd been forced to work at his hometown's local clinic treating scraped knees and the occasional broken bone. In a way, he should be grateful he could still practice medicine, and that the civil suits originally brought against him had been dropped. But he wasn't. He was determined to prove the drug worked. For Adeline's sake, he had to.

"Stick with what you know and stay out of my business," he finally said to his grandmother.

"As long as Adeline lives in my house, your need to fix her *is* my business. I know you're experimenting again. You need to stop this nonsense at once. You can't change what the devil has created. I've talked at great length with Pastor Landen about this, and about you."

Screw Pastor Landen. The man was a hypocrite who could probably use a dose of his drug. Rodney had seen the bruises on Landen's wife and their son. Either the two of them were the clumsiest people to walk the Earth, or the good pastor was beating them.

Ignoring the tears in Gramma's eyes, he continued to shovel. "I don't care what he has to say, and I don't want you talking about me or my business with anyone, understand?"

"Pastor Landen said that some people are born a certain way, while others are created."

"Nature versus nurture? It's a tired argument and one I don't feel like having with you right now."

"Adeline, she was born a certain way," she continued anyway. "I just know it. No one can create a person like Adeline. And no one can fix her. She has the devil inside and—"

"Enough." Rodney turned on Gramma. "I don't want to hear another word about the devil. Ever. There's no such thing. What's wrong with Adeline has nothing to do with demons and everything to do with her brain. This is a medical, not religious issue. And I *will* fix her."

"Why bother? She's a lost cause, hopeless and pure evil. You've already destroyed your career for her. She's killed your child, and I know to the marrow of my old bones that she killed the college girl and your cousin. Do you want to live with the guilt when she kills again? Because you *will* be guilty. You could have stopped her, but you chose not to."

"Like you could have stopped my father from beating my mother?"

Gramma stiffened. She lifted her chin and averted her eyes. "That was different. A woman has a place. That's what I was taught by your granddad, and your father needed to teach your mother the same."

"And you think Adeline is crazy." Rodney shook his head. "Go away and let me finish digging."

"Fine. I'll finish preparing the child for burial. Would you like to see her?"

"No. Just do what you have to do."

"Oh, I will. You have until the end of the week to make a decision about Adeline. Either she leaves, or I'm going to contact the sheriff and tell him about what she did to the baby."

Rodney stepped away from the small, shallow grave and crowded the old woman's space. His size should have intimidated her, but the tough old bag held her ground, despite being over a foot shorter and one hundred pounds lighter than him. "You will tell no one about the baby. You will not discuss me or Adeline to anyone. You will mind your business or the next grave I dig will be yours."

Gramma gasped. "How dare you threaten me? After all that I've done for you, for that crazy little ingrate. Your loyalty should be to me, not her." She took a step back and narrowed her eyes. "I won't go to the sheriff, but if you won't make her leave, then I want both of you out of my house. See how well you do on your own without the money you no longer have."

When the old woman turned away, he stared at the back of her gray head. If he were a different man, the mad scientist the press had claimed him to be, he'd sic Adeline on Gramma and give new meaning to the Big Bad Wolf.

A tap at his shoulder had him flinching. He quickly turned and glared at Adeline. "How long have you been here?" he asked.

"The entire time you've been. You should take off your shirt," she said, her tone seductive, as she ran her hand along his chest. "I love seeing my man's muscles work. It's so sexy."

"Stop it." He gripped her wrist, love and hatred hollowing his heart and soul. "You need help."

"Or Gramma's going to kick us out of her shitty, rotting house? Sounded like the old woman doesn't think anyone can help ease my wicked ways. Maybe I should go see Pastor Landen and let him try to drive the devil from my mind. A pastor's semen would be just as good, if not better than holy water, don't you think?"

Jealousy ripped him in two. He gripped her tighter and pulled her close. "Stay away from that man."

She shrugged. "Since my man won't touch me..."

"You shouldn't be thinking about sex, but about the baby you *broke*. My God, Adeline. You carried her for eight months. Your body kept her alive. She was part of you, of me. How could you do it?"

Adeline sighed. "How could I not?"

"Because deep down you're a good, kind, caring person. I know it. I feel it. It's why I can't ever stop loving you." He touched her cheek. "We used to be so close. We had the same goals, the same dreams. If I can make you better, we could still make those dreams happen." Like him, and despite being accused of murder, Adeline had graduated with a Doctor of Medicine degree and also had a Ph.D. in pharmacology. She had worked alongside him when he'd been developing his drug, and had quit her position with Medizen Pharma when he'd been fired. She was smart, creative and business-savvy. Once she was well, together they could become unstoppable. "Whether you want to go back into medicine or not, I'll support you. I just want you better. But you have to help me help you."

"What about Gramma?"

"What about her?"

"She's giving us the boot, unless you plan to stay here and want me to leave."

"You're not leaving."

"So, again. What about Gramma?"

He let go of her, then went back to shoveling. "I'll talk to her. She's upset about the baby. Once she cools off, she'll realize that she needs us here to help take care of the house and property."

"You and I both know that's not true. Gramma has plenty of money. She can hire someone to help her." Adeline walked over to the bright blue lobelia bush, then knelt next to it and plucked a flower. "How close are you to finalizing the new drug?"

"I feel like I'm close," he answered. "But even when I do have it right, I'm not sure how I can test it."

She plucked another flower, then stood. "Of course you know how." She grinned. "I'm the perfect lab rat. After all, it's for me, right?"

Satisfied the hole was deep enough for the tiny baby, he stepped out of it, then used the hem of his shirt to wipe the sweat from his face. "I told you before, I'm not experimenting on you."

"Afraid I'm going to off you and Gramma, then kill myself?" she asked.

He looked at her, saw her eyes trained on his bare abs, then dropped the shirt. "You know that won't happen. Someone at Medizen Pharma deviated from the chemical combination we knew worked."

"And yet you took the blame." She dropped the flowers into the grave. "We could experiment on Gramma."

He chuckled and looked toward the house. "Maybe the drug will knock the religion out of her."

Adeline smiled. "I'm being serious. What did Gramma say? No one can create a person like me. And no one can fix me. Right?"

"Gramma doesn't understand you the way I do."

She held up a hand. "The old woman understands me just fine, and you know it. Hear me out—if you can't prove the drug works, you'll never be able to move out from under the mad scientist stigma. Do you really want to work at the local clinic making thirty-five grand a year? After spending ten years studying your ass off, I'd think you'd want more from life."

Rodney hated everything about the clinic. The lack of equipment, resources and medication. Half of the six nurses who rotated shifts should have retired years ago. The receptionist was a gossip. One of the doctors was a drunk, while the other was a tree-hugging liberal who claimed he'd gone into medicine to help people and give back to society, not for the money or prestige of being a doctor.

That was well and fine for the tree-hugger, but not for him. He'd gone into medicine with the lofty notion that he could make a difference in other people's lives, maybe be the brilliant scientist who found the cure for cancer. Hell, if he found the cure for herpes he'd be lauded as a saint by those stuck with the virus. He'd wanted the prestige and money the tree-hugger hadn't. He still did. The only way he could salvage his career *and* his personal life would be to make his drug work. If he didn't fix Adeline and she ended up institutionalized or, even worse, in prison, he wasn't sure if he could go on with life. She understood him like no other. He loved her more than himself, even if he hated her for the horrible choices she'd made.

"Of course I want more," he said. "But I'm not going to experiment on Gramma."

"Then I guess you'll have to find a couple of psychopathic rats to test the drug. That should be easy," she said with heavy sarcasm and a roll of her eyes. "What's the difference? Gramma's pushing eighty. It's not like she has many more years in her."

His grandmother might be seventy-eight, but the woman was as spry as a sixty-year-old. "No. I will not even entertain the idea. I doubt Gramma would, either."

"Why in the hell would we tell her? Look, strap her to a chair, give her some hallucinogenic drugs, then fuck with her head. I have a journal filled with what to say to her while she's going through the change."

The change. Adeline's words chilled him. "A journal you wrote?"

She nodded. "There wasn't anything else to do while the baby was inside me and you were at work. I certainly wasn't going to hang out with the old bag of wrinkles all day. So, I started doing a little experimenting of my own."

"On Gramma?"

"Nope. But, damn, I was tempted." She moved a little closer.

"While you were trying to figure out where your drug had gone wrong, *I* had the foresight you didn't. Without a test subject, your drug is useless and your career is dead. Since it's not like you can run an ad offering money to any psychopath or sociopath willing to be a guinea pig, we would need to be creative."

He wiped a hand down his face and stared at her. "What did you do?"

She grinned. "I didn't hurt anyone if that's what you mean. But I did create a kickass hallucinogen that doesn't give the user rainbows and sunshine. It'll give them gray clouds and darkness. It agitates the brain and stimulates emotions, namely the darker ones like hatred, jealousy, aggression. The user doesn't care about the consequences of their actions or who they hurt."

"Stop," he shouted. "Who did you test this on?" Oh, God. She would go to jail and he would, too, if the police found out and thought he was mixing illegal narcotics in his home lab.

"Myself. But I wasn't a good test subject. After all, I already tend to head to the dark side, and I was six months pregnant."

"You took drugs during the pregnancy? Christ, our child—"

"Never had a chance anyway. Let's move on," she said with a sigh. "I video-taped myself while I was on the drug I like to call A-Line." Adeline gave him a quick grin. "The thing was, I didn't have to tape myself. I remembered everything I did. Yes, there were hallucinations, but it was strange how I could control them and make them work for me."

Rodney had smoked weed back in high school, but had never taken any other drug. He had no personal experience to compare to what Adeline was describing, yet he was intrigued. "Define control."

The glitter in her eyes should have scared him. He'd seen that same look before and knew what it meant. Adeline had been a bad girl.

"You know how much I hate Gramma, right? Well, this drug amplified my hatred. It made me want to kill her. I know, how is this so different from how I usually feel about Gramma? I can't explain it, but it *was* different. The drug showed me the ugly, spiteful, hypocritical bitch she is. I swear, I could see past the granny façade and straight to her cold heart. It was amazing." She let out a wistful sigh. "As much as I wanted to smash her head against the kitchen sink, then take a knife and split her wide open, I knew I shouldn't."

"Shouldn't or couldn't."

"Shouldn't."

"Because I'd be angry."

She laughed. "No. You'd get over it. You always do. I didn't kill her because it wasn't the right time. I knew I'd have to be smart if I were going to get away with murder." She gave him another quick grin. "Again."

He ignored that last remark. Adeline loved shocking people, and he wouldn't allow her the satisfaction. "So you think you've created a drug that could give the user temporary homicidal impulses, correct?"

"Oh, I know I did. But that's not all. I think if you continuously give it to a person, and heighten their surroundings with violent videos, music, subliminal messages, it'll warp them enough that they'll maintain those homicidal impulses even after the drug is out of their system."

Rodney folded his arms across his chest. "And you want to do this to Gramma."

She nodded. "Let me finish. Once the drug is out of their system, we give the psycho we created your drug and, *voilà*," she said with the snap of her fingers. "He'll be back to being a model citizen."

What Adeline suggested went beyond wrong. No matter how much he wanted to prove that his product had worked, he wouldn't experiment on his own grandmother.

"The journal I mentioned has the drug facts, along with pages of what I think we could use for subliminal messages." She took his hands, and forced them from his chest. "Rod, I believe in you. I always have. I know you can prove to the world that your drug works. Let me help you do that."

"You can help, but I'm not experimenting on people."

She gave his hands a squeeze. "Okay, so suggesting we use Gramma wasn't a good idea."

"It was a terrible one."

"What about someone who's homeless?"

Appalled with himself for being remotely intrigued by what Adeline presented, Rodney pushed her away, then bent and picked up the shovel. "This conversation is over." Gripping the shovel tight, he walked away.

"No one would ever know," Adeline continued as she followed after him. "We have acres of places to hide a body. That is, if something goes wrong."

He turned on her. "Listen to yourself. What you're saying has murder written all over it. I'm trying to stop you from killing, not encourage it."

"I know all that, silly." She tapped his chest with the tips of her fingers. "And I wouldn't let you get involved in anything that could jeopardize your career. If you went to prison, what would I do without you?"

She would become worse and have no one left to care for her. She could take a job and survive, but for how long? And how long would it be before she killed again? When he glanced away, she took his chin in her hand and forced him to look at her. "I love you. You've stuck by my side no matter what I've done. The choices I've made...I can't take them back. And I'm truly sorry that I've burdened you with my secrets. I'm also sorry that my actions don't show how much you mean to me."

This was the Adeline he missed and loved. He brushed her long, dark hair away from her face and cupped her head. "I love you, too. But we can't hurt people."

"And we might not. We're both doctors. We can make sure that the person is healthy enough to handle both of our drugs. We'll watch their reactions and make sure they can't leave and hurt anyone, or try to hurt themselves."

She made it sound so simple, yet there were a couple of huge flaws in her plan. "How do you suggest we keep the test subjects from going to the police?"

"We pay them. Just like the sperm donor clinics. We'll offer a homeless man seventy-five bucks per day, plus food and a bed."

"And Gramma? This won't be something we can keep secret from her."

Adeline wrinkled her forehead. "Yeah, the old lady's a problem." She brightened. "We can send her on vacation. Doesn't she have a sister or cousin living in Arizona?"

"A cousin." Good God. Was he seriously entertaining Adeline's idea? If they were caught drugging homeless people, they'd both go to prison. But, if they were successful, he could have Adeline and his career back. They could start fresh. End up working side-by-side developing new drugs to help people. Hell, if his drug was a success, he could help rid the world of violent psychopaths and sociopaths. He could possibly win the Nobel Prize in Medicine.

"See? We can send Gramma to the cousin's for a month, do our little experiment and not have to worry about her blabbing to her church people." Adeline looked over his shoulder and frowned. "Here comes the old lady now."

"Are you about done digging?" Gramma called.

Rodney stepped away from Adeline. "I'm finished," he said, walking toward his grandmother. "I'll take care of burying her."

Adeline took his hand in hers. "I'll help you." She looked between him and Gramma. "I'm sorry for what I did to her." Tears trickled down Adeline's cheeks. "I know that doesn't mean much now, but I truly am sorry. She deserved better. I think the both of you do, too." Her face crumpled as she let out a sob and bent her head. "I'm so sorry."

Adeline shocked him by falling against Gramma. Based on the widening of the old lady's eyes, Adeline had shocked her, too.

Gramma's face softened. "We need to get you some help, honey. Let Gramma make it all right," she said, hugging Adeline close. "You're sick. I know deep down you didn't mean to hurt anyone."

"I didn't," Adeline sobbed. "I'm so sorry. So, so sorry."

As Gramma comforted her, Rodney kept his hand in Adeline's and gave her a gentle squeeze. She looked over Gramma's shoulder and met his gaze.

Then smiled and winked.

PART II

"I really screwed up this time."
—*Jeffrey Dahmer*

CHAPTER 1

Tallahassee, Florida
Thursday, 3:42 p.m. Eastern Daylight Saving Time

AIR HISSED AS a baseball bat sliced past his head. Cash Maddox knocked the kickstand back, climbed on the Harley Davidson Fat Boy, then shot from the driveway, kicking up gravel in his wake.

"You son of a bitch," the motorcycle's former owner shouted. "I'm coming for your ass."

Cash gave the man the finger when he made the turn onto the main road, where Jude Kendrick waited for him in Cash's pickup truck. Once Cash rode past the truck, Jude made a quick U-turn and followed behind. When Cash saw his truck in the bike's mirror, he let out a sigh of relief and decided to enjoy the Fat Boy while he had it in his possession. He used to own one, but couldn't bring himself to replace the bike he'd lost. Not lost. Not exactly stolen, either. More like bike-napped for a ransom he'd been considering paying. He was damned tired of being alone.

Jude pulled alongside the Fat Boy when they reached a red light, and rolled down the window. "How close did the bat come to hitting your hard head?"

Cash held his index finger and thumb about an inch apart. "Not too much."

Jude shook his head. "I told you not to go alone. You should have—"

He revved the Harley and cupped an ear. "Sorry, man. Can't

hear you." The light turned green. Cash took off, saving himself an earful. Yeah, Jude was probably right. He should've gone in with another guy, maybe Pete or Sully, but he hadn't wanted to wait for them to come back from Pensacola where they were returning the boat they'd repossessed for the bank last week. The badass Harley he currently rode would earn him five hundred bucks. If he'd waited another day, hell, even another hour, his competition could have taken possession of the bike. And he was too competitive to allow that to happen.

With the Florida sun beating down on him and the wind keeping him cool, he rode through the outskirts of Tallahassee. When he reached the warehouse where he kept shop, he slowed to avoid running over his dog, Dolly, then eased the Fat Boy inside. Dolly rolled up behind him, tongue lagging to the side, eyes filled with affection.

Cash swung his leg over the bike, then bent and scratched the German shepherd behind the ears. "You like those wheels? You want Daddy to buy you some for Christmas?"

"Yeah, Daddy. Buy me some new wheels. All the dogs in the neighborhood are making fun of mine."

Cash chuckled and glanced over his shoulder at his mechanic, Ross. "You better not be making fun of my dog's handicap."

"Or else what? Are you gonna have her run me over?"

"Nope. After I get done kicking your ass. Jude will."

Jude climbed out of the Ford F-150, then slammed the door. "I'll do what?"

"Ross was making fun of Dolly's wheelchair. So I told him you'd run him over if he kept it up."

"Fuckin' A. I got more respect for that dog than most men I know."

Cash did, too. He'd been with Dolly for twelve years—four during the Army, eight stateside as civilians—and if it hadn't been for her, he'd either be dead, or the one in a wheelchair. "She's a good girl," he murmured to Dolly, bent his head and rested it on hers. When Dolly licked him, he smiled, then gave her another scratch and stood.

"You know I was only joking," Ross said, using a rag to wipe grease from his hands.

"Just bustin' your balls. If I let Jude run you over with my truck, you'd put a massive dent in the front end. Since you're the only one who could fix that, I'd be screwing myself."

"That's when you just take him out back and shoot him," Jude suggested.

"Then we'd have to figure out where to hide his body. And I'd still be out a mechanic."

"So does this mean I get to live?" Ross asked as he approached the Harley.

Cash stroked his dog's head. "For now. How's the bike look?"

The mechanic whistled. "Purty. How much is she worth?"

"Five hundred."

"Nice."

Jude snorted. "Except he almost took a bat to the head for it."

Ross looked away. "You want me to get the paperwork together?"

"You're such a kiss-ass." Jude pushed by Ross, clipping him in the shoulder. "I'll handle the paperwork. Christ, am I the only asshole around here who gives a shit?"

Ross looked at him. "You know I was only fooling about Dolly's wheelchair."

"Yep."

The mechanic glanced to the office, then jerked when Jude slammed the door shut. "You know Jude's just lookin' out for you."

"Got that, too," Cash said, trying his best to be patient. Ross, Jude, Pete and Sully, they'd been together since Cash had started his repair shop and repo business eight years ago. He knew them from when he'd been in the Army. Jude was a little more complicated. He wasn't just his business partner. He was his friend, confidant, and former Army captain.

"You want me to shut up now, right?"

"Pretty much." Cash sighed. "But I get it." He rubbed Dolly's back, then made sure the custom-made straps to the wheelchair attached to the dog's lower body weren't chafing her. "Clean the bike up, then we'll call it a day. Dinner and drinks are on me."

Cash gave Dolly a quick hand signal, indicating she should follow, then headed for the office. Once inside, he unstrapped the wheels from her hindquarters. "I can take care of the Harley if you want to head home," he said, laying Dolly on her dog bed.

Jude swiveled in the office chair opposite the one Cash used, and held up Cash's cell phone. "Why the hell didn't you have this on you?"

"Didn't think about it," he answered honestly. His sole focus had been on the sweet Harley.

Jude tossed the cell phone to him. "How thoughtful."

Cash caught it in his right hand, then unlocked it. "Let it go, man. It's over and done." He glanced to the screen, which told him he'd missed a text and a call. "But if you don't like how…" The text was from Pete, letting him know they'd dropped the boat off and were heading back to Tallahassee. The call? Nervous excitement shifted through his body, along with acute apprehension. Why would she call him now? He'd just spoken with Melanie last week, and the conversation had ended as most of their conversations had—both of them arguing. After she'd hung up on him, he'd sat with Dolly, wondering why he couldn't man up and give her what they both wanted. He also wondered why she couldn't accept him for who he was.

"If I don't like what?" Jude asked, reminding Cash he wasn't alone.

"Never mind." He clutched the phone and debated. Should he listen to her voice message? Should he care why she called?

Anger settled on his shoulders. She couldn't accept his lifestyle, but she sure as hell didn't mind using him when she saw fit. The last time she blew into town, Mel had used his men to help her transport a car to Everglades City, and used his body for old times' sake. She'd fucked him and left. Instead of being bitter about the way she'd treated him, he should be happy. The woman had a wicked temper when provoked and vindictiveness running through her veins. During the two years they'd been playing the occasional text, phone call and fuck game, he sure as hell hadn't needed her to be steady in his life. His business had done just fine without her. His personal life had improved once the sexy witch had moved back to the swamp where she belonged with her crazy-ass father.

"Screw that," Jude said. "What were you going to say? If I don't like how you run things, then I can get out anytime? 'Cause if that's how you want it, I'm outta here."

Jude's threat penetrated the haze of bitterness clouding his head. Cash stood at the same time Jude did and faced the man. "I was going to say that next time I'll make sure I have my phone with me and that I'll bring backup." He held up the cell phone. "Mel called me."

Jude's eyes widened, before a big grin split his face. He shook his head and chuckled.

"It's not funny."

"Maybe not to you, but I just won sixty bucks."

Cash rubbed the back of his neck where tension began to build and fought to keep his temper in check. "For?"

"Pete, Sully and Ross placed bets on which month Mel would call you for a fix. August happens to be one of the months I picked."

He would make them pay for this. Every one of them. He didn't know how or when, but placing bets behind his back was total bullshit. Especially a bet that had to do with Mel. His crew knew what she'd meant to him. They knew the low he'd hit when she'd left him. Even Dolly had shown signs of depression. Mel's abrupt departure had sucked the fun out of life, had left their home cold, empty. It had taken a while, but he and Dolly had managed fine over the past two years. But each time Melanie returned, he'd been forced to face the bitter reminder of what he'd lost.

The only woman he'd ever loved.

Cash pocketed the phone. He'd listen to her message once he was home. "I'm glad you guys have been having fun at my expense," he said as he placed Dolly in her wheelchair.

"We were just foolin' around," Jude said, apology clear in his voice. "We all miss Mel."

"I know." He sighed and rubbed the German shepherd's head. Even the garage wasn't the same without Mel working there.

"Just because I feel bad about the bet doesn't mean I'm okay with the shit you pulled today."

He understood where Jude was coming from. The man and the rest of his crew had been there for him when he'd nearly died. Because of them, and mainly Mel, during the past year, he'd been taking less repo jobs, handing them off to Pete and Sully, and focusing more on running the business. But he loved the rush of adrenaline he'd experience during a repossession, and still liked to take on a job now and then. "I know I put you through hell, and I know that's why you give me shit about how I handle some of our jobs. I'll be more considerate of your feelings."

Jude grinned. "Your therapist would be proud."

His cheeks warmed and he looked away. "Fuck off."

Laughing, Jude approached him and settled a hand on Cash's shoulder. "Look, I get that you still need the rush. You just need to be smart about it. Me? I'm good with taking the business from just a repair shop to total car care, and letting that replace the repo income. Pete's like an artist when it comes to doing bodywork. If I remember, Mel was, too."

Jude and Mel both wanted him out of the repo business. But neither of them understood why he couldn't put it behind him. His therapist called him an adrenaline junkie. Mel had called him a selfish prick and a wuss, saying he could risk his life, but not his freedom. Freedom wasn't the issue. He was cool with commitment. Being told what he could and couldn't do for a living? Now that was a problem.

"I still think we should repo for a couple more years," Cash said. "The extra money will help pay off equipment."

"Either way, when that time comes, I want to make sure you walk out of this warehouse with all bones intact."

"I hear you."

"As for your woman?"

"She's not my woman," he said, the admission like nails to a chalkboard. Knowing she'd never be his again—with the exception of an occasional weekend of sex which only left him craving more, and bitter that he couldn't have her—cut him deep. Being with her had been the best thing that had ever happened to him. Losing her had been, too. His therapist had called Cash's emotions a 'juxtaposition of the heart and mind'. Later, after Cash had looked up the meaning of juxtaposition, he'd come up with a simpler way to describe his emotions without the use of a big word: they were fucked up.

"You don't have any other woman and you've been faithful to Mel from the moment you two met."

Not interested in discussing his messed up relationship with Mel, Cash turned away. "I'm going to take Dolly home. I told Ross dinner and drinks are on me. Are you in?"

"If you're buying."

After they agreed to meet at Jimmy Mac's—Cash's favorite bar-restaurant—at six, Cash took Dolly to his truck. Fifteen minutes later, he pulled into his driveway, then hefted Dolly from the Ford's backseat. Once she was hooked into her wheelchair, he led her to the back of the house. But Dolly hesitated at the patio door and stared at the in-ground pool. Considering the temperature had peaked at ninety-two, the dog had the right idea.

"Do you want to go for a swim?" he asked. When Dolly barked and wheeled toward the pool, he chuckled and pulled his shirt over his head. "Hang on, girl. You've gotta wait for me." His contemporary, two-story home was surrounded by woods and backed up to a large pond, which was also part of his property, giving him the privacy he loved. Not bothering with a swimsuit, he stripped to his boxer briefs, unstrapped Dolly's wheels, then once he had her in her life vest, he helped her into the pool. The water wasn't as cool as he'd like, but the impromptu swim wasn't for him.

He grinned when Dolly swam to him and gave him a lick on the face. Although Dolly was adept at swimming with the use of the vest, Cash followed her around the pool. His thoughts might have been on Dolly's safety, but they were also crowded by images of Mel. She'd loved their pool, too. What he'd loved was when she wouldn't bother with one of her tiny bikinis and had skinny-dipped with him. He drew in a breath and dipped his head under the water. Resurfacing, he blinked and moved alongside the dog.

"I wonder what she wants," he said. Dolly looked at him. "Probably to nag me about something. It's not like she calls to see how I'm doing." He twisted to his back and swam in front of the dog. "I should call her tomorrow. Make her wait, like she does to me."

Dolly doggy-paddled toward the shallow end of the pool, signaling she was finished. "But what if something's wrong? Maybe her crazy-ass daddy is sick. Maybe she is."

Dolly held still as he removed her vest and dried her with a towel that had been left on the chair after yesterday's swim. The patience in her eyes had him realizing that his therapist was right. He couldn't continue on his current path. His best friend was a dog. He was in love with a woman who refused to be with him, yet couldn't let him go. He continued to unnecessarily place himself in dangerous situations for the rush and adrenaline without a thought for the people who cared about him. Yet he couldn't let go of the repo business, no matter that it had nearly killed him and had ruined his relationship with Mel.

He rubbed the towel beneath the dog's muzzle. "I'm being stupid. I should go with Jude's plan, take the garage to a new level, stop repoing and tell Mel she doesn't have to worry about me getting hurt." Satisfied Dolly was dry enough, he used the other towel to take care of himself before strapping on her wheels. "Before I go there, I should see what she wants first. Could be she's calling about insurance again. Or maybe Jude's right and she's coming to town for a quickie." He fished his cell phone from the pocket of his jeans, then after gathering the rest of his clothes and boots, he opened the sliding patio door. After Dolly made her way inside, Cash froze at the threshold, more of his therapist's words taunting him.

How can you wait on this woman? More importantly, Cash, how long do you expect her to wait on you?

Hell, Melanie could have been calling to finally ask him for a divorce.

Cap'n Ryan's Airboat Tours, Everglades City, Florida
Thursday, 5:22 p.m. Eastern Daylight Saving Time

MELANIE SCARLET TOSSED the rag into the stainless steel sink, then turned and slammed the ice cream cooler shut. Dang it, she knew she should have waited to call Cash. But she hadn't wanted to catch him at home, in *their* house, Dolly lying on the floor near the couch. She'd wanted to talk to him while he was busy at work, hoping to keep the conversation quick and to the point. Because if she gave Cash the opportunity to start talking, the temptation to make the seven-hour trip to see him and Dolly would be too great to ignore.

She opened the refrigerator and began stowing the condiments inside. Now she wouldn't be prepared for his return call. He could catch her off guard, maybe when she was home—alone—bored, lonely. Or in her garage where the smell of rubber, grease and fuel fed her imagination. Cash, dirty and sweaty after working on cars all day. His rough hands pushing her jeans down and her shirt up as he pressed her against the hood of a car.

With a frustrated grunt she shoved the rest of the condiments into the fridge. Why did he have to be such a selfish, stubborn fool? And why was she still hanging onto the hope that he would change? People didn't change. 'Can't change the stripes of a tiger,' her daddy liked to say, and he was dead right. Cash was, and always would be, more concerned about getting his rocks off risking his life, than anyone or anything else.

"Ice Cream Lady sound like angry gator."

Mel gripped the refrigerator handles and reined in her irritation. She was not in the mood for the Russian. "What are you talking about?"

"Mel growl like Polina."

She turned and dropped her gaze to the floor where Vlad Aristov's three-foot alligator, Polina, stood next to him, a band around her snout, a leash attached to the lacy pink collar Mel had bought for her. "I told you before, no animals where we serve food."

"Vlad know this."

"Then why are you breaking the rules?"

"Vlad and Polina need ride."

She did *not* want that gator in her newly restored 1978 Chevy Camaro Z28. "From me?"

When the Russian nodded his blond head, she picked up a fresh washcloth, moved to the sink, then ran it under hot water. "Why can't Harrison take you home?" Harrison and Vlad both worked at the boat shop and were roommates.

Vlad's eyes narrowed. "Harry become…нытье старуха."

"And that means what?" she asked as she wiped off the counter.

"Harry nag Vlad like old lady." The Russian frowned and his face hardened. "Vlad have enough. Harry and Vlad kaput."

"You're breaking up?"

Vlad nodded. "Like song say, it hard to do. But Vlad must." He punched his hand, the gator never flinching when the leash jerked slightly.

She rinsed the washcloth. "No offense, but I've got my own problems."

Vlad's face softened. "Vlad good listener. Tell Vlad why Ice Cream Lady filled with growl."

In a strange way, she loved Vlad, but she wasn't in the mood to talk with him or anyone right now. At this point, she didn't even want to speak with Cash. She needed to, though. Her cousin, Bobby, who was more like a little brother to her, occasionally worked for Cash. The past two checks she'd sent to Bobby hadn't been cashed and his cell phone was out of service. Since Bobby never passed up free money and never went anywhere without his phone, she was terrified something had happened to him.

"I was clearing my throat."

The Russian's blue eyes glittered with disappointment and anger. "Fine. Do not tell Vlad." He turned, and led Polina from the ice cream shop. "Vlad and Polina walk home."

"Oh, for cryin' out loud," she muttered. "Vlad, stop. If you need a ride, I'll give you one. But if that gator scratches up my upholstery, I'm making her into a purse."

He grinned and wagged a finger at her. "Ice Cream Lady act cold, but Vlad know."

She glanced around the shop. Satisfied the place was closed up for the day, she grabbed her purse, then met Vlad at the door. "You know what?"

"Mel have soft place for Polina."

She stepped aside to avoid being hit by the alligator's tail. "I don't have a soft spot for Polina. I have one for you, you big goof."

Vlad stopped and rested a large hand on her shoulder. "Vlad sorry. Vlad like Mel as friend."

"Whoa, that's not what I...wait, why don't you like me in *that* way?" Why did she care? *Except for sex, your own husband doesn't even want you.*

The Russian sighed. "Vlad have broke many heart."

"You're not breaking mine, I'm just curious."

"Vlad like blonde with big titties," he said as if she should be aware of his preference in women.

"Since I happen to be a blonde, I'll try not to be too offended that you just called me flat chested."

His eyes shifted to her boobs. "Vlad like Mel's titties, but Vlad have big hand." He held one up, palm out. "See? Mel could not fill Vlad hand."

"Oh, my God." She slipped on her sunglasses. "Someone needs to put a filter on you."

Laughter came from the entrance of the souvenir shop where tourists could also purchase their tickets for an hour-long airboat tour. Ryan Monahan, the owner of Cap'n Ryan's Airboat Tours, stood in the doorway laughing.

"Good, Ryan's still here," she said, honestly not offended by Vlad. She knew him well enough to know he'd meant no insult. "He can take you and Polina home."

Ryan stopped laughing and shoved off the doorjamb. "Why me? And why didn't you go home with Harrison?" he asked Vlad.

"Because Harry's nagging him like an old lady," she answered for the Russian.

Vlad nodded. "Да. Harry watch Vlad like mother chicken."

"Is this about you quitting smoking?" Ryan asked.

"Да. Vlad try. Vlad fail. Vlad try again. But Harry nag for Polina, too. Polina too big, Harry say. Vlad not allow to capture squirrel for Polina dinner. Harry say it illegal." He shook his fist. "Vlad know Harry full of shit from bull."

"Dang," Melanie said. "Harry's got you pretty fired up, huh?"

"Vlad fitness knotted."

Ryan frowned. "Come again?"

The Russian sighed. "Captain Ryan know…Vlad ready to explode a seal."

"What?"

Melanie laughed and touched Vlad's arm. "Oh, honey, you're too funny. Thanks, I needed that." She looked to Ryan. "Fit to be tied. Blow a gasket. Get it? The Russian is seriously ticked off."

"Ice Cream Lady know Vlad well."

"What I know is that I can't fit your gator in the back of my Camaro. But she'll fit just fine in Ryan's Suburban."

"Whatever. I have to wait for Lola to finish a few things in the office anyway." Ryan pulled his keys from his pocket. "Put your gator in the back while I go tell Lola I'm leaving."

"Vlad sorry for tittie comment. That rude," he said as he

walked Polina to Ryan's truck.

"It's fine. You're not my type, either."

"What man can melt Ice Cream Lady?" he asked with a grin.

Her husband. "When I find out, I'll let you know," she said, then headed for her car. Before she opened the door, her cell phone rang. Her stomach balled and her hand trembled as she glanced to the phone's screen. Since the water calmed her, and she would need to be calm to have a civil conversation with Cash, she started for the boat docks, and answered.

"Hey, babe. It was good to hear your voice," Cash said. "I just wish you were calling to check up on me and Dolly, instead of Bobby."

She loved and hated hearing his voice, too. The sound of him stirred so many memories, along with misery. She missed him. She wanted to be with him. By now, they should have a couple of kids. Instead they'd spent almost their entire marriage living apart because of Cash's selfish disregard for her and her needs.

"Don't call me babe," she reminded him. Once they'd separated, terms of endearment were no longer allowed. The only exception to her rule was during sex, which they hadn't had in nearly two months. No wonder she'd been ready to explode a seal lately.

"Sorry, *Melanie*." Dolly barked and she grinned. "Our dog misses you," Cash said. "I can't even say your name around her."

Her eyes misted as she pictured the German shepherd. "Tell her I miss her and give her a kiss for me."

"Are you missing anyone else?" he asked, hope in his voice.

She sat on the step leading to the dock and stared at the canal. Stubbornness had nothing to do with not admitting that she loved him. Resentment did. She resented him for not giving up the repo business and being the husband she needed. She also didn't want to hurt him—they'd both hurt each other enough. Still, misleading him by giving him any hope that they had a chance would be wrong.

"I'm missing Bobby," she said. "Have you seen him?"

"I think you need to take a break from standing over coolers all day. Maybe it'll help with the icy attitude."

"What were you doing when I called you? Repossessing someone's car? Maybe their boat?"

"Harley Davidson Fat Boy."

She instantly pictured the motorcycle she'd taken from Cash. It now sat in her garage, a dusty tarp protecting it. "Did they pull a shotgun or a knife on you?"

"Baseball bat."

"And you wonder why we're not together." Anger and disappointment deflated her. She slumped her shoulders, rested her elbows on her knees and her head in her hand. "Do you know where I can find Bobby or not?"

"I asked around before calling you. No one's seen or heard from him in weeks. He did a job for me about a month ago. I paid him, we went for a beer later and that's the last time I saw him."

"His phone is out of service and he hasn't cashed the last two checks I sent him. Something's wrong."

"Where'd you send the checks?"

She lifted her head. "To where I always do, the garage. Didn't you get them?" Bobby Scarlet was eight years younger than her. When he'd turned eighteen and had graduated from high school, he'd come with her to Tallahassee, where she'd had a job waiting and had eventually met Cash. Since Bobby hadn't been able to find work, Cash had given him a job at his garage. But her cousin had no interest in working every day. So Cash had Bobby do the occasional repo job, gave him one hundred dollars, then her cousin would disappear for a couple days until he needed money again.

She hadn't been, and still wasn't, always sure where Bobby lived, or how he could stand the lifestyle he led. The one constant with Bobby was that he'd always return to Cash's garage, which was why she'd sent the checks there. Since she doubted Bobby had struck it rich and was off on a vacation, and no one had seen or heard from him in nearly a month, something was definitely wrong.

"I'm meeting Jude later," Cash said. "I'll ask him if he remembers getting the checks. Maybe Bobby stopped in when I wasn't around. Ross did say he heard Bobby was hanging in Frenchtown with Quinell Willis. I don't know if you remember him, but he's bad news."

Frenchtown was known for its prostitutes, drug dealers, addicts, homeless and the mentally ill. Quinell was known to pimp and deal drugs. She hoped to God Ross was wrong. Bobby knew better than to run with people like Quinell.

"Yeah, I remember him." She rubbed her forehead. "I have to go."

"Already? Just hang on a sec. Before you get upset about Bobby, let me talk to Jude. Ross is going to be with us. We can head to Frenchtown and start asking around."

Cash, Jude and Ross were, collectively, seven hundred plus pounds of pure testosterone and muscle. They'd killed for their country, had been shot at and assaulted as civilians, and were all quick tempered. They might be badass, but if something happened to them while they were looking for her cousin, the guilt would crush her. She loved her husband, and Jude and Ross were her friends.

"Don't you dare. I'm going to check with the police and hospitals. If I don't find him, I'm coming to Tallahassee."

"Look, Mel, I think you're being a little extreme. Bobby's a grown man. He might've left town for a job or a girl. Hell, he could be drifting your way as we speak."

"Bobby's a fifteen-year-old inside a twenty-five-year-old's body. He's concerned with what goes in his stomach and gaming. You know as well as I do that he's not motivated enough to get a job on his own."

"I suppose you have a point. But if he did land himself into some trouble, it's of his own making, not yours. I've told you before, you can't keep bailing him out from his mistakes. The kid needs to grow up and learn to take care of himself. You coddle him too much. Instead of sending him checks, you should've told him to do what everyone else who needs money does—get a job."

Her daddy had told her the same thing, and while she knew it, too, she'd hated the idea of Bobby being forced to live on the streets to learn a lesson. Plus, she was responsible for him. When Bobby had been four, his mom had died. Her daddy had become his legal guardian and he'd moved in with them. She'd loved having him around. In a weird way, Bobby was like the puppy Daddy would never let her have because he'd worried the gators would make a meal out of a family pet. Bobby had been so dang cute, and would trail behind her whenever he had the chance.

Since her mama had died when she'd been about Bobby's age, Mel had been sure to give Bobby the love and protection any mother would give her son. What she hadn't given Bobby was the courage to do right by himself. She'd enabled him to be lazy, had made too many excuses for his behavior, and now she had to deal with the young man she'd created. Or the guilt, if something terrible had happened to him.

"I don't need the lecture. I need to find Bobby. I'll let you know if I'm coming to Tallahassee," she said, then decided to be mature and say good-bye rather than hanging up on him like she had last week. Before she allowed guilt and worry to fester, she headed inside the souvenir shop. After passing cases of trinkets and shirts, she moved behind the counter to the office. Lola Tam, Ryan's fiancée, and the head of their underground organization, Above the Law, sat at the desk, working on the computer.

Mel knocked on the door. "Got a sec?"

Lola turned and smiled. "Hey, I figured you left for the day."

"I needed to talk to you."

"It's about that last assignment, right?" Lola sighed. "I seriously had the 'flu, otherwise you know I would've gone undercover as a prostitute."

Melanie held up a hand. "It's not about the assignment, but now that you brought it up, I did question whether or not you were faking being sick. Until Ryan came down with it, too."

"Along with everyone else but you."

She shrugged and leaned against the doorjamb. "Maybe the 'flu gods decided to give me a break because I was forced to dress like a whore."

Lola grinned. "Wouldn't the medical world be impressed if that was the cure for the common 'flu?" Her smile waned. "What's going on? Is this about the ice cream shop or ATL?"

"Neither. It's personal."

Lola's almond-shaped eyes widened a fraction. If Melanie's stomach wasn't knotted with worry, she would have laughed. She liked Lola—as a boss—but they weren't close. She'd tried to make an effort to learn more about Lola, after all the woman was marrying Ryan, who she'd known since she could remember and was like a brother to her. But she'd grown up surrounded by men, had never had a girlfriend she could turn to, and didn't trust easily.

Growing up in a small town with a father who swore the Apocalypse was near, and the legacy of being from a family full of crazies hadn't helped. When she was young, the kids at school had ruthlessly teased her, especially the girls. Thank God for the Monahan boys and Barney Newton. Ryan and Shane Monahan's father, along with Barney, were Vietnam vets like her daddy. The men knew her daddy hadn't come back from the war with his head on straight, and had taken it upon themselves to look out for her and her mama when her daddy found himself too busy looking for Charlie in the swamps of the Everglades. Ryan and Shane had been a staple in her life. They'd protected her and had taught her to protect herself. Too bad they hadn't been around to help her influence Bobby when he'd been a teenager. If they had, maybe Bobby would have followed their lead, joined the service, learned the value of hard work and actually contribute to society.

"If it's personal," Lola began, "I'd think you'd go to Ryan or Shane. Don't get me wrong, I'm glad you feel comfortable enough to talk to me, it's just, you usually brush me off for the boys."

Melanie pushed off the doorjamb and approached the desk. "I can't. Not with this."

"Can you tell me why?"

"I'd prefer not to."

"I respect that." Lola gave her a small smile. "Okay, so what's the matter?"

"My cousin is missing. I need Harrison to see if he's in jail or in the hospital." During the ten months she'd worked with Harrison Fairclough, ATL's computer geek, she'd learned the man was a wizard when it came to finding information.

"That won't be a problem. Why don't you want Ryan or Shane to know?"

"Barney, too." Barney was her surrogate uncle and ATL's Jack-of-all-trades. He, along with Ryan and Shane, knew she'd once dated a repo man, but they didn't know she'd married him. If they found out now, they'd be ticked off she'd never told them, then they'd likely head to Tallahassee to beat some sense into the man who'd broken her heart. The thing was, Cash hadn't broken her heart. He'd disappointed her. Her daddy might be crazy, but one lucid day he'd talked about his marriage to her mama. He'd said that when it came to marriage, the only way to make it work was to put your spouse first. Always. When she'd met and fallen in love with Cash, he'd become the most important person in her life. She'd put him before everything and everyone. Too bad he hadn't done the same.

Lola made a slight nod. "Okay, we'll keep this between us and Harrison. Vlad can't keep secrets."

She chuckled. "That man is something else. Anyway, I also might need Harrison to go to Tallahassee with me," Mel said, then explained her concerns for Bobby without mentioning her relationship with Cash.

"That shouldn't be a problem, but I think you'd be better off having Vlad go with you. If your cousin is on the streets and involved in something dangerous, no offense to Harrison, but I'd be more comfortable going with Vlad."

"I know plenty of muscle in Tallahassee, but if Bobby's not in jail or the hospital, I might need Harrison's brain and computer skills to help find him." Which was the truth. What Lola didn't have to know was that Harrison would also be the buffer she'd need between her and Cash.

After the last time she'd seen her husband, and the weekend they'd spent together, it had taken her weeks to recover. She missed him, loved him, wanted to be with him every day, not just every few months when she'd found an excuse to see him. Thank God for ATL. Ten months ago, Lola had come to town to rescue her mom and the head of the private criminal investigation agency, CORE, which was ATL's northern counterpart—only more legit—from a killer. Mel had been given an opportunity to help with the mission, offering her more to do with her life than pining over her husband, fixing cars in her garage and scooping ice cream. Working for ATL not only gave her more purpose and money, it had allowed her to be part of something important.

Lola picked up her cell phone, then tapped at the screen. "Let's hope your cousin is fine and you don't have to go anywhere. I don't mind working in the ice cream shop, but if I can't, Vlad will have to."

Mel cringed. While Vlad was capable of scooping ice cream and making change, his customer service skills needed refinement.

"Hi, Harrison," Lola began, "I need you to do a favor for me. Can you run a search for…" She looked to Mel.

"Robert Edward Scarlet. Goes by Bobby," Mel said.

Lola repeated the information to Harrison, then minutes later ended the call. "Harrison said that if your cousin is a John Doe it'll take longer to find him, but if he's in jail or hospitalized he should have something for us soon." She set the phone on the desk. "The problem with that is if you two are close, why wouldn't he have called you?"

That was her concern. If Bobby had needed bail money, she'd have been the first person he'd turn to. If he were sick or injured and hospitalized, she would have known because he was still on Daddy's insurance. "I'm going to go home and let you get back to paying bills," she said, needing something to do to avoid considering the real reason why she hadn't heard from Bobby.

"That works. I'll call you when I hear from Harrison."

Mel thanked her, then headed out the door. Minutes later, she slid into her Camaro. As she backed out of the parking spot, she saw Lola waving to her in the rear view mirror. She stopped the car, kept the engine running, then opened the door. "You heard from Harrison already?" she asked as Lola met her at the car.

Lola nodded. "He found nothing. He said he not only checked Tallahassee, but Pensacola and Panama City."

Mel met Lola's worried gaze. "Did he..." She looked to the canal. "Did he check death records?"

"Yes. He didn't find anything in Florida, but said he could compare Bobby's driver's license photo to possible deceased John Does. I told him to go for it."

Her heart sank, but she forced herself to remain hopeful. "Thanks," she said, then slid back into the Camaro and closed the door.

"What are you going to do?" Lola asked. "If you don't want to be alone, come hang out with me and Ryan tonight."

Mel shook her head. "I'm good. I have a bag to pack. I have a feeling Harrison and I are heading to Tallahassee."

CHAPTER 2

The House of Archer, Bower, Georgia
Thursday, 6:06 p.m. Eastern Daylight Saving Time

RODNEY PLACED SALINE drops into their test subject's blood-shot eye. When the muscles around the man's eyes twitched involuntarily, the tape holding open his eyelids loosened. He tore another piece of tape off the roll and adhered it to the man's lashes for added reinforcement, then stepped away in order to give the man full view of the television screen.

Adeline had scoured the Internet, searching for DVDs that showed nothing but violence. What she'd had shipped to the House of Archer had been shocking and horrific. War footage, videos of genocide, homicide, suicide. His stomach had turned when he'd viewed only a small portion of one of the DVDs. Seeing the beheading of a pregnant woman should have that effect on anyone. But this test subject, along with the other homeless man Adeline had found, hadn't even flinched.

As the video recording played, Rodney checked the man's blood pressure and heart rate, avoided even glancing at the TV and tried his damnedest to ignore the seductively swaying words coming from their digital voice recorder. Adeline had spent hours creating recordings that were meant to encourage their subjects to hang on to the primitive and feral emotions her drug had created. He had to hand it to Adeline. The hallucinogen she'd developed was genius. One dose had knocked the hope and empathy out of the test subjects. Two had filled them with an uncontrollable amount of hatred. Three had been like sending pure evil into their veins.

This subject was well into the second day of their clinical trial. During the past forty hours he'd been given a steady stream of the A-Line drug without a moment of respite. One side effect they'd discovered had been their subjects' inability to sleep. A-Line worked as a stimulant, similar to an amphetamine, as well as an appetite suppressant. Also, like recreational amphetamines, A-Line caused the psychosis Adeline had said it would, but only for a short period. As if their bodies and minds had accepted the reality the drug had created, the test subjects had remained frighteningly lucid even as they'd spoken of murder and torture. But he and Adeline weren't creating a drug to counteract A-Line users, they were trying to stop psychopaths before they murdered.

Once they proved their drug worked, parents who caught their young children torturing animals could possibly stop a serial killer in the making. Had such a drug existed years ago and had been administered to Hitler, millions of Jews wouldn't have been murdered. When Rodney considered such infamous serial killers as Ted Bundy, Jeffery Dahmer or John Wayne Gacy, he wondered what would have become of them had they been helped before they'd hurt.

He wondered what would have become of the college girl and his cousin if Adeline hadn't murdered them.

Rodney finished checking the test subject's vitals, then noted that the man's heart rate had increased considerably. He glanced to the TV, tasted bile when he witnessed the gory act taking place, then turned away and listened to Adeline's recorded voice.

"Imagine splitting her ribcage open with your bare hands. Feel the warmth of her blood coating your skin. God, you want to taste it, but you want to hold her beating heart in your hands first."

The man groaned as if sexually satisfied. Rodney looked to the man's groin and quickly noted in his journal that the test subject had developed an erection.

"My God," Rodney muttered. "You're a sick man, aren't

you?"

Although tempted to rip the duct tape from the subject's mouth and hear his response, he refrained. He and Adeline had agreed to both be present when talking to their lab rats. Two sets of eyes and ears were better than one, and this experiment was too important to leave any, even the minutest, doubt in either of their minds. Especially when they'd stopped administering A-Line, which they'd already done to their other test subject.

The first man to receive A-Line had told them his name was Troy. If he'd been lying, neither he nor Adeline had cared. His identity hadn't been important to them, but his mind and what they could do to it, had been. Good God had they messed with his head. Between the constant stream of videos, Adeline's recordings and days of A-Line, they'd broken Troy. They'd scrambled his brain and had left him with nothing but thoughts of violence and antipathy—especially toward women. When they'd removed the duct tape from Troy, the first thing he'd told Adeline was that he planned to gut her while he raped her.

He'd had the urge to put the man down like the rabid dog Troy had become. But Adeline had laughed because Troy hadn't had a dose of A-Line in two days, and had been given a placebo in its place. Which meant they'd succeeded.

They'd taken a normal man and had turned him into a psychopath. Tomorrow would be the day they placed Troy on Rodney's anti-psychotic drug. Once the drug had been administered, in theory, it would take the subject over the rainbow and into a happy place where violence and utter hatred wasn't necessarily nonexistent, but it was deadened to the point that killing a spider would—again, in theory—provoke thought.

"Hungry or thirsty?" Rodney asked his subject, who went by the name Noah.

Noah made no sound and kept his focus on the screen.

He patted the man on the shoulder. "You keep watching. I'll be back in thirty minutes." He left the bedroom that had once belonged to his parents, closed the door, then set his watch to remind him to check on Noah and administer the saline drops. A muffled noise came from the room at the end of the hall that housed their other test subject, Troy. He paused at the top of the steps before heading downstairs to have dinner with Adeline, and stared at the closed bedroom door.

"Adeline?" he called. She shouldn't be with Troy, not without him. Once they'd realized Troy had a strange, sick fixation for women, they'd both agreed that Adeline would not see Troy without Rodney's presence. But Adeline was as unpredictable as their test subjects. Plus, she'd promised him meatloaf for dinner. He sniffed the air, searching for the aroma. Nothing.

"Adeline," he shouted.

A heavy thud from the guest room sent a shiver up his spine. He rushed for the door and turned the glass doorknob. Locked. Panicking, he pounded against the wood. "Adeline!" He threw his weight against the door. Once. Twice. It splintered, then gave. "Oh, God," he gasped, then rushed forward, knocking Troy to the hardwood floor.

Adeline fell with them, Troy's hands still clutching her throat, her blouse torn, breasts bared. Rage slammed into him. He couldn't see straight. Blood rushed to his head, muffling Adeline's choking gasps.

Rodney rolled off Troy, then punched him in the kidney. The man arched back, but held a firm grip around Adeline's throat. When he hit him again, Troy barely flinched, kept one hand on Adeline, and swung his arm behind him, backhanding Rodney in the jaw.

He fell on his rear and immediately focused on Adeline, on the blood trickling from her nose and mouth, the way her eyes bulged and watered. She slid her gaze toward his and mouthed, "Kill him."

"Let him try. I'm going to force him to watch me rape you." Troy laughed. "Wait 'til he sees how I'm gonna kill you."

The other man's mocking laughter and threats stoked Rodney's rage. He scrambled to his feet and searched the room for a weapon. Finding nothing, he unbuckled his belt, pulled it free, then rushed toward Troy. He wrapped the leather around the man's throat and made like a cowboy breaking in a bucking bronco. He straddled Troy's back and used his body weight to pull back on the belt.

Troy and Adeline gasped and wheezed in unison until Troy released her throat and clawed behind him. Rodney ducked and weaved to avoid the other man's groping hands, then using the belt and all his might, he drove Troy off Adeline.

Troy's head bounced off the floor when they fell in a heap. Rodney let go of the leather straps, gripped the man by the hair, then slammed his head into the floor again and again. When Troy stopped moving, Rodney dropped the man's head and leaned back on his heels. Shaking, breathing hard, he registered Adeline's coughing and wheezing. He glanced to her, saw that the bastard had not only ripped her blouse and bra, but her pants, too.

No one but him had ever touched her body. No one else ever would.

Rodney looked to Troy. Noticed the rise and fall of his chest, and the blood pooling beneath his head. For a split second, disappointment gave him a quick stab in the gut, but he shoved it away. Troy had been his and Adeline's creation. They'd taken a normal man and had made him a monster. What had just happened had been their fault.

"What are you waiting for?" Adeline asked, her voice raw, hoarse. "Kill him."

If he hadn't come to his senses, he would have. He would have kept slamming Troy's head into the floor until he'd crushed the man's skull and his scrambled brain had spilled onto the hardwood.

"I'm not murdering the monster *we* created."

She pushed herself upright, but didn't bother to cover her breasts. "Look what he did to me. Your drug didn't work, and until it does, this could happen again."

He stilled. "My drug didn't work? What are you talking

about? He was on the placebo, not...you went behind my back and gave it to him?" Damn it. She had no right. The drug was his conception and he'd wanted to be there during each step.

"I'm sorry. I shouldn't have done it, but I was too excited to wait. So while you were finishing up with Noah, I thought I'd check on him. He went crazy, somehow got loose and..." She touched her throat. "At least we know your drug doesn't work."

"Wrong. What we don't know is if A-Line was completely out of his system."

She stared at Troy. "You're right. But we still can't keep this one, or let him free. If he ended up on the streets, I wouldn't be surprised if he tried raping and murdering women."

He hated that she was right, and that she could act so damned nonchalant about it. For him, the guilt, the knowing he'd harmed other innocents in the name of science, would eat him alive.

"Even if we let him live, he'll probably die anyway. The trauma to his head could cause hemorrhaging, bleeding on the brain or—"

"I know all that," he shouted. "I told you this was a mistake from the beginning." He stood, then paced. "What we're doing is morally *wrong*."

"Screw your morals. Don't start acting as if you didn't know the risks we were facing." Adeline rose and stepped in front of him. "Look what he did to me," she said, her cheeks flushed as she stabbed him in the chest with her finger. "I don't care that we made him. I care that he tried to rape and kill me." Her eyes narrowed. "Obviously, you're more concerned about your conscience than me."

He grabbed her arms. "You know damned well that's not true. My God, Adeline. I wanted to kill the man with my bare hands for touching you. I almost did, and I'm ashamed to admit that a part of me still wants him dead. But the sensible, rational side of me knows that putting our test subject out of his misery isn't a mercy kill, but murder."

Her eyes softened. "You're a good man. You're not like me,

and I don't ever want you to be." She let out a deep breath. "I'll kill him."

He gave her a slight shake. "No. Absolutely not."

"What's the difference? It's not like I haven't killed before." He pulled her into his arms and held her tight. "I won't allow it. We're trying to find a way to stop the urge, not encourage it."

She sobbed against his chest. "I'm so sorry, Rod. I hoped it would never come to this. I don't want you to have to make the choice of who lives and who dies."

He leaned back and touched her chin. "You know I'd die for you."

She sniffed and nodded. "Then I'd die because I couldn't be without you."

God, he loved her so much. Their bond was so special, so strong, he doubted even death could keep them apart. But her sickness could. If Adeline murdered again and was caught this time, prison would separate them for life. So would the death penalty.

He cupped her cheek. "I don't ever want that to happen," he said. "You're right. I knew exactly what I agreed to when we decided to conduct our testing. I knew the risks to our subjects, but had been foolish to not consider what could happen to you." He dropped his gaze to the marks along her throat and breasts. Something inside him snapped. Unexpected fury clawed its way to the surface demanding vengeance. "I'd not only die for you, but I'd kill for you."

What if Troy survived? What if he was worse off once his head healed? He walked to the closet, opened it, then pulled a pillow from the shelf.

"What are you doing?" Adeline asked, shock in her tone.

"Protecting you."

Rodney kneeled next to Troy. He stared at the man's battered face, at the blood haloing his head. He glanced to the man's hands, remembered how they'd looked wrapped around Adeline's throat. With a grunt, Rodney slammed the pillow against Troy's face, freed the fury piercing his moral compass and scraping it raw...and smothered the man who'd dared to touch Adeline.

Denver, Colorado
Thursday, 4:31 p.m. Mountain Daylight Saving Time

LIAM FORRESTER FLUSHED the toilet. He moved in front of the mirror and turned on the faucet. After he'd splashed cold water on his face, then toweled off, he stared at his reflection and hated what he saw. Desperation, fear...guilt.

A horn sounded from outside. He shoved away from the counter, grabbed his backpack from the floor, then left the bathroom. As he walked down the hallway, the family photos hanging on the walls slowed his steps. He stopped and stared at one that had been taken twenty years ago. He'd been ten, his sister, Kiera, twelve, their parents in their late thirties. They all looked happy, and had been. He turned away and continued down the hall. He couldn't think about those days—they were long gone, just like his mom and dad. A car accident, they'd been told. But he knew otherwise, which was why he had to distance himself from his sister before they came for her, too.

When the horn beeped again, he rushed to the door, then opened it. His buddy, Mitch, waved to him from the backseat of the taxi. Liam raised a finger, indicating he needed another minute, then glanced around his sister's house one last time. The guilt intensified. Kiera would worry and wonder where he'd gone, but it was best she didn't know. He didn't want *them* to use her against him, which was why he'd asked William to stay behind and keep an eye on her. William would know what to do if they tried to use her to find him. Liam prayed to God that wouldn't happen, and that he would get to them first.

Maybe he should leave Kiera a note, let her know she was being protected. That he was doing everything in his power to stop them.

No. The less she knew, the better off she was.

Nostalgia wrapped around his heart as he pictured Kiera's smile. He loved her and never wanted to be the reason that smile was snuffed from existence. Determined to make sure that never happened, he hefted the backpack over his shoulder, then left the house.

William whistled from the hedges near the driveway. Liam quickly approached him. "Heard anything?" he asked.

William shook his head. "Nothing you 'aven't," the Brit said. "Either Mitch or I will contact you. If it's anyone else—"

William smiled. "I know the drill, mate. I'll get y'r sister to the safe 'ouse."

"Thanks, man. I know I can count on your badass."

The cabbie laid into the horn. William looked over Liam's shoulder. "Impatient son of a bitch," Liam said, taking a step back. "This will be over soon."

William gave him a two-finger salute. "God willing."

Liam turned, then rushed for the taxi. When he climbed into the backseat, he told the cabbie to take them to the Greyhound station, then glanced to Mitch. "Ready?" he mouthed, not wanting the cabbie to hear him.

Mitch opened his jacket slightly, displaying a gun and knife. "As ever."

Both anxious and nervous, Liam leaned into the cracked upholstery. After years of running, of being in a constant state of paranoia, he finally had the means and muscle to stop the government from unleashing mind-bending drugs into America's water supply. Now all he needed was proof. He slid his gaze to the six-foot-six, dark-skinned mercenary. With Mitch's team, he would obtain it and expose the bastards.

When the cabbie pulled into the bus depot, Liam paid the man, then exited the car. Mitch met him on the sidewalk. "Split up. I have my ticket, go buy yours. I'm going to case the area and make sure we're not being followed. I'll see you on the bus. Separate seats."

Liam nodded, then tossed his backpack over his shoulders and walked toward the ticket counter. Mitch was just as paranoid as him—which suited Liam just fine. Better to be paranoid than dead.

When he reached the counter, the cashier greeted him with a smile. "How can I help you?" she asked.

"I need a one way ticket to Miami, Florida." After she told him the price, he paid in cash, then asked, "How many stops will the bus make and where?" Mitch probably had all the information, but Liam wanted to make sure he was prepared for anything. Especially if something happened to Mitch.

"Let me pull up the information on my system," she said, tapping at the computer keyboard. "Okay, the trip will take two days and three and a half hours. It looks like you'll be making two transfer stops. One in St. Louis, Missouri, and Atlanta, Georgia. Is there anything else I can help you with today?"

He shook his head and thanked the woman. As he made his way onto the bus, he spotted Mitch, already seated a few rows behind Liam's assigned seat. He gave Mitch a slight nod, then sat. Minutes later, his cell phone vibrated, signaling a text message. He glanced to the screen and read the message from Mitch.

We have two days to rest. Take advantage of every hour. When we reach Miami we won't be getting any sleep.

The House of Archer, Bower, Georgia
Thursday, 8:12 p.m. Eastern Daylight Saving Time

RODNEY DROPPED THE shovel, then stepped out of the old barn to cool off and take a break from the hot, stagnant air. The temperature still hovered in the high eighties, making the barn as hot as a furnace. His shirt was soaked and clung to his skin. Sweat dripped from his forehead and stung his eyes. He used his shoulder to wipe away the sweat, then reached for the jug of water under the live oak tree. Empty. Damn. He didn't want to walk the half mile back to the house for more water. At least he wouldn't have to drag a body with him. He'd lugged Troy to the barn right after he'd killed the man and had definitely learned the true meaning of carrying around dead weight. Despite the fact that the man hadn't eaten once during the days he'd been with them, Rodney estimated that Troy had weighed close to one hundred and eighty pounds.

A whistle caught his attention. He shaded his eyes from the setting sun as he searched the field. Adeline emerged from a copse of gangly pines and held up a small cooler.

Although grateful to not have to walk to the house for water, he wasn't ready to see Adeline. He wasn't ready to face anyone, let alone his own reflection. He'd killed a man. As he'd dug Troy's grave, he replayed the man's death several times in his head. Like a scratched record stuck and tripping over a single note, one particular image had repeated itself. Troy's hands around Adeline's neck, the bulging of her watery eyes. Watching Adeline approach him now, her long hair caught up on the breeze, her billowy sundress pressing against the contours of her sexy curves, added to his self-loathing.

Because given the chance, he'd kill Troy again.

He didn't regret taking the man's life. Troy had come to them a leery, yet friendly individual. Although Adeline had discovered him at a homeless shelter in Tallahassee, and he'd needed a shower, shave and haircut, his clothes hadn't been in bad shape. When Rodney had asked him about his work skills—under the ruse that they would pay Troy seventy-five dollars a day, plus room and board, to work the land—Troy had explained that he'd been homeless for only three weeks. He'd lost his job, then his house and had lived in his car until that had been repossessed. The seventy-five dollars would have given Troy the chance to make his way north to where he had family. Instead, he and Adeline had turned Troy into a monster. And *that* he regretted.

If fate wouldn't have brought Troy and Adeline together, Troy might still be at the homeless shelter, or trying his damnedest to reach the family he had up north. But that man had disappeared the moment they'd sent the A-Line drug into his veins.

Too bad his drug hadn't been able to quickly reverse the damage. Too bad they had only one test subject left.

"Thirsty?" Adeline asked when she reached the barn.

He nodded and took the cooler from her. After pulling out a bottle of water and taking a drink, he looked to the marks on her throat, her swollen lip, the slight bruise on her cheek. "How are you feeling?"

"Sad."

He eyed her with skepticism. Sadness was one emotion he'd never seen from her. "Why's that?"

"I know how much you value life, and you had to end a man's today because of me."

He looked away. "What happened to Troy wasn't your fault. My drug didn't work, so the blame is on me."

She crossed her arms over her chest. "But if you weren't trying to help me, if I wasn't…sick, you wouldn't be creating the drug."

"If Troy hadn't lost his job, he would have never met you. He'd be alive and some other man would be dead in his place." He took a step forward. "We could go back and forth with this and it'll do neither of us any good. Don't blame yourself for being born a certain way. This is *not* your fault."

She reached for his shoulders and searched his eyes. "It's not yours, either. You know that, right?"

"I killed a man."

"In the name of science."

"Science? That's an excuse. I could have let him live. I could have tried to save him. I chose to smother him instead." He stared at the marks along Adeline's throat. "I allowed my emotions to rule my judgment."

She moved her hands from his shoulders. "You're sweaty. I brought you a shirt," she said, bending down and retrieving a plastic grocery bag from the cooler. "How are your emotions now?"

He pulled off the soiled, damp shirt in exchange for the clean, dry one Adeline offered him. "What do you mean?"

"Do you feel remorse?"

"Of course. We've been over this." He slid the shirt over his head, and let the hem drop. Adeline's hand stopped the material. "I feel sadness for you, because I love you. But I have no idea what it's like to feel true remorse," she said, running the back of her hand along his stomach. "Since Geoffrey was only fifteen, I thought I'd feel guilty for what I did to him. I waited for it." She inched closer, moved her hand to the waistband of his jeans. "I stared at his mutilated face, at the hole I'd put in his head, the bits of brain clinging to the knife and rock I'd used and felt nothing but the desire to do it again."

"Why?" Other than showing him Geoffrey's body, Adeline had never spoken of the murder.

Her lips tilted into a grin as she loosened the button of his jeans. "The rush. The shock and betrayal on Geoff's face. Knowing I had power over his life and how he would die." Her smile grew. "And, no, I don't believe I have a God complex."

"But you liked the power."

She closed her eyes and placed her hand over his crotch. "And the pain." She cupped him, and this time, he let her. Right or wrong, he loved when she touched him, loved touching her.

"I tasted his blood," she continued. "Not on purpose. When I smashed the rock against his face it splashed up at me and hit me in the mouth. It was warm, and knowing that only seconds before it had been pumping through his body made me want to see more of his blood."

His penis thickened. He grabbed her hand and held it still against him. "Is that why you stabbed Cindy forty-three times?" Adeline's college roommate, Cindy Cantrell, had been stabbed so badly, she'd almost been decapitated.

"No, I never liked the bitch. She was a slob and always stole my food. Even if I'd been able to take my time with her like I did with Geoff, I wouldn't have. She wasn't worth it. I just wanted her dead and out of my life."

"Most people would have gotten a new roommate."

She pressed her breasts against him and stared at his mouth. "I moved in with you, didn't I?" she asked, leaning her lips toward his.

He grabbed her mouth and forced her to look at him. "Geoff was going to move into Gramma's for the summer." He released her, then knocked her hand from his erection. "That's why you killed him and our baby. Isn't it?"

"I have no idea where you're going with this. I'm heading back to the house."

He gripped her arm and swung her around. "Admit it. You don't want anyone else in my life. If Gramma didn't have so much money, she'd probably be dead, too."

"A little egocentric, don't you think?"

Maybe. Or maybe killing a man, then spending a couple of hours digging his grave made him paranoid and edgy.

He turned away from her and picked up the shovel. "Just go back to the house."

"I saved dinner for tomorrow night, but there's plenty of lunchmeat in the fridge. I'll make you a sandwich once you're showered."

"I'm not hungry."

"Understandable, but you can't ignore your health. We still have another test subject to attend to."

"Stay away from him. I'll take care of his meds when I'm done here. I shouldn't be much longer."

"He's fine for now. I gave him the saline drops, changed the video and voice recordings out, and started the placebo. I'm hoping your drug works on him, but I still think we should get a couple of more test subjects. I think it would be interesting to see how my drug and yours works on a woman."

Stunned, he held the shovel in both hands and faced her again. "I'm about to put a man in the hole I just dug, and you're already planning to experiment on more people? Christ, you really are sick," he said with disgust.

Her chin trembled. She looked away and rubbed the back of

her neck. "I'll see you at the house."

Guilt had him dropping the shovel and reaching for her. "I'm sorry. I shouldn't have said that."

Not meeting his gaze, she shook her head. "No, you're right. There is something wrong with me." When she looked up at him, tears shimmered in her eyes. "I just told you why I killed Cindy, and that I tasted Geoff's blood. As for additional test subjects, I understand if you don't want to continue with the experiments. I just figured that if we're going to do this, we better be prepared, especially because we only have a short time before Gramma gets back from her trip."

Seven weeks and three days. Not the ideal time frame to run such a complex experiment, but they had no choice. Gramma couldn't know. The righteous old woman would go to the authorities. But if they succeeded and discovered the proper chemicals and dosage to 'fix' the monsters they created, governments around the world would want his drug.

"I'll think about it. When you go back to the house, stay away from the test subject. I don't want a repeat of this evening."

She nodded. A tear slipped down her cheek as she started to turn.

He stopped her, then touched her cheek. So smooth, so soft. "I didn't mean what I said." He captured a tear with his thumb. "I'm sorry. I was angry. Maybe when I'm done here and showered, we can have something to eat and talk about bringing in more test subjects."

She brightened a bit, but the earlier sparkle in her eyes hadn't returned. "Tomorrow? The subject needs to be on A-Line for at least three days. In theory, we should be able to see some results within a week of administering your drug."

"I agree. And since I took a leave from the clinic, it'll be good for both of us to get out of the house anyway. I'd like to wait another day, though. I don't want to leave the test subject alone the first day we administer the placebo."

"Good idea." She finally smiled. "Going to Tallahassee will

give me something to look forward to."

"I know you were wearing a disguise, but I don't want to run the risk of you being recognized. I think we should switch cities. How about Atlanta?"

CHAPTER 3

Tallahassee, Florida
Friday, 2:06 p.m. Eastern Daylight Saving Time

"WHO'S THE GUY we're meeting?" Harrison asked her as she exited I-75.

Melanie's stomach flipped as she made another left turn. In less than fifteen minutes they'd arrive at her house. And it *was* still her house. While she was here, she should have Cash remove the chandelier from her walk-in closet. The closet was actually considered a bedroom, but Cash had turned the small space into a frilly, girly, princess-like sanctuary for her. She sighed. Dang if it hadn't been a sweet place to house her clothes, shoes and purses. She pictured the enormous full-length mirror that had been too big to hang, but had looked fabulous propped against the wall. As she made another turn, her memory took one, as well. How many times had she and Cash made love in front of that mirror?

"Well, honey," Harrison began, hitching his voice and using an exaggerated southern drawl, "I'd tell ya' who we're meeting, but then I'd have to hide your body in my daddy's swamp."

She laughed and tossed her hair over her shoulder. "Sounds about right."

"Okay, then if you won't tell me, I won't help you."

"Lola said you have to. Or maybe you'd rather be back at Polina's Paradise hanging out with Vlad and his gator?"

Harrison groaned. "No thanks."

"I don't get you two."

"I told you I don't want to talk about Vlad."

They'd been on the road for nearly six and a half hours. One thing she liked about Harrison was that he didn't feel the need to fill the silence. Sure, they'd talked, but he'd also been cool with simply listening to the radio. She had to admit, she'd enjoyed this mini road trip and learning more about him. While she knew that he'd been incarcerated before joining CORE—the legit version of ATL—she hadn't realized why.

Holy moly, had he surprised her. With his laid back, computer geek attitude, she would have never guessed that he had helped stop a madman who'd murdered over two hundred innocent people. But Harrison hadn't been the only one to stop the killing spree. Vlad had been by Harrison's side through the ordeal. The two of them were like Oscar and Felix from *The Odd Couple*. They were best friends, yet total opposites.

"Then I guess we're even," she said. "If you won't tell me what's going on at Polina's Paradise, I'll make my own assumptions, since Vlad already gave me his side of the story."

"I guarantee his version made me look like the asshole."

"It did," she said, egging him on. She'd rather focus on Vlad and Harrison's issues than think about seeing Cash. Despite their problems, she knew one look from him—that cocky one that said, *I'm going to taste you, love you and make you come in a heartbeat*— could derail her reason for driving to Tallahassee.

"Right. Poor, innocent Vlad. Everybody's buddy," he said with heavy sarcasm. "Look, he's a good dude. But until you live with him, don't judge me."

"I get it. So you have an issue with his smoking."

"A big issue. Do you realize that he's been smoking since he was a kid? Like twelve or something ridiculous? He's also a total slob. He lets his stupid gator run the house, leaves his shoes and clothes all over the place and never, and I mean never, puts his dishes in the dishwasher, let alone unload the damned thing. *And*, you'd think by now the man would be done referring to himself in third person. Vlad this, Vlad that." He heaved another sigh. "You know, I don't care why I'm here with you. Just thinking about Vlad pisses me off. It's a good thing we're getting a little distance from each other."

That had been what she'd thought about Cash. A little distance. A little time and he'd change. But he hadn't. Which had made her realize she loved him more than he'd ever loved her. And that realization hurt. Badly. He'd obviously loved her enough to marry her, just not enough to change his destructive ways. How could he ever expect her to raise children with a man who risked his life on a regular basis? Not that the kid part mattered. After how Bobby had turned out, she had no business having any of her own.

"Maybe one of you should move out," she suggested. "You could move into Barney's trailer, let Barney move into Polina's Paradise, and—"

"No way. If anyone is moving, it's Vlad."

"Then let Barney move in with you and give Vlad his trailer."

"And listen to Barney's stories? Oh, my God. Where's the ice pick so I can pierce my eardrums?"

She stiffened. "I like Barney's stories."

"So do I. At least when he tells them, he doesn't refer to himself in third person. But I still couldn't see us living together, or Barney giving up his own space."

Her stomach tightened and her palms grew sweaty as she turned the Camaro onto the street leading to her and Cash's house. Harrison and his complaining were not enough of a distraction. The anticipation was killing her. She wanted to see Cash. Kiss him. Touch him. Run her hands along each and every one of his scars to make sure he was okay. Once she'd done that, she wanted to push and shove him for making her so miserable with constant worry. If only, for more than ten minutes, he thought about her rather than himself. But that was the way he was made.

Can't change the stripes of a tiger.

"Vlad has Barney snowed anyway," Harrison said, as she slowed the Camaro to a stop two houses away from hers and

Cash's. "Are we here?"

"Almost."

"Why are we stopping?"

She debated over how much she should tell Harrison. The truth would be the best route, but she wasn't good at that. Fibs and exaggerations kept people happy. But, like her, Cash had a temper and a severe jealous streak. He could take one look at Harrison and go territorial. After all, they were still married and Harrison was a good-looking guy. Just not her type.

She pulled lipstick from her purse. "I just need a sec."

"For what? Why are you putting on that?"

"Don't worry about it," she said, checking her reflection in the visor mirror and giving her hair a little volume with her fingertips. Once she had her hair exactly the way Cash liked it—draping her shoulders and wavy—she shifted into DRIVE, but didn't take her foot off the brake.

"What are you doing?" Harrison asked.

"What do you mean?"

"Who are we seeing that you have to make sure you look hot?"

"You think I'm hot?"

He shrugged. "Yeah, when you're not threatening anyone with a knife. But I mean that in a brotherly sense," he quickly added. "I don't want us to be weird or anything. No offense, you're not my type."

She turned to him. "Vlad told me my boobs were too small. Is that your problem with me, too?"

Harrison looked out the window. "No. And I don't want to discuss your body. It's almost...you're kind of like a sister, so that's just gross." He tapped his thigh with his palm. "Are you going to drive?"

Melanie looked toward the house, drew in a breath and lifted her foot off the brake. She eased the Camaro forward and moved the car to a crawl.

"So, are you going to tell me who we're meeting or not?"

"Cash Maddox."

"Perfect. That answers all of my questions. Now I know why you're making sure you look hot and are driving at five miles an hour."

"He's a repo man," she added.

"Are lipstick and big hair a requirement when meeting a repo man? If so, I'd better wait in the car."

She grinned. "That'd be a no."

"Unless you've dated the guy and want him to see what he's missing?"

She glanced at him before pulling into the driveway.

"I'm right?" Harrison asked. "Now I definitely have to meet this guy. Anyone who can handle the Ice Cream Lady—"

"We're not together, so don't go admiring him for what he *can't* handle." She threw the car into PARK. "And as far as Cash knows, all I do is work at the ice cream shop. Don't you dare mention a word about ATL or my garage."

"He doesn't know you chop cars and boats?"

"He doesn't think I do it anymore and I want to keep it that way."

"Why?"

"Because," she said, opened the door, then slid from the car.

"Awesome explanation. I really appreciate how open you've been with me." Harrison met her at the front of the car. "Is there anything else I should know about your repo man?"

"Just don't stare at my behind. Cash can get a little jealous," she said, remembering the time Cash had broken a guy's nose for looking at her butt. That'd been before the accident and she and Cash had been in a bad place. Too much partying, arguing, accusing each other of messing around. The fights, the make-up sex—looking back, she missed those days. The passion, the excitement, the dangers of the repo business. In a way, Cash's *accident* had saved her from the self-destructive life she'd been leading with him. But she was in a better place now.

Alone.

"Maybe I should wait in the car," Harrison suggested.

"C'mon, honey." She forced a smile. "You're a badass secret agent. Don't let a repo man bother you."

"Anyone who does a job like that is crazy," he said as he fell in step with her. "Crazy trumps badass, and I don't even carry a gun."

Harrison couldn't carry a weapon due to his felony. The computer geek would freak if he knew Cash had been part of the Explosive Ordinance Disposal unit while in Iraq. That was crazier than taking someone's car away from them for not making payments to the bank.

"Oh, stop. We won't be here long. Cash knows where to look for Bobby." She could have driven straight to Frenchtown, where Ross had said Bobby was last seen with Quinell Willis, but she didn't want to go there without Cash. He'd grown up not far from the area, knew the people and who to go to for answers.

When they reached the front door, she touched the faded, sun-bleached wreath she'd made over two years ago. Nostalgia settled over her heart. Although Cash had still been recovering from his injuries, those days had been happy ones. He hadn't been able to repo.

Betrayal and frustration gave nostalgia the boot. Dang it. They could have been good together. She knocked on the door. Instead, they were living separate lives because *she* wasn't enough. Not enough excitement, not enough of a challenge. His accident had taught her that she didn't need those things anymore. Then again, she had signed on to ATL and did still chop the occasional car or boat. Oh, God. There was also those bodies she'd disposed of in her daddy's swamp.

The door opened and Harrison took an immediate step back. Cash's large body filled the threshold. His t-shirt clung to his arms and chest, revealing the muscles she loved to hang onto when she rode him. Her heart beat hard as she shifted her gaze from his chest to his mouth. How she'd love to shove him against the door and kiss that arrogant, overconfident smile off his lips.

"How are ya', babe?" Cash asked, his tone rough, sexy.

She met his gaze. His dark-brown eyes held hunger, lust and smugness. During their two-year separation, they'd found excuses to see each other. Then they'd have a long weekend of hot sex. Cash was in for a rude awakening. Just because he knew how to make her moan didn't mean he'd be getting any action during this visit.

He took a step forward and crowded her space. She inhaled his cologne as he slid a finger along her jawline until he reached her chin. "I've missed you." He leaned forward, brought their mouths so close together his warm breath brushed her lips.

God, how she ached for him. If only he loved her enough. The reminder stung and bolstered the promise she'd made to herself: no sex, discuss making their separation permanent.

"Don't touch me," she murmured. "I have my period."

His lips, still too tempting and close to hers, slid into a big smile as Harrison released a groan from behind her. Cash's eyes narrowed. No longer smiling, he looked over her head. "Who's he?"

"Harrison Fairclough. He's here to help me."

"Tell him to go home. I'm all you need."

She gave his hard chest a shove, but he didn't budge or take his gaze off Harrison. "You're so full of yourself. I don't need anything from you I can't get somewhere else."

White-hot jealousy tensed his entire body. Cash looked down at Melanie—*his* woman—and gave her a menacing look that would intimidate most men. "Are you?" he managed, when he wanted to move her aside and kick the dick behind her off their property.

"Am I what?" she asked, her blue eyes wide and innocent. But he knew that look, knew she was fucking with him, and that Melanie Scarlet was far from innocent. She was sex personified. She was his late night fantasy.

She was the love of his life.

"Getting it from someone else. Maybe this scrawny guy with the pompous name," he said, not bothering to hide his irritation.

If anything, this time with Mel would give him something new to talk about with his therapist.

"Not everyone is as freakishly big as you, *Cash*."

"The ladies don't complain. If I recall, you didn't either, *Mel*."

She shoved her jaw forward and narrowed her eyes. "All the more reason I'm glad I'm bleeding. You're probably carrying more diseases than a rat."

"No worries, babe. They make condoms large enough to handle my freakishly big—"

"You're such a pig."

"I thought I was a rat."

"That, too."

"At least I have the decency *not* to throw my girlfriend in your face." Her eyes widened as she sucked in a breath. Damn, he'd pushed a little too hard. "Not that I have a girlfriend," he quickly amended.

"Rolled off your tongue easily enough." He saw the hurt in her eyes before she looked away. "On second thought, my scrawny, pompously named boyfriend and I don't need your help."

"You two realize I'm standing behind you, right?" the not so scrawny guy asked. If the guy had been a beanpole, he'd have blown the man off as Mel's legit friend. Even then, he'd probably still be jealous. In his opinion, men and women couldn't be friends without sleeping together. At least that'd been his experience and why he no longer had any female friends within ten years younger or older than him.

"Stay out of this, honey," Mel said, the term of endearment pissing him off. Yeah, she called everyone honey, but he didn't know this guy.

"It's hard to stay out of a conversation when I'm part of it. Plus, I thought we needed Cash to help find Bobby."

"Your boyfriend has a point."

"I don't care." She lifted her chin. "Maybe if you possessed an ounce of maturity, I could tolerate being around you. Since that's an impossibility, I'm going to pet my dog and leave."

"I'm not and never will be Mel's boyfriend," Harrison said, holding up his hands. "I can barely handle being friends with her."

Cash stared at the man who had obviously lost his frickin' mind. "What's that supposed to mean?" he asked, taking Mel by the arms and setting her aside. "Is Mel not good enough for you?"

"I didn't say that." Harrison stepped back. "I mean, she's pretty and all, but she's not my type."

"Why not?" he asked, wondering how any man could stay away from Melanie. Not only was she gorgeous, she was loving and loyal—when it suited her.

"Wait, you're asking me why I don't want to date a woman you apparently have or had a relationship with, correct?"

Hell, when the guy put it that way, it did sound like a stupid question.

"I believe he was," Melanie said. When Cash looked to her, she shrugged. "I don't want to date Harrison, either, but I am curious. At least Vlad was honest about telling me my boobs were too small."

When you feel your temper escalating, repeat the calming phrase we created.

He unclenched his fists and drew in a deep breath from his diaphragm. "Unicorns are magical. Unicorns are magical."

"I'm sorry, what was that?" Harrison asked.

"It's the phrase that's saving your ass from being kicked. Make fun of me and I'll kick it anyway."

Harrison nodded. "I'm going to the car."

"Wait," Melanie called. "I'm sorry. Cash tends to bring out the worst in me."

"Nope. I'm jumping off this crazy train, since I'm the only sane one on board." Harrison pointed a finger at her. "You want to know why you're not my type only to make him jealous." He turned to Cash. "And you want to know so you have an excuse to kick my ass. Clearly, you two have major issues."

"You're right," Mel said. "I'm sorry." She tossed him a set of keys. "I'm right behind you."

Harrison caught the keys and glared at him. "This has been *magical*," he said, then turned and walked away.

While he still wanted to kick Harrison's ass, especially for the 'magical' shot, he respected a man who had balls. Plus, this gave him and Mel a moment alone and the opportunity to kiss her the way he'd been dying to.

She brushed past him. "I'm going to say hi to Dolly."

He followed Mel into the house, grabbed her arm and hauled her against him. She looked up at him, her eyes glittering with anger and guilt. "Please let me go," she said with a hitch to her breath when he wrapped an arm around her and brought their bodies flush.

"I can't."

She reached up and cupped his jaw. "Neither can I," she said with so much damned sadness it made him ache.

Ignoring her tone and what it meant for them, he brought their mouths closer. "I've missed you." He brushed his lips against hers. "Nothing's the same without you."

"That's on you."

The disappointment in her eyes killed him. He could give her what she wanted, give them both what they needed, and end their two-year separation. But he didn't want to. He wanted his fucking cake, the whole damned thing, and to eat it, too. Right now, he wanted to kiss his wife.

"I want you on me," he said, taking the easy, immature way and making light of something serious. When she stiffened, he regretted his words and wished he could be the kind of man she deserved—smarter, well spoken, good with emotions.

"And I just want to see my dog." She pushed away, but he held her still. "I'm serious, let me go."

"I told you, I can't." He'd expected her temper to flare and for her to push him again, not her eyes to mist with tears. His chest tightened with panic. Mel never cried.

"Then maybe I'm the one who needs to put us both out of

our misery and do what I should've done a long time ago."

"Don't," he warned her.

"Or else what?" A tear slipped down her cheek. "I don't want the house or a piece of your business. I don't want anything except for you to stay out of my life, or be my husband in every sense—not just on paper."

He shoved his hand through her thick wavy hair and cupped her head. "I'm the same man you fell in love with eight years ago. Why does anything have to change?"

"Because I'm not the same woman, and we're not in our twenties. It's time to grow up, Cash. I'm ready to move on, with or without you."

He brought her mouth close to his again. "No divorce," he said, then pressed his lips against hers. When she didn't kiss him back, his panic intensified. She'd threatened him before, but not like this. She'd never brought another man with her or resisted his touch. He'd finally done it. He'd taken something good and pure and had fucked it up completely. With a sigh and regret weighing on him, he eased back. "I don't want a divorce."

"And I don't want to live seven hours from my husband."

Dolly let out a bark, then another. "I think she heard her mama's voice." He eased up on his possessive hold. He wanted to tell her that Dolly hadn't been the same since she'd left. That even after her brief visits the dog would be down for a few days. He would be, too. Only longer. But he wouldn't. Guilt didn't work with Mel, especially when it was his fault she refused to come back to him.

"Where's my girl," Mel sang.

He grinned. His woman could sing, and just hearing her now brought back memories of when he'd been injured. The late nights when the meds weren't working and the pain had been unbearable. How she'd eased his fears with sweet lullabies.

God, he was a dick. She'd nursed him back to health, and he'd given her nothing but heartache in return.

Dolly barked and wheeled over to see Mel.

"Such a pretty girl," Mel cooed. "Mama misses you." She hugged the dog, and he had another sucker punch of guilt when Dolly closed her eyes and rested her head on Mel's shoulder.

A horn blared from the driveway. Dolly lifted her head and perked her ears.

Mel hugged the dog tighter. "I have to go. Mama will be back soon with something pretty for you." She kissed the dog on the top of her head, then stood. After sucking in a shaky breath, she said, "I'll be by before I leave."

He grabbed her arm as she walked past him. "You're not staying here?"

"Harrison and I rented a couple of rooms at the Holiday Inn."

"You're seriously not staying here?" Since she'd left him, there hadn't been a time that she hadn't stayed with him when she'd returned to Tallahassee. And those times had been great, until the topic of their marriage and his job had come into play. Then they'd fight, she'd leave and they wouldn't speak for weeks. A vicious cycle, but one he'd become familiar with—until now. She was changing things up on him, and he didn't know how to react. He did, but his therapist would likely have a frickin' stroke.

"Well, you're seriously not going to change and I seriously want a divorce. So, yeah. I think it's best if I stay at a hotel."

He pulled her close. "Stay with me."

Her gaze dropped to his mouth. "No."

He pressed his body against hers and slid his hand along her rear. "Give me a few days."

"I've given you two years," she said, breathless, her gaze shifting from his mouth to his eyes.

She had him there, and he had nothing to counter her argument. She had given him two years, and he arrogantly figured she'd eventually come back to him.

"You're right," he said honestly.

"*I'm* right?"

He nodded and walked her backward. "I don't want a divorce, but we can't keep going on the way we've been." He pressed her against the foyer wall. "Give me the time you're here to prove we can make this work."

"I'm here to find Bobby, not deal with our marriage."

"I know, baby. We'll find him. I promise. I've already put word out on the street that we're looking for him." He leaned closer. "Just give us a chance."

Her eyes filled with tears again. "I can't keep doing this. It hurts too much."

Knowing he was hurting her left him hollow and shameful. "I'm sorry."

She punched him in the arm. "You've said you're sorry more times than I can count. Do something about it."

He kissed her.

She pushed him away. "Not with sex."

"That's right. You have your period."

"I lied."

"And I just want to kiss you."

She stared at him, her eyes unreadable. "Sometimes I hate you," she said, then shoved her hand through his hair and captured his lips.

His therapist would tell him to end the kiss, that they weren't solving anything, only prolonging the hurt. His therapist could go fuck himself. He had his woman in his arms and she was kissing him. Running her hands through his hair in that possessive way he loved. Pressing her breasts against his chest as if she couldn't get close enough. Skimming her tongue along his in a way that him hard and ready.

The damned horn beeped again. Mel tore her mouth away from his, then gave him a push. "I'm leaving."

"I'm coming with you."

"Fine. But the focus is on finding Bobby, not us"

Dolly rolled over toward them. Mel gave the dog another hug. "I'm leaving in two minutes, with or without you."

As he watched his wife walk away, he stared at her ass, and stroked the dog's head. "Well, Dolly, you heard your mama.

Looks like I either call it quits or lose my wife." He looked down at Dolly, who panted and hung her tongue to the side. "You've been retired for eight years. Is it so bad?"

CHAPTER 4

Tallahassee, Florida
Friday, 2:56 p.m. Eastern Daylight Saving Time

"ARREN'T YOU GOING to talk to me, honey?" Melanie asked Harrison, laying her southern drawl on thick. Harrison and Vlad usually melted around her when she added a little sugar to her words, but today she might've ticked Harrison off too much to make him budge.

"You egged on your boyfriend."

She saw Cash's truck in her rear view mirror, and was grateful her abrupt departure hadn't deterred him from helping her. She'd told him he had two minutes before she left, but he'd had her so worked up, she didn't want to be in the same car with him. She also didn't want Cash giving Harrison any more crap. "He's not my boyfriend, and I don't know what you're talking about."

He snorted and looked out the window. "Well, whatever the hell he is, the dude is crazy."

"Don't call him that."

"Of course you would defend him. You're just as crazy." He shook his head and folded his arms across his chest. "I bet you loved how jealous he got, didn't you?"

"That's ridiculous," she said, but if she were honest with herself, the answer would be yes. Her husband chose his career—and she'd use that term loosely—over her. When she'd come into town to torture herself with sex and heated arguments, she and Cash had rarely left their home. Anymore, she had no idea if he still thought she was worth a barroom brawl.

"That's a crock of crap." He sighed. "So what is he?"

Sexy, bullheaded, the love of her life. "What do you mean?"

He glanced to her. "Please don't play dumb. If you're not going to be honest, I'll assume he's an ex-boyfriend. And let me say, you made a good choice in making him an ex. That's not the kind of guy who knows how to treat women right."

"He treated me just fine. He's always been a gentleman. Would open the door for me, bring me flowers, take me to nice places."

Harrison chuckled. "Yeah, right."

"It's true. Cash might be selfish when it comes to certain things, and he might have a bit of a temper, but he's very generous."

"With his fist, I'm sure."

"He wouldn't have hit you," she said with less confidence than she projected. Several months ago, Cash had mentioned seeing a therapist for his anger issues and had assured her he had his temper under control. Today was the first time she'd seen him test whether those therapy sessions had worked. Thanks to Cash, she'd never think of magical unicorns the same way again.

"Whatever. So how long did you date him?"

"Five years. We stopped dating about three years ago." When they'd married.

She made a turn, bringing them closer to Cash's garage. In another ten minutes she'd have to face his friends. Sure, they'd treated her great, but those men had known Cash for years. Their loyalty was to him, not her. She'd been friends with them by association. While she hadn't planned on stopping at the garage, Cash had called when he'd realized she'd left without him, and informed her that they were picking up Sully, who'd also grown up in the same area as Cash and knew Frenchtown well.

"How'd you meet?" Harrison asked.

"I was stealing the car Cash planned to repossess."

"If you don't want me to know, then just say so. You don't

have to lie about it."

She grinned. "Who's lying? That's exactly how we met. I was in the process of hotwiring a sporty little BMW, when this bulging hunk of a man knocks on the window."

"Bulging hunk of a man." He wiped a hand down his face and chuckled. "Now I'm sorry I asked."

"I'm not. It's a good memory." Very good. She'd initially been terrified Cash was a cop. At the time, she'd been stealing and chopping cars for close to two months for a guy name Deuce, but hadn't been busted. If she'd gone to prison, it would have killed Daddy. Plus, who would take care of Bobby? She didn't want to think about how disappointed Barney and the Monahan boys would have been. Thanks to Cash, she'd quit the business. He'd showed her there were other ways to make money and life exciting. That loving him was enough of an adrenaline rush, and risking prison wasn't worth the income she could make legitimately.

"If you're going to continue on with Bulging Muscles, I don't need to know. Wait, you *stole* cars?"

"Don't judge me. You went to prison for robbing a bank."

He cleared his throat. "It was a virtual bank robbery. I did it with my computer, not a gun."

She shrugged. "You still did time. Whereas I didn't."

"Because you didn't get caught. And don't act like you're some innocent goody two-shoes. You're still chopping cars. Then there's the bodies in the swamp thing."

She pulled into the garage's parking lot. "Let's get a couple of things straight before we leave this car. These are very important. Like your life depends on it important." She put the car in PARK, then faced him. "No one in Everglades City knows I was stealing. I want to keep it that way."

"But you chop cars and boats."

"That's different. Barney, Ryan and Shane know all about it. It's how my daddy kept a roof over our heads."

"You learned about cars from your dad?"

"Don't forget the boats." When he cocked a brow, she smiled. "You need to promise not to tell anyone what I used to do in Tallahassee. Okay?"

"Promise," he said, looking out the front window. "Your ex is staring at me as if he wants to rip off my head. Maybe we should get out of the car. You can threaten me and make me promise you whatever later."

She waved to Cash, who glared at Harrison. "He can wait, this can't. I meant what I said earlier. Other than working at the ice cream shop, Cash can't know anything about what I'm doing with ATL."

"Don't worry about it. I heard you the first time." He gripped the door handle. "Great, Bulging Muscles is now walking to the car. Watch, he's going to drag my ass out, then kick it."

She half-laughed. "Oh, honey, that's just Cash trying to intimidate you. I've seen him do it plenty of times." She exited the car and closed the door. "You're supposed to open *my* door, not Harrison's," she said, just as Cash made his way to the passenger side.

He looked up at her. Sunglasses hid his eyes, the firm set of his jaw told her he was irritated. "You're right. I apologize."

The driver's side window opened a crack. "Can you get him away from my door?" Harrison asked as he leaned across the seat and continued to roll down the window.

She looked to Cash. "Let Harrison out before he has heat stroke."

"God forbid that happens," Cash said, stepping away from the Camaro.

Harrison quickly climbed out of the car, then met up with her. "He just wants to intimidate me, huh?"

"You need to stop whining. The guys who work for Cash aren't any different from him. Remember who you are and what you do for a living. You might not be as big as these guys are, but you're tough in your own way."

"Thanks. I'm sure that was hard to say with a straight face."

She stopped him. "Why would you say that? I meant what I said."

"Why? Mel, you pick on me like I'm your kid brother. If you think back, you have issues giving a compliment."

Did she? "Not true. Two days ago I complimented Lola on her shoes."

He rolled his eyes. "You know what I mean. Something else...for whatever reason, you think you need to shock people with the things you say. What you do with your knives? I don't get it. You're this total girly-girl, yet you can't let your guard down for a second to let anyone see who you really are. It's like you have multiple defense mechanisms."

"Are you two coming?" Cash called.

She held up a finger. "Are you taking online psychology courses or something?" she asked, irritated he took a simple compliment and turned it into a 'let's psychoanalyze Mel' session.

Anger flashed in Harrison's eyes. "Forget I said anything."

"That's a good idea," she said, and walked toward Cash. She didn't like to discuss herself, her shortcomings or faults, especially because Harrison was right. Before she'd walked away from her marriage, she'd been a different person. Nicer. Caring. She could still be nice, and she did care, but hiding behind walls of cynicism and bizarre eccentricities had helped keep her secrets secret. As for the knives? Daddy had taught her how to throw and wield one at a very early age. She could hit a bull's eye from twenty feet away, and later use the same knife to dice vegetables like a professional chef. After growing up in a swamp, she'd also learned that knives came in handy if she encountered unwanted critters—reptilian, amphibian, and mammals, humans included.

"Why does he look pissed off?" Cash asked, nodding back toward Harrison.

"You threatened to kick his ass."

Cash looked over his shoulder. "I dunno, he's glaring at *your* back." He gave her a nudge. "What'd you say to him?"

"Nothing. I think that's the problem," she admitted, and realized she needed to not only evaluate her relationship with Cash, but herself. The ATL crew were her friends and pseudo family, and she didn't treat them very well. They still didn't need to know about her and Cash, or anything else that had happened in their relationship. Especially Ryan, Shane and Barney. They would wonder why she'd foolishly stayed married to Cash, and would be hurt that she'd kept so much more hidden from them.

"You've lost me."

"Harrison is one of those talkie types. When I talk, I don't always say the right things."

"I never noticed that before. I think you're perfect."

"That's because you want to get into my pants."

He frowned. "You're right. You don't always say the right things. Because I do think you're perfect. There's nothing about you I'd ever want to see change."

Before she could comment or fully digest his words, or determine whether he was being truthful or not, they walked through one of the open garage bays. She stopped to let Harrison catch up to them, or maybe because she needed his support more than she'd realized.

"Well, I'll be damned. It's the Ghost of Christmas Past," Sully said with a chuckle.

Ross rolled out from underneath a Honda, and grinned. "Hey there, Mel. You're lookin' just as purty as ever. I hardly recognize you without a little grease on your face. Why don't you grab a wrench and a creeper, and slide on under this car with me. We need to get you dirty."

Cash leaned close to her ear. "You do look gorgeous. But if anyone is going to be dirty with you, it'll be me."

She rolled her eyes. "Nice line. I think you've been watching too much porn," she whispered back.

He leaned closer. "If I recall, that line had you spread out on top of a TransAm."

Memories of that night filled her head. She and Cash both underneath the TransAm. Brushing up against each other as he showed her how to change the oil. Her daddy had already taught her how, and she could've done it sleepwalking, but she'd been crushing on Cash so badly, she'd played dumb just to be near him. She'd been rewarded later. Small touches and lazy kisses had led to her on the hood of that TransAm and Cash's head between her thighs.

She sighed. They'd had great times together. But she was almost thirty-four. While she loved working at the boat shop serving ice cream, and loved being part of ATL, at this point in her life, she'd expected to be in a different place. She'd expected to be with Cash.

A low whistle drew her attention to the corner of the garage where the office was located. Jude sauntered over, his eyes filled with worry, but a smile on his face. "Aren't you a sight," he said, drawing her into a bear hug when he reached them. "Good to see you, Mel. Who's the guy?"

She pulled out of the embrace and glanced over her shoulder. "This is my friend, Harrison." She motioned for Harrison to step forward. "He's here to help me find Bobby. Harrison, this is Jude, Ross and Sully." She looked around. "Where's Pete?"

"Running an errand," Jude said, glancing to Harrison.

Harrison moved next to her and looked to the men. "What's up?"

"Kind of scrawny, don't you think?" Sully said to Ross.

"Yeah, name's kind of snooty, too. Not the kinda guy I'd expect Mel to go for."

Harrison shoved a hand through his hair and turned to her. "You might want to tell them that I can hear them."

"We know." Sully half shrugged. "What's your point?"

Harrison took a backward step. "Why are you friends with these people?" He shook his head. "I'm waiting in the car."

She grabbed his arm before he escaped, but he quickly pulled free.

"I've had enough insults for the day," Harrison said, then walked out of the garage.

Her temper spiking, she turned to Cash. "Harrison's right. Why am I friends with you people?"

Cash snagged her hand. "*You* people? What'd I do wrong?"

"You blew Harrison crap when we came to the house. Now you're letting your employees do the same."

"I was jealous," he admitted.

Before the accident, she used to be turned on by Cash's jealous streak. She'd never gone out of her way to make him jealous— that wasn't her style. But she'd loved that her man looked out for her. Thinking back to those days, she had a lot of regrets. To her, jealousy was now synonymous with mistrust, and she wished she'd been strong enough then to question Cash, to ask him if he had really thought she'd cheat on him. She never would. Again—not her style. Maybe Cash, her big, strong, badass husband, was insecure. That could explain why he'd been so possessive of her.

"Sorry, Mel," Sully said. "It's been a while, but we still like to look out for you."

"No, you're looking out for Cash." She crossed her arms over her chest. "FYI, Harrison is a good friend, so leave him alone."

Ross finally rose from the creeper. "I'm sorry, too. You want me to go talk to him?"

"I'll handle Harrison." Cash looked to Ross. "You told me you heard Bobby was hanging in Frenchtown with Quinell, when was that?"

"Two weeks ago," he said, wiping a rag along his sweaty forehead. "A guy I know saw Bobby and Noah with Quinell. You remember Noah?"

She did. Skinny, lazy, big time gamer just like Bobby. He also used to work for Deuce. "What was he doing in Frenchtown? There aren't many cars worth stealing."

"He stopped jacking cars when Deuce went to prison." Ross shook his head. "Anyway, this guy I know…I ran into him at a party, and he told me he saw them with Quinell. But later he saw them waiting in line at Hope House."

"What?" Her heart beat quickened. Oh, my God. A *homeless*

shelter. She should have forced Bobby to move back to Everglades City with her. She could have kept an eye on him, found him a job at the boat shop or with a fishing charter.

Cash rested a hand on the small of her back and narrowed his eyes at Ross. "You didn't say anything to me about a homeless shelter. Jesus, man, if I knew that, I would've dragged his ass to my house."

Ross shrugged. "The guy told me he saw Bobby and Noah standing in line, not going inside. I didn't believe him anyway. The guy's kind of a douche. And it's not like Bobby didn't have any money. He stops by and picks up the checks Mel sends."

"But why hasn't he cashed the last two?" she asked, confused and concerned over this entire situation.

"Sully," Cash began, "head to my truck. Let's find Bobby and let him explain." He turned to Jude. "If you don't hear from me in a couple of hours, send someone to check on Dolly."

"I'll take care of her while you take care of your girl," Jude said, glancing to her, and she realized it hadn't been worry she'd seen in his eyes earlier, but resentment.

Jude could kiss her butt. He might be Cash's closest friend, but the man hadn't been the one who'd played nurse to him, she had. Jude also had no idea how much leaving Cash had torn her apart. Not that she planned to explain herself to him or anyone else. Their relationship was their business.

"I'll follow you and Sully," she said to Cash, then turned away and headed for the parking lot. When she walked through the bay, she saw Harrison leaning against the Camaro. "I'm sorry those guys were jerks."

"Let's just get this done." He pushed off the car. "I want to go home."

"Please accept my apology. I knew Cash might be...Cash, but I didn't think those guys would act the way they did."

"Why should you apologize for them? I do seriously wonder why you're friends with them."

"I'm not. Not really. They're Cash's friends. I think they

made fun of you on Cash's behalf."

"Your ex did a fine enough job on his own." His face hardened when Cash and Sully exited the garage. "We're not driving with them, are we?"

"No." She moved to the driver's side, then opened the door. "Once I find Bobby, I'm putting him in the car and taking him to the hotel. We won't need Cash or his friends after that."

"Thank God," Harrison said, climbing into the Camaro.

Twenty minutes later, she followed Cash's truck into an unfamiliar alley in the heart of Frenchtown. As Cash parked, then climbed out of the truck, she rolled down her window. "Leave the car here," he said. "It'll be fine."

A black man exited one of the brick buildings leading to the alley. He exchanged a drawn-out handshake first with Cash, then Sully, before glancing to her car and Cash's truck. Cash slipped the man what she assumed was money, then turned toward her. He gave her a *why the hell are you still sitting there* look.

"I guess that's our cue," Harrison said, opening the car door.

She didn't want to. Yes, she wanted to find Bobby, but if you wanted to get stabbed, robbed, shot, or worse, this was one of the best places in Tallahassee. She double checked the knife she had hidden in her dark-brown cowboy boot, grabbed her leopard print purse, then exited the car. "Who was that?" she asked Cash.

"A guy I know from back in the day. He runs the bar we're parked behind. He'll make sure no one messes with our cars."

"What day would that be, and how can you trust him?"

"When his dad was selling drugs to my mom. Don't worry, about it. Quinell has a house a few blocks from here. Once we meet with him, we'll turn around and head in the opposite direction. Hope House is also just a few blocks away."

"Will Quinell be armed?" Harrison asked.

Sully grinned. "You never know."

"Are you two?"

Sully cracked his knuckles. "Not necessary."

"I didn't grow up in the best neighborhood. So I know a bullet packs more of a punch than...well, a punch."

"We're not carrying guns into a meeting with Quinell," Cash said, and looked to her. "Or knives."

"Good thing I'm not carrying one," she lied.

"I find that hard to believe."

"Then frisk me," she challenged.

Cash's eyes heated with desire, just before he slid on his sunglasses. "Let's go."

As they walked, Sully fell into step with Harrison, while she and Cash followed behind. "Frenchtown has a bad rep, but there's been quite a lot of revitalization here over the past few years," Sully said. "Want to know how the area got its name?"

Harrison glanced at him. "French settlers."

"Okay, easy guess. But did you know that one of the settlers was a prince and the son of the sister of Napoleon Bonaparte?"

Cash nudged her. She looked to him and couldn't help smiling when he repeatedly opened and closed his fingers to his thumb, indicating Sully was talking too much. She grinned. Dang, she missed Cash. Before she could think about him, and all that she missed, Sully tapped Harrison on the shoulder and looked back to them.

"You recognize the guy on the stoop?" Sully asked Cash, referring to the biracial man with sleeves of tattoos along both arms.

Cash nodded. "Quinell's half-brother. He's the good one."

"Good one?" Harrison echoed.

Sully nodded. "Yeah, Quinell has six or seven brothers. Can't remember which. Me and Cash went to school with a couple of them." He waved to the man on the stoop. "What's up, Demetrius?"

Demetrius frowned at first, then grinned and came onto the sidewalk. "You lookin' to get your ass kicked, *Sullivan*? You know no one but my mama calls me that, or maybe Prescott's been feeding you stupid for breakfast."

"Fuck you, Dizzee," Cash said with a grin, and shook the man's hand.

"Who's Prescott?" Harrison asked.

Demetrius, aka, Dizzee, laughed. "Oh, shit. I guess I just blew your cover, bro." He nodded his head toward Cash. "Cash's real name is Prescott. His crack-head mama named him after the rich dick who'd knocked her up, hoping he'd pay for her baby." Demetrius looked to Cash. "Is your mama still trying to get you into your daddy's will?"

Mel tensed. While there had been no love lost between Cash and his mom, she knew it hurt him to know that his father had wanted nothing to do with him. His mother had no proof that Cash was Prescott Chandler Maddox's son, or that the man even existed. Cash had tried to find his father, but had been unsuccessful, leaving him to believe his mom had made up the man and the name.

"She's dead," Cash said.

Demetrius sobered. "Sorry, Cash."

Cash waved him off. "We're looking for Quinell. Is he around?"

A rickety screen door opened. Four African-American men spilled out, three of them making their way onto the sidewalk. The fourth man remained on the stoop, glaring at them. "I know you're not here for drugs and I see you got a girl, so I'm thinking you don't need one of those, either." He looked to Demetrius. "What do you think, Dizzee? Social call? Maybe Cash and Sully want to talk about our high school glory days? Or maybe they came here looking for a fight."

Demetrius nodded. "Probably want to impress Blondie."

"Do you impress easy, Blondie?"

She didn't know what these men were doing, and didn't understand their association to Cash and Sully. Yes, she heard them mention school and that they grew up knowing one another, but Quinell clearly had an issue with them.

"She stays out of the conversation." Cash took a step in front of her. "We're looking for someone and heard they were seen with you."

"People do love Quinell's charismatic personality," Demetrius said, eliciting chuckles from the four men behind him. "Why, Quinell has been known to do a comedy act from this very stoop and draw a crowd."

"A crowd of po-nine," one of the other men said, and they all chuckled again.

Police. Outnumbered, and worried about their safety, she wished the cops were around now.

"For real." Demetrius grinned and shook his head. "Okay, Cash, who you looking for?"

"His name is Bobby Scarlet."

"I have a picture of him," Mel said, pulling the photo from her purse, then handing it to Cash.

"What else do you have in there, Blondie? Any money for me?" Quinell asked as the picture was passed to him.

"She stays out of the conversation," Cash repeated.

"She engaged with me," Quinell said, looking at the photo. He snorted. "Yeah, I know this guy. He wanted me to cash a couple checks."

"What'd you tell him?" Cash asked.

"To get the fuck outta here."

"How long ago?"

Quinell shrugged. "Don't know, don't care."

"About two weeks ago," Demetrius said.

"Shut it, Dizzee. We don't owe Cash no favors. I'll reconsider maybe once I see what Blondie has in her purse."

These men were no help. She'd rather head to Hope House and flash Bobby's picture around there. "Sorry, I don't have much in my purse. Lipstick, compact, tampons…girl stuff. Can I have my picture back?"

Quinell nodded to the man closest to him. "Get her purse."

"Are we really going to do this?" Cash asked, moving alongside Harrison and Sully, creating a barrier between her and Quinell's men.

"You were stupid enough to come where you don't belong,

what do you think?"

"You'll be sipping from a straw."

Demetrius whistled. "Damn, Cash. Those bombs you used to play with must've rattled your brain. Are you lookin' to get your asses kicked?"

"Just looking for information. Since we got what we came for, we can be on our way."

"Not without paying," Quinell said, taking a few steps to the sidewalk. He crumpled the picture, then tossed it at Cash.

Not good. She did not want Cash's temper flaring and a fight to follow. She quickly pulled a twenty dollar bill out of her purse, then stuck her arm between Cash and Harrison. "Here's a twenty. It's all I've got on me. Thanks for your time."

Quinell looked at the money and nodded to Demetrius, who took it.

Cash motioned for them to step back. "Let's go."

Harrison walked backward, then stopped. He took a few steps forward, then bent to pick up the crumpled picture. Quinell nudged one of his men, who grinned and kicked Harrison in the stomach. Harrison grunted and dropped to his knees.

"Son of a bitch." Sully, who was closest to Harrison, rushed forward. He swept the man's leg before he could release another kick. The man dropped to the concrete, but there was another right behind him, fist cocked.

As Sully reacted, blocking the blow and delivering his own, Cash jumped in, knocking the next man to the ground with a double jab and swift uppercut. Mel quickly bent and retrieved the knife from her boot. Harrison moved next to her, clutching his stomach. "Don't go there. Come on, back to the car."

"Not so fast." Demetrius blocked their path, rushed Harrison, knocking him onto his back.

Keeping the knife at her side, she whacked Demetrius over the head with her purse. Over and over, until the man reached back to block the blows. She straddled him. Dropping the purse, she latched onto his wrist, twisting his arm up and behind his back.

When she took him to the point where a few more inches would cause the arm to break, she quickly brought the tip of her knife near Demetrius's eye. "Enough," she shouted. "Or I'm blinding him."

Quinell wiped blood from his nose and told the last of his men standing to stop. Cash and Sully were sweaty and breathing hard, but appeared to be okay.

When Demetrius went to move, she pressed his arm higher. "I'd remain absolutely still. It'd be a shame if you accidentally jerked your eye into my knife."

Demetrius winced. "Call her off, Cash."

Cash picked up the crumpled photo, then moved next to her. "If you're not going to stick him, let him go. We're done here."

Since she had no intention of going to prison for mutilating the man's face, she removed the knife, released his wrist and jumped off him. She kept the blade in front of her. Not until they were far away from these men would she put it back in her boot.

Demetrius stood, and rubbed his wrist as he moved toward his brother. The two men on the ground slowly rose. "Either Blondie doesn't know our rules, or you're fighting dirty now," Quinell said.

Sully wiped his hands on his jeans. "She didn't know. And since when do you guys start stealing purses from women?"

"Now? What's he talking about?" Harrison asked. "Do you guys get together for impromptu fights?"

Cash shrugged. "Not on purpose. They sometimes happen. When they do, no one is allowed to pull a weapon, which is why I said no knives. Sully's right, though. Trying to steal from my girl wasn't right." He nodded to Quinell. "I wanted to kick your ass for suggesting it."

"And I wanted to see if you still had any fight in you since your accident." Quinell wiped blood from his nose and looked to her. "We've been doing it since we were kids."

"How did I not know this?" she asked Cash.

"Because I didn't want you looking at me the way you are

now," he said.

Demetrius laughed. "I wouldn't, either. She looks like she wants to stick *you*, bro."

Good Lord. Her husband was certifiable. Pre-accident, when he'd been his most reckless, there'd been many occasions when he'd come home wearing the unmistakable signs of a fight. She'd assumed something had happened during a repo job or he'd been in a barroom brawl, but had never figured he'd actually gone looking for a fight.

"So this was like a little reunion of sorts?" She should be furious. Instead, the disappointment weighed heavily on her. This moment solidified just how reckless and selfish Cash truly was, and why they could no longer work. "Quinell could have simply told us what we needed to know and we could already be on our way to Hope House. In the meantime, I'm terrified something has happened to my cousin, and instead of helping me, you chose to continue with this juvenile fight thing. And you wonder why we're not together."

"In Cash's defense," Sully began, "they started it."

"By kicking my friend." She sighed. "Quinell, did Bobby tell you why he came to you for money instead of going to a bank?"

"Yeah, he said he got mugged. His wallet and phone were stolen. Without an ID he couldn't cash the checks."

Mugged? Oh, God, Bobby. Why didn't you go to Cash for help?

She slid the knife back inside her boot's built-in sheath. "Let's go find my cousin," she said, then, ignoring Cash, fell into step with Harrison.

"Hey, Cash," Demetrius called. "Better watch your back with that one. She's got crazy written all over her."

"Better watch how you talk about my wife, or I'll kick your ass for real."

Harrison tripped over a crack in the sidewalk. "You're his wife?"

She quickened her pace. "Not for long."

CHAPTER 5

Hope House, Tallahassee, Florida
Friday, 4:22 p.m. Eastern Daylight Saving Time

"YOU'RE SERIOUSLY MARRIED?" Harrison asked as they made their way toward the homeless shelter.

She glanced over her shoulder. The anger radiating from Cash's eyes should have burned a hole in the back of her head. Whatever. She faced forward. "I'm seriously married. This is another item to add to the list of things I don't want anyone in Everglades City to know."

"You know, I thought you were…different, but I didn't realize just how out there you really are."

"What's that supposed to mean?" Cash and her daddy thought she was perfect. Barney doted on her and treated her like a daughter. Even the millionaire owner of CORE thought she was all that. Granted, she had disposed of a couple of bodies for him that, if discovered, could shut down his agency and send him and his employees to prison. Still. She was cool with who she was. She liked herself. If no one else did, that was their problem.

"Give me a break, Mel. You know exactly what I mean."

"I honestly don't. If what I've done in my past, or what I'm currently doing seems out there to you, maybe you should consider that who I am is natural to me."

He gave her a sidelong glance. "In the weirdest, scariest way, that made absolute sense. But I still don't get why you would keep being married a secret."

"I don't plan on explaining myself with my husband walking five feet behind us. This will give us something to talk about on the drive home."

"When?"

"When can we go home?" At Harrison's nod, she said, "If we find Bobby today, we're leaving first thing in the morning."

"Why not tonight?" he asked. "We can take turns driving if you're worried about being too tired."

She stopped at a crosswalk and waited for the light to change. "I have unfinished business that needs attending."

"Cash?"

She nodded and tried to maintain a blasé attitude about the finality of their marriage. On the outside, she probably looked in control but, dang, if her insides weren't a jumbled mess. She loved Cash, but she hated that he wouldn't budge, wouldn't even make an effort to change. Today proved just how far apart they'd grown, or maybe how much she didn't really know him. Had she ever truly known him? Or had she'd been attracted to his looks, his kisses and touch, his dangerous aura. Maybe she should check *herself* on this one. Instead of faulting him for being the man he was, she should take a look at the woman she'd become. What right did she have to expect him to change because she had?

Memories of seeing him lying in a hospital bed filled her head. Swollen, bruised, practically unrecognizable. Tubes running in and out of him. Watching the monitor, and hoping to God he wouldn't flatline.

She glanced at Cash when he and Sully reached them at the crosswalk. His lower lip had swelled since walking away from Quinell and his crew, and a bruise was developing on his cheek. There was a small cut above his eyes, which still held anger. He could choke on it. As it was, she was having a hard time containing the fury coursing through her body. What grown man purposely provoked fights to let off steam? Why would Bobby come to Frenchtown in the first place? Why—

"Light changed," Cash said, and she realized she'd never

stopped staring at him.

She quickly looked away. "How much longer before we reach the shelter?" she asked as they crossed the street.

"Next corner," Cash said, catching up with her.

Knowing they were close had anxiety replacing her anger toward Cash. "And if we don't find him?"

He took her hand in his. "There are other shelters in Tallahassee we can try. If he's not at those, we'll go to the police."

She held his hand tight and wished they could always be a team. A solid partnership without the Jerry Springer drama. As Sully fell into step with Harrison, and began telling him more about the history of Frenchtown, a crowd of people came into view.

Her heart sank. Men and women lined the sidewalk and spilled into the vacant lot next to the two-story building. Those who weren't hovering around the shelter doors, like groupies hoping to snag tickets, were sleeping against the side of the building, or on the grass next to various pieces of litter.

Some looked as if they'd given up on life. Others looked lost, yet hopeful. She stared at them and realized that as crazy as her daddy was, he'd been smart enough to keep them five steps from having to live this way—and this was no way to live. Just thinking that Bobby had to turn to a homeless shelter tore at her heart. She pulled away from Cash, but he held her still.

"Be cool," he said, leaning close. "Some of these people don't want to be found. We don't want to spook anyone."

She nodded and drew in a shaky breath. "I don't understand why Bobby wouldn't have come to you."

"I don't, either. You know I would have let him stay at our house, right?"

She met his gaze. The anger had disappeared—for now—in its place was nothing but concern. "I know."

"Got him," Sully said.

"Where?" Mel asked, combing the crowd for Bobby.

"By the back of the building. See him? He's propped up

against a backpack."

When she spotted him, overwhelming relief filled her to the core.

"Be cool," Cash reminded her.

She nodded. But as they made their way toward Bobby she had the urge to rush to him, hug him, then give him an earful for what he'd put her through. When they reached him, and she realized he was sleeping against his backpack, she swallowed a sob and looked away. Cash wrapped an arm around her. She leaned into him, soaked up his comfort and strength, then cleared her throat. "I've got this," she said to Cash, then stepped toward her cousin. "Bobby? Honey, it's Mel. Wake up."

Bobby flinched, quickly snapped open his eyes and grabbed his pack. "Mel?" He grinned. "What are you doing here?"

She touched his dirty cheek. "Honey, I'm wondering the same thing. Come on, let's get you out of here."

"I can't. I'm waiting on Noah."

"Bring him with us."

"But I don't know when he'll be back."

She glance to Cash, who mirrored her confusion. "Back from where?"

"What time is it?" Bobby asked, instead.

"About a quarter to five."

Bobby hung his head. "It doesn't matter now. She's not coming."

"Who?"

"Madeline."

Chuck's Diner, Tallahassee, Florida
Friday, 5:56 p.m. Eastern Daylight Saving Time

CASH SHOVED HIS half-eaten burger aside and watched as Bobby inhaled his food like a wild animal. While he was concerned about Bobby's welfare, he was more worried about how Mel was dealing with her cousin. Once Bobby realized the woman he'd been waiting for was a no-show, he'd agreed to let them take him to dinner and to stay in Mel's room at the hotel. But after Cash dropped Sully back at the garage, Bobby insisted that tomorrow he'd head to the shelter to wait for his friend.

Mel placed a napkin over her plate. The disappointment crossing her face was all too familiar. At least it was directed at Bobby and not him. He knew he wasn't off the hook, though. Then again, Mel was so focused on Bobby becoming homeless, she might forget all about the fight they'd had with Quinell and his crew.

Bobby picked up his Coke and took a long drink. "I'm stuffed," he said, but tossed another French fry into his mouth.

"Now that you've eaten, you have questions to answer," Mel said. "Like why didn't you go to Cash for help?"

He let out a sigh. "Because by the time I really needed to, it was too late."

"Sounds like a load of crap," Cash said, picking up his water. "What else you got?"

"Cash," Mel gasped. "That was completely unnecessary."

Harrison leaned back in the booth. "I dunno. There were times when all me and my brother had between the two of us was five bucks and a roach-infested, one-room apartment. Guess what we did? Got a second J.O.B."

"Exactly right," Cash said, deciding he liked Harrison the more he was around the man. He'd noticed the way Harrison looked out for Mel, had liked that the man had the balls to pick up the crumpled picture Quinell had thrown—Cash rubbed his sore jaw—even if he could've done without a fight this evening. He also liked that it was clear Harrison and Mel were only friends. Based on how she'd left things earlier, he'd needed the reassurance. If quitting the repo business was what it would take to keep her happy, then he'd do it. Not once during their two-year separation had she brought up divorce. Since he didn't want that, he wasn't going to test her.

What bothered him was the shock on Harrison's face when

the man realized Mel was married. Was he a dirty secret or something stupid like that? If so, then maybe he'd reconsider his plans for retirement. He loved Mel, but if she was ashamed to be with him, then the only solution was divorce. Prescott Chandler 'Cash' Maddox had gone from living in poverty, to making a name for himself in the Army, to starting his own lucrative business, and deserved better—even if his mom had made up his frickin' name.

Bobby rested his elbow on the table. "You guys just don't get it." He dragged another fry through ketchup. "With the economy, it's hard to find a job."

"You had a job at Cash's garage," Mel reminded him.

"The hours weren't flexible," Bobby countered.

Cash tried to rein in his irritation, but decided what the kid needed was more than tough love. He needed an ass-kicking. "Screw that. Working eight to five is what most people do. What the hell did you expect? Maybe you thought I'd say, 'Hey, Bobby, why don't you work the hours you feel like working today.'" He shook his head. "You need to grow up and contribute to society."

Bobby snorted. "Contribute to society," he echoed. "I'm not for feeding into the system and giving my tax dollars over to the government."

Mel slammed her hand against the table, rattling glasses and plates. "You've never paid taxes, so don't you dare go there. Cash and Harrison are right. You're giving us a load of crap. Are you on drugs?"

"God, no."

"Then what is it? Why didn't you go to Cash or try to find another job? Jesus, Bobby, after you moved out of our house, I was never fully aware of where you were living. Don't you want to have something of your own? Don't you want to wake up in the morning knowing you're good, that you have a few dollars and a roof over your head?"

Bobby narrowed his eyes. "Save the lecture, *Mom*." He tossed his napkin on the table, then stood. "Thanks for dinner, but I'm out of here."

Cash started to rise, but Harrison blocked Bobby before he could slide from the booth. "I think you owe your cousin an apology."

"For what? Telling me how to live my life?"

"Absolutely," Cash answered. "Because if she didn't care, you'd still be sitting in a dump and your stomach would be empty."

"Sit," Harrison said.

Bobby glanced at all of them, then took a seat.

"How could you?" Mel asked, her voice shaking. "*Mom?* When your mom—my aunt—died, I took care of you. If you don't remember, let me give you a refresher...I was the one who helped you learn to read and write. I made sure you were enrolled in school and had all your supplies. Clean clothes and sheets? That was me. Daddy supplied the money, but I supplied the love. What do I get in return?" She flipped a lock over her shoulder. "Since we know the answer, there's no point in continuing with this conversation. Go ahead and go. Go back to the shelter. Sit outside and hope you can get in there tomorrow night, or that this Madeline woman shows up and makes your money worries disappear." She stood. "I'm done losing sleep over someone who doesn't care enough about me to do anything to make themself better."

Ouch and holy shit. Never, ever had Mel gone off on Bobby like this. While impressed, her words hit him hard. He knew his woman, and she'd hit a wall. The men in her life weren't manning up like she'd expected, wanted or needed. Bobby wasn't the only issue she was facing, he was, too. She'd had expectations for him, and he'd failed.

Cash snagged her hand. Instead of pulling away, she twined her fingers through his and looked to him. The disappointment in her eyes made him ache inside. It also made him want to smack Bobby upside the head for being an idiot. "Sit down and let Bobby apologize," he said, tugging her hand.

She glared at Bobby. "Is that what you plan on doing?"

He nodded. "I'm sorry. You know I appreciate everything you

do for me, and how you took care of me when I was a kid."

Mel eased back into the booth, but fortunately didn't let go of his hand. "How I took care of you?" She let out a sarcastic chuckle. "Honey, I wasn't your babysitter, I was the closest thing you had to a mother. I might've done all right with getting you through school and making sure you were healthy, but when it came to setting goals, I did a terrible job. I gave you what you needed without ever making you work for it. Now you think you're entitled to do as you please."

Bobby widened his eyes. "Entitled? I had to grow up in a swamp." He turned to Harrison. "Ever eat frog or squirrel? Or how about snake or gator? I had to wear clothes from the thrift store or hand-me-downs. Yeah, I had it really great living with you and Uncle Daddy."

Anger boiled inside Cash's chest. He tried to tell himself unicorns were magical, but he couldn't see the magic past the rage. Still holding Mel's hand, he leaned forward. "Boy, in another second, I'm going to throw you in the back of my truck and dump your body in Frenchtown. Be glad you had food, clothes and a roof over your head. After spending time on the streets, you should be on your knees thanking Mel for what she's done for you, instead of putting her down. You grew up poor. Get over it. So did I. Only I didn't always have food, or a steady home."

"We grew up poor, too," Harrison said. "I'm not sure how I feel about squirrel meat, but I could've done without the beatings from my mom's many boyfriends. Did Mel or her dad ever hit you? Until you *chose* to live on the streets, did you ever go to bed hungry, then wake up in the morning feeling like your stomach was eating itself?"

"I know he didn't," Cash said, adding Harrison to his list of friends. "Because I know Mel. If there was nothing in the pantry and you were hungry, I bet she was in the swamp, gigging until she brought home supper."

"Gigging?" Harrison asked.

Bobby's cheeks and ears grew red as he stared at Mel with

shame. "You take a pole with sharp prongs on the end, and use it to spear fish or small critters like frogs or snake. Mel used to make crispy frog legs, squirrel stew, barbeque snake...you've never tasted anything until you've had her southern fried catfish." He reached across the table toward Mel. "I'm sorry for what I said. I didn't mean it."

She tightened her hold on Cash, and took Bobby's hand. "I know, honey." Her eyes misty, she gave her cousin a reassuring smile. "You used to be quite the gigger, too. I loved cookin' for you and Daddy." Her smile faded. "I meant what I said. I did you wrong by not making you pull your weight as much as you should've. Now you have no drive. You don't care about having a place of your own, a job, a car, a girl. Anymore, I don't know what you care about."

"You. Uncle Daddy." Bobby let go of her hand. With a sigh, he leaned into the booth. "Hanging with my dudes. Gaming."

"If you have so many dudes, then what were you doing at the shelter?" Harrison asked.

"They ditched me. Some for a girl, some for school or work. All except for Noah. I suppose he's as pathetic as me."

"You're not pathetic," Mel said.

"Yes he is," Cash replied, not holding anything back. He'd been telling Mel for years that the kid needed tough love. "He had a job, he had a place to stay until he could afford his own. Remember the car I offered him?"

Mel stared at Bobby. "You never fixed it?"

"Nope," Cash answered for him. "He could have used my materials and my garage, and had himself a nice ride. But that was too much work, right, Bobby?"

The kid crossed his arms over his chest and looked down at the table. "I don't know what my problem is. I want money, an apartment, a car. Hell, I'd love to have a girl, but who'd want me? The only thing I've got going for me is that I don't do drugs."

"You have more than that," Mel said. "You have me. But I can't hold your hand anymore. You need to grow up and be responsible. Go back to working for Cash, find a roommate and get an apartment. Or come back to Everglades City and work for Ryan until you find something else."

"No offense, but I don't want to move back to the Glades. I like it here." He drummed his fingers on the table. "When Noah gets back, he'll have some money. If Cash lets me work for him again, in a week or two, we could have enough to put down on a cheap apartment."

Harrison wrinkled his forehead. "What's this Noah guy doing that he's coming back to the shelter with money?"

Bobby shrugged. "I'm not exactly sure."

"Where did he go?"

"Don't know that either."

"Are we back to this Madeline woman?" Mel asked.

"Yeah." Bobby nodded. "What's today?"

"Friday?"

"Friday?" He frowned. "I think she picked him up on Monday. She took Noah and another dude, Troy. Me and a couple other guys were hoping she'd take us with them, but she said she only needed two men for now."

"For what?" Cash asked. Having grown up near Frenchtown, he knew there were people who preyed on the homeless or addicts living on the streets, and hoped this woman wasn't one of them.

"She said something about helping restore her house. She offered seventy-five dollars a day, plus a room and meals."

"Did she say she planned to come back and hire more men?" Mel asked.

Bobby nodded. "Maybe women, too. She asked about the women at the shelter, but most were already inside for the night. The ones hanging on the street were either older or had kids with them."

"So, your plan was to stay homeless until this woman *maybe* came back and picked you to work for her." She gripped Cash's hand tighter. If she kept it up, he didn't think he'd have any circulation left by the end of the conversation. "You do realize how ridiculous this is, right? You could have a solid job, with a weekly paycheck. Instead you choose to live on the streets and wait for a job to *maybe* fall into your lap."

"I was desperate. When me and Noah had no place to go, we made our way to Frenchtown. We heard about a pawn broker who'd pay top dollar for any gaming system that's up to two years old. I got mine from one of the dudes who ditched me for a job, Noah grabbed his from his mom's, and we went to see the broker." He shook his head. "We were robbed three blocks from the pawn shop. They beat us up, took our systems, our wallets and our phones. We spent the night in an alley."

"And the visit to Quinell?" Cash asked.

"I still had Mel's checks in my pocket. I was hoping he'd hook me up. He didn't." Bobby took a drink of his Coke. "We ended up at Hope House that night. I told Noah we should go to his mom's, but I guess after he stopped there to get his gaming system, his mom told him not to come back." He looked to Cash. "I thought about coming to you, but I was too embarrassed. The last time I saw you, you called me a pathetic waste to society."

Mel let go of his hand. "Did he?" She gave Cash a narrowed glance.

"Damn right," Cash said. "It pissed me off that he'd rather mooch off you and anyone else he could, than be a man and get a job."

"Don't be mad at Cash," Bobby said. "He's right. When I was sitting around, hoping I'd get a bed for the night at the shelter, I thought long and hard about what Cash said. The problem was, I had nothing. Not an ID, not a phone or a dime. Who'd hire me? Hell, the only way I could've made it back to the Glades would've been by foot. I didn't know what to do next. Then Madeline came along. She gave me hope, but you're right. It was stupid for me to count on someone like her when I have you."

"You'll always have me," Mel said. "But you need to start counting on yourself."

Cash picked up the check their server had left behind earlier.

"Before Bobby does anything, he needs a shower and new clothes. I suggest burning the ones he's wearing."

After everyone, including Bobby, agreed, Cash paid the bill, while the others left the diner. When he finished and met them outside, Mel told him that she and Bobby were going to walk to the drug store on the corner, and that she'd like for him to wait for her. He'd do anything for her. As he watched them walk away, he stood next to Harrison wondering why he'd waited two years to give her the peace of mind she'd needed. Why had he been so damned stubborn about quitting the repo business? Yes, he was an adrenaline junkie. But he could have received the same kind of rush that happened during a repo job doing something else. He could skydive, strap a bungee cord to his body and jump off a bridge, or meet Mel's crazy daddy in the swamps of the Everglades.

Harrison kicked a pebble. "So…"

Cash shifted his gaze to the man and remembered Harrison's reaction when he'd realized Mel was married. Irritation tightened his shoulders. "So…what?" he asked.

Harrison let out a sigh as he looked across the street. "Want a beer?"

Cash eyed the bar, and nodded. "Text Mel or she'll be pissed."

"She's your wife, you do it," Harrison said, crossing the street.

"You seriously didn't know?"

Harrison reached the bar door, then opened it. "Nope."

After they took a seat at the bar and sent Mel a quick text, he ordered them a couple of draft beers still part of the happy hour special. "Does anyone in Everglades City know?"

"No clue. I met Mel last November when I moved there." Harrison reached for his beer and turned to him. "Dude, I gotta know, were you really pissed that I wasn't interested in dating Mel?"

"You make us sound like swingers."

Harrison laughed. "I don't know about that."

"Well, why aren't you interested in my wife?" Cash asked,

then quickly added, "Don't worry about me kicking your ass if you answer honestly."

After taking a drink, Harrison said, "Your wife is an attractive woman."

"She's fucking gorgeous."

Harrison nodded. "You know she runs the ice cream shop at the airboat company, right?"

"Yeah." Why, he couldn't understand. When it came to fixing cars, the woman's hands were frickin' magical. She used to love making old, ugly cars pretty again. He'd bet the Camaro she drove to Tallahassee was something she'd restored. Jude had been right. If Cash added auto body work to his garage, and had Mel helping out, there'd be no need for the income from the repo business.

"It's kinda fitting that she's the Ice Cream Lady."

Cash grinned. "She can be cold. No doubt. If you piss her off, watch out." He lifted his beer. "This, I know *all* too well." His therapist had called their relationship *toxic*. If he hadn't liked the guy, or hadn't liked working on the man's car, he might've told him to fuck off. They weren't toxic. A little dysfunctional at times, but when they were good, they were really good. When things were bad…he was an asshole. He'd shut down, and find trouble to blow off steam. Thanks to therapy, he'd realized that communication was important to women. The problem was, every time he tried to communicate with Mel, they either fought or wound up having sex. Or fought, then had make up sex.

"She does tend to enjoy showing off her knives. Is that why you two are separated?" Harrison asked.

His mind still on sex, he frowned. "No. Mel never tried to stick me. There were a few times I wouldn't have blamed her for trying."

Harrison laughed again and shook his head. "That's not what I meant."

Cash picked up his glass, and wondered how much he should say to Harrison. Jude knew what was going on—or not going on—between him and Mel. The other guys from the garage were aware, minus the details Jude knew. But Harrison was Mel's friend. Until today, the man hadn't even known he'd existed. That hurt. Why would she keep him a secret? Yeah, he could be an ass, but he'd given her everything. He'd made sure she would be taken care of, should anything happen to him. If he bit the bullet today, she'd be set for life. He'd done that because he loved her, but it hadn't been enough. While he understood why she'd walked away, sometimes he wondered if she'd find some other reason to want to leave him. People left. They died. Or they just didn't care if you existed. A quick image of his mom filled his head, but he shoved it away. She wasn't worth his time.

"Mel doesn't like that I'm in the repo business," Cash admitted. "It can be dangerous."

"She never struck me as the type to run from danger."

"Oh, she wasn't." He grinned. "Mel likes living on the edge. At least she used to, but I had a little accident and she kinda went ape-shit after that."

Harrison raised a brow. "By ape-shit, do you mean she left you?"

He nodded. "Not right away. She waited until I was better, then left."

"Did this accident happen during a repo job?"

"Yeah, I was repossessing a pickup truck just like the one I own. Should've been routine. Unfortunately for me, the truck's owner had a buddy at the bank who gave him a heads-up that I'd be coming for the truck. The guy and a couple of his friends were waiting for me. Ambushed my ass and beat the hell out of me."

Harrison blew out a breath and reached for his beer. "You went there by yourself?"

"Jude dropped me off and was waiting about a quarter mile away. He had no clue what was happening until those pricks threw me in the back of their pickup, drove toward where Jude was parked, and dumped me onto the road."

"Holy shit, man. How bad did they hurt you?"

"Broke my back, both my legs, couple ribs and my jaw. My

face and head were so swollen, I looked like the frickin' Elephant Man. It took almost eight months and a whole lot of physical therapy before I was walking right."

Harrison drained his beer, then stared at him. "You couldn't walk?"

"I had swelling around my spine that caused temporary paralysis. No biggie. I got through it."

"Wait a sec. You're telling me you were paralyzed—"

"Temporarily."

"Are you kidding me? I don't care if you were paralyzed for only fifteen minutes. I don't blame Mel for leaving you."

Damn. And he was just starting to like Harrison. "Go fuck yourself."

Harrison half-smiled. "Dude, what's funny is how badly *you've* fucked yourself. Your buddies at the garage? I can't believe they don't tell you how stupid you are every time you go out to do a repo job."

"Look, man," Cash said, trying his damnedest to keep his temper in check. "You don't know me, or my buddies. Doesn't sound like you know Mel all that well, either. So you might want to keep your mouth shut."

"I know Mel well enough to get why she left you." Harrison pushed the barstool back and stood. "Watching a person you care about continue on a self-destructive path sucks. I've seen it with my mother, my brother, my best friend. What's funny is how you had no problem telling Bobby what a dumbass he is and how he's screwing up his life, but you can't see what you've done to your own."

Cash stood, knocking his barstool to the floor, and purposefully entered Harrison's personal space. Screw this asshole. He didn't know him or Mel the way he thought. "Let me tell you something about *my* life. I have my own business, I'm two mortgage payments away from owning my house. I have no debt, own my truck and have money in the bank. Don't even try to compare me to Bobby."

Harrison gave him a mocking smile Cash wanted to punch off his face. "At least Bobby still has Mel. Can you say the same?" He threw a ten dollar bill on the bar. "Beer's on me."

After Harrison left, Cash righted the barstool, then finished his beer. He wanted to hate Harrison. At the moment, he did. The prick was right. Mel used to talk to him like she'd done with Bobby this evening. She used to be sympathetic and understanding. She used to be easy. When she'd gone all hard ass on him about his job and lifestyle, things had changed between them. The love was there—at least on his end—but the fighting had become out of control.

Then she'd left him.

Cash, I want you to put yourself in Melanie's position. How would it make you feel if she had been the one to sustain the same injuries you had?

He hated Harrison *and* his therapist. Again, why couldn't he have his fucking cake? Why did everything have to be talked out and analyzed? Was everyone around him deep, or was he just that shallow?

Shallow enough not to care that his wife had left him simply because he'd refused to quit a job that—according to his tax returns—he honestly didn't need. He owed Mel an apology. He might've already decided to retire from repoing to coerce her into coming back home, but he realized that might not be enough.

His stomach clenched with the nausea that came on whenever he thought about losing her for good. He left the bar and looked across the street. Harrison stood in front of the diner, gave him a nod, then jerked his head to the left. Cash shifted his gaze in that direction and saw Mel walking along the sidewalk with Bobby. Her arm was hooked through his and she was smiling. She didn't smile like that at him anymore. The kind of smile that made him warm inside, that let him know she cared.

With panic tightening his chest, he quickly crossed the street. He had no idea if she'd stay with him tonight, but he'd somehow find a way to talk with her alone. At their house. Once she was there, he'd right everything between them. He'd tell her that he planned to quit the repo end of their business, and ask what it would take to get her to come back home. He didn't want her to be done with him, or losing sleep because of the possible consequences of his job. He wanted her to know that he *had* been trying to become a better man. He just hoped she'd give him the chance to talk before she took off for Everglades City. Now that she'd found Bobby, she could leave first thing in the morning.

He didn't want that. He wanted his wife home. For good.

CHAPTER 6

Cash and Mel's House, Tallahassee, Florida
Friday, 8:58 p.m. Eastern Daylight Saving Time

MEL WANTED TO have sex with her husband. Sex and nothing more. She wanted to pretend to be the kind of woman who could turn off her emotions, not think, just enjoy the pleasure she knew Cash could give her. Tired of nagging, of giving him ultimatums, of the occasional weekend together, she wanted a divorce.

She parked in their driveway, then checked her reflection in the visor mirror. Divorce was the last thing she truly wanted, but living separate lives wasn't working for her. While she couldn't imagine dating or being with anyone but Cash, and she refused to consider another woman touching Cash's body, she wasn't being fair to either of them. Mostly herself. She knew Cash. He liked things easy and uncomplicated. For him, their marriage was easy. He could do what he wanted, when he wanted, without answering to her.

She closed the visor. He could risk his life, start fights and continue to go about his business as if she only existed on the occasional weekend. She was done being a part-time wife and a second thought.

After she slid from the Camaro, she reached into the back for her overnight bag. As she made her way toward the front door, she pressed a hand to her nervous stomach. Cash would expect sex, which she also wanted. Should she bring up their dysfunctional marriage prior to sex, or wait until they were both satisfied? Since she figured she'd end up sleeping in the guest room once she'd had her say and they'd argued about it, they should have sex first. Considering the way he'd reacted when she'd first arrived, and how his gaze had kept shifting to her breasts, she doubted Cash would object to that plan.

She rapped on the door. Dang it, *she* objected to that plan. She didn't want tonight to be the last night she'd spend with him, and she certainly didn't want to spend it arguing or sleeping in separate rooms. But what else was there for her to do? How much longer could they live like this?

The door opened, and Cash greeted her with a scowl. Well, there went her plans for sex first, argument later.

"Since you're so happy to see me, maybe I should head back to the hotel," she said, making no move to enter.

"Who says I'm not happy?"

"The nasty look on your face. But you're not repeating your unicorn phrase, so you must not be that mad."

"I prefer the sweet Mel to the bitchy one," he said, opening the door wider, revealing his worn jeans and bare feet.

She stepped inside and set her bag on the tiled, foyer floor. "And I prefer a real man over a boy who likes to get into fights and still thinks he's invincible," she said, then walked into the living room in search of their dog. "Where's Dolly?"

"Kitchen, sleeping in her bed." He grabbed her arm, forcing her to face him. "Well, I prefer to be with a woman who isn't ashamed to be married to me," he said, his voice low, unforgiving.

She met his gaze, saw the anger and hurt, and realized her choice to not tell anyone but her daddy about Cash had been a mistake. "I'm not ashamed of you."

"Then explain why Harrison didn't know we were married."

"The subject never came up."

"Bull." He let go of her arm to hold her left hand. "Where's your wedding ring?" He released her and held up his to show off the simple black tungsten carbide wedding band she'd bought him. "Mine doesn't come off, but I see yours does. You usually have it on when you come to town, now I'm wondering if that was only for my benefit."

She jerked her hand away. "Considering the only time we act like a married couple is when I'm here, that seems appropriate to me."

He took a step back and turned. "Wow." He shook his head, then faced her again. "So you *really* never told anyone from home you married me?"

The ache and disbelief in his dark eyes had regret twisting her stomach in knots. "Daddy knows." Tears filled her eyes. "Daddy might be a little off, but he's not stupid. He knew I was hurting. I stayed with him for about three weeks after I came home."

"You didn't tell me that, even after we started talking again."

"You didn't ask. By the time I came out of hiding and left Daddy's swamp, I didn't see any point in telling anyone about us."

"Didn't see any point?" he echoed. "Here I thought you loved me."

"I do," she shouted. "But you can't change the stripes. You're selfish and pigheaded. You want what you want and that's all that matters to you. And what you want is to risk your life for a job." Memories of when Cash had been found broken and beaten filled her mind. When she'd first walked into the ICU, he'd been unrecognizable, and in those early days, no one was sure if he'd fully recover from his head injuries or walk without assistance. She swiped her cheeks where tears began to fall. "Don't try to make me feel guilty for not telling my friends that my husband chose his work over me."

He looked away, and rubbed a hand down his face. "I didn't choose my business over you. Sorry if I wanted to make sure I provided for us. You grew up about as poor as I did. I doubt neither of us wants to go there again."

"You keep tellin' yourself that."

"What the hell does that mean?"

She took a few steps and stabbed his chest with her finger.

"You own a garage. That's how you make the majority of your money. You don't need to repo to maintain the business or this house. You're like a drug addict. You need to repo to get your adrenaline fix. Because *I'm* not enough."

He gripped her by the upper arms and pulled her close. "That's not true and you damn well know it."

"You let me leave."

"You were upset about the miscarriage. I thought you needed some time."

She hadn't been upset, she'd been devastated. After nearly losing Cash, the pregnancy had represented hope and second chances, both of which were torn to shreds when she'd lost the baby and Cash had selfishly gone back into the repo business.

"Time?" She fisted the front of his shirt as anger sliced her wide open. "I needed *you*. I needed to know that if we got pregnant again, you'd be around to raise our child, not bound to a wheelchair or dead." She shoved at his chest and tried to step away. When he forced her to remain still, her temper erupted. "I'm done. I want out. For good."

"I told you. *No* divorce."

"Doesn't matter what you want. In Florida, only one of us has to want a divorce for the request to be granted."

"I won't sign."

"Why?" She shoved him again. "Why are you hanging on to something that's making us both miserable?"

"What's miserable is this entire conversation."

"You're right. We were never great conversationalists. Let's do what we always do when we get together, and just have sex," she said, wanting to hurt him the way he was hurting her. "That's what we're best at—that and fighting."

"Agreed. We'll have sex. You can leave me—*again*—tomorrow, and file for divorce. I'll sign your papers so you don't have to deal with me again."

"Good, because that's exactly what I want."

He let go of her and crossed his arms. "So what are you waiting for? Take off your clothes."

The fury in his eyes challenged her confidence. She also questioned his motivation. Cash was predictably unpredictable. He'd been too adamant about his 'no divorce rule' to roll over so easily. Sure that he didn't want a divorce any more than she did, but unsure of where this would actually go, she shook her head. "Since you're treating me like a whore, maybe you should pay me first."

His hand shot out, and he gripped her by the back of the head. The intensity in his eyes, his closeness, the roughness had desire curling through her belly.

She gasped and held her ground. Fought to keep her gaze on his, not his mouth.

"Don't talk like that," he said. "I've never treated you that way. No matter what, I never will."

He was right. Cash had always treated her like the lady she'd spent her life working hard to be. Despite her love of clothes, jewelry, and anything frilly and girly, she could kill and skin a squirrel, chop a car, or throw a knife. Her skills weren't something she'd advertised—most men were turned off by a woman who liked playing with knives. Not Cash. He'd always treated her as his equal, yet he also liked to take care of her. She couldn't count the times he'd buy her flowers from the gas station, just because.

Cash might be rough, but she liked rough.

He loosened his grip, then ran the tip of his finger along her cheekbone. "Let's play a game," he said, inching his mouth closer to hers. "Kind of like truth or dare, minus the dare."

"Do I have a say in the rules?"

"Maybe. Here's how we'll play. I ask you a question. If you get it right, then I remove one article of clothing. But whatever answer either of us gives has to be the truth."

"And if I answer wrong?"

He skimmed his finger along her collarbone. "Then you'll be the one to remove the clothes, not me."

"After all these years, is this your way of finding out how well I truly know you?" she asked, loving and hating that he was derailing their argument. She didn't want to fight, but she did want their marital problems to come to an end.

"Nope." He nudged her chin. "This is my way of showing you why we're supposed to tough it out and make our marriage work."

Although she'd place bets that the removal of clothes portion of this 'game' was Cash's idea, the rest had to be his therapist's. This wasn't Cash's M.O. He didn't play games. He said what was on his mind, expected the same in return and if he didn't like the outcome, he walked or shut down.

"Okay," she said. "I'll play along. Who goes first?"

He took a step back, taking his heat and pure male scent from her. "I will. Ready?"

"Wait, am I asking you the question?"

"No, I'm asking you a question about me. Better answer it right or you lose something. Got it?" When she nodded, he asked, "When's my birthday?"

Cash was a bullheaded Aries. "That's simple. April seventeenth."

He pulled his shirt over his head. "My turn."

"Hold on a sec. That was *way* too easy. You had to know I'd get that one right."

He shrugged. "Maybe I wanted you to see how I've been working hard for you, babe," he said, tightening his ab and chest muscles.

Good Lord, the man was sexy and cheesy in the best way. She stared at his tanned, toned chest and stomach. Envisioned kissing a path from his pecs to the waistband of his low-riding jeans. "My turn?" she asked, snapping out of the brief fantasy before it went too far. They were supposed to be proving something, not having sex. Yet.

"Yep."

Since she wasn't quite ready to shed her clothes, she asked, "What do I want in a marriage?"

He pressed the heel of his hand to his temple. "Do you even know the answer to that?"

"That's not an answer, but yes, I do." Sort of. She'd never truly been exposed to how loving, married couples acted around each other. Her mom had died when she was young. Barney was divorced. The Monahan boys only recently met their women, so they didn't count.

"Okay," he began, "Fidelity." He grinned. "Yes, I know what the word means."

She smiled back. "I don't doubt that."

"Honesty." His stance was self-assured, while his eyes were filled with understanding. "You want to know that your husband will come home to you every night. You don't want a drunk, but someone you can have fun with. You want to treat marriage like the way you treated the garage—as a business. How am I doing?"

"Good."

"I can keep going."

"Please do."

"You want a husband who isn't afraid of hard work. A man who doesn't procrastinate. You want to wake up and go to bed knowing that everything is awesome. You want the impossible."

"Nice," she said, disappointed. He'd been saying everything right, and describing the qualities she loved about him. Then he went and screwed it up in the end. "That'll cost you your jeans."

"The hell it will." He glanced to her chest. "Lose the shirt. I'm right."

"Thanks, Jiminy Cricket, but I already have a conscience and can think for myself. Since you were only half wrong, we'll call it even and neither of us loses anything."

He shrugged. "You're cheating."

"How?"

"Because it's true. You want everything to be just so, and that's not how life is. What's funny, I don't think you want perfect, anyway."

"I don't even know what to do with that ridiculous statement."

"Tell me to shove it up my ass, for all I care. It's true." He took a step forward. "Do you know why I got back into the repo business after the accident? Don't answer, because *you'll* be half wrong. I went back because I couldn't handle what you couldn't—us, pretending to be cool with doing normal couple things."

"What in the world are you talking about? You were still on your meds and—"

"I hated taking drugs. You know that. But what you hated was that everything was becoming too perfect."

"Now that's crap."

"Is it? Think back. You were bored. I couldn't take us out on the Harley—which I'm still pissed you took. You missed going to the bar and meeting up with our friends. You missed that edge. The badass boyfriend who used to fuck you against the wall after a stupid argument." He crowded her space. "Admit it." He sifted his hand through her hair, then tugged, forcing her neck to arch slightly. "Admit you liked it when I was rough, and how you hated playing Melanie Homemaker. Working eight to five, cooking dinner, gardening, sitting on the couch watching TV."

God, she'd hated it. She *had* missed the old Cash, but dang if he wasn't back and in rare form tonight. Except, she wasn't the same woman she was two years ago. She had a regular job like she'd had then, came home and did regular things. When she was bored, she worked on whatever car she had in her garage, or tried new recipes—which Daddy loved, since he was her guinea pig. She didn't need the hard partying, a cocktail or two was just fine. She had her favorite shows she liked to DVR. Crap, she had ATL. Her mind worked quickly, honing in on the night she'd disposed of a dead bodies in her daddy's swamp. Oh, God. If Cash knew the truth…

"Remember the rules," he reminded her. "Honest answers."

"I missed the old Cash," she admitted.

He brushed his lips along hers, then released her hair and took a step back. "As pretty as you look in it, lose the shirt."

Holding his gaze, she gripped the hem of her lilac shirt that accentuated her cleavage and waist, then pulled it over her head.

"Your turn."

"Did you leave me because you thought I was half the man I was before the accident?"

"God, no. I left because I loved you so much it ate at me. I know that sounds stupid, but I don't know how else to describe it. Seeing you…" Images of him bandaged, swollen and bruised slammed into her. "I don't ever want to see that again. It's bad enough I can't erase it from my memory. But knowing the risks, you went back for more. The moment you had the chance, you took another repo job. Even after the last one nearly cost you your life. Lose the jeans and tell me why."

"Because I missed the rush," he said, unzipping his jeans. "Because I thought you'd get bored with me—which you did."

"Check yourself. I admitted to missing some parts of our pre-accident life, but you never gave us the chance to adjust to being a married couple once you'd recovered. Without any thought of me, let alone my opinion, you just dove right back into the repo business."

He tossed his jeans on the floor. "Get rid of your pants and tell me this…do you blame me for the miscarriage?"

She let the denim capris pool around her ankles. "Not once. It just wasn't our time," she said, the anguish, the heartache in his voice, made her chest hurt. She'd never forget the agony in Cash's eyes when her doctor had informed them they'd lost the baby. Cash had been just as excited as she'd been over the pregnancy. After growing up without a father, he couldn't wait to show his child all the love he'd missed. Needing to hold him, she kicked off her sandals and capris, then reached for him.

"Game's not over." His gaze cautious, vulnerable he took a backward step. "Do you miss me?"

"You changed up the rules and skipped my turn," she said, her throat tightening. She didn't just miss him, she ached to be back home and in his arms, where she belonged.

"I don't care." He glanced to her pale pink bra and panties. "You have on extra clothes, so answer."

Straightening her spine, she reached behind and unhooked her bra. "Every day." She dropped the bra next to her capris and held his gaze. "My turn. Why didn't you try to stop me from leaving?" "I did."

Half-heartedly. Sure, they'd argued, and he'd given her a few lines as to why she should stay, but that had been it. She knew Cash. Knew that if he wanted something, he made it happen. He was a fighter, didn't quit and never liked to lose. "Liar. If you don't have the guts to be honest, then don't bother taking off the boxers. I'm getting dressed and leaving."

"You want to know the truth?" He shoved a hand through his hair. "I didn't want you to reject me."

"Reject you?" she echoed, utterly confused. "I *left* you. Most people would consider that a rejection."

"So?"

"So that makes no sense."

"To me it does." He took a step forward. "You missed the old Cash, right?"

"Not enough to give up on our marriage."

"Maybe not then, but what about later?" The vulnerability was back in his dark eyes. She hated it. Hated that for whatever reason he had in his mind, she was the cause of it. "You didn't reject me when you left. You didn't leave because you didn't love me, or because you were bored with me. You were pissed off that I went back into the repo business, and that was your way of trying to get me to stop." He cupped her cheeks. "We remained married, stayed connected, and even though we still fought, I got to see you, touch you, tell you I loved you. It wasn't ideal, but it worked."

She rested her palms over his hands. "How can you say that?"

"Because it meant I still had you. You'd left because of my job, not because of me." He slid his hands from her face, then twined his fingers through hers. "What if I had quit, and you couldn't adjust to married life? What if you missed the edge, the fights, the parties? What if you decided I was too much of a regular guy? Leaving me for those reasons would have been harder for me to accept, than leaving me over a job."

While she seethed inside, she searched his eyes, took in the regret, the worry, and kept her temper controlled. She loved the man, and that he was finally being honest. Even if the truth hurt. "You rejected me before I rejected you," she said.

"That's not what I did."

"You're right. You've been stringing me along because you were worried about getting your feelings hurt. Lemme ask you, did you ever consider *my* feelings?"

His eyes narrowed. "I love you."

"You love knowing I'm still around, even if it's seven hours away."

He gripped her arms and drew them chest to breast. "I gave you everything I have, including my last name, which I doubt you've bothered to use."

"You married me when you were lying in a hospital bed and thought you might not make it." She struggled to break free, but he kept her pinned to him. "Maybe I should be the one worried about you rejecting me. Maybe I left here thinking you wished to God that you hadn't impulsively married me."

"We were engaged before the accident. Marrying you was what I wanted. The only regret I have about our wedding day was that it was in a hospital, not on a beach like we'd planned." He set her back, then shoved his dark boxer briefs over his lean hips. "My turn. If I quit the repo business, do you still love me enough to give us a shot?"

"You should quit for you, not me."

"Not an answer," he said, folding his arms across his chest. "And not what you've been preaching for the past two years."

No, it wasn't. But after this game of honesty, she wasn't sure if she could commit to anything without giving it thought. Cash had been so worried about being rejected, he'd allowed them to live separately—yet still be a couple. He'd brought up his worry that she could become bored with him, and he was right to be concerned. Yes, she'd changed. Yes, they'd lived together for years before the accident, but they'd only lived as a married couple for a short time. During their first year of marriage, she was either busy putting in extra hours at the garage or taking care of Cash as he finished his therapy. Then there was moving back to Tallahassee. Being back in the Glades had been healing for her. She loved living close to Daddy, working at the airboat company, being part of a big family. Was she ready to give that up, along with ATL?

"Don't bother taking off the panties. Your answer is clear. I'll take the guest room."

She blinked away the tears blurring her vision and stared at her husband. Watched as he turned his back, exposing the scars from hours of surgery. The scars represented so much physical and emotional pain. As he knelt to grab his clothes, she wiped at a tear. "What if you end up resenting me?" She shoved off her panties. "What if you decide I'm boring and want someone else?" she asked, and threw them at him.

Her underwear landed at his feet. He glanced at them, then turned and tossed his clothes back to the floor. Instead of staring at her nude body like she'd expected, he locked his possessive gaze onto hers. "I'll never want anyone but you." He moved toward her. "Do you ever think about being with another man?" he asked, the heat in his eyes causing her nipples to harden.

"Not since the day you caught me stealing the car you were repossessing."

He ate up what little distance was between them. His erection brushed her belly. Her nipples grazed his chest, yet he kept his hands at his sides. "I don't want to lose you," he said. "I'm done taking risks, and don't want to risk our marriage over a job."

He was saying everything she'd been dying to hear. With his warmth radiating against her skin, the barely-there touches, the need to be with him, to be his wife, she refused to worry about what she'd be leaving behind in the Glades. Cash was a man of his word. If he was willing to give up a job he loved for her, she would do the same for him. If they still didn't work out, then at least they'd given their marriage a fair shot.

She twined her fingers through his. "Yes," she said, then gasped, when he moved their joined hands behind her back.

"Yes, what?" His eyes were filled with need, hunger and the hint of uncertainty. He pressed her body against his until they were completely flush. "I need to know."

Despite the sexual tension, the desire rushing through her body, images of the faces of the people she'd leave behind quickly ran through her mind. But she'd had a life here, too. And she was only seven hours away from home.

Home. It was time to come home to her husband.

She rose to her tiptoes, then brushed her lips along his. "Prepare yourself, honey. Mel's comin' home."

"About damn time," he said, then captured her lips in a searing kiss that left her breathless and wanting more.

She writhed against his body, struggled to move impossibly closer. To break free from his hold so she could touch him, run her hands along the hard contours of his body.

"Let me touch you," she demanded.

He tore his mouth away to kiss her neck. "I need you in our bed," he said, releasing her hands, then lifting her in his arms.

She twined her arms around his neck and kissed him. Tangled her tongue with his in a sultry open-mouthed kiss. She loved this domineering, he-man side of Cash. Loved knowing she was his. Loved the way he branded her, took control. Loved that he loved her, no matter that others thought she was nothing but a crazy, white trash girl from the swamp.

When he reached their bedroom, he eased her onto their bed. He pinned her arms over her head, then broke the kiss. "I hate it when you're not here with me." He kissed her again, then dragged his lips along her neck. Releasing her arms, he cupped her breasts. "So sexy," he said, thumbing one nipple, while taking the other into his mouth.

Desire shot straight to her core. She ran her hands along his neck and shoulders. Wrapped her legs around his and lifted her pelvis. It *had* been too long and she wanted, needed him inside her.

He met her gaze as he shifted to her other breast. She let out a harsh breath when he slowly traced a circle around her areola. Frustration tore through her. She gripped his head. "Please."

He flicked his tongue along her nipple. "Please, what?"

He was going to play sex games now? Breathing hard, anticipating the pleasure he could give her, she'd play whatever game he had in mind. "Suck it," she said, then drew in a sharp breath when he did. As he rubbed his calloused hand over her hip, then brushed it along her labia, she held his gaze. How many nights had she gone to bed wishing she could look at him this exact way? Every night. She'd missed the intimacy. The skin to skin contact. The pleasure.

She leaned forward slightly, touched his jaw and brought his mouth back to hers. Kissed him with urgency, with unabashed need, until they were both breathless.

"I've missed the way you taste," he said, cupping her breast. "Six weeks is too long."

Six weeks and three days to be exact. That had been the last time she'd seen him, touched him. "No more waiting."

A small, smug, sexy smile tilted his lips He pressed her against the pillows and leaned back. After moving her legs apart, he ran his hands along her inner thighs and stared at her sex. "I'm going to make you come," he said, pressing his finger between her folds, then slowly pulling out and rubbing her clit. "When I'm done, I'm going to do it all over again."

She grew slick from his touch, his words. Her nipples had grown so hard, they ached. She shifted her gaze from where he leisurely glided his fingers, to his thick length. If she could angle her body over a foot, she could take him in her mouth. Licking her lips, imagining the taste of him on her tongue, she moved. Cash pressed her back down, brushed his hand along her breast, before moving between her thighs.

"Cash, let me."

"Nope." He raised her calf to his shoulder. He kissed her behind the knee, then slowly leaned forward, placing more open-mouthed kisses along her skin. When he grew closer to her sex, he gripped her bottom with both hands and looked up at her. "I told you, I'm going to make you come."

The man was too damned sexy and sure of himself. But she knew how well he could use his lips and tongue, and counted on him being right. "All I'm hearing is a lot of talk and no action."

The smug grin returned. "Then I guess I better shut up and fuck you." He swiped his tongue between her folds. When he flicked it along her clit, she pressed her heels into his upper back and arched her pelvis closer to his mouth. Humming his approval, he tightened his grip on her rear and kissed her sex as he'd kissed her mouth. Possessive, greedy, his lips and tongue driving her crazy with desire.

She shoved her hands through his hair and held his head still. "Right there, baby," she encouraged him. His dark eyes glittered with determination and lust. Each flick of his tongue along her clit brought her closer and closer to the orgasm he'd promised. Goose bumps cascaded along her skin. Her inner thighs tightened. Pure pleasure suddenly blurred her mind and shot through her body. Groaning his name and still holding his head, she arched her back.

Before she could catch her breath, Cash knelt, moved her pelvis toward his until the head of his erection was pressed against her. "Ready to come again?"

She moved to one elbow and reached for him. "Always," she said, running her hand along his hard abs.

With a swift thrust, he entered her. She dropped to her back, and groaned as he rubbed his thumb along her clit. Dug her heels into the mattress to match each push of his hips. Oh, God, it was too much, yet not enough.

As if he somehow knew, Cash raised her legs and placed them on his shoulders again. Resting his hands on her thighs, he thrust. When his breathing grew labored, he fell forward, used his arms to brace his body and drove deep. With Cash's big body sheltering her, his hard length inside her, pleasure, comfort and a strong sense of security filled every crack in her heart their arguing had caused. She loved Cash. Not for his body, not for the material things he could give her, but for his heart. No matter what the future held for them, he was her man. No matter if they ever parted ways again, no one knew her, understood her and accepted her, like Cash. And no one could replace him. Ever.

He lifted his chest. "Take your legs off my shoulders. I want to feel your breasts against me." When she did, he let out a satisfied sigh. "God, did I miss this," he said, placed his hand under her head, then kissed her, the thrust of his tongue mimicking the thrust of his hips.

Surrounded by him, by the love she knew couldn't, wouldn't ever fade no matter how many miles were between them, she hugged him close. He broke the kiss and pressed his forehead against hers. "Come with me," he said, grinding his pelvis against hers.

The friction of his coarse hair against her clit sent waves of pleasure through her body. Her breath quickened. Her heart raced. More goose bumps coated her skin as she ran her hand down his back to grip his tight rear.

He moved faster, harder. "Come on, baby."

She panted, met each thrust until she shattered. Her sex gripped him, convulsed around his length, held him deep inside as he let out a harsh breath and tensed. Moving her hands from his taut butt to his scarred back, she hugged him again. Tilted her chin and sought his mouth.

His warm breath puffed against her lips before he captured them in a slow, sensual, soul-tugging kiss. When he rolled to the side, taking her with him, she rested her head against his shoulder and ran her palm along his chest.

He kissed the top of her head. "I told you I'd make you come."

She tweaked his nipple. "Bet you can't do it again."

Chuckling, he squeezed her close. "Give me thirty minutes

and you'll lose that bet."

"Thirty? Used to be fifteen," she teased, tracing his pec with the tips of her fingers.

"I'm not in my twenties anymore."

Cash had celebrated his thirty-seventh birthday last April. The reminder of his age stung. Being in his arms again, encouraged that after finally hashing out their issues, they could make their marriage work, she still had an enormous amount of regret. Because they were both stubborn, they'd spent two years apart when they should have been together as husband and wife.

"Why'd you go quiet?" he asked.

"When you brought up your old age, it made me think about how we've let two years slip by us."

He rolled her onto her back and pinned her beneath him. "I should spank your sweet ass for the old age comment." He smoothed her hair from her face. "But I'm going to let you off the hook this time, because I was just thinking the same thing. I was wondering where we might be if I would've told you I was worried about losing you. Do you think we'd have kids?"

She grinned. "Do you think we should? Neither of us are very level-headed."

He cocked a brow and nodded. "I suppose not. But we have this big house, the pool and yard. Plus, I think it'd be fun to teach a kid how to fix a car."

"Don't forget there's also knife throwing and defusing bombs."

He smiled and brushed his thumb along her lips. "We might get a visit from child services if we do that."

"Then maybe we should stick to baseball or football."

"Probably a good idea." His smile faded. "Will you marry me?"

"We're already married."

"We didn't do it proper and I never took you on a honeymoon. So, I'm asking you again. Will you marry me?"

She wrapped her arms around his back. "I want my daddy and

friends from the Glades at our wedding. I'm sorry I didn't tell them about you. I didn't think about how that would hurt you, I was too busy worrying about my own hurt."

Regret and guilt darkened his eyes. "I deserved every word you've said to me."

She placed her hand along his hardened jaw. "Words like I love you? I want to move back to Tallahassee and marry you all over again?"

"You know exactly what I meant."

"Of course I did. But how can we move forward if we keep bringing up the past? We're going to make us work."

He relaxed. "Absolutely," he murmured against her lips. As he kissed her, his length hardened along her thigh.

She grinned. "What happened to needing thirty minutes?"

"You. There's nothing sexier than hearing my wife say she loves me, is moving home and marrying me again."

She moved her hand between their bodies. "Then I guess there's no point in giving this any special kisses," she said, stroking his arousal.

He gave her lower lip a light nip. "I wouldn't go that far."

When his stomach grumbled, she said, "Let's go to the kitchen. I'll make you something to eat."

He climbed off her, then went he-man on her again, and lifted her in his arms. "I need a shower that involves special kisses first. Then while *I* make us something to eat, we can talk about when we'll move your stuff back."

Her chest tightened. She was really going to do it. Give up everything she'd done the past two years since moving back to Everglades City, and come home to Cash. As he carried her in his strong arms, the panic lessened. She knew in her gut it was the right move.

Without Cash, no place felt like home.

CHAPTER 7

Cash and Mel's House, Tallahassee, Florida
Saturday, 1:28 p.m. Eastern Daylight Saving Time

CASH'S SMILE GREW as Mel swam alongside Dolly in the pool. With determination and Mel's help, the dog paddled toward the ball Bobby had just tossed her way.

"This is nice back here," Harrison said, as he toweled off and took the chair next to Cash's. "I'd love to have a pool in my backyard."

"What's nice is having people here using it again. It's usually just me and Dolly." Since Mel talked Harrison into staying one more night, he'd even have the opportunity to break out the grill and cook up burgers and brats.

Life was good. He had his woman back, his dog, and the beginnings of a small party. Jude and the boys from the garage planned on stopping over after they closed for the day. Once he had a beer in his hand, his afternoon would be complete. When he realized Harrison stared at him, he looked away from the pool. "What?"

"I'm sorry for what I said at the bar. I had no place, and what you've got going with Mel is none of my business."

"It's all good, man. I like knowing she has someone looking out for her when I'm not around."

"So you two talked?"

Cash glanced at the man. Other than his therapist, and occasionally Jude, he didn't talk about his relationship with Mel. He wasn't proud of how he'd screwed them up, but their relationship was their business. "Yeah, we talked. Didn't she say anything to you about it?" While he cleaned up around the yard, and took care of the pool, Mel had gone to the hotel to pick up Harrison and Bobby.

He shook his head. "She just said she wanted to stay another night."

Yeah, he could definitely use a beer. Why wouldn't she tell them she was moving back to Tallahassee? Especially Bobby. Like him, the kid had been lost without her here. Then again, he shouldn't read into what she had or hadn't said. Could be she wanted to talk with each man privately.

"I think Dolly's ready for a break," Mel called as she swam the dog near the shallow end of the pool.

"That's my cue." He rose from the chair and grabbed a towel. After laying it on the concrete, he stepped into the water, then lifted Dolly. "That swim will zonk her out for a couple of hours. Won't it, girl?" he asked the dog as he carried her to the towel.

"I wouldn't mind a nap," Mel said, as she left the pool, wringing her long blonde hair.

He loved her naked, but damn if he didn't love seeing her in a sexy bikini. Remembering Harrison, he glanced over his shoulder. But the man wasn't paying attention to Mel. He had his sunglasses on and his head tilted back against the chair.

"If anyone should complain about being tired, it should be me," he said when she knelt beside him.

"You weren't complaining last night," she countered, and took Dolly's life vest from him.

He grinned. "You're right. Which is why I think we should do everything we did last night, again tonight."

"Everything?"

He drifted his gaze from her breasts to the front of her tiny, hot-pink bikini bottoms. Pictured them off, his mouth replacing them. "Maybe a couple of new moves, too."

"Interesting." She bent close to his ear. "There are only so many ways to insert A into B."

"True. But I'm talking about foreplay."

She looked to where Bobby still swam in the pool, then to Harrison, who now had his mouth open and was snoring away. "I'm intrigued," she said quietly, and narrowed her eyes. "Where did you come up with these new moves, and have you used them on anyone?"

He finished hooking Dolly into her wheelchair. Once the dog rolled off toward the covered patio, he slid his hand behind Mel's neck. "You ruined me for anyone else. There hasn't been another woman since the day I caught you trying to steal the BMW. It pisses me off that you'd even think I'd cheat on you."

"Sorry. You know I can get a little jealous."

"Oh, I know." During the first six months they were together, an old girlfriend tried to mess things up between him and Mel. They'd been out one night when the ex had pulled Mel aside in the women's restroom and told her a made-up story about him and her. Mel was escorted from the bar after she pinned the woman against a bathroom stall, and pulled a knife on her. In Mel's defense, the woman *had* goaded her. Plus, he knew Mel well enough to say confidently that she wouldn't have cut his ex. She was all about leaving a lasting impression.

She gave him a sexy pout. "Does this mean you're too mad at me to show me those moves?"

"I'm sure you can come up with a few ways to help me get over it."

She slid her gaze to his dick, then licked her lips. "Definitely."

His cell phone rang, but he was too busy staring at her mouth to care.

"Aren't you gonna answer that?" When she stood, the triangle of her bikini bottoms was right at his eyelevel. If they were alone, they'd be around her ankles before she could blink.

"Cash, your phone," Harrison called.

"Go ahead and answer," he said, and looked up the length of Mel's curvy body. He stood, maintained a reasonable distance from her so as not to embarrass their guests, then leaned toward her ear. "I can't wait to fuck you later."

"Dang," she whispered. "I can't wait until later."

"It's Jude." Harrison rushed over with the phone. He looked to where Bobby swam laps, then said, "Noah showed up at the garage, claiming Madeline drugged and tortured him."

CASH HELPED MEL from his truck, then took her hand. Bobby climbed out of the back passenger seat, and fell into step with them and Harrison.

"Noah must've decided to come here when he didn't find me at the shelter," Bobby said as they made their way toward one of the opened bays.

Cash didn't respond. Everyone except Bobby knew the truth, but they agreed to keep quiet until they saw Noah and could assess the situation.

"I hope he made some money," Bobby continued. "The more I think about going back to work and getting my own place, the more I...oh, God." Bobby froze. "Noah? What happened to you?"

Mel tightened her hold on Cash's hand and leaned toward him. "That could be Bobby," she whispered.

Cash didn't want to think about that. "Stay here," he said, letting go of her hand. He looked to his men as he neared Noah, who sat in a metal folding chair near a Toyota Ross should be fixing. The kid's lips were cracked and bleeding. The circles under his eyes were so dark, it looked as if someone had used him as a punching bag. His eyes weren't just bloodshot, the whites were almost completely red. His pale, hollow, dirty face had been scratched, as if someone or something had clawed him. Cash looked to where the man's folded hands jerked in time with his shaking legs. Blood stained Noah's fingernails, and Cash wondered if Noah had sliced up his own face.

"Noah, it's me, Bobby. Talk to me, brother. Who did this to

you?"

Noah looked up at Bobby. His entire body trembled as he slowly flipped his hand to reveal the underside of his forearm. "M-M-M-Madeline."

"What about Troy?"

"D-dead."

"Did you see a body?" Cash asked, not sure what to believe.

Noah shook his head. "Sh-she told me."

"Madeline told you Troy was dead?"

Noah nodded. "Drugged us. No, no food. Sick. Sick. Sick!" Noah gripped his face. Before he could damage his skin more than he already had, Sully and Ross grabbed his arms.

"Calm down," Cash ordered, and looked to Jude. "Has he had anything to eat or drink?"

"No."

Mel stepped forward. "I'll go in the break room and find something for him."

After she headed toward the back of the garage, Cash knelt next to the man. "How'd you get here?"

"W-walked."

"How far? Do you know where Madeline lives?"

He closed his eyes and frowned. "I-I think Georgia. I-I can't remember. There's so much blood. So much. You don't understand what I saw. What they made me watch."

"They?" Bobby asked.

"I-I don't know his name. He was nicer. He-he was going to fix me."

Cash glanced to Jude, who raised a brow and shook his head. "Fix you how?" Cash asked.

"Take a-away what M-M-Madeline did to me. The drug." He tried to break free from Sully and Ross's grip. "Let go!"

When Cash noticed the chafing around Noah's wrists he nodded to his men. "Let him go." The moment they did, Noah scratched his forearm where the telltale signs of needle punctures remained.

"Here," Mel said, as she approached, carrying a Mountain Dew, chocolate bar and chips. "Sugar and carbs always takes the edge off when Daddy has a crazy spell." She handed the soda to Cash, and tore the wrapping off the chocolate bar. "Eat this, honey, and then we'll get you to the hospital."

Noah bit into the chocolate and hugged himself. "No h-hospital. Can't help." He looked at the soda Cash held, reached for it, then took several long swallows.

"Tell us about the blood," Sully said. "Did you see these people hurt Troy?"

He shook his head, and explained how Madeline and a man had brought him and Troy to a large plantation house in the middle of nowhere. Once there, they were bound, gagged, then separated. "They drugged me and made my eyes stay open," he said, finishing the chocolate. "And...and forced me to watch videos." A tear slipped down his cut cheek. "Gory videos. So much blood. The whole time, all I could hear was M-Madeline's voice, even when she wasn't in the room. Sh-she kept telling me to do bad things. To kill. H-hate." He grit his teeth and fisted his hands. "I wanted to. I wanted to cut the bitch wide open. Cut her and watch her bleed for what she was doing to me."

Noah drew his knees to his chest. More tears fell as he looked to Bobby. "Why would I even think that? I-I would never hurt anyone." He slammed his feet to the concrete, anger and outrage contorting his face. "She wanted to make me a monster like her. She told me so. She would build her own army of monsters to feed on the weak and innocent."

Bobby wiped a hand down his face. "Noah, man, you're no monster. You're a good dude. Tell us what happened to Troy."

"Madeline said the guy killed him. Smashed his head against the floor until his brains spilled out, then choked whatever life was left from him."

Cash took the bag of chips from Mel. "Head to the office until we're finished."

"It's okay," she said.

None of this was okay to him and he didn't want Mel exposed to Noah. "Just for a few minutes."

"No." She stepped around him, then in front of Noah. "Noah, why did they let you leave?"

"I-I escaped. I heard them talking. Th-they were going to get more *subjects*," he said with a snarl. "That's what me and Troy were. Test subjects."

"What the hell?" Ross shook his head. "Are you saying these people were experimenting on you?"

Noah nodded. "Th-the shot they gave me this morning didn't do anything to me. Not like the d-days before. But the video kept playing, and I still could hear Madeline telling me to be bad. When I thought they were g-gone, I knocked my chair over. It t-took a while, but I got free. And then I ran." He looked to Bobby. "I thought they'd get you, too. They needed more subjects, and I thought they'd go to the shelter, so that's what I did." He dropped his gaze to his trembling hands. "I ran into the guys that kicked the shit out of us and took our money and stuff." He leaned forward, reached in his back pocket, then threw a wallet to Bobby. "I hope they're still alive," he said on a sob. "If I killed them, I didn't mean to. There's something in my head now, and I gotta get rid of it."

Mel blew out a slow breath. She turned to Harrison, said something, then faced them again. "You need to go to the hospital. They can draw blood and test it. That's the only way to know what kind of drug they gave you. Doctors will notify the police and—"

Noah laughed without humor, and Cash didn't like how the man stared at Mel with pure hatred. "I'm fucking homeless. Half the homeless in Frenchtown are addicts. Do you think the police are going to believe me or even give a shit?" He shook his head. "What a stupid bitch."

Cash lunged for the man, but Sully and Ross stopped him. "Get him to a hospital and out of my garage."

"Cash, this isn't how Noah is," Bobby said. "It's whatever they gave him that has him weaving in and out. Trust me. I know this guy. He's not like this."

Mel knew Noah and knew this wasn't him talking, but the drugs. Before Cash had a meltdown and kicked the crap out of the man, she'd remove herself from the room. Plus, she wanted to discuss this situation with Harrison, and how it should be handled. She held up a hand. "I'm stepping outside, while you guys talk some more with Noah. Harrison, why don't you keep me company?"

"Good idea," Cash said, relief in his eyes. He straightened his shirt once Sully and Ross let him go. "I'll come get you when were finished."

When she and Harrison stepped into the sun, Mel slipped on her sunglasses, then motioned for him to follow her. "What do you think?" she asked, leading him toward a picnic table under an awning behind the building.

Harrison stepped around an old coffee can filled with sand and cigarette butts, then sat at the table. "He should go to the hospital. But I don't think the police are going to believe the guy. They'll assume he pushed some bad crank into his veins and is tripping."

She sat across from him. "Do you think that's what happened?"

"Bobby said he saw this Madeline woman, so we know she's real." He frowned. "How far is Georgia from here? Noah thinks that's where he was taken."

"Not far. Half hour by car. So it's possible he could've walked here. Just depends on where Madeline lives." She took off her sunglasses, then rubbed her chin with the back of her hand. "What if Noah is telling the truth?"

"And Madeline and the guy with her are experimenting on people?" He let out a breath. "Do you want to call Lola and ask her if she can find a contact with the Tallahassee PD? Once we figure out where Madeline lives, we might have to deal with law enforcement in Georgia, too."

"What about Ian?" she asked. Ian Scott, CORE's owner and the man who also created ATL, had begun his career with the FBI. According to Lola and Harrison, Ian had many friends in both high and low places.

He shrugged. "We should still go through Lola first. But Ian might know some people. He could also worry about exposing ATL, which none of us wants."

No, they didn't. Some members of their team had criminal records.

"We could ignore it," he said.

"Just pretend Noah wasn't kidnapped, held against his will and used as a test subject?" She nodded. "We could."

"And, if we called Lola and she gave the green light to investigate, how would you keep your involvement with ATL from Cash?"

That was a huge problem. "He's quitting the repo business." She toyed with her sunglasses. "I'm moving back to Tallahassee."

"I see." Harrison stood, took a few steps from the table, then came right back. "Are you serious? What's wrong with you?"

"What's that supposed to mean?"

He tapped his fingertips to his head a few times. "Think. You're going to give up everything we have going in the Everglades to move back in with a man who went back into a business that nearly paralyzed him."

"Did he tell you?" she asked, stunned. Cash never talked about the accident with anyone outside his main circle. Even then, he was tight-lipped.

"Yeah, when we had a beer at the bar last night. Then I told him he was stupid, and that I didn't blame you for walking."

She gave him a small smile. "Dang, Harry, you've got a set on you."

"If you make a hairy balls joke—"

She wrinkled her nose. "That's just gross. Now sit down and tell me why you're flippin' out."

He rolled his eyes, and sat. "I just told you. Mel, men like

Cash don't change. If he quits the repo business, he'll find something else to do that's dangerous. Like go into the ghetto and pick random fights."

Her stomach knotted. "I don't want to hear this."

"Because you know I'm right."

"Shut up. I love him."

Harrison reached across the table and settled his hand over hers. "I don't know about that kind of love. You're my friend. I don't want to see you hurt. If we get involved in this case, I'm afraid you're going to get hurt either way."

While she understood where Harrison was coming from, he also didn't understand the bond between her and Cash. He was right about one thing—after all the crap she'd given him about the repo business, Cash was going to be angry about ATL.

She rested her cheek in her hand, and held Harrison's with the other. "My conscience says we call Lola. My head tells me we pretend this didn't happen."

"I'm wrestling with the same. We could flip a coin."

"So the fate of future test subjects will rely on a quarter toss?"

"That sounds bad." He let out another sigh. "Let's call Lola and let her decide. If she says no, we walk."

"Fair enough." She let go of his hand, and waited while he placed the call. As the phone rang, he put it on speaker and set it on the table between them.

"Hey, Harrison," Lola answered, worry in her voice. "Don't tell me something else happened with Mel's—"

"Lola, yeah, Mel's here with me and we're on speaker."

"Hi, Mel."

Mel raised a brow at Harrison. "Did you tell her about Cash?"

"No. I told her I hated it here. I wanted Shane to fly me away from crazy town. But that was before Cash and I had a beer."

Lola cleared her throat. "Listen, guys. We've got a bunch of tours running, so if it's nothing important, let's catch up when you come home tomorrow."

"It's important," Harrison said. After he told her about Noah, the phone went silent. "Are you still there?"

"I'm here. I need to call Ian about this. Remember, we get paid for the cases he assigns us. But I don't like knowing there's someone out there possibly turning humans into lab rats. The question is, how do we find this woman?"

Harrison lifted a shoulder. "If she's hitting homeless shelters, I can go undercover."

Mel didn't like that idea. At all. Harrison had a backbone, but he was a computer geek, not a trained fighter like Vlad, Shane or Ryan.

"When you call Ian," Harrison continued, "ask him if he could ship us the GPS chip they used during the Honey Badger case."

That investigation had been the one where Harrison and Vlad had met. Together they'd put an end to a mass murderer, and secured their future with Ian and his agencies.

"Last I heard, the chip was in another round of testing," Lola said. "But that's not a bad idea. The problem is, Madeline might not return to the same shelter."

"She might if she's worried Noah went to the police," Mel suggested. "Her and her partner could attempt to go to Hope House to find out if Noah made it there, or if anyone is looking for them."

"Good point," Lola said. "But I'm not comfortable with Harrison going undercover. I think we should bring Vlad in for this— *if* Ian approves."

"Vlad?" Harrison shook his head. "Yeah, a six-foot-six Russian is the perfect candidate. Let the woman take me, then send the muscle."

"He has a point," Mel said, even if she hated to see Harrison put in a situation where he could be the subject of sadistic experimentation.

"Okay, I'll check with Ian. Even if he says no, I suggest getting Noah to a hospital. I agree, the police likely won't become involved, but at least he'll have the proper care. I'll call you back."

The phone went silent. Harrison picked it up, then tapped his hand on the table and stood. "We should ask Noah if he heard where Madeline was heading for her next test subjects."

"Let's wait until we hear from Lola," she said, part of her hoping their boss would give them a big fat no-go. If they tried to find Madeline, she would have no choice but to tell Cash about ATL. The other part of her wanted to investigate the hell out of this. She'd grown up poor, but had been lucky enough to have a roof over her head, even if it leaked. Cash had grown up with nothing, too, minus the love of a parent. They both knew people who'd been so down and out they'd had no choice but to live on the streets. Madeline was going after the forgotten, the ones most people turned a blind eye to or sloughed off as drug addicts or alcoholics who'd made their own bad choices. Even if that was the case, no one deserved to be treated the way Noah had. And if Noah was telling the truth, Madeline and her friend had murdered Troy.

"I wonder if Madeline is already on her next *shopping* trip," Harrison said with heavy sarcasm.

"What's with you? You're really ticked off about this. We've worked plenty of cases together and I've never seen you this way."

"It's like we talked about last night with Bobby…I grew up with nothing. I knew people who lived on the streets. So, this rubs me wrong. It also pisses me off that no one thinks I can do anything outside of typing on a laptop."

She stared at Harrison, really looked at him. He was more passionate than she'd realized. She always thought he was cute, in a boyish way, but when his temper was high, he had a different air about him. More masculine. For whatever reason, he always seemed smaller to her, but these past two days, she'd noticed his height, his broad shoulders. She supposed even a guy ranging around six-one would look small next to Vlad.

"None of us think that," she said. "The difference between you and Vlad is that he's a killer, you're not. Personally, I'd like you to stay just the way you are."

"Thanks." He gave her a shy smile. "I hope Lola doesn't take too long. I don't want her calling when Cash is around."

"If she does, you take the call, then tell me about it later." She rested her head in her hand again and thought about what Harrison had said regarding Madeline's 'shopping' trip. "Wouldn't you love to be a fly on the wall when Madeline and her partner discover Noah escaped?"

He let out a low whistle. "I'm betting that won't go over well. Considering what she was filling Noah's head with, she'd probably say…"

PART III

"I am a serial killer. I would kill again."
—Aileen Wuornos

CHAPTER 8

The House of Archer, Bower, Georgia
Saturday, 7:36 p.m. Eastern Daylight Saving Time

"**S**ON OF A bitch."

Adeline threw a pillow across her room, then paced in front of the mirror. "I'm going to find him and cut him," she said to the walls, and fisted her hands. "I'll start with his testicles." She paused and tapped her chin. "Maybe I'll make him eat them." Grinning, envisioning the pathetic bastard choking on his own balls, she sat on the bed. She would make Noah—test subject number two—hurt. Badly. Noah would truly understand the meaning of pain when she was through with him.

Damn it. She fell against the mattress. Everything had been going perfectly. She'd had the test subjects and even Rodney under control. Now Rod was downstairs in the parlor drinking bourbon and convincing himself they were doomed. "All doomed," she said, mimicking Rodney's deep voice. They were fine. Noah wouldn't be once she found him. The two new subjects they had secured in the attic bedrooms wouldn't, either. But, she'd have to wait to play with them until after Rodney had calmed himself. She knew just the way, too. She'd wait until he drained some of the bourbon first. God forbid he let his guard and stupid conscience down for a bit to have fun. All he was concerned about was making her better.

She pushed off the bed and approached the mirror again. "What if I like who I am?" She reached behind and unzipped her sundress, then let it pool to the floor. After adjusting the straps of her bra, she eyed her reflection. Her breasts were still larger than usual, thanks to the baby. Same went for her curves. She liked how she looked. Liked looking voluptuous, and knew Rodney liked it, too.

It was a shame she'd had to push out a kid to get a curvy body.

Since she broke the baby, she knew Rodney would never let her have another. He'd use every precaution possible the next time they had sex. *If* they had sex. The man needed to send his morals to hell and fuck her. She knew he wanted to, could see it in his eyes. God, how she loved the battle he waged with himself. The lust was there, along with hunger. He would stare at her with a molten combination of love and hatred…mmm-mmm. She slid her hand between her legs, then quickly fisted it as frustration and need magnified the outrage of Noah's escape.

The dimwitted ass had screwed up everything. She reached behind, unhooked her bra, then tossed it in her drawer. After taking off her panties, she slipped a flimsy, see-though nightgown over her head, then used her fingertips to give her curls a little volume.

She stared at her reflection again. Rodney had refused to have sex with her since she'd found out she was pregnant. God forbid a psychopath beget another one. Tonight, that changed. She needed him, not because she was upset about Noah's escape, but because she knew sex could convince a man to do just about anything.

Poor Rod. She might have been a virgin their first time, but there'd been others since him. She hadn't graduated with a four-point average because of her strong study skills.

She looked to the mirror and made her best frowny face. Made her chin tremble as if she were going to cry. Happy with the results, she headed for the door. Once she was in the hallway, she paused at the main staircase leading to the second floor and attic bedrooms. God, how she wanted to go play with their subjects. If she did that, Rodney would know the truth. She couldn't have that. Not yet. For now, she had to convince him they needed to bring home more subjects. They also needed to retrieve Noah.

She knew the chances of finding the homeless man were slim to none. While she was concerned about Noah going to the authorities, she doubted anyone would believe him. Well, unless they found out Rodney lived here. After all, he had made the cover of *Time*. This would be the argument she'd use tonight. They *needed* to diffuse the situation before the law came knocking on their door.

She continued down the hallway. When she reached the parlor, she paused at the open doorway. Rodney sat on Gramma's hideous floral sofa, his head down, a tumbler in his hand. She put on her frowny face again, and gave a soft rap against the doorjamb. "Rod?"

He straightened, and turned. His gaze drifted from her mouth to her breasts. "Go to bed," he said, taking a drink and keeping his focus on her breasts.

"I can't sleep. I'm so worried." She stepped into the parlor, then slowly walked toward him, giving her hips a slight sway, drawing his attention to them. To the possibilities, if he would stop being so damned rigid. "Come to bed with me. Please. Just for tonight."

He dropped his gaze to his glass. "I can't," he said, his tone filled with anguish.

She closed her eyes, fed off the agony, the torment that must be tearing him in two. He wanted her, she knew he did, saw it in his eyes. But his morals, his concern for her mental health, stopped him from taking what he wanted.

She shot her lower lip out and forced her chin to tremble. "Fine. But I'm warning you now that I'm sleeping with a knife under my pillow," she said, and turned away.

"No knives. What if you mistake me during the night?"

"That won't be a problem since you don't bother to come to bed with me. I'm worried about the other subjects. Now that Noah has escaped, I'm terrified one of the two men we brought home today will, too."

He drained the rest of the bourbon. Then his face twisted in anger. He threw the glass against the ugly, weathered fireplace. As it shattered, he gripped her by the arms. "No knives." He pulled her close, until they were nose to nose. "You wanted this. It was all your idea."

"No. I just wanted you. But you couldn't let that happen because you're too worried about fixing me. Why can't you just love me for me?" she asked, playing off his emotions.

He rested his forehead against hers, and shook his head. "It's not right. Wanting to be with you is not right. You *have* to know that."

Oh, she did. She just didn't care. "We love each other." She held his face in her hands. "Who cares what anyone else thinks? Who cares that I've been accused of murder? No one but you and I know the truth."

He lifted his head and searched her eyes. "But that's just it. You're a murderer. Now I am, too. My God, Adeline. I love you." He grabbed the front of her nightgown and tore it from her body. "I want you. God, how I want you," he said, cupping her breasts.

Taking a calculated risk, she stepped back and covered herself. "Come to my room. Show me how much. Stay with me tonight and make sure I'm safe."

He looked away from her body. "No. Go to bed."

Moral prude. "Fine. I'll go to bed alone and masturbate like I've been forced to do since you won't come to me." She started for the door, then stopped when she reached the threshold. "I'm going to Tallahassee tomorrow. Don't try to stop me."

That should light a fire under his ass. She headed down the hallway and back to her bedroom. She really did intend to go to Tallahassee. Noah was homeless, where else would he go but back to the shelter? Although there were others in the area, and he could have walked off in the wrong direction and wound up deep in the forests leading to Appalachia, she *needed* to know. Had Noah told the police? If so, had they believed him? Would shelters throughout the state be on alert?

She'd disguised herself with a blonde wig when she'd gone to Hope House, just like today when she'd hit the homeless shelter in Atlanta. Noah had been so doped up when he'd been at the House of Archer, she doubted he could describe Rodney or what she truly looked like.

Still, she wasn't ready to call it quits yet and didn't want one homeless dick screwing with her plans. So, with or without Rodney's consent, she'd head for Tallahassee.

She entered her room, didn't bother putting on another nightgown, then crawled into bed. With the extra padlocks— something they hadn't added to Noah's room—securing their latest guests, she wasn't worried about them killing her in her sleep. Plus, they'd strapped their subjects to beds, rather than chairs, to avoid the same mistake they'd made with Noah. Yeah, she wasn't worried about the subjects, she was worried whether or not Rod would cave in and come to her.

Minutes passed. The wood floor outside her bedroom creaked, signaling Rod had followed behind. But would he go to the other room, or join her tonight? Anticipating his arrival, needing sexual release anyway, she slid her hand between her legs and touched herself. She was a woman of her word. She had told him she'd masturbate if he wouldn't join her, and that was exactly how she wanted him to find her. Taking pleasure. Alone. Knowing the sensitive and sensual side of him, he would respond to this.

When the door to the room opened a crack, sending in a small stream of light, she moved the covers aside hoping he could see what she was doing, then put on a show for him. She didn't have to look at him to know he liked what he saw. His labored breathing said it all. Then the door closed. Close to orgasm, she continued anyway, until the mattress dipped.

She stilled her fingers.

"Don't stop," he said, moving a hand over her breasts, then down further until his fingers joined hers.

"Will you stay with me?" she asked.

"Yes."

She smiled.

The strong scent of bourbon tickled her nose as Rodney moved over her. "I love you," he said. "I'd never let anything happen to you."

She touched his jaw. "I know."

"And we'll discuss Tallahassee in the morning."

She helped him pull his shirt over his head. "Why not now?" she asked, in a teasing tone.

"I don't want to talk," he said, then kissed her.

Cash and Mel's House, Tallahassee, Florida
Saturday, 8:07 p.m. Eastern Daylight Saving Time

"I STILL THINK you should've told him," Harrison said to Mel when Cash went inside to grab a few more beers for them.

Guilt made her nervous stomach queasy. "It's too late now. They'll be here any minute."

"Warn him."

"Back off. I know Cash. He'll be fine." She hoped.

Damn it. She honestly planned to tell Cash about ATL and how they were going to look into what had happened to Noah, along with Ian's interest in the case. But Noah had been such a wreck. They'd finally talked him into going to the hospital. Of course, once he was there, nurses and doctors had immediately assumed he was a user and on a bad trip. And it was quite possible Bobby didn't know his friend that well, and Noah was hallucinating. But that didn't add up. Bobby had been there when Madeline had chosen Noah and Troy to go with her, and the Noah she knew didn't do drugs. Fortunately, Harrison had distracted one of the nurses with his cute smile and witty charm—that she hadn't realized he possessed—long enough for her to snag a vial of Noah's blood. Whether Ian's people could do anything with it or not, she didn't know, but the opportunity was there, so she'd taken it.

She could have told Cash about ATL after they'd left the hospital, but selfishly wanted another great evening with him. And they were having a good time, up until an hour ago. That had been when Lola had called to let her know they were coming. To tell Cash now would only set him off to the point where he might be rude to Lola. An excuse on her part? Maybe. Or maybe she wanted to be surrounded by other ATL agents when Cash learned what she'd been up to during the past ten months.

They could reassure him that she hadn't ever been in real danger. Not really. Well maybe the one time when—

"Thinkin' about me," Cash murmured against her ear, then pressed the cold beer bottle along her neck.

She shivered and grinned. "I was thinking about later."

He skimmed a finger along the straps of her sundress. "I've been thinking about your bikini."

She took the beer from him. "Maybe we'll have to go for swim," she said, keeping her eyes on his as she took a drink.

"I'm going to throw up," Harrison said, and walked over to where Dolly lay on a blanket near the corner of the patio.

"What's his problem?" Cash asked.

"Maybe the two brats he ate weren't cooked through," she suggested.

"Or maybe I don't want to know what you two are going to do later," Harrison said. "I'm not invisible and have excellent hearing. Either you two don't care what people hear, or you're oblivious to your surroundings when you're in the same room together." He looked around the backyard. "Or just together, period. Whatever. You know what I mean." He stroked Dolly's head. "If Mel wasn't Mel, it might be kind of hot. Like watching the beginning of a crappy, soft-core porn movie."

She looked to Cash, who burst into laughter. She did the same, and walked toward Harrison. "I'm sorry I gross you out and that we act like porn stars."

Harrison chuckled. "I said the beginning of a porn movie. I don't want to see either of you in action." He shook his head and looked at her. "You're like family. That's what grosses me out."

He frowned. "That didn't come out right."

"Works for me," Cash said, sitting on one of the patio chairs. "I like the brother-sister angle. It saves me from having to kick your ass if I feel slightly threatened."

"Like he could feel threatened by me," Harrison said quietly, his head down as he continued to pet the dog.

Mel took another drink and studied Harrison. She realized she—maybe no one from ATL—hadn't given him the credit he'd deserved. Since no other man compared to Cash, she'd never looked at Harrison in any way other than...well, Harrison. Vlad's little buddy. ATL's computer guy. But if her heart hadn't belonged to Cash, she could see how women would find him attractive. She liked her men tall, and Harrison had her by almost a foot. He was lean, but muscular. Svelte came to mind. While she preferred Cash's short hair, Harrison's longish, thick brown hair would be something fun to run a hand through. Too bad she didn't have any girlfriends. A woman could knock the block off Harrison's shoulder, and also help give him and Vlad some space.

The doorbell rang. Harrison looked up at her, his eyes wide with concern. She took another quick sip of her beer. "No worries, honey." She forced a smile. "Mel's got this covered."

He gave Dolly a final pat. "You need to seriously stop doing the Vlad thing."

"I have it." Cash rose from the chair. "It's probably Jude. He said he might stop by."

Mel met him at the patio door. "It's not Jude."

The doorbell rang again. This time Dolly gave a tired bark.

"How do you know?"

Her stomach swarmed with angry hornets. "Harrison and I called in a couple of people we know to help with Noah. I'm going to need you to be open-minded about them. Can you do that for me?"

He grinned. "No problem, babe. You know how laid back I am."

When it suited him. "Great," she said. "Then I'll just get the door."

He kissed her cheek. "Hang out with Harrison. I got it."

"You should go with him," Harrison said from behind her.

"I should." But she made no move. She might've screwed up this time. Instead of chickening out, she should have been upfront with Cash. Now she'd have to deal with his temper. She took another sip of beer. Would there ever be a day they didn't argue?

CASH MADE HIS way to the front door. He hoped whoever Mel and Harrison had invited over didn't stay too long, and took Harrison with them when they left. He had plans for his wife.

He opened the door. The dying sun silhouetted the shapes of three people, one who was blowing out a stream of smoke.

"Hi, I'm Lola." An Asian woman with long black hair pulled back in a ponytail, stepped into the foyer, offering her hand. She had a pretty smile and carried herself like a dancer. "We're here to see Mel and Harrison."

"Cash." He shook her hand, and stiffened when the other two men followed behind. The guy who had his long, dark-blond hair slicked back was an inch shorter than Cash, with a similar build, and maybe weighed a little less than him. Either way, Cash could take him if needed. The other guy, who'd just snuffed out his cigarette on the front porch, might be a different story. The man with short white-blond hair turned a broad shoulder and ducked his head as he stepped into the foyer. When he straightened, Cash realized the man wasn't that much taller, but damn if he wasn't huge. With his massive arms and chest, Cash wasn't sure how many blows he could take from this guy. Not that he planned on fighting anyone. These people were friends of Mel and Harrison. Nope, he just liked to be prepared.

"Cash, this is Shane." Lola introduced him to the slicked-back hair guy. "And this is—"

"Vlad," the big guy said with a thick accent, and shook his

hand. Based on the name, Cash was going to go out on a limb and guess the man was Russian. "Where Harry?"

Yeah, definitely Russian. "He and Mel are on the patio. Want something to drink?"

"Vodka," the Russian said.

Shane shook his head. "I'm good. I gotta fly home."

"Where's home?" Cash asked, leading them to the backyard.

"Everglades City."

Cash stopped and glanced over his shoulder. Two of his three new guests stared at him with concern and confusion. The Russian looked angry enough to chomp on broken glass.

"You flew in from the Glades?" Cash asked, keeping his temper in check. Mel had some serious explaining to do. "Do you do charity work for the homeless?"

Lola's brow rose. "No."

"Then you must work with drug addicts."

Lola cleared her throat. "Do you think we can talk with Mel and Harrison, please? Oh, and I'll take a water, thanks."

He would not wait on these people or leave them alone with Mel and Harrison until he knew exactly who they were and why they were here. Mel was up to something. He'd sensed it earlier at the garage. At first, he'd thought Noah's outbursts had upset her. Then, once they'd taken him to the hospital, she'd relaxed and he had blamed paranoia over their marriage for making him see things that weren't there. Just last night they'd set everything straight between them. He was going to marry her again, give her the wedding and honeymoon she deserved. He was going to try his damnedest to be the husband she needed. Now he knew he wasn't paranoid, he was right.

"Sure," he said, opening the patio door. "Mel, your friends are here."

Mel walked over wearing a forced smile. He knew his woman, immediately noticed the fear in her blue eyes. Who the hell was she afraid of? Them? Or him?

"Hey, y'all," she greeted them. "I take it you met Cash."

Just Cash, *not* my husband, Cash. So much for straightening everything out between them.

Lola nodded. "We did." She looked over Mel's shoulder. "Hi, Harrison."

"Lola, Shane," Harrison said, but ignored the Russian.

The Russian's frown deepened. "Harry no talk to Vlad?" He shrugged a shoulder. "That fine. Harry bore Vlad to crying anyway."

"Whatever, dude. Why don't you go smoke a carton of cigarettes and play in the swamp with your stupid gator?"

"Why do not Harry pull stick out of ass?"

"I'll pull the stick out, then hit you upside the head with it. Maybe it'll knock some sense into that Russian brain of yours."

Damn, did Harrison have balls. Cash couldn't believe the man was provoking Vlad.

"Boys, enough," Lola said, then gave Cash a tolerant smile. "Sorry about that. I don't mean to be rude, but I'm really thirsty."

She was trying to dismiss him. In his own house. He hooked his fingers in the front pockets of his jeans. "I'll get right on that. First, let me see if Harrison or my wife need anything." He turned to Mel. "Babe, need another beer?"

Her plastered smile fell. "Don't be mad."

"Who said I'm mad?"

"The nasty look on your face."

"You used that line yesterday, I'm seeing a trend."

"Is this a joke?" Shane asked, irritation in his tone.

"Our marriage is a laugh a minute," Cash responded.

"Vlad call shit of bull. Mel have no husband."

"Mel?" Lola stepped forward, looking confused and upset. "Is this true?"

Mel nodded.

"But what about…" Lola glanced to Shane, then quickly looked away. "When did you get married?"

Jealousy rooted itself deep in Cash's chest. He stared at Shane, and wondered just how good of friends he and Mel were. "Three years ago," Cash answered, then turned to Mel and nodded toward Shane. "Are you fucking that guy?"

She cringed. "God, no."

"Nice," Shane said.

Cash ignored the man and stared at Mel. "He seems a little upset that you're married."

"That's because I've known him since we were kids. Shane and his brother, Ryan, who is Lola's fiancé, are like family to me."

"Family you don't trust." Shane shook his head. "Ryan's going to be thrilled when he hears about this. Does Barney know? Did you at least tell your daddy?"

"Daddy knows, Barney doesn't."

"That'll go over well, since it's normal for a woman to marry a guy no one has ever met, and not tell her uncle and brothers."

Mel pressed her hands to her temples. "I had my reasons. But I'm not getting into them now. Besides, you knew I was dating the repo man when I was living in Tallahassee, and you were in prison when I married him."

"I've been out for eight months. And you could have told Ryan and Barney." Shane glared at Cash. "What'd he do to you?"

She turned to Cash. "This is the other reason why I didn't tell anyone about us."

"Because you thought your family would head to Tallahassee to kick my ass?"

"I hoped eventually we'd get back together and didn't want them hating or resenting you when that happened." She glanced to Shane. "I'm sorry I didn't tell you. Or anyone else. You and Ryan always accused me of being too impulsive. I wasn't when I married Cash, but I was embarrassed that I couldn't make our marriage work."

Guilt erased any traces of jealousy. Cash wrapped his arms around her. "You didn't do anything wrong. I wasn't man enough to step up. I'm sorry this is coming back to haunt you now." He touched her cheek. "I got your back, though."

Her smile filled his hand. "I love you."

"I love you, too."

"Christ." Shane let out a sigh, and shoved a hand through his hair. "I'm glad I have witnesses, because I never thought I'd see the day when Melanie Scarlet told a man she loved him." He grinned, then stepped over and offered his hand to Cash. "Belated congrats, man. Next time I'm around, we'll have to have a few beers. I've got some stories about Mel you might like to hear."

Cash chuckled. "Sounds good to me."

"Not to me. And the last name is Maddox," Mel said, then gave Shane a hug. "I'm sorry. Please don't say anything to Ryan or Barney. Let me be the one to tell them."

"You got it."

"Ice Cream Lady woman of many secret. Vlad impressed." The Russian wrinkled his forehead. "Vlad have confusion."

"Why's that, honey?" Mel asked.

"Lola have confusion, too." Lola crossed her arms. "Did you tell Cash?"

"Tell me what?"

"I warned you, Mel," Harrison said.

"Tell me what?" Cash repeated, wondering if the Russian was right and Mel was a woman of many secrets.

"I didn't tell him," Mel said. "Even if I did, Cash can be trusted."

Frustrated, his temper rising, Cash turned to Vlad. "Talk, and I'll get you the vodka."

"No," both Mel and Lola said in unison.

Cash shrugged. "Then anyone who isn't a Maddox can't get out of our house."

The Russian chuckled. "Vlad like Repo Man."

Lola rubbed her eyes, then dropped her hands and released a breath. "This entire conversation has gotten *way* out of control. It's time to rein it in. Cash, your wife works for me."

"Right. At the ice cream shop."

"At a private investigative agency."

Cash grinned. "Mel's a PI? Okay, what else you got for me?"

"Our agency is real, but we're operate around the system so we're not exactly legit."

Good God, the woman was dead serious. He froze. His heart rate rose and his chest tightened.

"When Mel and Harrison called about Noah and their suspicions of what had happened to him, I notified my boss," Lola continued. "He's kind of a big deal in the legit world of law enforcement, and he's interested in investigating Madeline. One of his agents is arriving in the morning." She looked to Harrison. "She's bringing the GPS chip."

"GPS chip for what?" Cash asked, still trying to soak in that his wife worked for this woman—and not in the way he'd thought.

"Harrison is going to go undercover as a homeless man. With any luck, this woman Madeline will come back to Hope House. Most criminals like to return to the scene of the crime. In this case, I wouldn't be surprised if Madeline makes a return to ensure that the police aren't aware of her. If she's bold enough to go for a couple of new victims, hopefully she'll take Harrison. We can find out where she lives, then go from there."

"Sounds like a simple enough plan," Cash said, when on the inside he wanted to pick up the patio table and smash the glass door. "I like it."

"Good." Lola eyed him with caution. "The agent will be here around eight. We need to drive Shane back to the airport, and check into our rooms. Is Harrison staying here?"

"I have a room and can use a lift," Harrison said. "If this works, I'll need the rest."

"Harry need head examination."

"Don't start, Vlad," Lola said. "We've been over this before. Harrison is perfect for this job. Nothing is going to happen to him."

Harrison shook his head. "Like Vlad gives a shit."

"Harry right. Vlad give no shit. Get killed to prove Harry big tough guy. Дура," he finished in Russian.

"What did you call me?"

"Stupid fool."

"Enough," Lola shouted. "Please." She shifted her gaze between Cash and Mel. "Should we meet here or at the hotel?"

"Here is fine," Cash said, shocked and disturbed by the emotions running through him. Anger should have been the top dog. Although pissed, he was...hurt that Mel had kept this secret agent crap from him. A sense of betrayal was there, too. After all the hell she'd put him through for his job, and she'd been walking a dangerous edge the entire time.

When Mel left the patio to walk the others to the door, he went to Dolly, didn't bother to hook her back into her wheelchair, and lifted her into his arms. He carried the dog inside, then laid her on her bed in the kitchen next to her water. He'd noticed his girl had been eating and drinking less, and sleeping more each day. He stroked the fur behind her ear. Dolly would leave him soon, too.

"Is Dolly okay?" Mel asked softly.

"Just tired." He stood. "I am, too."

"Yeah, it's been a long day."

"That's not what I meant." He left the kitchen, and headed for their bedroom.

She caught up with him in the hallway. "Then what did you mean?"

"I'm tired of this." He motioned between the two of them. "I'm tired of the lying and the secrets. You want a divorce. No problem."

Tears filled her eyes as she shoved him against the wall. "Is it really that easy for you?" She shoved him again. "Maybe you're right. We should officially split. I don't want a man who's going to up and walk the moment things don't go his way, or when he can't control every situation." She wiped her tears with her hand, and drifted her gaze over his body before meeting his eyes. "I need a man who can handle me."

CHAPTER 9

S HE DIDN'T THINK he was man enough to handle her?
Cash blocked her path, before she could walk away. "Better check yourself," he said, trying like hell to keep his temper under control. "I think it's the other way around. Remember, you were the one who left."

She narrowed her eyes at him. "Get out of my way."

"No."

"Damn it, Cash." She pushed at his shoulder and tried to move down the hall. "I'm done with you, let me leave."

He rotated, took her by the shoulders and pinned her against the wall. "No." He pressed his cheek along hers, inhaled her scent, loved her soft skin, her breath against his neck. "What happened to last night?"

"The sex was great, everything else was a mistake."

"There's my woman." He kept her against the wall, but leaned back enough to see her eyes. "You love to cut deep when you're hurt, don't you?"

Her chin trembled slightly before she hardened her jaw. "You'd know, since you've been hurting me for years."

"Is that what tonight was? Payback?"

"No."

"Why didn't you tell me? I have you by well over a foot and one hundred pounds. I have a mean temper and like it rough." He slid his hands down her arms, gripped her wrists, then quickly turned her until her back was flush against his chest. "Why is it you can trust me with your body?" he asked, running a hand along her breasts, then lower. When he reached the hem of her short sundress, he shoved the material out of his way, then pressed his palm against her sex. "Why is it you'll let me fuck you any way I please, but you can't trust me enough to tell me what's in your head?"

"You can't handle what's in my head *or* my heart," she said, trying to wriggle free.

"Try me. Start by telling me why you'd take on a dangerous job after complaining about mine." When she didn't say anything, he rubbed his fingers over her silky panties and along her swollen lips. "I want to know," he said against her ear.

Her breathing grew rapid. The rise and swell of her chest made him crazy with need. He wanted her dress off so he could see her breasts, her nipples. He might be tired of fighting, but he'd never be tired of her.

"Maybe I wanted the edge, to know what kept you from me." She stopped wriggling and arched into him. "Maybe I wanted to feel like I belonged, like I mattered."

He stilled his hand. "You matter to me."

She glanced over her shoulder, her tear-soaked cheeks punching a hole in his chest. "How could I know?"

"I gave you everything when I didn't think I was going to make it. It'll always be yours." He loved her so damned much he'd made sure he had made her his wife, should he not survive the surgeries after his accident. She would get the house, half his business, his money, everything.

"And then you let go." Keeping her head against his chest, she faced forward. "I know you love me. I know you didn't leave the hospital regretting that you married me. But there were times when I wondered if guilt was what kept you from divorcing me, and I admit to moments of insecurity." She let out a shaky breath. "I'd come for the weekend, and you'd love my body just like before the accident. Then you'd let me go again and a part of my heart would shrivel. A piece of my soul turned gray. I'd go home feeling worse about me, us. Spend my days scooping ice cream to cute kids I'd never have, my nights working on cars or watching TV. You want to know what I do when I go to bed?"

No, he didn't. He wanted to drop to his knees and beg her to forgive him. To trust him with her heart and soul. To give him the chance to prove that he'd do everything and anything to make sure she never had a single moment of loneliness or insecurity.

"I lie in bed pretending the pillow I'm holding is you. I hum the lullaby I used to sing to you when you were having trouble sleeping, then imagine I hear you breathing next to me."

He moved his hand from under her dress, then smoothed the fabric back in place. He also let go of her wrists, but she made no attempt to move.

"Why'd you let me go?" she asked.

"I have no business using force to keep you with me. Touching you the way I was…it's no way to prove a point. You deserve better. I'm sorry. I feel like I keep disappointing you."

She shrugged, then stepped away from him. "That's okay. You didn't this time. I knew you couldn't handle me."

He grabbed her by the arms and pulled her against his chest again. "Why do you have to be so mean?" He dragged his mouth along her neck and his hands over her breasts. "You open up, then shut down before giving me a chance."

She reached behind and hung onto his hips. "A chance to do what? Keep hurting us both?"

"You're the one who's doing the hurting this time." He slid his hands down her stomach, bunched the sundress in one hand and gripped her panties with the other. "You could have told me about your other job last night. You could have told me how bad you were feeling. I was honest. I told you something that embarrasses the hell out of me."

"Cash Maddox embarrassed?" She let out a raspy chuckle. "Please."

He pulled her panties taut, let go of the dress and cupped her chin and jaw in his hand. "Don't. I opened up. I admitted to being a coward. I told you I let you go because I was afraid of losing you. Stupid or not, those were *my* feelings. I would never laugh at yours. Are you going to laugh at me if I tell you that I wake up every morning tempted to drive to Everglades City and drag you home to me? That I hate my life when you're not in it? Maybe it'll amuse you to know that I like getting punched in the face because the physical pain sometimes helps deaden the constant dull ache in my chest?" Her tears slipped onto his fingers. He ignored them, let go of her panties and cupped her sex. "I think about your body. Imagine sliding my dick inside you, or running my tongue between your lips. You have no idea how much I love the way you taste." He nipped, then kissed her exposed neck. "Well, go ahead and laugh. I can *handle* it."

"You're such a bastard," she said, gliding her hands from his hips to the fly of his jeans. She moved his shirt out of the way, slid the top button free, then the zipper. "There are days when I hate you."

She let out a low groan when he slipped a finger beneath her panties and ran it along her clit. "Like right now?" he asked, then drew in a sharp breath when his jeans hung around his hips and she took his dick in her palm.

"Yes," she said on a hiss.

He pulled his fingers from her heat, unzipped her dress, then pushed the straps down her arms. After moving her hand from his erection, he shoved her panties over her hips. "You'll get over it," he said, kissing her shoulder and unhooking her bra.

She pressed her hands against the wall. "Arrogant ass," she said, rubbing her rear along his dick.

"Call me whatever the hell you want." Damn, he needed inside her. "But I'm starting to realize our separation wasn't entirely my fault."

"Don't go there." When she glanced over her shoulder, her eyes glittered with both passion and anger. "Like you, I'm tired of talking about our marriage."

"So it's sex or nothing?"

"That's all it's been until yesterday."

"And it's my fault. You didn't do a thing wrong. Wait." He leaned forward and kneaded her rear. "You were working a job you didn't want me to know about." Reaching under, he pressed two fingers between her slick folds. "How dangerous is it?" he asked, hating that what she'd been doing intrigued him, and hating being jealous of a frickin' job and how that had fulfilled something inside her he couldn't. "A fast ride on my Harley used to turn you on. Does the danger of the job?" He circled her clit with his thumb. "Do you come home and touch yourself? I bet you do. I can see you now. Legs spread, one hand playing with your nipples, the other rubbing your clit. Yeah, what do you need me for, now that you have all that going for you?"

"I told you to stop talking," she said, her sex gripping his fingers.

"Right. Back to what we're good at. Fucking." She gasped when he pressed his fingers deep. "I can handle that, babe."

With a groan, she shoved his hand away, then quickly turned and faced him. "Fuck you."

He tensed. When the F-word came flying out of Mel's mouth, that meant she was beyond furious.

"We were good at everything," she shouted, as tears began to stream down her cheeks. She cupped his face. "We've both made mistakes, and we've both done our share of hurting. Neither of us are innocent." She grazed her fingertips along his lips. "When I touch myself, I think of you, not a job. When I'm sad, I think of the good times we've had. When I'm happy, I wish you were there to share the moment with me."

God, she humbled him. He lashed out and said mean things out of pride and anger, and she turned around and told him something private and special.

"What do you want me to do?" he asked, needing guidance in unfamiliar territory. "I told you I'd quit my job and do everything in my power to make us work. I want you home. But now I understand why you hesitated yesterday when I asked if you'd come back to me. You aren't sure about quitting your job." That realization sucked. Talk about having the tables turned. Now he could understand why Mel had been angry with him. His wife might be tough, but he didn't like knowing her life could be in danger.

"It's a job. That's all. Yes, I enjoy it, but I like working with the people even more."

"Then you'll quit?"

"After this investigation."

"Promise?"

She took his erection in her hand. "*I* wouldn't chose a job over my husband."

The little swamp witch always had to have the last word, and it always had to be laced with barbed wired. He took a fistful of her hair and brought their mouths close. "That stung."

She nipped his lip, then soothed it with her tongue. "I wanted it to."

Anger simmered in his chest. "Are you done now?" he asked, keeping his irritation from his voice.

She rubbed her thumb over the head of his penis. "It's out of my system."

"About time," he said, then kissed her. Hard. Open-mouthed. If she wanted slow, she'd let him know. Even then he'd have a hard time going easy on her. He'd eventually get over the secret agent job, but knowing she'd kept it from him still had him wound up and furious. They'd talked enough about it and he wouldn't bring it up again, unless she went back on her word. Then all bets were off and he'd play dirty. For now, he'd take his anger, his love and lust, out on her body.

Tearing his mouth away, he pushed her against the wall and raised one of her legs. Bent his knees slightly, then with one swift thrust, entered her. When he met her gaze, she gave him a small challenging smile. "That's all you've got for me?" she asked, then let out a soft moan when he thrust again. "What happened to those new moves?"

"Are you complaining about my performance?"

She gasped when he gripped her rear and pumped his hips harder. "Never."

"Are you going to come?" he asked, loving being buried in her heat.

"Yes," she said, wrapping her arms around his neck.

"Good." He pulled free.

"What the hell, Cash?"

Without responding, he went to his knees and tasted heaven.

She ran a hand through his hair and moaned. "I didn't expect you to...never mind. Don't stop."

He would, just not yet. After drawing in one lip, he slid three fingers between her folds, then flicked his tongue along her clit. The throaty sounds she made, the way her muscles tightened around his fingers told him she was close.

"Yes, right there," she panted.

That was his signal. As much as it pained him, he pulled his fingers and mouth away, then stood.

She shoved at his shoulders. "What's wrong with you?" she asked, her cheeks flushed, anger and desire in her eyes.

He turned her around, then bent her over. "Ass in the air," he said, giving one rounded cheek a light slap before entering her.

After calling him the bastard that he was, she did as he demanded and pressed her hands against the wall. "Are you going to let me come this time?" she asked.

"Will it make you mad if I don't?"

She glanced over her shoulder. "Why don't you take the risk and find out? You like a little danger."

The heat and challenge in her eyes should have sent up red flags, but she was right. He did like danger. He loved how it made him come alive, loved how his wife did the same for him. As he gripped her hips and pressed himself deep, he realized she was all he'd needed. Living with Mel would always be exciting, and based on the threat in her tone seconds ago, maybe even a little dangerous.

His plan to torture her by making her wait to orgasm was a

bad idea. Because her pleasure meant everything to him, he was only torturing himself. He slipped free.

"Not again," she said on a groan.

He picked her up and carried her into the bedroom. "Not again," he said, and gently set her on the mattress.

"What are you doing?" she asked, as he moved over her.

He held one of her legs, then slid himself between her wet folds. "Do you need to ask?"

She caressed his chest. "You were punishing me, weren't you?"

"You pissed me off." He leaned forward until her nipples grazed his chest. "The last shot you threw at me wasn't necessary. You even admitted you wanted it to sting."

She twined her legs around his lower back, and her arms around his neck. "I'm sorry."

"Me, too." Now that his anger had subsided, he gave her a slow kiss. Explored her lips, teased her tongue with his. When he raised his head, he pressed his pelvis deep. When Mel gasped, he grinned. "No more talking, I'm trying to make love to my wife."

Despite the pretty smile crossing her face, tears slipped into her hair. His throat tightened at the sight of them. He swallowed and slowly rocked his hips. The only tears he ever wanted to see Mel shed were tears of joy. Neither of them had had an easy life. They'd both been forced to grow up before their time, had to learn to fend for themselves, and knew that love wasn't a gift, but something earned. He might not always deserve Mel's love, but he never wanted to lose it.

Her breathing grew ragged, and matched his own. He stared at her face. She'd closed her eyes, and that was okay. It gave him the freedom to watch her, witness the beauty of her pleasure.

"Cash," she whispered, then gasped.

The moment her muscles tightened around him, his body tensed and he closed his eyes. As his orgasm shot through him, tightening his core, giving him that intoxicating satisfaction he craved, Mel's image filled his mind. Dragging in a deep breath, he opened his eyes and met Mel's. "Were you watching me?" he asked.

"Yes. I couldn't resist. You looked so happy and sexy. What were you thinking about?"

"You."

She touched his jaw. "I loved making love to my husband."

He brushed his lips along hers. "I loved making love to my wife."

"I think we should make a promise to each other."

"Anything you need. I'm tired of fighting."

"See how perfect we are for each other?" she asked with a smile. "That's what I was going to suggest. That, and a no more tit for tat rule."

"I wouldn't have withheld the half dozen orgasms you could've had if you hadn't bit me." When she pinched his nipple, he chuckled and gave her a kiss. "I think you just broke your new rule."

She sighed. "I have a feeling we'll both struggle with it."

He did, too. But as long as he had Mel back, he didn't care.

The House of Archer, Bower, Georgia
Saturday, 10:48 p.m. Eastern Daylight Saving Time

STILL GROGGY, LIAM Forrester slowly awakened. When he realized there was no subtle jostling from the bus, he came alert.

Panic clawed at his chest. As he gazed around the room, memories of yesterday assaulted him…

The stop in Atlanta. Climbing off the bus. Mitch dragging him behind the depot and quickly explaining that they couldn't board the next bus. The government was onto them. They knew their names, their faces and had men searching for them. Mitch had told him to hide his wallet and backpack, go in the opposite direction, then meet him at the diner five blocks northeast of the depot.

He'd done as Mitch had instructed and…damn it. Then what happened? God, he didn't know. Everything was hazy and blurred.

The drugs.

He glared at where the IV had been stuck in his arm earlier. The woman would pay. He just prayed to God they hadn't captured Mitch, too. Otherwise, he was on his own.

He looked around the small room, touched on the small, blackened TV screen and remembered...the blood, the gore. The way they'd taped his eyelids open in order to force him to watch such despicable violence. Her voice. The woman's sexy, soothing words shouldn't have been sexy *or* soothing. She'd spoken of atrocity, of the joy, the euphoric pleasure of killing.

She'd encouraged *him* to kill.

He wasn't a killer, but he'd have no problem ending the life of the people behind the government's sick experimentation. The door to his room opened. *She* stepped inside, then shut the door behind her. Yes, he'd have no problem killing and would start with the woman—after she told him what he needed to know.

"Who are you?" he demanded.

"Forgot so quickly? Interesting. My name is Madeline." When she stepped around the heart rate monitor, he realized she'd dressed inappropriately. Wearing a sheer nightgown, her long, dark curly hair an arousing mess, she approached him. "How'd you sleep?" she asked.

The bed he'd been strapped to suddenly moved. As he was taken from being seated to lying flat on his back, he held her gaze.

"You're an interesting one," she said, tiptoeing her fingers across his chest. "I think you and I are going to have a *good* time." She slid her hand from his chest to his crotch. "Yes, indeedy. I'm going to train you right. You'll be perfect."

As she stroked him, he thought about his hatred for her, for everything the government was doing to innocent men, women and children. He thought of his sister, how her life could be in danger. About how they'd killed his parents.

She frowned. "You *are* an interesting one. Since you're too young for erectile dysfunction, either you don't like girls, or you have extreme willpower."

He refused to answer her, or take part in whatever game she played. When she unzipped his jeans, the heart rate monitor began to ping in rapid successions. "This is rape," he said, as she drew his penis from between his fly. He wouldn't deny wanting fellatio from an attractive woman, but he wanted it on his terms. And definitely not by a woman who'd taken part in holding him captive and drugging him.

"I hadn't thought about it that way." She stroked him. "So you don't want me to give you a blow job?"

"No."

"You really don't want me to do this?" she asked, and holding his gaze, circled the tip of his thickening penis with her tongue.

He quickly brought to mind the violent films he'd been forced to watch. Suddenly sickened, his penis grew flaccid again. "No," he repeated.

Grinning, she readjusted him, then zipped his jeans. "I am going to break you," she said, as she raised the bed back into its original place. "Don't worry." She ran the back of her hand along his cheek. "It's going to hurt *so* good. Nighty-night," she sang, then turned off the light and left the room.

Once the door was closed, he let out a deep breath. *She will not break you. You're strong. You can adapt and overcome.*

Could he? He was a pencil pusher. A former accountant who had stumbled on numbers that hadn't made sense. With Mitch and William at his side, he'd been confident. He'd been scared for his life and his sister's, but he'd also had faith that justice would prevail. And he needed to hang onto that faith, otherwise millions of innocent people would be poisoned.

CAREFUL NOT TO disturb Rodney, Adeline slipped back into bed. Their new subject was quite interesting, as well as very attractive. While she'd always loved Rodney's dark good looks, she rather liked this fairer subject, his light-brown hair, sexy five o'clock shadow, muscular physique. Or maybe she liked that he'd resisted her. Yes, Rod was *always* resisting her, so nothing new there. But Rodney was her equal. Same education, same everything, and she would never want him on his knees kissing her feet. One of the things she loved about him was that he challenged her spirit and mind.

But Rodney didn't always fulfill her needs. She rolled her head to the side. The moonlight filtered into the room revealing hints of his handsome face. She loved Rod as much as she was capable, loved it more when he satisfied her. Too bad she had to constantly seduce or trick him into her bed. Wouldn't it be interesting to create a sex slave who would never tell her no? Better yet, a monster who would do whatever she asked? He could help her keep the others she would create under control. If need be, he could help her keep Rodney under control, too.

She pulled the comforter around her shoulders. This new subject required serious thought. Something was off about him. When she'd found him on the street, he'd acted lost and out of sorts. Paranoid.

Tomorrow they would assess him, along with the other man they'd picked up near the Atlanta shelter, then give them both a healthy dose of A-Line. Then, later in the afternoon, she and Rod would head to Tallahassee to find out what—if anything—had happened to Noah.

She snuggled deeper under the comforter and closed her eyes. Noah had better hope she never found him. Her bitch roommate's wounds would look like paper cuts compared to what she'd do to him.

Adeline smiled into the darkness. Damn, she couldn't wait for tomorrow.

CHAPTER 10

Cash and Mel's House, Tallahassee, Florida
Sunday, 7:23 a.m. Eastern Daylight Saving Time

MEL ENDED THE call with Daddy. "That went well," she said, then curled next to Dolly on the living room area rug. "How you doin', pretty girl?" As she ran her hand along the dog's back, sadness settled around her. Dolly turned her head and nuzzled her with her nose. "I'm sorry I wasn't always here. I've missed swimmin' with you and going for long W-A-L-K-S." Dolly's tail went crazy. She lifted her head and licked Mel's cheek.

"I swear she can spell," Cash said, kneeling next to her.

"Or maybe she saw you walking into the room. You make me want to wag my tail, too."

He chuckled, then kissed her. "How's your dad?"

She sighed and tried not to let guilt take root. "He thought Charlie was settin' camp up on the north side of his swamp. Turns out it was a family of 'coons. Which he promptly killed and is in the process of skinning. He's wantin' me to cook 'em up for him in the crock pot." She rubbed her hand along her head as she realized how she must have sounded. "Sorry. When I start talking to Daddy, my twang gets a little...twangy. Can you remind me again why you married me? Good Lord, who talks about imaginary Viet Cong and skinning raccoons on a Sunday morning?"

Laughing, he cuddled next to her so the three of them were one giant spoon on the living room floor. "Makes for interesting conversation." He smoothed his palm along Dolly's coat. When their fingers touched, they joined hands and petted their girl. "I want to talk about your job."

"With ATL?"

"Is that the name of the agency?"

Since they'd been too busy fighting, then making up, they had never discussed the details of her side job. "Yeah, it stands for Above the Law. Harrison's a big Steven Segal fan and named it after one of his movies."

"I'm more partial to Chuck Norris, but to each his own."

"We're weird."

"Why do you say that?"

"Viet Cong, skinning 'coons, Above the Law, Chuck Norris…we're weird."

"Maybe I think people who don't have these types of conversations are weird," he said.

She glanced over her shoulder. His teasing, dark-brown eyes held amusement, curiosity and hunger, and she fell in love with him all over again.

"Why are you smiling?" he asked.

"Because you're looking at me the same exact way you did when we met. I fell hard for you that day."

He kissed her shoulder. "After all these years and you're just telling me this?"

"You were already cocky enough." She bent and kissed Dolly's head. "I miss this. Just lazing around, cuddling with our dog."

"Waiting for an agent to bring a GPS chip."

"Not funny." She rolled onto her back. Dolly did, too. "This is serious business. The man we work for was one of the first profilers for the FBI. His agents all come from a government agency or have military background. Of the three I met, one was former FBI, the other CIA, the last, Navy SEAL."

"SEAL? Does he know your friend Ryan?"

She nodded. "It's a long story. But because of Ryan, that's how we all became acquainted."

"Except *you* don't have a military background. So how'd you get hired?"

Oh, boy. Should she tell him about the bodies she disposed of for Ian?

"I heard Ian thought I looked like Farrah Fawcett."

"Red swimsuit picture?" He let out a wistful sigh. "He's right. And it makes me want to kick the man's ass."

"Would you stop?" Grinning and tightening her hold on his hand, she rolled back to her side, then rubbed their joined hands along Dolly's belly. Memories of last night, of their heated argument, of the two of them standing naked, vulnerable, exposed, had her closing her eyes. "I'm sorry I didn't tell you about ATL. Even though we were apart, I should have. Because now it does affect you."

"Tell me honestly, did you join the agency as a way to get even with me?"

"No. I told you the truth. I wanted to experience a little of your danger, and I like the people. I'm not always sure how Lola feels about me, though. Sometimes I get the impression she thinks I'm a little…out there."

He kissed her shoulder again. "If that's what she thinks, then she should probably go fuck herself."

She laughed and rolled back toward him. "You are so bad. Telling or thinking someone should go diddle themselves because you don't like what they say or think is not going to take you places."

"I have my woman, my dog, my garage." He touched her cheek. "You bless me with a baby, and I don't think my life could be any more complete."

She panicked. "Too fast."

"What?"

"I said that out loud." Dang. "I want a baby. I wanted the baby we lost."

He frowned. "But?"

She drew their joined hands away from the dog and pressed them against her stomach. "Cash, honey, I love you. I'm not sure if you've noticed, but my family has issues."

His eyes danced with amusement as he grinned. "Hell, we all got issues. My mom made up my name after an imaginary millionaire. I don't know anything about her family, except I might have a relative in Alabama. An aunt, I think. Or maybe you're worried about my background?"

"No." She gripped him and realized just how lucky she'd been to have Daddy, Barney and the Monahans. "Not at all. It's just, we Scarlets are known to be…eccentric."

He cupped her cheek and grinned. "Baby, eccentric is what rich people call their crazy relatives. Just own where you come from, because I love it."

"This coming from a man who used to diffuse bombs for a living."

"And newly retired from the repo business," he added with a kiss.

"Love the sound of that."

The doorbell rang. Cash's smile waned. "Duty calls *one* last time."

She moved to answer, but he stopped her.

"I'm coming along for this ride," he said.

She stiffened. "You worked alone on repo jobs."

"Reckless and stupid on my part."

"Harrison is the one going undercover. Don't be offended if Lola doesn't want you involved."

"Make it so I am."

She kissed him. "You got it."

After he helped her up, Mel headed for the door. When she opened it, Lola stood front and center. "You're going to love this." She brushed by her and headed for the patio.

"Asian Lola woke on wrong side of bed," Vlad said, and followed Lola.

Harrison stepped inside. "I don't know what Ian was thinking," he said quietly, then turned when a tall woman, with striking, ice-blue eyes and dark hair, cut in a short angled bob, approached the threshold. "Gillian, this is Melanie. She's with ATL."

Gillian assessed her. "They kept calling you Mel, so I assumed you were a man."

"I can assure you she's not," Cash said as he entered the foyer. "I'm Cash."

"My husband," Mel added.

"Is this important to the investigation?" Gillian asked.

Mel shook her head, unsure if the woman was joking, rude or asocial. "Just making introductions."

Gillian tugged at her suit coat, which fit loosely yet didn't hide her well-endowed chest. "I didn't realize ATL had a husband and wife team."

"Cash isn't with ATL," Mel said as she and Cash led Gillian to the patio.

Once everyone had taken a seat, Gillian cleared her throat and looked directly at Cash. "If you're not ATL or CORE, you'll need to leave."

"He stays," Lola said. "This is his and Mel's house."

"Should we go somewhere else?"

"No."

Gillian drew in a deep breath and set a small case on the patio table. "I want you to call Ian and confirm this is okay with him."

Lola shook her head. "He's with my mother, picking out flowers for their wedding."

She glanced around the table. "Right. Very unconventional."

"Have you been with CORE long, honey?" Mel asked, still trying to decide what to make of the woman.

Gillian glared at her. "The last person who called me honey ended up with his penis severed. They sewed it back on, but I'm not sure why the government wasted tax dollars since he was heading for death row."

"Good thing I don't have a penis." Mel said, deciding that maybe she didn't want Cash sitting in on this after all. "But you still didn't answer the question."

"Three months."

"Before that?"

"DEA. Are we done?"

"Honestly," Mel began, "I'd like to be finished with you. You're not a very nice person. If you didn't have something we needed, I'd tell you to get out of my house."

"Agreed," Lola said as Dolly wheeled onto the patio. "Let's get to why you're here so we can part ways as quickly as possible."

Gillian watched Dolly, and Mel swore the woman melted. "Your dog?" she asked.

God, had Gillian heard a word she or Lola had said? "Cash served with her in Iraq. She lost her legs, but saved my husband's life."

"What a brave and noble dog." A wistful smile softened Gillian's face. "I had a German shepherd when I was growing up."

"How nice."

"Not really. My father snapped his neck to punish me and my brother."

"Jesus," Harrison said. "Why would you even tell us that?"

Gillian glanced around the table. "I'm sorry if I come across rude. I lost my filter when I was a kid and never found it."

"Vlad have no filter."

"So?"

"Vlad have also lost many animal."

"I don't know how to respond to that." She opened the case. "Lola's right. We'll need to part ways soon. I have to be in Dallas this afternoon." She turned to Mel. "Not to be *rude*, but we need to move along."

Mel hid a grin when Cash gave her a light kick from under the table. "Of course," she responded.

After pulling out the small device, Gillian looked to Harrison. "We're going to implant the chip into your armpit, which is an area we'll assume the perpetrators won't examine. It's almost like a shot." She stood and approached him. "Raise the sleeve of your shirt and your arm."

As soon as he did as she'd instructed, Gillian pulled the device's trigger. Harrison flinched as quickly as she took the device away. "Now to the fun stuff." Gillian pulled her laptop from her case and instructed Harrison to do the same. "Since I'm flying to Dallas, one of you will have to quickly learn how to follow the GPS program I'm syncing to Harrison's computer as we speak. The program is simple and just like the GPS you'd use in a car. If you do run into a problem, contact Rachel Davis at the CORE office. She helped develop the program." She looked to Lola. "Who will be taking the lead on this?"

"I will," Lola said.

Gillian explained how the program worked, that they would be able to follow Harrison's whereabouts at all times. "Be aware," she continued, "the chip will also remain active, even if he's deceased."

"Nice," Harrison said, and rubbed his armpit. "This itches."

"According to Ian's product developer, it's a minor side effect." She closed her case. "In other words, suck it up."

"Why didn't you say you were former DEA when we met?" Lola asked.

"You didn't ask."

Lola released an exasperated sigh. "We're dealing with a man who was drugged. It's also possible someone is using the homeless for experimentation purposes."

"Anything is possible," Gillian said. "Trust me. I'm fully aware that there are pharmaceutical companies taking advantage of the homeless. When I was DEA, there was an issue in Philadelphia. Homeless people were being approached, offered money and a consent form. But here's the problem with that. Some of these people can't read. Some don't care to read the consent form, all they see is a way out. Money in their pocket. An opportunity to get off the streets."

"Since you obviously have experience in this," Lola began, "would you stop by the hospital and meet with Noah before you leave?"

"Already done."

"When?"

"Before I came to the hotel. Noah was clearly detoxing and completely incoherent. I wouldn't be surprised if ninety percent of what he told you was a hallucination. *But*, what's bothersome is that there were eyewitnesses who saw Noah, sober and drug free, leaving with an unknown individual." The agent looked to her watch. "If there's nothing else, I'll need to call a taxi, or can one of you take me to the airport?"

"Vlad can take you," Lola said, handing the Russian the keys to her rental car.

Once Gillian gave them a curt good-bye and left, Harrison itched his underarm. "I think she liked putting this thing in me."

"She did her job," Lola said.

"Whatever. Once ours is done here, I'm cutting it out of me. I don't like the idea of knowing I can be tracked."

The House of Archer, Bower, Georgia
Sunday, 8:08 a.m. Eastern Daylight Saving Time

ADELINE ADJUSTED THE volume of the recording device, while Rodney checked the test subject's vitals. This subject, Jim, wasn't like the one in the neighboring room. When she'd approached Jim at the Atlanta shelter, he'd come with her willingly and had been eager to work. Based on his girth, she'd thought he'd be a perfect subject: healthy, able to survive without food, which was good, since the amphetamine tended to suppress the appetite. Except once they'd brought Jim to the house and he had shed his coat, they'd discovered Jim's extra padding wasn't fat. The man had layered his body with clothes, a blanket and a small bag filled with his personal items—ID, brush, bar of soap, toothbrush and a picture of an ugly woman. Turned out Jim was a skinny, boney man and, based on his ID, much older than she'd thought.

Which meant Jim would die. Even if his heart could survive the drug and treatment, she'd kill him. The man served no purpose to her. Now that his face had been cleaned, he was as ugly as the woman in the picture.

She turned and stared at Rodney's back, drifted her gaze lower and remembered gripping his ass last night while he fucked her. Actually, she'd have Rodney kill him, just like he'd murdered Troy. Excitement filled her stomach. She had the urge to touch herself. God, how she'd loved the way Rodney had come to her rescue and had fought Troy. She could have done without Troy nearly choking her to death, not that he would have succeeded. She'd come to the room with a razor in her pocket, just in case her plan had fallen apart. Fortunately, it hadn't. Troy had also proven that A-Line and psychological torture was a maddening combination. She had taken a normal man and had turned him into a bloodthirsty animal. Too bad she hadn't been able to control her creation.

Memories of the way Rodney had wrapped his belt around Troy's neck, how he'd slammed the man's head against the wood floor, then smothered him, played in her mind. The torture crossing Rodney's face when he'd realized he had murdered a man. She grinned. That he could be like her.

Now *that* had been something special.

As she walked past Rodney, she purposefully brushed her breasts against his back. When he stiffened, her grin broadened. She went to the TV, turned it on, then the DVD player. After she hit PLAY, and the screen came to life, she faced Rodney. "Do you think he's strong enough?"

Rodney finished taping Jim's eyelids open by wrapping a layer of duct tape over the surgical tape keeping the man's lids from closing, then around his head. After trial and error, they'd learned this was the best method, aside from toothpicks. Rodney, out of concern that his patients might accidentally poke themselves in the eye, had disapproved of that idea.

"I'm honestly not sure," Rod said. "He has to be about twenty pounds underweight. I didn't want to upset you last night, but I also noticed his hands were trembling yesterday. Now his entire body has the tremors and his heart rate is elevated."

She'd been so damned angry about Noah's escape, then furious when she'd realized Jim was practically nothing but skin and bones, that she'd dismissed the man from her mind, and had let Rodney give him the first, small dose of A-Line without her presence. She stared at Jim, at the sheen of sweat coating his face, the way his body shivered. Yep, Jim was going to die.

She stepped closer to the raised bed and checked the straps around his ankles. "You like alcohol, Jim?"

The man grunted. "Rodney, be a dear and remove the tape?"

Rod rolled his eyes and tore the duct tape from the man's mouth. "Why are you doing this?" he asked, panic lacing his raspy voice. "Please let me go. I won't tell anyone."

"Do you like alcohol?" she asked again. "Shot of whiskey, gin, vodka? Or maybe you're not into the hard stuff and stick to beer or wine."

Jim licked his lips and stared at her with bulging, bloodshot eyes. "Whiskey."

"Would you like some now?"

"Yes," Jim sobbed as tears streamed down his face.

She nodded to Rodney, who muffled Jim's cries with the strip of tape. He then turned on the recording device. Once her recorded voice filled the room, she stepped into the hall and waited for Rodney. When he closed the door behind him, he shook his head. "Unless we continue with mild doses, Jim's not going to make it. I'm worried about shocking his system and sending him into cardiac arrest."

"Do you want to take him back to the shelter?"

He turned away and walked toward the room housing the sexy test subject. "It's bad enough we don't know where Noah is, or what condition he was in when he escaped."

Interesting. She hid her excitement. "What are you saying?"

He glanced over his shoulder. "You know exactly what I'm saying. These people can't leave, which means I won't allow any more inside this house."

He wouldn't *allow*? "But we still have plenty of time."

"I don't care. I've killed one man, and we have no idea if Noah has gone to the police or if he's dead in the woods." He slammed his hand against the wall, then turned on her. The fury in his eyes ignited her lust. She loved when he was angry, loved it when he warred with his morals, how he fought his cravings and the urge to join her on the dark side. "I want to blame you for this, for everything that's fucked up in this house."

"Go ahead. You'd be right. It is my fault. My sickness created this situation. If you remember, I coaxed you into experimenting on people."

He grabbed her by the arms and gave her a hard shake. "Your sickness isn't your fault," he said, his eyes softening slightly. "And you didn't coax me into anything." He shoved her against the wall. "Do you think I didn't know what you were doing when you suggested drugging homeless people? Do you honestly think that I'm that gullible and simple-minded?"

Oh, no. For the first time in years, her chest tightened with panic. He couldn't be onto her. Not yet. She wasn't finished, not even close. Her heart sped. A wave of dizziness blurred her vision. When she went slack, Rodney helped her to the floor.

"Adeline, honey, what's wrong?" he asked, concern in his tone.

"I'm so sorry, Rod. You know I don't think you're a stupid man. I love your mind." All true, except the apology. But she knew Rodney, knew what her man needed to hear, that he needed to see she could have a small amount of regret and empathy. He needed a glimmer of hope and a sign that she was…fixable. "I'm so scared you'll give up on me and leave," she said, and *that* was the truth. No one knew her better than him. No one but him loved her, and she'd hate to have to kill him if he ever tried to leave her.

He cradled her against his chest. "I could never leave you. There've been moments when I've wondered what my life would be like without you in it. Would I have chosen a different career path?"

She inhaled his spicy aftershave and clung to the front of his shirt. "Or a different woman?" she asked, curious as to how he'd answer. Rod could've had any girl he chose. Fit and muscular, he had a great body, thick dark hair, gorgeous eyes, and a sexy smile. She'd seen the way women looked at him, and couldn't blame them—even if she'd wanted to slice out their eyes.

He kissed the top of her head and stroked her back. "You're the only woman I've known. I can't imagine being with another."

She hid her shock. While she knew Rod had been a virgin when they'd had sex the first time, she had assumed that he'd hooked up with a couple of girls during college. She supposed it made sense, though. The man had high moral standards. If he'd cheated on her, the guilt would've eaten him alive.

"And you're the only man who's touched my body," she lied, and looked up at him. "If you love me, why do you deny me?"

He glanced to her lips, then to the hallway floor. "I'm tired of this same argument."

"Do you regret last night?" she asked, and rubbed his chest.

"No. I only regret being too weak to resist you."

"I have needs." With her head clear again, she pushed herself from the floor. "If you want to keep denying us both, then maybe I should see if our test subject would be willing to give me physical satisfaction," she taunted him, hoping to drive him over the edge of depravity. "He's young, attractive. I doubt he'd turn me down, and I'm sure he'll be able to get me off."

The fury in his eyes returned. He quickly stood and shoved her back against the wall. "Don't you dare." He grabbed the front of her blouse and tore it. Buttons fell to the floor as he undid his pants. "No one touches you but me," he said, ripping the button and zipper of her shorts, then pushing them over her hips. "If I find out you've fucked him, I'll kill him and beat you."

When he thrust himself inside her, she decided she just might have to let Rodney catch her with their subject after all. She'd loved watching Rod kill for her, but would be thrilled to see him murder out of passion and pure jealousy.

"You wouldn't beat me," she said on a groan, and envisioned him taking a paddle to her ass. "And you're not a killer."

Holding onto her hip with one hand, he grabbed her mouth and drove himself painfully deeper. "I killed for you once," he said, his eyes possessive and dark with hatred. "I'll do it again. Don't test me." He moved his hand from her face, held onto both her hips, then with a grunt, pulled away and spilled himself across her stomach. Breathing hard, he staggered back and righted his pants. "Clean yourself up. I'm going to take care of the subject."

She stared at the door Rod had closed behind him, and used the shredded blouse to clean her stomach. She was good with the impromptu fuck, but to leave her unsatisfied was just wrong.

The son of a bitch would pay for his little show.

LIAM PULLED AT his restraints and squinted against the harsh light. Once the room came into focus, and he realized the man from yesterday had returned, he momentarily relaxed. The man had been clinical and had said little. While that should have him on edge—and it did—the woman worried him even more. There was something in her eyes. Something sinful. A mischievously evil promise that he had no doubt she would deliver.

"People are expecting me," Liam said. "When they realize I'm missing, they'll come looking for me."

The man turned to him and Liam suddenly wished the woman, Madeline, had come to the room instead. The man's eyes narrowed with hatred and rage. "They won't find you."

He swallowed, but his mouth was too dry to gather spit. "What are you going to do to me?"

"More of yesterday. A lot more."

The drug, the videos, the voice. "Is this part of the government's plan? Or is this your way of torturing me to find out what I know? Because if that's the case, you're better off killing me now. I won't talk."

The man studied him for a moment, and wrinkled his brow. He glanced to the IV, then back to him. "Is your vision blurred?"

"No."

He picked up a tiny flashlight, pressed his fingertips to Liam's eyes, then forced the lids open. He shined the light in his eye. "How old are you?"

"I'm sure you have that information, so cut the bullshit, small talk."

He set the flashlight near the heart rate monitor, which pinged faster. "I wouldn't have asked if I knew," the man replied, lowering the monitor's volume.

"Tell me your name and I'll answer you."

"Roderick."

Liam's stomach tightened when Roderick snapped on a pair of latex gloves. "I'm twenty-nine."

"And your name?" he asked as he checked the IV bag and tubing.

"Not until you tell me why I'm here."

Roderick ran a finger along the underside of Liam's forearm, near the crook of his elbow, then tied a tourniquet. "I'm going to break you," he said.

Oh, God. "The woman said the same thing, but that's not an explanation."

Roderick looked at him, and Liam swore he saw a brief glimpse of betrayal in the man's eyes. "Madeline? When did she come to you?"

In the darkness, he'd lost track of time. "I'm not sure."

He raised the needle. "Remember, or this will go into your eye instead of your vein."

"I swear, I don't know," he said, staring at the needle.

"Was it the middle of the night?" The veins along the man's neck grew taut. "Answer me," Roderick shouted, and brought the needle closer to his face.

Liam flinched. "I have no idea if it's day or night now. Please believe me."

"Tell me your name."

"Liam."

Roderick eased away, then after giving Liam's arm a tap, he pressed the needle into his skin. "This is nothing but a saline drip to keep you hydrated. If you have to urinate, hold it. I will supply you with a bedpan." Once he had the IV taped in place, he picked up a roll of duct tape. "I'm sure you remember this from yesterday, correct?"

"Please don't do this. If you want me to watch the videos, I will. You don't have to tape my eyes." *Please, God, not this again.* Panic welled in his chest as utter helplessness enveloped him like a smoldering, hot blanket.

"Sorry, Liam, but I do." Roderick cut a piece of tape. "Look to the ceiling."

Liam stared at the tape. "Yesterday you used surgical tape."

"I know, that was to make you more comfortable. Today, I'm not interested in your comfort. Now look to the ceiling or I'll physically torture you."

"This isn't torture?"

Roderick smiled without humor. "Not. Even. Close."

His heart hammering, Liam quickly looked to the ceiling. He tried his damnedest to be strong, to fight the tears, the fear. But he couldn't stop from shaking. His throat tightened and thickened with phlegm. The tears blurred Roderick's calm face. When the tape tugged his left eyelid back, terror settled on his chest, knocking the air from his lungs. He couldn't breathe. He gasped and fought the restraints at his wrists and ankles.

"Calm yourself, Liam. Almost there," Roderick said, as he took the eyelashes along Liam's right eye between his gloved fingers. "Just a little panic attack. Once the tape is in place and you've been administered A-Line, you'll be in a better place."

Wheezing, trying desperately to drag in a deep breath, Liam's eyes had already begun to burn. His right cheek and lower lid twitched involuntarily as Roderick finished applying the duct tape.

When the man stepped away to retrieve the entire roll, Liam finally filled his lungs. He was strong. He could endure this. If he was going to survive and tell the world what the government was doing to its citizens, he had to maintain hope.

"Why didn't you scream?" Roderick asked as he wrapped more tape around Liam's head, securing his eyelids in place.

"What good would it do?"

"True." Roderick set the tape on the monitor in exchange for a syringe filled with clear liquid. "Except I was rather looking forward to your cries."

Liam shifted his gaze to where Roderick pressed the tip of the syringe next to the IV in his arm. "What are you giving me?" He winced when the syringe pierced his skin, then sucked in a breath when the liquid shot into his veins.

"I told you. A-Line." He removed the syringe. "You were given a quarter of this dose yesterday to see if you would have any kind of allergic reaction. Since you're healthy, today you're getting it all. Soon enough, you'll start to feel the effects." He stepped back, then turned on the TV. When he moved away from the television the images of a man having his bound hands beaten with a mallet filled the screen.

Liam turned his head, then sobbed with frustration when he couldn't close his eyes. The torture was too much to bear. How could he last? How could he be strong?

His sister's face filled his mind. Kiera always knew the right things to say, the right things to do. Peace settled over him as he imagined her soothing voice. His fingertips tingled. His lips grew numb. Heat radiated from his ears and he pictured smoke coming out of them. The thought made him smile.

"Feeling better?" Roderick asked, his voice muffled, distant as the man placed a leather strap around his head, forcing Liam to face the TV.

"My ears burn."

"The others complained of the same side effect," Roderick responded. "But it passes within minutes." Madeline's bewitching voice suddenly filled the room. "Listen to her voice, watch the TV and don't fight what's happening to you."

Oh, he'd fight. He'd find a way to fight his way out of this hell and expose the sick bastards.

Roderick's face blocked the television. He stood so close, Liam could see the pores in the man's skin. "After I break you, I'm going to fix you."

"Why fix me at all?" he asked, and swore he could count each individual eyelash Roderick possessed. Such a strange thing to notice, and yet the clarity intrigued and excited him.

Roderick grinned. "So I can kill you." He drew back, tore a piece of tape from the roll, then slapped it over Liam's mouth.

When the man left the room, turning the lights off before shutting the door, Liam tried to look at anything but the TV. Only he could still catch glimpses of the horrifying footage from his peripheral vision. Plus, moving his eyes without blinking created a dull ache in his eye muscles. Forced to watch the screen and listen to Madeline's voice, he began humming, trying desperately to block her from his mind.

Something moved in the shadows. He darted his gaze from left to right. Saw nothing.

"Do you feel it moving inside you? The ache festering in your chest like an infected wound? It claws at you, begging for release."

Madeline's seductive voice eased the paranoia. He understood she wasn't talking to him, and was lucid enough to know this wasn't an attempt at subliminal stimuli. But a form of hypnosis? Maybe.

"There are no rules," Madeline continued. *"Only the sweet satisfaction of having the power over life and death. Of knowing you can decide who will live and who will die. How they die. How will they die? What will you do to them?"*

He stared at the TV, watched as someone in a HAZMAT suit hosed off a nude man. Except water wasn't coming out of the hose. As blisters bubbled along his skin, the man screamed without a sound. But Liam imagined it. The high-pitched cry pierced his ears, along with Madeline's words.

"Will you cut them? Watch their blood spill. It's a beautiful shade. So sticky sweet. Can't you taste it?"

As the man's silent screams echoed through his head and the flesh fell from his skin, the only thing Liam could taste was revenge. The images on the TV played but he didn't see them. He saw Roderick, dead, a bullet wound in the center of his forehead. He saw Madeline. Her slender neck arched. His hands wrapped around it.

Tears trickled down his cheeks. They might break him, but not before he broke them first.

CHAPTER 11

Cash and Mel's House, Tallahassee, Florida
Sunday, 12:42 p.m. Eastern Daylight Saving Time

VLAD TOSSED A cigarette into the unlit fire pit Cash had built at the edge of the backyard, then pulled another from his pack. Mel shifted her gaze to the pool, where Harrison swam laps. Lola sat on a lounge chair beneath an umbrella working on Harrison's laptop, while Cash was by Mel's side at the patio table under the covered porch, leafing through a car magazine. By all accounts, anyone who stopped by would see a group of friends enjoying a lazy Sunday afternoon. Too bad that wasn't reality.

Her phone chimed, signaling she'd received a text message. She picked it up, then read the screen. "Dang," she murmured.

Cash set down the magazine. "What's wrong?"

"Bobby. Noah went into septic shock."

"From what?"

"He didn't say. I'm assuming the cuts Noah gave himself. Or, it could be from the syringe Madeline used on him. I honestly don't know much about it."

"Yeah, cars are easier to deal with than people. Is he going to be okay?"

She sent her cousin a text, asking about Noah's prognosis. He replied: *Dr. unsure. Have him stable.* After she relayed the message to Cash, she set the phone back on the table. "I'm not comfortable with Harrison going undercover."

"Madeline might not show. Worry about it if it happens."

"I know." She did, but couldn't help herself. While she didn't doubt Harrison could handle a couple hours in Madeline's house, as far as they knew, the woman and her partner—if Noah was to be believed—had killed one man. If doctors didn't find a way to control Noah's infection, he could be next. Plus, too many things could happen in a matter of a couple hours. And what if the GPS failed? What if they couldn't find Harrison?

"Good," he said, picking up the magazine. "Someone needs to tell Vlad. I think he's smoked a half a pack in the two hours he's been sitting out back."

"He's mad at Harrison."

Cash kept his focus on the magazine. "Do I want to know why?"

"I don't know." She pulled her hair back as she stretched. With the way Cash had pinned her arms last night, she'd awoken with sore muscles not only in her chest and shoulders, but her inner thighs. Not that she'd complain. The muscle strain, the tears and the fighting had been worth it. There were no more barriers for her or Cash to hide behind. They'd torn them down last night, and rebuilt their relationship with promises she was confident they'd both keep.

"You don't know if I want to know?" he asked, raising a brow until he noticed the way she stretched. His gaze shifted to her breasts. Placing the magazine on the table, he leaned forward. "Why don't you help me change a light bulb in the bedroom?"

She leaned forward, too. "Is that code for sex?"

"No. I really do need to change a light bulb, and it'd be easier if you handed it to me so I don't have to climb up and down the step stool. You don't want me to risk breaking an ankle."

She chuckled. "You're so full of it."

"Yeah, I know. Okay, tell me why Vlad's mad at Harrison."

"I can tell you," Harrison said, rising from the edge of the pool.

Cash reached for his water bottle. "You have ears like a frickin' bat."

Harrison frowned as he approached them. "No, your voices carry." He turned toward Lola. "Could you hear Cash and Mel talking?"

Lola looked up from the laptop. "Noah is septic, and light bulb is code for fooling around."

Mel's cheeks warmed. "Then I guess you heard me say I'm worried about you going undercover."

Harrison nodded and took a seat. "Which is one of the many reasons Vlad is pouting like the overgrown child he is."

"Man, I gotta ask you," Cash began. "No offense, but aren't you afraid Vlad's going to kick your ass?"

Harrison snorted. "If he does, he better make sure I can't get back up, or I'm putting his gator in the swamp where she belongs."

Mel gasped, then gave him a quick grin. "Shame on you. I had plans on makin' a purse out of Polina."

"You're sick, Mel." Lola closed the laptop. "It's also close to one. We should probably leave in a few." She called to Vlad. The Russian looked over, blew a stream of smoke, then tossed the butt into the pit. "I suggest you and Vlad work things out," Lola said to Harrison.

"I didn't do anything wrong."

"Honey," Mel began, "he's upset about you taking a risk with Madeline. You're his buddy. He's looking out for you."

"And I'm looking out for him when I ride him about smoking."

"Are you and Vlad dating?" Cash asked with a grin.

Harrison gave him the finger. "Not funny."

"Asian Lola need Vlad?" the Russian asked, his frown so deep Mel wondered if she could rest a spoon on his brow.

"We're going to leave soon. I'd like to be in Frenchtown by one-thirty."

"Bobby told us she came around four the last time," Mel said.

"I know, but I don't want to take the chance of missing her. Not after Ian made the effort to get us the GPS chip." Lola motioned to Vlad. "Please sit."

Vlad walked to the furthest chair away from Harrison. Once he was seated, he glared at him.

"What the hell, dude?"

"Vlad give Harry smell eye."

"I know what you're doing, I just don't get why you have to be such an immature freak. Do you really think giving me the *stink* eye is going to intimidate me?"

"да."

"Should be easy enough. Have you smelled yourself? No wonder you can't get laid. Your mouth is like an ashtray and your big ass body smells like nasty swamp water from hanging out with your gator."

Vlad's gaze never wavered. "Vlad can change smell. Harry cannot change monkey-ass face."

Harrison stood. "You're an asshole."

"Harry smell like one."

"You would know."

"Enough," Lola shouted. "You're both acting like nine-year-old boys."

Cash rested his chin in his hand. "I think that might be an insult to nine-year-olds. Hell, when I was nine, I would've been wiping the streets clean with your faces if you talked like that to me."

Mel rolled her eyes. "Does everything have to be physical?"

He slid his gaze to her. The heated look in his eyes had her fighting a grin. "As I was saying," he continued, looking between Vlad and Harrison, "I don't care why you two are mad at each other, but if you're gonna fight, man up and do it right."

Lola's eyes widened a fraction. "Do not listen to Cash. Let's just go over a few points, then leave."

"No, I think Cash is onto something." Harrison stood, then motioned to Vlad. "Let's go."

Vlad chuckled and also stood. "Vlad former Russian heavyweight boxer. Harry no match. Throw in towel while all teeth are in head."

Harrison moved toward the pool. "Bring it."

When Vlad fell into a boxing stance, Lola turned to Cash. "See what you started. You need to stop them. I don't want Harrison screwing up the GPS chip."

"She's right, baby. As fun as this would be to watch, Harrison's our undercover man."

Cash sighed. "Fine."

"Just forget it," Lola said, marching toward the pool. "I said enough." She pivoted on her left leg and delivered a sidekick to Harrison's side, knocking him off balance and into the pool. When Vlad turned and laughed at Harrison, she rushed behind him and sent a front kick to the man's rear. Water splashed to the concrete and all over Lola when Vlad fell into the pool. She brushed droplets from her arms. "We are leaving in fifteen minutes. Get out of the water and get ready." Lola pointed at Mel and Cash as she made her way toward the patio door. "Now I see why you two are good together. Harrison's right, you're both crazy."

Mel reached for Cash's hand. "I don't think we're crazy."

He kissed the underside of her wrist. "I don't, either," he said with a grin.

Vlad sloshed over, wringing the front of his shirt. He pulled a soggy pack of cigarettes from his pants pocket then crushed them.

"Serves you right," Harrison said, walking past him and into the house.

When Vlad hung his head, Mel's heart went out to the big goof. She gave Cash's hand a squeeze, stood, then went to Vlad. "You okay, honey?"

"Ice Cream Lady see through Vlad." He let out a tired breath. "Vlad must ready."

"Are you sure Vlad and Harrison are agents?" Cash asked when he came up behind her.

"You'd be surprised what they can do."

"What about you? What'd you do for ATL?"

She thought about the bodies in Daddy's swamp. "I'm mostly the lookout," she said, not totally lying. She'd done that job a couple of times.

"Good." He kissed her cheek. "I know you can handle yourself, but I'll be honest, I don't like the idea of my woman being involved in something that could kill her."

Or put her in prison. But Cash didn't need to know about that, either. "After this job, neither of us will have to worry about anything, except fixing cars."

"I like the sound of that."

She did, too. She just hoped it was enough—for both of them.

Hope House, Tallahassee, Florida
Sunday, 4:42 p.m. Eastern Daylight Saving Time

"I COULD NEVER be a cop," Cash said, moving the vent so the AC hit him in the face. If he was warm sitting in his air-conditioned truck, Mel and Harrison had to be sweating their butts off.

"Vlad cannot be cop."

"Right. Stakeouts are about as fun as watching a snail fight."

The Russian turned to him and frowned. "How would snail fight? Can Vlad find this on the YouTube?"

Cash chuckled until he realized Vlad was serious. "No, man. I'm making a joke. You know, because snails are slow and they don't have arms."

"That disappointing." Vlad stared out the window toward where Mel sat in the shade, leaning against a backpack. "Vlad do not mind the stakeout. It boring, but safe."

"You don't look or act like the kind of guy who likes boring and safe."

"Describe to Vlad how boring and safe look."

Cash immediately pictured the garage he owned. "Not sure."

"Then how Repo Man know this?"

"Got me again."

"Vlad see white car."

Both Bobby and Noah had claimed Madeline drove a white sedan, but had been unsure of the make, model and year. Bobby knew better, considering he'd been around the garage enough. He'd said he had been too distracted to pay attention. Bobby and Noah had also told them Madeline had long blonde hair.

When the white Lincoln slowed about a half a block from Hope House, Vlad's phone rang. "да," he answered. "Vlad see." He ended the call. "Asian Lola say black male drive car." Since Hope House sat on a corner, Lola had parked Mel's Camaro along the street facing north, while he and Vlad had taken the street to the west. If Madeline showed, one of them would be able to quickly spot her.

Cash relaxed against the driver's seat. "It's almost five. They'll be closing the shelter doors soon. I don't think Madeline's coming tonight." Once the shelter locked its doors, most of the homeless who hadn't been able to obtain a bed for the night left to search for a place to stay that wasn't as open or exposed as the field next to the shelter.

"Vlad agree. Vlad and Cash stakeout tomorrow."

The joy. "Unless Lola wants to switch up and let you take Mel's car." To keep Lola from standing out, Mel had suggested Lola use the old Camaro rather than the new rental car. With how well Mel had fixed up the Camaro, it was probably worth more than the rental, but he still agreed.

The Russian shook his head. "Ice Cream Lady do not allow Vlad to drive."

"Why's that?"

"Harry have nose of Pinocchio. Ласка tell lies."

"Come again?"

"Harry weasel. Say Vlad cannot be trusted with car. Ha! Vlad have perfect drive record." The Russian pointed to the right. "Vlad see Mel."

Thank God. He was tired of hearing Vlad complain about Harrison, and didn't know how Lola put up with the two of them.

"I got her," Cash said, shifting the truck into DRIVE and heading in her direction.

Although he'd wanted ATL's investigation to go smoothly, and stop Madeline and her partner from taking any other people, a part of him was relieved she hadn't showed today. While he didn't look forward to spending another three to four hours in the truck with Vlad tomorrow, or for Mel to have to sit in this God-awful heat, he'd worried about how Harrison's undercover job might affect Mel. His wife put on a superficial mask when it came to people she cared about, using sarcasm or dark humor, even anger, to hide her worries.

She cared about Harrison, and not in a way that made him want to kick the man's ass. With the way Harrison had acted around her, Cash doubted the man had a clue how lucky he was to have a friend like Mel. She knew the true meaning of loyalty, and had more decency and compassion in her manicured pinky than most people possessed in their entire body.

And she was finally coming home to him.

This was where the other part of him had wished the woman would've showed today. He couldn't wait for them to start over again, and hadn't been kidding about wanting to renew their vows. He was also anxious to start the new detail business at the garage. Mel was going to love it. He already had Jude working on purchasing the necessary equipment. Not too much, though. He wanted Mel to be part of the new venture that would replace the repo business.

He stopped the truck along the curb. Mel's skin glistened with sweat. The short-sleeved light gray shirt she wore stuck to her torso, and had dark spots under her arms and along her stomach. She'd probably have to peel off her jeans, but wearing shorts hadn't been an option. She'd needed to look like she was homeless, not heading out for a day at the park. Plus the jeans covered the tall socks she wore to hide her switchblade.

As soon as she slid onto the backseat bench, he passed her the cold bottle of water he'd had waiting for her. "Where's Harrison?"

After she took a long drink, she leaned against the leather seat.

"He went with Lola. I'm diving in the pool when we get home," she said, then took another drink.

He glanced at her in the rear view mirror. "Your face is red. Didn't you wear sunscreen?"

"It's from the heat." Her face saddened as she looked out the window. "I couldn't imagine having to live that way. It's depressing and scary." She crushed the plastic in her fist. "I'm so thankful for Daddy. We didn't have much, but at least I had a bed and a leaky roof over my head."

Growing up, he hadn't always had a steady home, but he'd had enough people looking out for him and his mom to keep them from being forced into a shelter. "I saw you talking to a few people. Anyone know about Madeline?"

"There was one guy. He seemed like he was strung out on something, so I don't know how reliable he is. Anyway, he said he's been sleeping in the field because the shelter rules are you have to check your belongings at the door. He doesn't want to do that, so I'm guessing it's because he has drugs or paraphernalia—which is also against the rules. He did confirm that he hasn't seen Madeline all week, and that she drives a white car with Georgia plates. A 1999 Buick LeSabre, to be exact."

"This good," Vlad said, handing her another cold water.

Cash grinned. "Yeah, it is. Did he happen to get the plate number?"

She shook her head. "No, and I feel bad for the guy. He said he used to own a car just like Madeline's. Then he went on to tell me how he'd lost his job and fell on hard times. When he started on the second coming of the Messiah, I found another place to sit. Part of me wants to give the guy some money, but I'm worried he'll either get robbed for it, or use it for drugs or alcohol."

He loved Mel's big heart. "If you want to give him money, do it. Don't worry about how he spends it."

"I'd rather give him a job." She met his gaze in the mirror and grinned. "Don't worry, honey. I'm not gonna start bringing in strays."

After Cash had caught her trying to steal the BMW, he'd brought her back to the garage, and later, had given her a job. Jude had referred to her as a stray they hadn't needed. His business partner and friend had thrown a fit, until Mel had flashed him the same smile that had knocked Cash flat on his ass. "I don't know, some strays are worth taking a chance on," he said, thanking the Lord for placing Mel in his path.

Her grin broadened into a smile as she rested her head against the seat. "No doubt." When her cell phone rang, she adjusted the seatbelt and leaned forward, grabbing it from the center console. "It's Bobby," she said, then answered. "Hey, honey, how's it—"

Cash pulled into a gas station, then parked the truck. He and Vlad both shifted in their seats and stared at her. She looked between them, worry banked in her eyes.

"What about the police?" she asked. "I see. I'm so sorry, honey. We'll come get you. I want you to come stay with me and Cash." Her face reddened again, and Cash suspected she was about to blow her top. "You do what you need to do."

She ended the call and dropped the phone in her lap. "Noah is dead. The police aren't involved because even the doctors and nurses thought Noah was on a bad trip. Thank God I stole a vial of his blood."

Cash tensed. "Come again?"

"Please don't start. I did it the day we took him to the ER. I didn't tell you because I was hiding something, I just forgot about it."

"How do you forget about stealing a vial of blood?"

She leaned forward. "And how do you so easily forget that we made a promise not to argue?"

He gripped the steering wheel and tried to keep his temper in check. "I'm not arguing with you, I'm trying to understand where your head is sometimes."

She crossed her arms over her chest and stared out the window.

"Now you're not speaking to me?" he asked.

"Not in my current state of mind."

He faced forward, then shifted into DRIVE. He knew she was hurting on Bobby's behalf, so he wasn't about to start a fight over something that had happened before they'd hashed things out between them. "Fair enough. Vlad, please ask Mel if I need to pick up Bobby from the hospital."

The Russian cleared his throat. "Vlad think Mel hear Cash."

"Perfectly well, thank you. Vlad, you can tell Cash that Bobby is using the money I gave him to check back into the hotel. He wants to be alone. He also wants to move back home with Daddy."

"Does that mean you will, too?" Cash asked, glancing in the rear view mirror.

Tears shimmered in her eyes as she met his gaze. "My home is with you."

Relieved, he let out the breath he was holding and drove them home. The moment he parked the truck in the driveway and killed the ignition, he hopped out, then quickly opened the back passenger door. When Mel went into his arms, he held her and kissed her head. "I'm sorry about Noah," he said, as Lola parked behind him.

"I know this is bad, but I keep thinking that Bobby could be the one in the hospital morgue." She hugged him tight. "Wednesday evening, I had Harrison checking death records and hospitals looking for him or a John Doe who fit his description. Today I spent a few hours around people who could've been put in the same position as Noah." She pushed away and pulled her ponytail free, letting her blonde hair spill around her shoulders. "While we were sitting by the pool, joking about sex and goading Harrison and Vlad to continue on with their ridiculous fight, which—by the way—is absolutely stupid…" She wiped her cheeks and drew in a breath. "A twenty-five-year-old kid was dying. What makes it even worse? Bobby said Noah's mother refused to come to the hospital and see her son. So you have a mother who doesn't care, the police and hospital employees who believe Noah caused his own death, and—"

"Us." Lola stepped forward. "I spoke with Ian while you and Harrison were at the shelter. He said the lab CORE uses is still running more tests on Noah's blood. They haven't been able to identify the exact drug Noah was given, but were able to come up with the molecular make-up."

"And?" Cash asked, impressed with how quickly the agency had worked, but worried about what they'c found. Noah had been in a bad way, and he didn't want to think about anyone else suffering the same fate.

"We have a poly-drug with molecular formulas of methylphenidate, methamphetamine, amphetamine and crack cocaine—all of which, taken alone—could cause psychosis. That's what they've found so far. Like I said, they're still running more tests."

"Vlad know not this psychosis."

"It's when someone has a disconnect from reality."

Disgust simmered deep in Cash's chest as he wrapped an arm around Mel. "Did they say what kind of effect a combination like that would have on a person?"

Lola nodded. "Extreme violent behavior toward themselves and others."

CHAPTER 12

The House of Archer, Bower, Georgia
Sunday, 6:28 p.m. Eastern Daylight Saving Time

ADELINE FORKED A slice of roast beef, then dragged it through the lake of mashed potatoes and gravy on her plate. "How are our subjects?" she asked, breaking the silence that had hung between them since Rodney had taken her against the wall.

Rodney sipped his whiskey. "I'm concerned about Jim. His heart rate has been irregular throughout the day."

"Too fast? Too slow?"

"Fast. Constantly."

She dropped her fork, the clang against the ceramic plate forcing Rodney to finally look at her. "Now that I have your attention, do you mind telling me *why* you're not sharing information with me about *our* subjects?"

"I just did."

"Then tell me about the other subject."

He drained his glass, then slammed it on the table. "No."

She didn't bother to hide a smile. "No?" Pushing her plate away, she tossed her napkin on the table and stood. "Then I'll find out myself."

"Don't," he warned.

"Because you'll be forced to *beat* me?"

Rod looked away. "I...I'm sorry. I shouldn't have treated you the way I did."

Oh, but she'd wanted him to rough her up and show the

backbone she knew he carried. He was her equal in everything, except he had a conscience. She lifted her plate, then smashed it against the edge of the table. The beef, gravy and potatoes erupted, splashing on the ceiling, the front of her clothes and Rodney's shirt. "You're so full of it," she said, dropping what was left of the plate.

Rodney's eyes darkened as he stared at her with loathing and hunger so acute, if she were anyone else but her, she might be frightened. Instead, he aroused her. Fascinated by the way she'd been able to manipulate him, she decided to push him further, harder.

"You have no right to ban me from our testing. Without me, you wouldn't have the opportunity to even see if your drug would actually work."

His chair fell back as he stood. Remnants of her dinner stained the front of his shirt and face. "You're right," he said, his calm tone belying the fierce storm brewing in his eyes, as he scraped his napkin across his chin. "We're colleagues, scientists, and A-Line *is* your drug. But we'll visit him together."

"Now?"

"Why wait?"

She was beginning to think Rod was fucking with her. But her need to see the sexy subject outweighed common sense. Rodney had a jealous streak she hadn't anticipated, which only stirred her excitement. Maybe, finally, he'd shove his stupid morals aside. If he did, when he did, life would actually mean something. Instead of dying a slow, torturous death as a prisoner in the House of Archer, they could leave this place. God, how she longed to rid herself of this decrepit home. The plantation house was suffocating and there had been days when she'd thought it would swallow her whole. Rodney had been the only reason she hadn't run away. Her need for him had kept her shackled here. Soon enough, without even realizing it, he would break her free.

As she followed him up the stairs, a flood of anticipation filled her belly. Whatever she'd sensed about the sexy subject had been pure. Of that she was sure. Even if she hadn't been able to pin-point what that purity meant, or how it would work in her favor, she knew he was her ticket out of hell.

When they reached the closed door, Rodney stopped. "Re-member. Don't test me." He opened the door. Her recorded voice floated into the hallway.

Ignoring the sound of her own voice, she entered the room. And there he was. Bulging eyes fixated on the TV, silver duct tape wrapped around his head, concealing his mouth. She glanced to the monitor and noted that his resting heart rate was fifty-six beats per minute. Excellent. This one was strong and fit. She brushed past Rodney and shut off the recording device.

"What's his name?"

"Liam."

"Tell me about him."

Rodney placed a few saline drops into the man's eyes, then tore the tape from his mouth. "Find out for yourself."

Rod was definitely fucking with her. Since she did enjoy a good fucking...

"How are you feeling?" she asked.

His cheeks and lower lids twitched. He licked his lips. "Thirsty."

Rodney picked up the water from the table near the monitor and held the straw to the man's lips. But he clamped his mouth shut.

"Drink," she said.

"I have to urinate. I'm so thirsty, but I don't want to go."

She cocked a brow at Rodney. "Are you telling me this man hasn't peed since he's been here?"

"He can piss himself for all I care."

"That's because you're jealous." She picked up the bedpan. "You're a *doctor*. If you want the experiment to succeed, you need to act like one." When she reached for Liam's fly, Rodney gripped her wrist. She glared at him. "I'm not going to give him a hand job. I'm going to let the man relieve himself."

"I'll do it." Rodney knocked her hand away, but Liam bucked his pelvis. "Don't touch me. Let the woman."

She chuckled. "He must be homophobic."

"Not at all. I don't trust him. I don't trust you, either. But, I'll take you over him."

"Gee, Rod, you must've made a fantastic first impression," she said, reaching for Liam's fly again. She held Rodney's gaze as she unbuttoned, then unzipped the man's jeans. When her fingers connected with the velvety soft skin of the man's penis, she fought against closing her eyes. Memories of tonguing him last night made her nipples hard, made her heart race. She held Liam in her hand as he urinated in the bedpan, but never broke eye contact with Rodney. Once the man had emptied his bladder, she handed Rod the bedpan, put Liam's penis where it belonged—for now—then righted his jeans.

She gave Rodney a small smile. "Why don't you get rid of that?"

"When I come back, we leave." Rodney glanced to Liam, the abhorrence in his eyes shockingly fascinating. Rod, her do-gooder, her crusader, the man who would *fix* her, hated Liam, all because she'd suggested she might have sex with their subject. The power of persuasion at its finest.

Once he left the room, and knowing she had a minute at most, she bent her head toward Liam's ears. "Do you enjoy the sound of my voice?"

"I hate it, and you."

"Oh, pooh. I don't believe you." She ran her hand along his chest. "Have you thought about my tongue on your cock?"

"You disgust me. The only thing I've been able to think about is figuring out a way to close my eyes."

"What if I can make that happen?" she whispered in his ear. "What if I gave you that power back? What would you do for me?"

His bulging gaze darted back and forth. The monitor showed an increase in his heart rate.

"Calm yourself, Liam. We can't let Rod know." The attic stairs creaked, signaling Rodney's impending return. She looked to the monitor, grinned when it slowed again. "Very good. I promise to reward you."

She stepped away from the man. "Would you like that drink now?"

"Please," he begged.

As she held the straw to Liam's mouth, Rodney entered the room, slamming the bedpan on the small table. He picked up a syringe of A-Line.

"A little soon for that, don't you think?" she asked as she took the straw from Liam's lips. With their last subjects, they'd doubled up the dosage the second day.

He tapped Liam's arm and searched for a vein. "This is day two."

"Yesterday didn't count. We both agreed. The small dose we gave the subjects was to ensure there would be no allergic reactions."

"He can handle it," Rodney said, then sent the drug into the man's veins. When he was finished, he tossed the syringe on the table. "Turn on the recording."

She did, then left the room. Rodney quickly joined her in the hallway, slamming the door shut. "Happy?" he asked.

"Not at all. Why did you do that? Are you trying to kill him?" The man would die eventually, anyone they brought into the house would. But so soon? Liam was a fighter. She wanted to break his mind and spirit, see if she could mold him. Use him to stoke Rodney's jealousy, push Rod to his limits. She didn't want him to OD within twenty-four hours.

"Not at all," he responded. "Ready to pay Jim a visit and relieve his bladder?"

"I can't believe that you'd let insecurity and jealousy ruin your experiment. What happened to the man I love and trust? The doctor and scientist who was bound and determined to create a drug that would fix me, along with all the other psychopaths out there?" She turned away. She'd feed Rodney every line of bullshit she had to avoid touching skinny-Jimmy's penis. "I never thought I'd say this, but I'm disgusted by you."

"Does this mean you don't want me in your bed tonight?"

Of course she wanted him in her bed, but she didn't want to come across as needy or predictable. She faced him. "I'm not sure. The last two times you bothered to touch me, you were either drunk, or threatened to beat me and kill a man. You also treated me like a whore."

He stepped forward, bent until his nose nearly touched hers. His breath warmed her lips. "Do you have any idea how hard it was to watch you touch him?"

"Had to be brutal."

"Bitch." His mouth curled into a snarl. "I'll see you in the morning."

She grinned. "Aren't you curious about how it felt for me?"

"Not at all," he said, and turned away.

"Since he was flaccid, and I'm not overly experienced, it was hard to tell if he was as big as you." When he stopped, and his back stiffened, she decided to test the waters. "I noticed his penis had a slight curve." She hadn't, but it sounded believable. "I wonder if something like that helps a woman have a better orgasm?"

"You're pushing me on purpose. Knock it off."

"Don't tell me what to do." She walked toward Liam's door. "You don't own me or my body. If I want to find out what another man is like, I'll—"

Stars shot from behind her eyes as pain radiated through her skull. Her head bounced off the wood door and she dropped to the ground. She blinked several times until Rodney's face came into focus. The hatred in his eyes fueled her desire to punish him. "Hit me again. Like father, like son. Put the woman in her place."

Rod's face knotted in shame. He dropped to his knees. Reached for her, then drew back. "I...I didn't mean." He gritted his teeth. "I'm *nothing* like him."

Her head hurt. Yeah, she'd really pushed him too far. Now it was time to smooth things over. She still wanted to go to Tallahassee tomorrow to check on Noah's whereabouts, and snag a couple more subjects before Rod completely nixed the project. She couldn't do that if he beat the hell out of her, or drank himself into a guilty stupor.

Forcing her hand to tremble, she touched where her forehead had connected with the door, then pressed on the goose egg. Tears of pain immediately filled her eyes and she went with it. "I know you're not," she cried. "I did push you. The way you treated me today, after all the times I've begged you to come back to me and be the man you'd promised you would be...I wanted to hurt you."

He cupped her face with shaky hands. "That's no excuse. I'm so sorry. Let me take you to your room. I'll get some ice for your head."

"No," she said, holding up a hand, warding him away from her. Funny how she'd always begged for his touch, but now that he was offering it freely, it empowered her to be the one to tell him no. "I can take care of myself. You take care of Jim. I need to be alone."

The regret in Rodney's eyes disappointed her. How long would it take to weaken the morals he clung to so desperately? "I understand." He stood and took a jerky step back. "Whatever time you need. I'll be here."

She pushed herself up, fought a wave of dizziness, then pressed a hand to her head—this time avoiding the bump. "Good night, Rodney," she said, and made her way toward the staircase.

"Adeline," he called.

She stopped, but didn't look at him. At this point, she just wanted to make it to her bed before she collapsed.

"I love you," he said with so much pain and heartfelt devotion, she couldn't resist looking at him.

I love the misery on your face. "I'll see you in the morning," she said, then gingerly walked down the steps, smiling when Rodney's quiet sobs echoed throughout the stairwell. While she wasn't a fan of a crying man, she'd milk this one, for sure. The moment Rod gave her a hard time about bringing a couple of new subjects home, she'd show him the knot on her head.

Then watch him crumble to his knees.

LIAM GRINNED AS he watched guerillas hack the heads off of villagers, and Roderick's soft crying overpowered Madeline's recorded voice. He didn't care about whatever was going on between the couple, all he knew was that he'd enjoyed listening to the show. As he stared at the atrocities on the screen, he imagined how it must have felt to be Roderick, to slam that sexy bitch's head against the door.

His dick stirred. That's how he would have handled her.

The thought startled and frightened him. He would never hit a woman, and never had. His stomach soured. He'd been raised to respect women.

A shadow moved in the corner. He shifted his eyes, strained to catch a glimpse. Madeline's voice recording droned in the background like white noise.

When his eye muscles began to ache he looked back to the TV. The guerillas were still busy. Their machetes coated in blood. So much blood. Was it as sticky sweet as Madeline had claimed? Would she know? Would she *like* to know?

Would you?

"No," he grunted. The sound of his voice startled him. He pressed his teeth into his numb lip, then opened his mouth wide and drew in a deep breath. Air might have no taste, but he sure as hell tasted freedom. A scrap of it.

His ears grew hot as the drug worked its way through his veins. He knew better than to mistake that scrap of freedom for hope. Hope didn't belong in this place. After spending what seemed like days sitting in this bed, watching violent images, hearing Madeline's voice as she soothingly suggested he act like a vicious barbarian, he wondered if there was such a thing as hope.

When he caught the shadow in his peripheral vision again, he didn't bother to look. The drug created the shadows, along with thoughts he'd never in his life possessed. He wasn't this man. He didn't find gore entertaining. He certainly didn't fantasize about snapping a woman's neck.

The burn in his ears moved to his chest. The tips of his fingers tingled. He clenched his hands and tugged at the restraints around his wrists. Saw Madeline. The evil glint in her eyes. Her lush lips. His abdomen tightened. Her hand wrapped around his penis as he relieved himself.

"Oh, God," he whispered, then cried with frustration when he couldn't close his eyes and block out the shame.

What would you do for me?

Madeline's whispered promises of removing the tape from his eyes fueled his hatred. *Why* would she betray Roderick? And what kind of doctor was the man? He wasn't foolish enough to believe the two of them were part of the agency he and the others were trying to stop. Madeline and Roderick hadn't operated like any of the government employees he, Mitch and William had studied prior to deploying on their mission. Thinking of William had him longing to see his sister, Kiera. To be back in her house, sitting at the kitchen table talking about their day over dinner.

When his tears wet his lip, he captured them with his tongue. Instead of tasting salt, he tasted irony. He'd been so damned close to helping stop the government from poisoning the minds and bodies of millions, only to be kidnapped and drugged by a sadistic couple.

The drug. Other than the few acute side effects of what Roderick had called A-Line—tingling limbs, burning ears, heightened awareness, dry mouth—his mind remained lucid. God, he'd love to know what they were giving him, and why. That's what he needed to remain focused on, he decided, as he stared at the guerillas tossing the dead into a large pit. Both Madeline and Roderick had said they'd planned to break him. Roderick had gone further and had claimed he'd fix him afterward. He swallowed. Then kill him.

Would Madeline let him? Although he didn't trust what he saw in her eyes—malicious mischievousness, cruel passion—she had made silky sweet promises and had defended him. Roderick would have let him urinate himself. According to Madeline, he'd also given him the extra dosage too soon.

The shadow crept along the wall again. He shot his gaze to the left.

"Liam."

He held his breath. His name had been nothing but a whisper. A trick of the mind. A shiver along his skin. Roderick had given him too much of the drug. That was all, nothing more.

"Remain calm and do as I say."

Mitch? No, don't let the drug get to you. Stay focused. Stay calm. Fight it.

He took in a deep breath, then slowly released it, but he couldn't slow his heart rate.

"I don't have much time." Mitch's shadow ran along the wall near the TV, before he stepped to the side of the bed. "We're all in danger," he said when he finally came into view. The man studied Liam's forehead and eyes. "Torturous."

Liam gave his friend a tired smile. "You have no idea. Hurry, free my hands," he said in a hushed tone, trying his best to contain his relief and excitement.

Mitch looked to the closed door. "It's not that easy."

"Sure it is."

The grave look crossing Mitch's dark complexion sent dread to his core. "They've been drugging me. Are they part of the government operation?"

He shook his head. "Worse."

"I don't understand. What could be worse than the government poisoning our water supply?"

Sympathy filled Mitch's eyes as he gave Liam a small sad smile. "Finding out that *this* is reality."

"Of course it's reality. I'm *really* strapped to a bed with my eyes taped wide open, and those two whack-jobs are *really* drugging me." He fisted his hands. "Cut the bullshit and get me out of here."

"You honestly don't know." Mitch stared at him with mild fascination. "What happened after you got off the bus?"

"You know. You were there."

"Tell me anyway."

They didn't have time to waste. "Fine, we went behind the depot. You told me we couldn't take the transfer bus to Miami because the government knew our names and faces, and had men searching for us."

"And then?"

"What the hell, Mitch?" When the man crossed his arms and said nothing, Liam let out a frustrated breath. "And then you told me to hide my wallet and backpack, which I did. We went in opposite directions with the intent of meeting at the diner five blocks northeast of the depot."

"But what *really* happened?"

Confused, he shifted his gaze to the heart rate monitor and noted the lines moved at a rapid pace. "That *is* what happened." Why was Mitch doing this to him?

He chuckled as hatred burned a hole in his chest. The drug. The extra dose Roderick had given him because the man couldn't stand seeing Madeline holding his dick. Mitch wasn't really in the room. He was hallucinating, seeing shadows on the walls, hearing voices to block out Madeline's.

"Why are you laughing?" Mitch asked, urgency in his tone as he moved in front of Liam's face. "This isn't funny, man. You are in serious trouble. You need to think, you need to focus. Fight the drug. You *have* to fight it. Your mind can't handle another break."

I am going to break you.

He sobered. How could Mitch know what Madeline had said, or how Roderick had threatened him? He swallowed around the unease tightening his throat. "What do you mean by another?"

"Think. When did we meet?"

His mind raced. "Outside my office building."

"How did you find me?"

"You contacted me," he said, remembering talking to the man on his cell phone. "I was at my sister's. I sat on my bed, phone to my ear. You told me you'd been watching me, that you and your people suspected my client was being paid hush money and wanted me to look into it. But I was already all over it. I knew something wasn't right. You helped me confirm it."

"I never called you, Liam."

"Of course you did. I remember," he said quietly, when he wanted to scream at Mitch.

"Your sister was home. Did she hear the phone ring?"

He thought back to that night…

"Liam." Kiera knocked on the door, then tried the knob. "Who are you talking to?"

Worried for her safety—based on what the mysterious man had told him—Liam asked Mitch to give him a sec, then pressed the cell phone to his chest when she opened the door. "My cell phone provider," he said. "I want to upgrade my plan."

"When you're finished, come in the family room and watch a movie with me. I'll make us some popcorn."

How could he sit on the couch, watching a movie and eating popcorn, knowing a sector of their government was conspiring to poison them? "Sure. I'll be right there," he said, knowing he'd have to spend the next two days pretending he was just as blind, deaf and dumb as the rest of the country. Mitch had told him that he and his colleague, William, wouldn't be in Denver until then.

"Okay." She frowned and stared at his phone. "Don't be long or I'll start the movie without you."

He grinned. "Just don't eat all the popcorn."

"What did you see, Liam?" Mitch asked.

"I saw…" Liam stared at the man, wondered how he could know his thoughts. Or had he spoken out loud?

"Go back to your sister's house, to the bedroom," Mitch said.

"Look at the phone."

Mitch was being a prick. Maybe this was his way of testing him. Or maybe this was the drug screwing with his mind.

The wooden floors groaned. Mitch glanced to the closed door. "Hurry. Look at the phone before he comes."

"Why is this so important?" Liam whispered, and pulled at his restraints. "Free me. We can take them down together."

Mitch shook his head. "You have to look first."

When Kiera left the room, his smile fell. Hoping Mitch hadn't hung up on him he looked to his hand and saw the remote for the guest room TV. Confused, his hand shaking, he set it on the nightstand, then rushed from the room and into the kitchen.

Kiera stood in front of the microwave, the bag of popcorn inside popping rapidly. She glanced over her shoulder, her long, wavy hair concealing part of her face. "Since I'm making our snack, you're on drink duty. I'll have water. Lots of ice."

"Sure," he said, reaching for a glass. "Kiera?"

"Hmm?"

"Where's my cell phone?"

The understanding in her eyes chilled him. She pushed away from the counter, then gave his bicep a gentle squeeze. "You don't have one."

A door banged shut, jolting him away from Kiera, and back to *reality*. Quick images rushed through his head. The doctors. The hospital. Sitting across from a man who played with the string of drool hanging from his lip. More memories slammed into him. The constant paranoia. Being afraid to open the door and leave the house, to watch TV because he wasn't sure who could be watching him from the other side of the screen. *The voices.* So many of them. Telling him what to do, echoing over each other, contradicting what his doctors, sister and parents told him. His parents…

He stared at Mitch, tried to blink away the tears, but couldn't move his fucking eyelids. "Oh, my God." His parents had died in a car accident—one week after he'd been institutionalized.

"How were their deaths labeled?" Mitch asked.

The man could read his mind. He shuddered. His skin crawled.

He could read his mind because—

"You created me, Liam."

Had he? "That can't be true. People have seen us together. Seen us talking. If I was walking around a bus station talking to myself, people would have stared, I would have noticed."

"In your mind I was with you, but you never spoke to me. If you did, we were out of the public eye—either in the bathroom or behind a building."

"What about the taxi? The driver saw you. And when he dropped us at the bus depot, we talked on the sidewalk."

The pity in Mitch's eyes had bile rising in his throat. He swallowed it down, along with the urge to scream. This couldn't be true. This couldn't be happening. Not again. Not when his life was on track.

"Your life was never *on track.*"

He clenched his jaw. "Get out of my head."

"You're the only one who can do that. Now think back to the taxi. What did you see? Hurry, Liam, there's not much time. You need to do this before they come for you."

This had to be a test. Mitch was assessing his strengths and weaknesses. Madeline and Roderick must work for Mitch's people.

Then how does he know your thoughts?

Determined to prove Mitch wrong, he took himself back to his sister's place. "I was in the bathroom..."

He flushed the toilet, but didn't tear his gaze away from the swirling water until every last pill had been sucked into the sewage pipe where they belonged. He could no longer trust his doctors, or even the pharmacist who'd filled the medications. They could have gotten to them, too.

"Leave the bathroom and go outside," Mitch ordered. "Hurry."

He shoved away from the counter, grabbed his backpack from the floor, then left the bathroom. He hurried down the hallway, ignored the family photos and rushed to the door. He quickly opened it and saw the taxi.

"Do you see me?" Mitch asked. "Look hard, Liam. It's important.

The late afternoon sun reflected off the closed, back passenger window.

"No."

"That's because I don't exist."

Liam went back inside his memories, and to Kiera's house. *He raised a finger to the taxi driver, indicating he'd only be a minute, then hopped off the stoop and jogged toward the hedges near the drive way.*

"I talked to William about watching over Kiera," he said to Mitch. "He promised to get her to the safe house if anything went wrong."

"Did he?" Mitch asked.

Liam reached the hedges, moved behind one and buried the empty pill bottles in the soft mulch. Once he was satisfied Kiera wouldn't find them, he headed for the taxi. When he climbed into the backseat, he told the cabbie to take him to the Greyhound station, then glanced out the window. He leaned into the cracked upholstery and watched as his sister's quiet neighborhood segued into a school, then a park. When the cabbie pulled into the bus depot, Liam paid the man, then exited the car.

"In your mind, we met up on the sidewalk." Mitch said. "But you didn't say a word, did you? Years of fighting the voices told you never to trust yourself in public. So you nodded, then went and bought your ticket. The woman at the counter was real. The people entering the bus with you were, too. Do you remember where I sat?"

His head ached as if someone were driving nails into his skull. "In the back, several rows behind me." Despite the pain, he gave Mitch a sarcastic smile as he remembered something important. "And once we were seated and underway, you sent me a text telling me we had two days to rest, that I should take advantage because once we reached Miami, I'd need it."

Mitch cocked his head to the side. "How could you get a text from me when you don't own a cell phone?"

The past two days suddenly filled his mind. Memories twisted and tumbled over themselves, rotating round and round like a tornado eating up houses, pulling trees and cars from the ground. The stops made during the bus trip. Hiding behind the buildings of the various bus depots, seeing the giggling couple and snapping his mouth shut before they'd heard him. Sitting at a fast food restaurant staring at an empty booth while he ate. Becoming confused in Atlanta.

"You left the bus depot to go to the diner, after you heard several passengers say that's where they were going," Mitch began, filling in the foggy memories his mind couldn't capture. "But you stopped to use the bathroom first. When you were finished, the others had already left. Thinking you knew the way, you continued on, only you didn't know the way. The crowded streets, people bumping into you...you became desperate, paranoid."

He shoved his hands into his pockets and avoided anyone near him as he frantically searched for the diner, for the other passengers in his group. Sweat trickled down his back and along his forehead. His mouth had gone dry. He should turn back and buy a bag of chips and a soda from the vending machines at the bus depot. He swiveled, began walking again and realized he had no idea where the bus depot was located, and that he'd stumbled into an area he shouldn't be. Trash—cardboard, newspapers, plastic bottles and wrappers—hugged the sidewalk along old buildings coated in graffiti. A glass broke. He looked to the left. His heart hammered as a group of men approached him, telling him he didn't belong here. Liam took several steps back, a white sedan drove by as he turned and hurried around the corner.

The white car pulled along the curb. The front passenger window rolled down.

A beautiful woman with long, blonde hair leaned across the seat. "Do you need help?" she asked with a smile.

He glanced back. The group of men loitered at the corner, staring at him. He looked to the woman, and nodded. "I'm lost. I need to get to the bus depot."

"I'm heading in that direction. Hop in and I'll drop you there." She looked in her rear view mirror. "I don't like the way those men are looking at you."

He gripped the door handle. "I don't either," he said, sliding into the seat. "Thank you. I know it's not safe for a woman to pick up a stranger like this, so I appreciate that you're willing to take the risk."

"Without risk, life just wouldn't be any fun." She looked into the rear view mirror again, and grinned. "Isn't that right, sweetie."

Sweetie? Liam turned to the left to see who was in the backseat. A sharp prick pierced the right side of his throat. He stiffened, reached for his neck. A hand shot out from behind him, and gripped his wrist, stopping him from pulling out the needle. The woman beside him chuckled. The world around him grew fuzzy and gray. His eyelids drooped, then everything went black.

He stared at Mitch. "You're not real. No one is coming for me or knows I'm missing." Mitch's words clicked into place. No, not Mitch's—*his*. Mitch, William, the rest of the team were in danger of being erased from his mind. Because *this* was reality. There was no government conspiracy. No source waiting for him in Miami. There were two sick fucks keeping him prisoner and drugging him.

"You need to stay strong," Mitch said.

"Go away," he replied, disgusted with his imaginary friend, with himself. Why hadn't he listened to his sister? Kiera would never lie to him. She was the one person left in the world he could trust. She had told him repeatedly that he'd needed to stay on his meds to keep the voices at bay. But a missed dose had been all it had taken for them to return and to blot out the truth. He wasn't an accountant. He didn't even have a job, but was on disability. Their father had been schizophrenic and had purposefully driven the car—with Liam and Kiera's mom in it—off the side of a mountain. A murder-suicide, homicide detectives had said, and the medical examiner had confirmed.

With his tears bathing him with clarity, Madeline's recorded voice filled his head again. Mitch still stood in front of the TV. He spoke, but there was no sound—nothing but Madeline.

The door swung open. Roderick stepped into the room, his expression angry, suspicious. "Who are you talking to?" he asked, his tone accusing.

Mitch's image dissolved to dust, leaving Liam looking at what he must've been watching the entire time: an autopsy of a woman who had been beaten and clearly stabbed. He should be disgusted. His stomach should be revolting. The water Madeline had given him a short while ago should be climbing up his throat. Instead, acceptance settled over him. Given the chance, he would fight. But he would be the one fighting, not a figment of his imagination. A part of him wanted to believe that he could be imaging his current situation. But he wasn't imagining the tape around his head and holding his eyes open, the horrific video, the IV in his arm or Madeline's voice.

Or the hatred in Roderick's eyes.

"I suggest you answer me," Roderick said. "Who were you talking to?"

"My imaginary friend," he answered honestly.

A smile crossed Roderick's mouth as he picked up a small bottle and an eyedropper. "Who was this imaginary friend?"

"His name was Mitch," Liam said, finding the autopsy fascinating. Either the filmmakers had hired topnotch special effects and makeup artists, or he really was watching the top of a skull being removed from a person's head. "He was a mercenary hired to help stop the government from poisoning the water."

Roderick leaned over him, then dropped cool liquid into Liam's eyes. "Was this mercenary successful?"

"How could he be successful if he isn't real?" Liam asked, laying on the sarcasm. He didn't care what the man did to him. At this point, he saw no reason to live. His life was a figment of his imagination. He made up his friends, his job. The only things that were real were his sister and this place. Kiera would be sad once he was gone, but death would be easier than living like this. Tortured by Madeline and Roderick, by his own sick mind.

Roderick swapped the bottle and eyedropper for another syringe. "How often do you see your imaginary friends?"

"How often do you watch Madeline hold another man's dick?"

Roderick's face reddened.

Knowing he'd hit a nerve, Liam pushed further. What did he have to lose? "I heard you two fight. Did you hit her? Did it feel good? I'm going to assume it didn't, since you were crying like a little girl."

Roderick pressed the needle into Liam's vein. "I can't wait to kill you."

Liam grinned. "Better do it soon."

"Why is that?" he asked, setting the syringe aside, then picking up the roll of duct tape.

He focused on Madeline's recorded voice, listened to her talk about death, about murder. Liam met the man's eyes and smiled. "Because there's nothing scarier than a man with nothing to lose."

CHAPTER 13

Cash and Mel's House, Tallahassee, Florida
Sunday, 8:22 p.m. Eastern Daylight Saving Time

"HOW ARE THINGS in the Glades?" Mel asked when Lola returned to the patio table after spending the past ten minutes on the phone with her fiancé, Ryan.

"Fine," Lola responded, and nodded toward the backyard where Cash had a fire going. "What are they playing?"

She watched Cash toss a small beanbag. "Cornhole. It's like horseshoes, but not really."

"Well, that explains it."

Mel grinned. "You have a propped board about thirty feet away from another propped board. The goal is to toss a beanbag into the center of the hole in the board."

Vlad let out a triumphant yell.

"Cash must've missed the hole," Mel added, and watched Harrison stoke the fire. "I hope Vlad and Harrison get over their issues."

"Me, too. I don't like seeing them at each other the way they've been."

"I'm sure you're worried about how it'll affect ATL," Mel said, edging toward a subject she knew she needed to address.

"Since when do you hold anything back?" Lola asked with a grin. "Say what's on your mind."

"Did you tell Ryan about me and Cash?"

"No. Shane did."

Damn it. She knew Shane would go behind her back. Even when they'd been kids, he'd been a snitch.

"Did you expect anything less?" Lola asked. "Shane's upset, Ryan is, too."

Guilt balled in her stomach. "I explained my reasons. Did Shane tell Barney, too?"

"No, they're leaving that to you."

That was a conversation she dreaded. She loved Barney, and how he'd treated her like a daughter. She should have trusted her gut and told him the truth about her and Cash the moment she'd moved back to Everglades City. But she'd been so disappointed in herself, she hadn't wanted to disappoint him, too.

She'd been angry, mostly at Cash for going back into the repo business, but also because she'd allowed herself to be blindsided. After the accident, she'd busied herself taking care of Cash and the garage. She'd fallen into a comfortable pattern and hadn't paid attention to the signs. Cash growing restless, taking long rides on the Harley when he knew she wouldn't be around. Picking small fights with her, going out with Jude and the boys from the garage when he should've been taking it easy. Yeah, she should have known, she should have been prepared. Because she hadn't been, the only thing she could think to do had been to hightail it back to the Glades.

She'd been in a dark place then, where hope hadn't existed, and bitterness and resentment had become her new best friends. She'd spent that time living in Daddy's swamp, gigging, fishing, practicing knife throwing and assessing her life. When she'd left Daddy's, she'd walked out with her head high. She hadn't looked at the six years she'd been with Cash as a waste. He'd helped bring her around and to realize it was okay to depend on someone, that she didn't have to go it alone. And she hadn't and wouldn't be alone in the Everglades. Not with Daddy, and her extended family—no matter that they weren't blood. Without knowing what she'd been fighting internally, they'd kept her from going insane. Yeah, she owed Barney a beer, an apology and a big bear hug. Ryan, too.

"How'd you end up in Tallahassee anyway?" Lola asked, pulling her from the past.

Lola was a woman who could be trusted. Mel had been around her long enough to know this, and was confident anything she said to Lola would remain between them. If she were a different woman, she'd open up and tell her everything on her mind—her worries and her hopes for and about the future. That she was torn about leaving the Glades, Daddy, her friends...ATL.

"It's a long story," she said.

"In other words, you don't want to tell me." Disappointment flickered in Lola's eyes before she masked it with a smile. She raised a hand. "No worries, I expected as much, but thought I'd give it a try."

"Give what a try?"

"Being your friend."

Dang. Lola definitely knew how to work the guilt. Mel stared at the woman. She could use a friend and supposed Lola could, too. Since she'd known the woman, other than the ATL crew, Lola had socialized with no one.

"I love my daddy," she began, deciding she had nothing to lose at this point. "But the man checked out mentally more times than not, leaving me responsible for me, Bobby, the house." She shrugged. "I had the Monahans, but both Shane and Ryan had gone into the service. You have no idea how mad I was that they volunteered for positions that'd had me so worried, there'd been nights I couldn't sleep."

She picked up the beer she'd been nursing. "With them gone, I also realized I had a whole lot of nothing going on in the Glades. Working on cars with Daddy had been okay, but it wasn't Bobby's thing. And I wanted better for him. So I started looking for work, heard about a job in Tallahassee that paid well, and figured with the money I had saved, I'd take the job, rent an apartment for me and Bobby, and enroll him at the community college." Although Bobby had showed no interest in going to college, she'd hoped that once he was away from the Glades, away from the lazy, pot-smoking boys he'd hung with, Bobby might have a shot at doing something good with his life. Find a nice job, a pretty wife, have a kid or two. "So we got settled in, things went fine for a few months, then I was let go from my job when the company was sold off and the offices closed."

"Ouch," Lola said. "What'd you do?"

"I picked up a serving job at a restaurant. But I wasn't able to make enough money to take care of me and Bobby, and pay for the community college." That had been about the time she'd met Deuce and had started stealing cars—a little something Lola did *not* need to know about. The money had been great, but the risk, the worry that she'd get caught and go to prison had kept her in a constant state of fear. She'd had more anxiety attacks than she could count, until the day she'd met Cash. Aside from being the sexiest man she'd ever laid eyes on, he'd had his life together. He had a business, goals, a nice condo and the sweetest dog. He'd also treated her right—with respect, with consideration. He'd treated her like a lady.

"Then I met Cash, and started working for him a few days later. The pay was good, not as good as the job I'd lost, so I kept the waitressing gig for a while. Six months later, he asked me to move in with him, and even offered up the guest room for Bobby." She stared out into the yard and watched him. She smiled. "I was so crazy in love with him, I jumped at the offer. Bobby wasn't as cool with the idea, and I couldn't understand why." Her smile faded. "Then I found out he'd quit school and was spending his days hanging out with losers with no ambition. He would work for Cash on occasion, crash for a few months at one buddy's place, then move on to another." She sipped the beer and shrugged. "Once in a while he'd spend a week or two with me and Cash, but then he'd be gone again." Leaving her guilty and thinking the way he'd turned out had been her fault.

"Ryan mentioned that Bobby always seemed kind of lost. You do know that none of what's happened to him is your fault?"

"I know," she lied. Cash had been right all along. She was an enabler and had allowed Bobby to take advantage of her love and her money. Knowing Bobby the way she did, she doubted he even realized how he'd been treating her. He'd spent his childhood with her bailing him out of trouble and taking care of him, why would he think any different as an adult? "Sorry, I know I'm talking your ear off and it's nothing exciting."

"Do I look bored?" Lola asked. "Keep going. So, you started working for Cash, then you two moved in together."

She grinned. "They were good times. I took on more duties at the garage, made more money, and quit the restaurant. Me and Cash bought this house a year later." Almost all of the down payment had been his money, and he'd insisted that she keep hers in the bank. But they were partners, and she'd been proud to be able to contribute even a few thousand dollars to their home. Those really had been good times. She missed them, but wouldn't go back now. She'd learned all she could about herself during those years, then learned more about herself when she'd left him. Funny, she hadn't realized there was still much more to learn.

These past two days had her reassessing the future. While scooping ice cream in the Everglades, she would daydream about the day that Cash would come to his senses and quit the repo business so she could finally go home to him. Now those day-dreams were becoming a reality. She still loved Cash and still wanted to come home. But she was scared. She worried that she'd eventually have to run back to the Glades, once again embarrassed that she couldn't make her marriage work.

You can't change the stripes of a tiger.

Lola cleared her throat. "You know, the key to a good conversation is to talk out loud."

Mel chuckled when she realized she'd gone in her head. "I'm used to dealing with problems on my own. Anyway, about the ice cream shop...I'll keep working until you find someone to replace me."

"Back to business?" Lola reach for her beer. "I'm sure Harrison can fill in until we find someone. There's no need for you to hold up your move for that."

"Yeah, but what if he needs to go on assignment?"

"Vlad can fill in, or I'll do it."

"We all know Vlad doesn't do well with customers. Plus, if you're in the ice cream shop, who's going to cover the souvenir store and handle booking tours?"

Lola leaned forward. "Who's going to hide the bodies?" she asked, her tone quiet, thoughtful. "You haven't asked about who's going to take over your position with ATL."

Mel looked away. "Getting rid of those bodies and chopping the car and boat were the only major things I've done for ATL. Otherwise, I'm just a warm body. I'm sure you'll eventually find someone to replace me."

"Wow." Lola sank back in the patio chair. "It must be exhausting being you."

She looked away and watched as Vlad tossed a beanbag and missed the hole. "I don't know if I want to talk anymore."

"That doesn't surprise me. You have no problem adding to the conversation when we're brainstorming a case, or getting along with customers at the boat shop, or enjoying a burger and a beer if we're all hanging out at Polina's Paradise. Try to get a little personal, and you shut down. Like now. We were doing just fine, then you just stopped talking."

Lola was describing Cash, not her. At least the old Cash. "Then I guess now you know better than to ask personal questions," Mel said, still not meeting Lola's gaze.

"I'm going to ask one anyway: how could you drop everything you have in Everglades City?"

"Finish the question."

"What do you mean?"

"Talking about saying what's on your mind," Mel said with a sigh, and finally looked at her boss. "Why don't I finish the question for you? How could I drop everything I have in Everglades City *for a man*?"

"I got the gist of it from the little you told me. You met him, fell crazy in love, bought a house. From there, it's none of my business."

"You're right, it's not." She watched as Cash tilted his head back and took a drink from his beer. He picked up a beanbag, then grinning and saying something to Vlad, tossed it. *Bull's eye.* "How long have you and Ryan been together?" she asked, her focus still on Cash. She'd wanted to be back with him for so long, she was waiting for the fantasy to burst and return her to the swamp.

"You know it's only been ten months.'

"I do." She faced Lola. "So, if Ian shut down ATL and told you he'd like you in Chicago working for his CORE team, what would you do?"

"My home is with Ryan."

"After only ten months? I suppose working together to hunt and kill a man would definitely bring a couple close. I've known Cash for over eight years, but we never killed anyone. Maybe that's what's been missing from our relationship."

Lola smiled. "I see what you're doing."

"Good, then you get that me and Cash have history. It's hard for me to walk away from that."

"My concern for you is that history will repeat itself."

"Meaning?"

"Meaning nothing will change, you'll be unhappy again and forced to leave. And that worries me."

This was why she'd never been too bent out of shape about not having any female friends. They wanted to dive right into all the dark and heavy emotional stuff. "Well, until you're in the situation, I think you should save your advice and worry. You say your home is with Ryan, but after only ten months, I'm not sure I buy it. You love running ATL."

"It's a *job.* Yes, I love doing it, but I don't see myself chasing bad guys forever. Ryan and I want to expand the airboat business, partner up with Shane more than we have. We want a family."

She hadn't thought about Lola's wants outside of successfully closing a case. "I want a family, too. With Cash."

"A man you've been separated from during two out of the three years you've been married." Lola held up a hand. "I'm playing devil's advocate. I want you to be happy. I also want you to know we're here for you if you need us."

"Devil's advocate or not, you have me and Cash doomed before we get anything started again."

"I'm sorry, I really don't mean to—"

"Cash is the best thing that has ever happened to me. Every tear I cried over him was worth the good times, and what he's given me. And I'm not talking clothes or jewelry. He wanted to give me those things, that's for sure. He always wanted to buy me something nice. So I told him, 'Baby, I'm fine hittin' the discount racks and wearin' fake jewelry'. I wanted us to have a home. A nice yard for our dog. A place we could raise a family. He gave me more than that." She looked across the yard again, and stared at her husband. "Cash is strong. He can be mean when he wants to, and he doesn't back down from a fight. He will work his butt off and do whatever it takes to make sure there's money to pay the bills. He has a big heart, and a temper to match. He gave me hope when I was desperate, and the kind of love I'd never had before. He survived war, survived a beating that should have him wheeling around in a chair alongside Dolly." A tear slipped down her cheek. "There had to be a reason he'd survived all that, don't you think?"

Lola rested her hand over hers. "Harrison told me why you left him. You're stronger than I would have been."

"Don't sell yourself short. I've seen you in action." She rested her hand over Lola's sandwiching it in place. "Look, I have to believe he'll keep his promise and stay out of the repo business. From the moment I met Cash, I knew he was the man for me."

"Listening to you describe Cash, you could have been describing yourself. Knowing Cash is—was—in the repo business, it doesn't surprise me why you'd joined ATL. You like excitement."

"I do, but that's not the reason."

"Why'd you join?"

"This is going to sound really bad, but I did it for the money. Ian gave me ten grand to hide the bodies, another five for chopping the car and boat—which I made another fifteen grand on when I sold the parts. I needed the money. No offense, but being the ice cream lady isn't the most lucrative job."

"Didn't Cash send you money?"

"I got a check twice a month for my percentage of the business, but I gave some to Bobby to keep him from being homeless." She rolled her eyes. "Lotta good that did. Some of the money went toward helping Daddy fix up his house. I was tired of him having to deal with the leaky roof. I split the rest between my savings account and this family I adopted."

"You adopted a family. Of what? Raccoons?"

Mel chuckled. She gave Lola's hand a pat before leaning back in her chair. "No, a human family of five. About seven years ago, I got this idea in me that I needed to take up running. So I took Dolly to the park, ran for about fifteen minutes before deciding that if I was gonna run, someone had better be chasing me," she said with a grin. "Now I stick to Pilates. Anyway, I stopped at a picnic bench to catch my breath. A couple of minutes went by and I heard this little boy yelling to his mommy that Dolly was just like his daddy. The boy came running over. Meanwhile, the mom looked like a dang zombie. Too skinny, dark circles under eyes, tired smile. She was pushing a double stroller, one side with a toddler in it, the other with a tiny baby." She glanced to where Dolly lay on her bed in the corner of the patio. "While the boy, his name is Dustin, was loving Dolly, I got to talking to the mom, Diana. She explained that her husband came home two months ago from Iraq. He'd been walking along a roadside in Baghdad looking for IEDs, unfortunately one found him and he lost both of his legs. Just like Dolly."

"You mentioned to Gillian that Dolly saved Cash. What branch of the service did he serve in?"

"The Army. He was an explosive ordnance disposal specialist."

"So how'd you go about adopting this family?"

"Diana and I ended up talking for a long time. She did most of the talking. I think she just needed to vent to a stranger. Her husband had a long road ahead of him, and was having a difficult time adjusting to not only being back home, but accepting the loss of his legs. The government was taking care of his pay and housing, but money was still tight. Diana couldn't get a job because paying for daycare would eat up her salary, and her husband was in no position to take care of the kids. After I told her about Cash and Dolly, we exchanged phone numbers. Later that night, I talked to Cash about her." She smiled. "He was ready to give that family whatever they needed. So, between him and me, and the boys at the garage, we started paying for daycare so Diana could go to work."

"If you met her seven years ago, aren't their kids in school full-time?" Lola asked.

"They are. But Diana became a single mom about five years ago. Her husband overdosed on painkillers. I know it's not easy for her to raise those kids on her own. I can't afford to send a whole lot, but I'm sure she appreciates every cent."

Lola set her elbow on the table, rested her chin in her hand and stared at her. "I don't know what to do with you. You have to be one of the hardest people to understand, one of the strangest, too."

Mel took a drink, then regretted it. The beer had gone warm and flat. She also now regretted telling Lola about Diana. "I've been told worse."

"Don't be offended. I wasn't insulting you. I mean, look at you. You're this fluffy girly-girl who always has her nails done, always looks gorgeous, always has men turning their heads. You're sweet and mean. You're compassionate, and yet you didn't even blink when you disposed of two dead bodies. How do you do that?"

"I need a fresh beer. Want one?"

"Yes, but I still want to know."

Mel pushed back the chair, then stood. "How did you handle cleaning brains off the floor?" she asked, bringing up the night that had started ATL.

"Once I was back at Ryan's, I cried, then had sex with him."

"You weren't cryin' for the dead men, though," Mel said, as she pulled two beers from the cooler.

"No. I think the whole situation had finally caught up with me. That was a growing period for me."

Mel set the beers on the table and thought back to that night. Although her main focus had been making sure Ryan hadn't been hurt, she'd had the wherewithal to make a mental note of each person in the room. Lola had immediately caught her attention. The haunted look in her eyes could have been mistaken for anger, but Mel had seen that same look in her daddy's eyes when he went deep inside his head and couldn't tell the difference between what was real, and the men he'd fought during the war. What Lola had experienced had been more than real. Because of how she'd handled herself that night, Lola had earned Mel's respect.

"Not the best way to grow, but there could be worse things." Mel twisted the bottle open, and took a seat. "As for me, it wasn't as if I didn't feel anything when I was rolling those bodies off my daddy's dock. I had. I felt relief. Those men couldn't hurt anyone else, and Ryan was fine." She took a sip of the beer. "You have to understand how I was raised. I didn't go to the grocery store for my meat. I hunted for it. Killing an animal for food is natural to me. Dumping a body isn't, but I have more respect for the animals who gave their lives so my family and I wouldn't starve, than for men who have no regard for human life. Those men weren't worth thinking about or feeling any guilt for. After hearing what they'd done to all of you, I was glad I could help." She shrugged. "I don't think that makes me strange."

Lola gave her a small apologetic smile. "I'm sorry. Strange wasn't the right word. Interesting and admirable are, though. I think it's amazing that you can rationalize a situation to the point where your logic can clear your emotions."

Mel chuckled as she pictured Cash's reaction to what Lola had just said. "Don't go admiring me. When it comes to certain things, I've been known to be *highly* emotional and irrational."

"Like Cash?"

Dang, back to him again. "Yep, like Cash. He's promised to quit the repo business, and it's why I'm moving back, otherwise I'd be filing for a divorce I don't want. But Cash went from bomb disposal to repoing. He's spent his life placing himself in dangerous situations. I'm wondering how he's going to replace the rush."

"You're worried he's going to break his promise."

"Cash has always been a man of his word. I'm worried he's going to resent me for forcing him to keep his promise."

Understanding softened Lola's eyes. "I hope that doesn't happen. I don't want to lose you, and I'll miss seeing you every day at the boat shop, but I want you happy. If things between you two don't work out, you know you'll always have a place with ATL, and a job at the shop." She cleared her throat and reached for Mel's hand. "And a friend if you need to talk."

Sweet Baby Jesus, this was weird, but in a good way. "Thanks. I'm going to miss working with all of you, but it's not like I'm moving that far away. I think one of the hardest things is going to be leaving Daddy again."

Harrison walked toward them. Cash and Vlad followed behind, having what she hoped was a friendly argument.

"If your dad needs anything, you know any one of us would help," Lola said. "We'd have to meet him first."

"Barney, Ryan and Shane know Daddy, they can check up on him for me."

"Yeah, but what if I'd like to meet him?"

"Meet who?" Harrison asked as he reached into the cooler and pulled out a water bottle.

"Mel's dad."

"Vlad have curiosity for Daddy."

"I haven't met Mel's daddy, either. I'm not even convinced he exists," Cash said as he walked over and planted a kiss on her head.

"I'm thinking Mel's an angel sent from heaven."

Harrison shook his head. "Do you really like it when he says stuff like that?"

Mel grinned. "Love it. Give him another one, baby."

Cash rested his hands on her shoulders. "Wanna know why I have so many pictures of Mel on my cell phone?"

Harrison rolled his eyes. "Gee, Cash, why is that?"

"So that I have proof that angels do exist."

"That's awful," Harrison groaned.

"I think it's sweet," Mel said, laying her palms over his hands.

"Hey, Vlad," Cash began, "can I borrow your cell phone?"

"Vlad have no phone." The Russian frowned at Harrison. "Harry took away from Vlad."

"Here, use mine," Lola said, offering the phone.

Knowing the goofy line Cash was going to lay on them, Mel chuckled. "I think you lost them, honey." She patted his hand.

"Yeah, I do, too."

Lola held onto her phone. "I'll bite, what's the line."

"The moment's over," Cash said with a sigh, then he leaned down, pressed his mouth to Mel's ear, and whispered, "I need to call animal control because I just saw a fox."

Cash blew against Mel's ear, smiling when goose bumps rose along her skin. She giggled—Melanie Scarlet Maddox actually giggled. Next to her crying out his name as he gave her pleasure, Cash had never heard a prettier sound. Now that they'd reconciled their differences, he hoped to hear more.

"Now Vlad know."

Mel rubbed her hands along her arms and looked up at the Russian. "What's that?"

"The man who can melt Ice Cream Lady," he said with a grin.

The sweetest, shyest smile curved her lips. "You really are a big goof."

Vlad beamed, then looked to Lola. "Vlad tired. Asian Lola take Vlad to hotel."

"He just wants to call Barney and check up on his gator,"

Harrison said. "But I'm tired, too. I wouldn't mind going back and falling asleep to the TV." He glared at Vlad. "Something I don't get to do in my own house because someone is always complaining about it."

"Vlad feel this bad habit for Harry."

"Right. It's way worse than smoking."

Vlad pulled out a pack of cigarettes.

"Don't bother," Lola said as she stood. "And I don't want to listen to you two argue during the drive to the hotel. I've had enough of it." She looked to Mel. "You're good with me taking your car?"

"I trust you," Mel responded, and Cash swore the look exchanged between the two women solidified some sort of secret pact.

"I'm glad. I really love driving your Camaro."

"It is bitching," Vlad added.

"On that note…" Harrison said, then opened the patio door.

He and Mel followed their guests to the front door. Once they'd left, and Mel shut the door, he was tempted to pull her into his arms. They hadn't had the chance to talk after they'd returned from the homeless shelter. He'd wanted to, but the others had decided to stay rather than go back to their hotel rooms. While he had entertained them, and prepared chicken to cook on the grill, Mel had hidden herself in the bathroom for a long shower.

"It's still early, are you ready for bed, too?" he asked as he helped her clean up the patio table.

"No, I wouldn't mind watching TV."

Sounded fine to him. After having a good meal, a couple of beers and a little fun in the backyard with Vlad and Harrison, he wouldn't mind doing something that didn't require much thought. "Lemme get Dolly settled for the night." He headed for where their dog lay on her patio bed. When he lifted her, he looked at the purple collar Mel had made for her. "You're looking awfully pretty tonight. Your mama knows how to dress you up," he said, setting her on her bed in the kitchen.

"She does look pretty." Dolly lifted her head and her eyes went alert. Mel came over, then took the dog's head in her hands. "I've missed our nighttime routine," she said, scratching Dolly behind the ear.

He had, too. Before Mel had left, and he'd been back to his old self, they'd fallen into the habit of putting Dolly to bed as if she was their child instead of their dog. Dolly would, as she was now, eat up the attention. Give them those big, brown puppy dog eyes, nuzzle them with her nose for just one more scratch, then groan and roll on her side as if the process had exhausted her.

"Want something to drink?" she asked, taking a water bottle from the fridge.

"I'll just steal some of yours."

She grinned and grabbed two bottles. Once they were in the family room and on the couch, he raised the remote. "So what do you want to watch?"

"Doesn't matter," she said, resting her head in his lap.

Well, hell. He wanted to throw the TV on and not think. But with Mel laying the way she was, it was hard not to think about touching her, or her touching him. She'd had a rough afternoon, though, and he wanted to show her she could lean on him. That nothing had changed, even if he had. He was still the man she could count on, still the only man she'd ever need.

He started flipping through channels, found a few things that might interest him, but doubted Mel would want to watch. Or maybe she did. During the past two years, when they'd spent a weekend together, they hadn't been watching TV. He searched back into his memory bank, trying to remember what she used to like to watch. A couple of the shows she had liked were no longer on the air. She had a strange liking for old sitcoms from the sixties and seventies, but he didn't know where to find them.

"You're making me dizzy," she said. "Just pick something."

"I'm trying. I want to find something for you."

She rolled onto her opposite side and looked up at him. "Do you still like to watch shows about cars and the military?"

"Don't forget sports. And I've gotten into history."

Her face saddened. "I feel like it's been forever since we've watched TV."

Not forever, but two years. "It's been a while."

"Sometimes I feel like I don't know you. I mean, I *know* you, just not the little things."

"Like what I watch on TV."

"That and other things you might be interested in doing. I know you go to work, then usually meet the guys out after. I know you've been doing things around the house—I forgot to tell you I like the color you painted the guest bath."

"I only meet the boys once a week. Twice if we have something to celebrate."

"Why don't you go out as much?" she asked.

When she curled toward him, he turned off the TV, then set the remote on the couch. "You know all this," he said, smoothing her hair from her face. "I've told you before. I don't like going out. If you think back, nine out of ten times when we talk, I'm at home or at work. Not at a bar." He gave her earlobe a light tug. "You didn't believe me, did you?" He couldn't blame her. When she'd left, he'd been so damned determined to prove he could be the man he was before the accident, he'd gone back to working hard and playing harder.

"I'm sorry. I know you did. It's not that I didn't believe you, it just hard to picture you relaxing."

"We used to relax together all the time. Our old hammock doesn't owe us a dime."

She grinned. "Those were some fun, lazy Sundays."

He couldn't agree more. There'd been nothing like holding Mel while they lay in the hammock, talking, kissing, then later dozing off for a nap. "I think about those days all the time."

"It's nice knowing I'm not the only one." She touched his chest. "How come you took the hammock down? I noticed it wasn't up the last two times I was here."

"Why didn't you ask me when you first noticed?" He suspected why, but had learned over the years to never assume anything when it came to Mel. How she could ever think he could be bored with her, he didn't know. The woman knew how to keep him on his toes.

"I don't know," she said, her gaze on his chest as if his old t-shirt was fascinating. "I guess I was afraid of your answer."

"You didn't think I took it down as a way to show you I was done with those days, did you?"

"That would have been a reason I could've handled." She finally looked up at him, her eyes cautionary. "I think if you told me you took the hammock down because it hurt too much to look at it, that would have hit me hard."

What was she talking about? "I told you how much I missed you every time I saw you or we talked."

"Hearing is one thing, seeing is another."

He took her right hand from his chest. "Kinda like you not wearing my ring or using my name." He kissed her ring finger. "Knowing you don't acknowledge that I'm your husband…" He drew in a deep breath hoping to keep the disappointment at bay and from his voice. They were supposed to be healing, not hurting each other. "I get why you didn't tell anyone from home about me."

Her eyes filled with tears. "I told Lola about us."

"What'd you tell her?" he asked, worried it couldn't have been good when she looked about to cry.

"I told her how I ended up in Tallahassee, how you gave me a job—minus the fact that I used to steal cars—and how we bought this home together."

"When you have your mind set to something, you get it. I would probably still be in my old condo if it wasn't for you."

"This coming from a man who grew up with nothing, and became a hero and a successful businessman."

He wanted to look away, yet he wanted to keep looking into her expressive eyes, eyes that don't lie, and make sure she was telling him the truth. "I'm no one's hero."

"You're mine. You helped me get my life on track."

"I gave you a job. You're smart. You could've found one without my help. That doesn't make me a hero."

"It's not just the job. I've told you before I liked the excitement of stealing cars, but hated myself every time I did it. I was risking too much, and for what?"

He tucked a lock of hair behind her ear. "People say money doesn't buy happiness, but it's nice to have some to pay the rent and buy groceries." This, he knew all too well. If he hadn't joined the Army, he probably would have wound up getting into all kinds of trouble. When he'd been a kid, his mom would have him shoplift for her. He could remember thinking stealing was so damned easy, why pay for what you could take?

"I know you understand better than most people would. Still, you took a chance on swamp trash, and treated me better than I'd ever been treated. No matter what happens between us, I'm grateful for you, and for the hope you gave me."

"You don't think you gave me the same? I never planned to get married. Ever. I never wanted kids and the responsibility that came with it. I didn't want to have to worry about disappointing my wife and kids when I screwed up."

Her eyes widened a fraction. "You never told me this."

"Because when I met you, that saying, 'Never say never,' dropped on my head like a four hundred pound car engine. Once we started dating, I still worried about screwing up, but I figured you'd keep me on track and make sure that didn't happen." He ran his finger along her soft cheek. "I never had anyone love me the way you did."

"Do," she said, a tear slipping down her cheek. "The way I do love you." She rubbed her hand along his chest again. "When I was talking to Lola, I told her how you survived war and a beating that should have left you dead or paralyzed. I believe there's a reason you survived Iraq and the accident, not to mention a childhood that would've landed most people in prison."

"I never thought about it like that. But now that I do, maybe that was God's way of making sure I'm around to be here for you." The only church he'd been in was the Army chapel. He'd never had any religious schooling, and his mother had certainly never said much about God unless she'd been using His name in vain. He still believed, though. He had since he'd been a kid. Lord knew he'd needed something to give him hope. Years later, He'd placed Melanie in his path.

He stroked her cheek, then her hair. "Do you think Bobby's doing okay?"

She sighed. "I think Noah's death opened his eyes. I'm hoping he learns from everything that's happened to him in the past week, and betters himself like he'd promised."

While she wasn't talking about him, she could've been. Cash had made promises to her, too, and he planned to learn from everything that had happened to him, remember the loss of his wife these last two years and the pain that had come with it. He didn't want to be without her again.

"What if he really moves back to Everglades City?" he asked.

"What do you mean?"

"Will you want to stay in the Glades for a while until he gets settled, or maybe split your time between here and there?"

She lifted her head off his lap, then straddled him. "You know how they say there's no such thing as a dumb question?"

He grinned and ran his hands along her back. "I just asked one, huh?"

She nodded. "I'd like to go into our bedroom and fool around with my husband," she said, grazing her lips along his. "Are you good with skipping TV?"

He could have pointed out that she'd also asked a dumb question, but kissed her instead. He'd be a fool to turn her down, and didn't want to anyway. After spending two years separated, they had plenty of making up to do.

CHAPTER 14

The House of Archer, Bower, Georgia
Monday, 7:38 a.m. Eastern Daylight Saving Time

"JIM'S DEAD."

Adeline looked up from her over medium eggs and stared at Rodney. "How?"

He shrugged and walked toward the coffee pot. "I'm assuming from a heart attack. When I checked on him before bed last night, his heart rate had been over one hundred and forty beats per minute."

She picked up the jelly spoon, then dipped it into the jar of strawberry jam. "We knew he could be at risk." Setting the spoon aside, she used her knife to swipe the jam across her toast, and shifted her gaze toward him. "And how is our other test subject?" She smiled when Rod's back straightened and his shoulders squared.

"He's fine."

"Should I go see for myself?" she asked, then took a bite of the toast.

"If you feel it's necessary." He faced her, apology clear in his eyes. "I gave him his saline drops, his next dose and made sure that he'd relieved himself before he urinated in his pants."

"How kind. After your outburst last night, I've been concerned about your bedside manner. Maybe I'll check on him anyway. Or will you hurt me again?"

His hand shook as he reached for the creamer. "You have no

idea how horrible I feel about hurting you. I let my jealousy get the best of me. Please accept my apology."

"I'm sure I'll get over it." She already had. If anything, she had new respect for Rodney. He'd showed a backbone, had proven that when pushed hard enough, he would retaliate. *That* had been what she'd been waiting for from him. She'd wanted him dark, dirty and ready to push the limits. And she planned to compel him to stretch his imagination. By the time she was finished, he'd no longer have a conscience. His morals would be a thing of the past. In its place would be her desires, her wishes. She didn't want an obedient dog—she was saving that role for their test subject, Liam. She wanted a strong man at her side. A man who would think nothing of killing. She wanted Rodney to be that man and to be her equal.

He set the creamer back on the counter, then rushed to her. He fell to his knees. "I need you," he said, his eyes imploring and filled with worry. "I need us to go back to where we were before I struck you."

She set her toast on her plate, then rotated in the chair until she faced him. "You mean, when you ripped off my clothes, then fucked me against the wall."

His eyes simmered with hunger as his gaze dipped to her breasts. "Before that."

Not bothering with untying the sash of her robe, she lifted the hem of her nightgown. "To when I was constantly begging you to come to my bed? Did you like having that kind of power over me?" She raised the nightgown higher and spread her legs.

"I hated you for tempting me," he said, sliding a hand along her inner thigh. "There were nights I laid in bed stroking myself, imagining your mouth on me, my tongue inside you."

When he moved her panties aside and pressed his fingers deep, she fought against groaning, against giving him an ounce of satisfaction. She wanted him to suffer just a little longer.

"I hated that all I could think about was licking you." He twisted his hand, and brushed her clit with his knuckle. "Sucking your nipples." He pulled his fingers from her body. "Fucking you," he said, then drew them into his mouth.

"Do you still hate it?" she asked, unable to stop staring at his mouth.

"Yes."

She grinned. "Good." She adjusted her nightgown and robe. "Don't you have a body to bury?" she asked as she turned and picked up her toast.

"Bitch." When he stood, his crotch was level to her face, his arousal evident beneath his old jeans. He rubbed himself, which only made her want to resist him more. She loved making him suffer. She wanted him hard and hungry for her. She wanted him angry, jealous. Because later the reward would be that much sweeter.

"Call me what you want. I don't care." She watched as his hand continued to move along the outline of his erection. "While you're burying Jim in the old barn, I'm going to drive to Tallahassee to see if there's any word on Noah."

He dropped his hand away, and moved back to the counter. "I would prefer if you waited for me. It could be dangerous."

If she found him, Noah would be the only one in danger. "I don't want to wait. I also think I should try to bring back another subject. We need more to make sure our results are accurate."

"No."

Right. Because she was going to obey.

"If you can't promise me that you won't pick up another homeless person, then I will hide the keys from you. Better yet, I'll chain you to the bed."

She scooped jam onto the tip of her finger, then swept it off with the tip of her tongue. "Now I'm tempted to disobey you."

A smile tugged at his mouth. "Well, are you going to promise me?"

"Fine. I promise not to pick up a homeless person." *For now.*

"Good. There's something else I need to tell you. It's about Liam," he said, and she swore his small smile became mocking. "I heard him talking to someone."

"Do you think the drug is affecting him differently than the others?" The previous subjects had experienced mild hallucinations, but they hadn't lasted long. She was quite impressed with the drug she'd created. A-Line had left the user lucid enough to understand what was happening to them, but compliant enough to accept what her voice recordings and the videos suggested. Add on the violent urges, and she'd created the perfect recipe for a future killer.

"I don't think A-Line had anything to do with it," Rodney said with a frown. "I heard him mention something about reaching Miami. Then he said, 'No one is coming for me or knows I'm missing.' Just before I opened the door, he said, 'Go away.'"

"Maybe he was talking to you. As I recall, you weren't very nice to him."

He sipped from his coffee mug. "Initially, I thought the same thing. I figured he was having a mild case of psychosis. So, I went into the room and asked him who he was talking to. He told me it was his imaginary friend, Mitch, who was a mercenary hired to help stop the government from poisoning the water."

No longer interested in breakfast, she pushed her plate aside. "I'm sure it was the A-Line talking. Think about it, we're injecting him and he doesn't understand why. His mind could be fabricating a story to justify what's happening to him. Did he say anything else?"

"Not a word," he said, and she knew he was lying. She'd spent too many years with the man to not know the signs. She doubted she'd be able to coax him into telling her what had been said, but knew who might enjoy talking with her.

She shoved her chair back and picked up her plate. "I think I'll shower and get ready to drive to Tallahassee," she said, setting her plate in the sink.

Rodney came up behind her, but didn't touch her. "You didn't get to come yesterday. I want to take care of that later."

She glanced over her shoulder. "Who says I didn't come?"

He turned her around and pinned her against the old farm-house sink. For a second, she regretted her words. The anger, the possessiveness in his eyes suggested she shouldn't push him.

"Who says I didn't go back to my room and pleasure myself?" She moved to her tiptoes and ran her tongue along his lower lip. "While I was thinking about the way you fucked me against the wall."

On a groan he kissed her, then quickly stepped away. "I'm heading to the barn. I'll have my cell phone on me. Call me when you're leaving."

"Do you need help moving Jim's body from the attic room?"

"No. I doubt the man weighs more than one hundred and thirty pounds."

She flicked her gaze to Rodney's strong biceps, and couldn't wait to hold them when they had sex later. "How are you taking his death? I realize the circumstances are different compared to Troy's, but I know you. I know you think about these things more than I do."

"If the man hadn't gotten into our car, he'd still be alive. Probably sitting against a building, either passed out from whatev-er rotgut he'd found the night before, or hung over, or going through withdrawal because he couldn't find any booze." He shoved a hand in his front pocket. "I feel guilt for not feeling guilty, if that makes any sense. And I think I don't feel guilty because Jim probably would have died a slow, painful death on the streets anyway."

Very interesting. But how would Rodney feel if he killed Liam out of jealousy? Not anytime soon, though. She had plans for their subject.

"I think I understand," she said, even if she didn't at all. For her, guilt didn't exist. It never had. When she'd been scolded as a child, she'd taken the beating and just was smarter the next time, making sure she didn't get caught. When she'd killed her room-mate, the only emotion running though her had been relief. The bitch had been dead and she'd had an excuse to move in with

Rodney. Geoff? Rodney had been right the other night. She'd killed him because she hadn't wanted the boy at the House of Archer the entire summer. She hadn't wanted the kid in her way, invading her privacy, infringing on her time with Rodney. That wasn't to say she hadn't had a little fun with him first. Fifteen-year-old boys were very eager to please.

Rodney took a few steps back, his gaze drifting over her body. "Call my cell phone before you leave." He turned and headed for the stairs, but stopped at the first step without turning to face her. "Stay away from Liam. I don't want to make good on my promise."

If I find out you've fucked him, I'll kill him and beat you.

As Adeline turned to the sink to take care of her dirty dish, she smiled. The lump on her head, curtsey of Rodney, was still tender. She now knew what he was capable of when provoked, but couldn't wait to test the limits. He was so close to breaking that she suspected it wouldn't take much more for him to truly accept the truth.

He was just like her.

She'd finished cleaning up the breakfast mess, when Rodney came down the stairs carrying Jim's body—wrapped in a sheet—over his shoulder. She watched him, stared at his straining muscles, at his ass as he exited to the back porch, then let out a sigh.

She had plenty of time to kill before Rodney would finish digging Jim's grave. Time enough to play with Liam.

"THERE'S SOMETHING IN the corner."

Liam quickly looked.

"No, the other corner," another voice said.

He shifted his gaze.

"Don't listen to him, listen to me," the first voice said, its tone higher, and holding more urgency.

Liam didn't know who to listen to, who to believe. The two

voices had been battling and contradicting each other from the moment Mitch had disappeared. *Focus. Focus.* But when he tried to focus, all he heard was Madeline's voice.

She was a bad, bad woman. She wanted him to do bad, bad things.

"*Smash her teeth,*" Madeline told him through the recording, but she might as well have been in the room. Filling his head with images of violence that matched the scenes on the TV.

"*Listen to her,*" the lower voice said. "*She will help us.*"

"*No, she won't,*" the other voice countered.

"*She will.*"

He wanted to tell the voices in his head to shut the fuck up. Unfortunately Roderick—the bastard—had taped his mouth before leaving him, but not before sticking another needle in his arm. Whatever Roderick had given him, he wanted more. The drug helped make Madeline's words less appalling, the images on the TV less offensive. That didn't mean he hadn't been thinking about Roderick and what he'd like to do to the man, should he find a way to escape.

"*Fuck with him hard,*" the lower voice suggested.

"*Yes, do it,*" the other one concurred.

They were all in agreement. Roderick needed a good fucking with before Liam smashed the man's teeth into the back of his throat.

The door opened, and Madeline stepped into the room.

"*Don't trust her,*" the higher voice said. "*Don't listen.*"

"*Wait. She could help,*" the lower voice advised.

She smiled. Such a pretty smile. Her sun-kissed cheeks had slight dimples. Her green eyes held amusement. But there was nothing amusing about his current situation. He wanted to blink his eyes so bad that he'd kill for the chance.

"How are you feeling?" she asked as she moved alongside the bed. She caressed his face, the touch feather-light, soothing before she ripped the tape from his mouth.

He let out a grunt and tamped down the pain and hatred.

"Thirsty."

"Last time you said that, I held your big cock in my hands. Is that a correlation or just coincidence?"

"I don't think Roderick liked you touching me," he said, unsure why he'd encourage her. He was helpless, vulnerable. If he pushed Roderick too much, the man could amplify his current position in hell.

"Good thing Rod's not here," she said, tiptoeing her fingers along his chest. "How do you feel?"

Her recorded voice, although once again background noise, penetrated his mind, urged him to kill. "Hungry," he said.

"For what?"

"I'm not sure."

She leaned close, so close he lost sight of her in his peripheral vision. God, she smelled good. Like strawberries. "Food?"

His stomach turned. "No."

Her breast pressed against his arm. "Me?"

Hell, no. "I hate you."

She slid her hand to his dick. "Revenge?"

He sucked in a breath when she cupped him. Yes. He wanted revenge. He wanted out of this place, but he wanted to make them pay for what they were doing to him first.

"I can help you with that." She moved her hand over him. "Roderick doesn't know I'm here. He's busy burying the man who died in the room next to yours. If we're not careful, that could be you. I doubt you want that."

Death would be easier.

"Listen to her," one of the irritating voices in his head said.

"Yes, listen," the other one agreed.

"What happened to him?" Liam asked. While he didn't remember seeing another man, he'd heard noises from the next room. He also wanted to know his possible fate.

"Rod's a very jealous man. When our test subject tried to fondle me, Roderick let the man know that wasn't allowed."

His breath quickened. Despite his hatred for Madeline, his

penis grew under her talented hand. "He beat the man?"

"Until his face was unrecognizable." Her lips brushed his ear. "Until his eyes were swollen shut and blood poured from his ears, mouth and nose." She ran her tongue along the shell of his ear, before whispering, "Then Rod slit the man's throat. There was so much blood, Liam. I wish you could have seen it."

He wished the dead man was Roderick. Picturing himself beating the man until he'd become nothing but a bloody pulp, then slicing his throat would become his new fantasy. But then what to do with Madeline afterward?

When she groaned, he snapped out of the fantasy and realized he'd become harder than he'd ever been. Damn it, he had to keep his body under control.

"Feels so good," one of his voices murmured.

"Yes, let her. Maybe she'll let you go," the other said.

Doubtful. While their names were likely fake, he'd seen their faces. He knew what they were doing to people. "You called the dead man your test subject. Is that what I am?" he asked, hoping the reminder of his place in this situation would control his sexual urges.

"I don't want you to be," she said, moving a step back and untying the sash of her robe. Even if his eyes weren't taped open, he doubted he could look away. Although nearly thirty, he'd only been with two women. The first had been in high school and had ended in disaster—him fumbling, trying his best to be the stud he wasn't, then climaxing within fifteen seconds. The second had been a few years later when he'd been in college. Her name had been Jane and she'd been pretty and sweet. They'd dated for a few months before she'd finally let him go all the way with her. Two weeks later, he'd had his first schizophrenic breakdown. Jane had never bothered to contact him during or after his month-long stay in the psych unit.

The bitch.

He forgot about Jane and the slut from high school, and stared at Madeline's breasts. Her flimsy nightgown teased and tantalized. Revealed the outline of her areolas, her hard nipples.

"Suck them," one voice suggested.

"This could be a trick," the other said.

"Who's with you?" Madeline asked. He shifted his gaze to her mouth, where she rubbed her index finger along her pouty lower lip. "If you're honest, I'll let you see my breasts." She cupped one full mound. "I might even let you touch them with your mouth. I also might be able to help you get rid of whoever's bothering you."

"Don't tell her," both voices shouted.

When she used her other hand to lift the hem of her nightgown, his balls tightened. She had beautiful shapely legs. He could picture them around him as he drove himself deep.

"Tell me, Liam. Let me help you. I don't want you to end up like the others. You're special to me." She slipped her fingers beneath her panties. Her forehead wrinkled slightly as desire crossed her face. "*So* special. God, I wish these were your fingers instead of mine. Please tell me. Please, Liam."

Wishing he could touch her or at least stroke himself, he pulled at his restraints. The voices in his head kept cautioning him, kept telling him to keep their secret, to not be fooled by her act of seduction. He wasn't fooled. He wanted her. He wanted to hurt her as he took pleasure from her body. "I want to strap Roderick to the bed, then fuck you in front of him," he said, not meaning to speak out loud. He didn't care, though. He had nothing to lose.

"Your life," the high-pitched voice said with urgency.

"We'll be fine," the other countered.

"No, no! She'll hurt you. Roderick will know."

Madeline's smile told him she liked his idea. "That would be fun. But you still didn't answer the question. Tell me, and I'll make sure this doesn't go to waste," she said, reaching for his erection.

"I hear voices," he admitted on a groan. "I was diagnosed with schizophrenia when I was twenty."

She unzipped his pants. "Mitch was one of those voices?"

"Roderick the dick told you?" He sighed, but didn't allow his hatred for the man to lessen the pure pleasure of having Madeline's soft hand wrapped around his erection.

"He did, but I'm not judging you. I'm curious. You told Rod that Mitch was gone. What happened to him?" she asked, sliding her thumb over the head of his penis.

"Show your breasts."

The corner of her mouth turned up in a sly smile. She removed her hand from her panties, then pulled aside the strap of her right shoulder, exposing her breast.

He licked his lips. "I don't know."

"Mitch was a mercenary, correct?" she asked as she slowly pumped his penis. "How long did you know him?"

He stared at where she held him. The voices had quieted. Even Madeline's recorded voice had become nothing but a faint buzz. "Months," he said, then blew out a breath. God, he wanted her mouth on him, which made him hate her even more. He didn't want to depend on her, need her, trust her.

"Months? What if I told you I could make Mitch and all the other voices go away?" She leaned in, then rubbed her nipple along his cheek, but not close enough where he could capture it with his mouth. "Permanently," she added, bending until her lips were so close he could bite them. Puncture the soft flesh and tear it from her face before she could scream for Roderick.

Tempting. So damned tempting. But hurting her would likely lead to his swift death. He wasn't ready to die, not when he was on the brink of the greatest orgasm of his life.

"How?" he asked.

With a smile, she eased back. "It's simple," she said, shifting her body until her mouth was only inches from his straining erection. "Obey the rules." She ran her tongue along his length. "Focus on only my voice." She did it again, her gaze locked on his. "Watch the videos." She circled the head of his dick with her tongue. "Don't fight the drug, Liam. Let it break you free." Rubbing her lips along him, she grinned. "Imagine life without psychosis, without voices. I promise, once you let the drug break you, allow yourself the clarity you deserve, the acceptance, the power..." She drew him into her mouth.

His eyes rolled back. The suction from her mouth was exquisite, until she released him. "Once the drug has broken you, I will give you something that will define you as the man you truly are, not the man doctors and pharmaceutical companies want to use as their guinea pig. Did your doctors prescribe you lots and lots of pills?"

The memory of watching the colorful pills swirl down his sister's toilet rushed through his mind, along with outrage. "Yes. I hated taking them. I hated the way the nurses looked at me as if I was a side show freak, and the way doctors wanted to dissect my brain with their tests." God, how he'd hated every moment. He'd endured, for the sake of his sister. Kiera had believed in him, and was probably the only person who had accepted him for who he was—until Madeline. But Madeline was the enemy. She was holding him against his will. Drugging him, using him as one of her subjects.

"*She said she didn't want you to be one of their subjects,*" one of his voices quietly reminded him.

"*I still don't trust her, but what other hope is there?*" the other asked.

None. Without Madeline, there was no hope. Not until he could free himself and escape. But what if she was right? What if this drug *could* help him? It had made him realize Mitch hadn't been real, and had given him the memories he'd been suppressing.

She gave him a wry smile. "You're not sick, maybe a little cracked, but after I break you and put you back together like Humpty Dumpty, I think you and I could make history."

"Except Humpty *couldn't* be put together again."

She stroked him. "I've got a special kind of glue. Don't worry, Liam. By this time tomorrow, *if* you cooperate, Rod will remove the tape from your eyes. But you have to be good. It's the only way I can help you, and stop Rod from killing you. Understand?"

"What'll he do to you if he finds out you're touching me?" When she looked away, he remembered the thud he'd heard last night against the door, followed by Roderick's crying. "He'd hurt you," he said, desire rushing straight to his balls.

"That's why he can't ever know." She licked him again. "Promise you'll be good for me. Promise you won't tell."

"Don't promise her anything," the high-pitched voice said.

"Shut up and listen to me. Promise her. Use her," the other voice urged him.

"How can I trust you?" he asked, tormented between telling her to go to hell, and demanding that she suck him.

She raised a dark brow and released him. After hiking up her nightgown, she nudged her panties down over her hips, exposing her dark curls. "You can't." She climbed onto his lap. He groaned when she guided him in her tight, wet sex. "But I'm all the hope you have," she said on a moan. "So, do you promise me?"

"Yes," he said, and meant it. Right now, he wanted release. As irrational as that thought was—considering his current situation—his body demanded it. Maybe because of the drug…it didn't matter. Having her heat surrounding him did. He'd think about all the rest later.

Madeline glanced over her shoulder as she rode him, a smile playing on her lips. "How fitting. Look at the TV, not me." She undulated faster. "Whenever the voices start talking, focus on only mine. Listen to the recording when I can't be with you. Picture this moment. Imagine your big cock inside of me. Imagine a future where you hold power."

As his orgasm neared, he stared at the television. Ironically, a clip from *A Clockwork Orange*—the rape scene—played. He'd seen the movie years ago before his psychotic break, and had been appalled and unable to finish it. With Madeline's wet warmth taking him in, he wouldn't close his eyes even if he could. He wanted that power she'd promised. He wanted her on her knees, begging him for forgiveness, begging for her and Roderick's life. And yet he suddenly couldn't imagine not knowing Madeline.

Intriguing, sexy, manipulative...what could they do together if Roderick wasn't alive? Who could *they* break?

"*What are you thinking?*" the high-pitched voice asked. "*This isn't you.*"

"*It could be,*" the other countered. "*Wait and see what she does for you. If she can be trusted.*"

"*You only care about getting off,*" the high-pitched voice accused.

Laughter from the other voice filled his head. They needed to stop and leave him alone. He was schizophrenic, not stupid. He was fully aware that Madeline was a self-serving bitch. With the way she rode him, and knowing there was a chance he could possibly leave this place alive, he didn't care what she was.

Madeline clutched his shoulders. She let out a low moan, her sex clenching him as she rode out her orgasm. He was about to join her when she quickly moved off him, then took him in her mouth. She licked and sucked him as he'd always fantasized a woman would. Jane had been too much of a prude to bother. The slut from high school had simply spread her legs and told him to stick it in her. Between them, there'd been no one. After, it had been him, his pills and his hand.

Primed, his body tense, he watched her. Wished he could make the bindings around his wrists disappear so he could grab her hair. Rip it from her head. See the tears in her eyes.

She took him deep in her throat and he came in a rush, grunting his pleasure and frustration, wishing he were buried deep inside her again and choking the life from her body. As she let him slip from her mouth, she licked her lips, then righted his pants. Once he was zipped, and his clothes were in place, she put on her panties, then fixed her nightgown.

"You're something special, Liam," she said, touching his cheek. "When you were coming, were you thinking about me?"

"Yes."

"Were you thinking about hurting me?" she asked as she tightened the sash of her robe.

"Yes," he answered honestly. Based on the videos and her voice recordings, his desire to harm her shouldn't be a surprise.

"You really *are* something special." She slapped the duct tape over his mouth, then stared into his eyes as she kissed his sealed lips. "One day, when I'm certain you won't bite me, maybe I'll give you a real kiss." She grinned and moved toward the door. "Enjoy the video and remember what I said. When the voices come, focus on only one. Mine."

As the door closed behind her, he listened to Madeline's words and watched as the video segued into what he hoped was another horror movie clip. Bludgeoning a person with a bat wrapped in barbed wire had its merits, but was damned gory. And strangely appealing...

CHAPTER 15

"THIS IS CRAZY," Cash said as he parked along the curb several streets over from Hope House.

Mel agreed, allowing Harrison to remain wherever Madeline took him—*if* she took him—for a minimum of thirty-six hours was insane. So much could happen during that time.

Even Lola had originally wanted Harrison out of there within less than twenty-four hours. But after a morning conference call with Ian, and the way their boss had explained the need for hard evidence in order to make this bust as legit as possible, Lola had reluctantly agreed to give Harrison the thirty-six-hour window.

"We've been over this before," she said, then took a drink from her water bottle. They had another scorcher and, while she had a bottle of water stashed in her backpack, she wanted to be sure she was hydrated before stepping out of Cash's truck and into ninety-degree weather. "He knows the drill and he's wearing the GPS chip. He'll be fine." At least that had been what she'd been telling herself since their conversation with Ian.

"Harry no fine," Vlad said from the back seat. "Harry have strong bone in back. Vlad know this. Vlad also know Harry not strong like horse."

"Physical strength isn't what he needs," she said. "If Madeline takes him, he's going to have to use his head. Harrison is one of the smartest people I know. So for this job, he *will* be fine."

Vlad sneered at her. "Mel have delusion. Either swamp have warp effect, or maybe Ice Cream Lady spend too much time in cooler. Harry *not* fine."

"You might want to watch how you talk to my wife," Cash said. "Remember why we're here. Or do I need to remind you."

She choked on the testosterone in the truck. "Enough," she said when Vlad glared at her husband. "Decisions have been made and we're moving forward. Madeline might not even show—ever. Who knows? She could be done. In the meantime, keep your nasty remarks locked in your Russian brain before I come at you with something worse than an ice cream scooper."

Cash grinned. "I bet we have tools at the garage that could turn one of those scoopers into a sharp object."

"Vlad do not like threats," he said, his tone surprisingly menacing. While she'd heard him threaten suspects and had witnessed Vlad's aggressive side, it had been on the job, and he'd been able to joke easily afterward. This Vlad was one she wasn't sure how to handle.

Her cell phone rang, saving her from having to deal with Vlad at the moment. Since the caller ID showed Lola's name and number, she hit speaker. "Hey, Lola."

"Hi. Harrison just left the car. He's heading to the shelter. I'm going to wait a few, then follow behind and park where I did yesterday. Mel, are you ready?"

She instinctively touched the switchblade she'd hidden in her sock, then smoothed her old jeans in place. "I'm ready."

"Okay, let's hope today we get a lead. Watch Harrison's back and get the full license plate if you can."

"Got it," she said, before the line went dead. She glanced to Cash. "That's my cue. Give me some sugar before I go melt in this heat."

She hated the worry on his face, but loved the sweet kiss he gave her. Afterward, she took another long drink, then looked back to Vlad. "See ya' later, gator."

Vlad gripped her shoulder, the intensity in his eyes scaring her. "Harry will not speak to Vlad. What if...?" He shook his head and released her.

"Nothing is gonna happen, honey. Harrison always had faith you—anyone could see it—maybe you should give him some credit."

"Vlad cannot help worry."

She smiled. "That's 'cause he's your best bud. So, while you're sitting here twiddling your thumbs, why don't you think about that and how to resolve your problems? I'm sure we'll all be back at our house, hangin' poolside by dinnertime anyway."

"You don't think she'll show?" Cash asked.

"I like the theory of Madeline coming back to find out if Noah came here or if he went to the police, but it's a long shot." As soon as she cracked open the truck door, the heat took her breath away. "Dang, it's hot. I see frozen froo-froo drinks in my future."

"You got it, babe," Cash said. Despite his smile, worry lurked in his eyes. "Be careful."

"Always," she replied, then closed the door. After slinging the backpack over her shoulder, she made her way down the street and around the corner toward Hope House. Using her hand to shield her eyes from the sun, she searched for Harrison and spotted him stepping out of the street and onto the sidewalk. He gave her a nod of acknowledgement, then headed toward what little shade was near the building.

Deciding it didn't matter if Madeline saw the two of them talking, she walked over to him and realized there was no room for either of them in the shade. "Let's go across to the vacant lot and hang out there. There's not that many people along the brick wall, and in another hour or so, the sun will shift and it should be shady."

He agreed and fell into step with her. "Man, is it hot," he said, wiping sweat from his brow. "Yesterday wasn't as bad."

"There was a slight breeze. I have a full water bottle if you need it. It's not that cold, though."

"That's okay, I still have mine," he said. "I don't think I can do this for another three days. I don't care what Ian wants."

Ian had suggested they give it five days before walking away from the case—which, fortunately, included yesterday and today. "Just picture later this evening…drinkin' a cold beer, coolin' off in the pool. I'll have Cash grill us up some country ribs loaded with my special sauce."

"Special sauce, huh? Would this sauce be made from some critter you caught in the woods or pond?"

She elbowed him. "No, but there ain't no guarantees on the hash."

"I'm never eating anything you serve me unless I watch you make it."

"Would you stop? I'm only kind of joking."

"Only?" He grabbed her hand. "White car at two o'clock."

She looked to her right, just as a white sedan came to a stoplight. Once the traffic slowed, she gave Harrison's hand a squeeze. "Georgia plates. Should we turn back to the shelter?"

"Let's hang tight and see who's driving and where they head. It's early."

Anxious to see if the driver was a blonde female, yet terrified this could be Madeline, her stomach rolled and she regretted the water she'd guzzled earlier. She wanted to put an end to anything sinister this woman and her partner had planned, but did not want Harrison risking his health and life for a case.

The sun glared off the windshield as the car pulled forward, then turned left. The driver veered the sedan close to the curb and, as if searching for a street address or a place to park, drove slowly. Out of the corner of her eye, Mel noticed a few men rising from their resting spots in the shade. She glanced over her shoulder and saw several men who'd been standing near the shelter, walking in their direction. "People are coming toward the car. Early or not, it's gotta be her."

"Yeah, I see the guys coming up on my left." He let go over her hand. "One guy is on her. I'm heading over before I get shut out. Did you memorize the plates?"

Harrison was right. The man, who looked to be in his thirties, must have been sitting along the abandoned storefront. "Already done."

"Good. See you in thirty-six hours," he said without a backward glance, and walked toward the car.

Nervous, her stomach sick with worry, she hugged herself and moved toward where she and Harrison had planned to set up camp for the day. Before she reached the brick wall, the man who'd first approached the car was climbing into the back seat. Now she wished she could have brought her cell phone. She wanted to call Lola and let her know what was happening. But she'd left it with Cash, just as Harrison had left his with Lola, both of them deciding they hadn't wanted to carry anything worth being robbed for.

While five men gathered near the car, Harrison bent toward the opened, passenger side window. Hoping to appear inconspicuous, she took a seat against the wall and watched, waited. When Harrison glanced over his shoulder at her with narrowed eyes, she tensed. He looked back to the driver—a woman with long, bleached-blonde hair—stepped away from the Buick, then turned and walked toward her.

Crap, Madeline didn't pick him. At least they had the woman's plate number. Unless those were stolen, they could try and track her down that way.

As soon as Harrison neared her, she said, "Once she drives off—"

"She's leaving in one minute. With or without us."

Mel stood. "What? I don't understand."

"Her name is Madeline," he began. "She needs people to work on her house."

"It's the same story Bobby gave us."

"She saw me with you and asked who you were. I told her you were my wife and that I could use the money to help get us on our feet. She agreed to hire me, but only if *you* come along." The car horn honked. He gripped her hand. "We don't have to do this.

We have her license plate number."

"Which could be stolen."

"Cash will kill me."

He'd be furious with her, too. But she'd promised him this would be the last case she'd work for ATL, she hadn't promised how much she would involve herself with it. Then she pictured Noah, the way he'd mutilated his face. Pictured Bobby, grief-stricken over the loss of his friend. She glanced around, her gaze touching on the dozens of people near the shelter. There was no laughter or hope in their eyes, only despair. And this woman preyed on their misery.

Grabbing her backpack, she pushed off the ground. "Cash is a pussycat. I don't want to miss the opportunity to stop this woman." She took his hand. "We need to try and stay together as much as possible," she said as they approached the car.

"Madeline promised us a room together, plus meals and seventy-five dollars a day—each."

"I'll be sure to act excited about it. How long have we been married?"

"Two years. We went bankrupt three months ago and we're from the Orlando area, trying to make it up north to my brother's place."

Dang, Harrison had done a great job selling his story to Madeline. "Easy enough to remember," she said. When they reached the car, she gave Madeline what she hoped was a shy smile.

"Joining us?" the woman asked.

"Yes, ma'am. Thank you so much for hiring us," Mel said.

"Please call me Madeline. Harry said your name is Melanie?"

"Yes."

"Glad to meet you. Why don't you sit up front with me? We'll let the boys have the backseat."

Her fingers trembled as she reached for the door handle. She told herself not to worry. They only had to endure this woman and whatever she had in store for them for a day and a half. If

Cash had his say, maybe less. She and Harrison would have each other's back. They were both survivors and would come out of this unscathed.

Once she and Harrison were both seated, and the passenger window was closed, Madeline cranked up the AC, then shifted the sedan into DRIVE. "Melanie and Harrison, meet your other co-worker, Eliot."

Mel clicked her seatbelt in place and nodded to the man, who looked as if he'd been saved from a gator attack. If only Eliot knew the truth. Madeline wasn't his savior, she was Satan in a blonde wig.

"Eliot," Madeline began, "there's a small cooler at your feet. Open it up and hand Melanie and Harry a water bottle. I'll take one, too."

As Eliot did as she'd instructed, it took everything in Mel's power to not look back at Harrison. Not trusting Madeline, she didn't want to drink the water, even if it was clearly store bought, and her nerves had her mouth and throat dry.

"What's your house like?" Harrison asked.

Mel took the opportunity to look at him, but her gaze immediately dropped to the half empty bottle he held. She glanced to Eliot, who had drunk all of his water. She tested the cap of her bottle. Properly sealed. Still looking into the backseat, she scanned the cars behind them, looking for Cash's truck or Lola's rental car. Nothing.

"It's incredibly old," Madeline said, as she made a turn. "It was built over two hundred years ago." She grinned. "If the walls could talk, I'm sure they'd have tales to tell. Anyway, I inherited the plantation a few months ago. At first I was going to sell it, but I hated to let it out of the family. So, I decided to fix it and try to bring her back to what she used to be."

"I'm not a carpenter," Eliot said. "But I'm handy. My dad used to have a remodeling business and taught me how to frame in a wall, windows, closets."

"Excellent. I've recently discovered that the wooden beams in the attic rooms have dry rot and need to be replaced." She glanced to Mel. "Harry says you two have been married for two years? It's a shame about the bankruptcy. Fortunately, I haven't had to file, but there'd been plenty of lean years. It's why I came to Hope House. If someone hadn't taken a chance on me, I could have wound up homeless."

"It's terrible," Mel said.

"It sucks," Eliot added.

Madeline frowned. "I have no doubt. Since you were the first to come to my car, does that mean you've heard about me?"

Eliot nodded. "Yeah, I was jealous that you picked Noah and Troy. There were so many people standing around your car that day, you probably don't remember seeing me."

"I'm sorry, I don't. Should I assume Noah and Troy had good things to say about their boss?" Madeline asked with a grin.

Eliot shook his head. "They never came back to the shelter. I figured they were still working for you."

Her grin widened into a big smile. "Then that must mean they'd made enough money to keep from having to go back to living on the streets."

Eliot smiled, too. "I like the sound of that."

"Same here," Mel said, looking back to Harrison. "When we're done working for Madeline, we could have enough money to take a bus to your brother's."

"Your brother couldn't send you money?" Madeline asked as she drove past a small sign indicating they'd just entered Georgia.

"Mickey lives check to check," Harrison said, and Mel was glad he'd used his dead brother's name as part of their story. If they could stay close to the truth, there would be less of a chance at being caught in a lie. "But he has an extra room in his apartment and a job lined up for me."

"Well, I'm glad I can help all three of you," Madeline said. "We have another twenty minutes before we arrive. Since I plan on putting you to work right away, you might want to close your eyes and rest."

Eliot yawned, and did as Madeline had instructed. "I got shut out from the shelter the past few nights. I wouldn't complain if you had me sleeping in the car instead of a bed."

"Don't worry about that happening. I have plenty of room for you. You're going to think you're in a hotel. Comfy beds, and each bedroom even has a TV."

"I've missed TV," Eliot said, his head lulling to the side.

As he finished his water, Harrison looked at the man. "Eliot's got the right idea. The heat is draining," he said, resting his head back. Within seconds, his eyes were closed and he was snoring.

"I swear, Harry can zonk out just about anywhere," Mel said, concerned that both men had fallen asleep so quickly. Could Madeline have drugged the water? Her cap had been properly sealed and even Madeline had asked for a bottle. She hadn't opened it, though.

"I wish I could be like Harry," Madeline said. "But I'm a creature of habit and need my favorite pillow. I'm sorry. That sounded terrible, especially since you and your husband have been forced from your home." She glanced at Mel. "If you'd prefer something other than water, I have a couple of cans of soda in the cooler."

"That's okay. I'm not thirsty right now. I'll save the water for later."

"Don't worry about me putting you to work the moment we arrive. I'm sure you'd all like something to eat." Madeline turned down an unpaved road. "I'll make us sandwiches while I divvy up everyone's jobs."

Mel hid her panic. She'd grown up in the swamps and was familiar with many parts of the Glades. But now she was entering unfamiliar territory and terrified Madeline had somehow spiked their waters. "Are we close to your house?"

Madeline nodded. "You're going to love how peaceful it is in the country. Later, after you're done with your jobs, you and your husband should take a walk on the property. There're a few spots that I think are very romantic."

Mel studied Madeline's profile. The wig was horrible. If the woman had been going for unassuming, she'd failed. People would remember the big bleach-blonde curls. Plus, the hair color didn't match Madeline's olive complexion and dark eyebrows. With plump lips, a pretty smile and intriguing green eyes, Mel would bet that once Madeline's natural hair was showing, she would be a very beautiful woman.

"It *has* been a long time since Harry and I have been able to be alone," Mel said, keeping up with the charade Madeline was playing. "It'd be nice to take a long walk with him and not have to worry about stepping over a homeless man, or being afraid of running into some of the thugs we've seen in Frenchtown."

"I know there are bad seeds throughout that area. With as pretty as you are, I can only imagine how worried Harry must've been for your safety."

"I think I'll feel better about myself after a long shower," Mel said, staring out the windshield. "Is that your house?"

Madeline slowed the car to a stop. "Grand, isn't it? From here, it's stately and beautiful. You can't see the cracks in its foundation, the rotting front porch, the missing shingles. Sometimes I'll walk to around this point and stare at the house for long hours, imagining what it had once been, and what it could be again."

Mel had never seen a house as big as Madeline's. The gigantic white columns dominated the front porch and commanded respect. She loved the Juliet balcony off the second floor, and could picture a Southern Belle, dressed for her cotillion ball, gazing down as horse-drawn carriages made their way along the winding drive. While Mel couldn't see anything wrong with the house, other than a yard that needed tending, she knew what the woman had meant. In her gut, she knew that the house's grand beauty hid something disturbing. Something that had compelled Noah to claw at his face. She looked to Madeline…some*one* who was using humans for experimentation.

She could suspect and speculate all she wanted, but without proof, Madeline would not be stopped. Now she and Harrison had less than thirty-six hours to obtain that proof.

"Regardless of the repairs your house needs, I still think it's beautiful." Mel turned, then reached in the back and gave Harrison's knee a shake. "Honey, wake up. We're here." Harrison's head fell forward, before he slumped against the window. Alarmed, she shook his knee again. "Harry, wake up. I need you to see the house," she said when she really needed him alert and ready to take on whatever Madeline had in store for them.

Madeline let out a wistful sigh. "If only you drank the goddamn water."

Mel stiffened. To hell with thirty-six hours, she had the water bottle as proof. She fisted the hand she'd used to try and wake Harrison, then swung it toward Madeline. She connected with the woman's chin, just as Madeline stabbed a needle into Mel's arm.

The puncture mark burned. Mel pulled the syringe from her upper arm. Before she could turn it on Madeline or reach for the small switchblade hidden in her sock, the woman opened the car door and stumbled onto the ground. She tore the wig from her head, revealing a mass of dark hair, then rubbed her chin with her knuckle. "I'm going to enjoy breaking you and your husband," she said, her voice becoming tinny as vertigo set in, making Mel's head spin.

"What did you give us?" Mel asked, her arms and legs becoming heavy, her neck too weak to hold her head straight.

"The boys got your run-of-the-mill sleeping potion. You, my dear, were lucky enough to get a taste of one of my own creations. It's a little something I like to call A-Line. This first dose is going to knock your pretty ass out for a while and give you freakishly entertaining nightmares. But the next dose is when the fun stuff starts happening." She climbed back into the car, then grabbed Mel by the hair and forced her head back. "So much fun," she said, cupping Mel's breast.

Unable to work her muscles and push Madeline's hand away, Mel endured her touch. "I'm going to kill you," she managed, her words slow, slurred.

Madeline grinned. "That's what they all say. Now take a nap.

We have a long night ahead of us," she said, then slammed Mel's head against the passenger window.

As the world faded to black, Melanie prayed to God Cash had forced Lola to take immediate action. Otherwise, they'd end up like Noah…dead.

Lola's Hotel Room, Tallahassee, Florida
Monday, 2:43 p.m. Eastern Daylight Saving Time

"I DON'T CARE about what your boss wants," Cash said, shoving his hands into the pockets of his jeans to keep from plowing his fists into the wall. "My wife is now in danger."

Lola looked up from the laptop. "We've already been over this. We have a lock on Harrison's GPS signal. Once we can verify where they are, we'll leave."

"If they get split up, that won't do us any good."

The Russian punched his hand with his fist. "Vlad say storm building."

"I'm with Vlad. You didn't see what Noah looked like. I don't want them giving Mel whatever they gave him. The man clawed his face. Are you hearing me?"

"Oh, I'm hearing you loud and clear. And for the record, Harrison is like a brother to me. I care about both him and Mel." She let out a breath and looked away. "I don't know why Mel got in the car, but she did. So we need to put our emotions and concerns aside, and focus on finding out who we're dealing with before we take action."

"Vlad still say storm building."

"Heard you the first time," Lola said, glancing back to the computer screen. "First we need to know where this building is."

With Noah's face still seared on his brain, Cash turned away. He didn't want to sit in Lola's room and *investigate*. He wanted to take action and worry about the danger later. He wanted his wife home. And once she was safe, he planned to give her all kinds of hell. She'd seen Noah, knew how the man had died, and had been well aware that they were dealing with people who were possibly running experiments on humans. Why would she purposefully place herself in danger? Was this her way of having the last word again? Another one of her tit for tat moments? She'd promised to leave ATL. Promised her involvement with this case would be minimal. He sure as hell never made a promise he couldn't keep. Now he wondered if she'd go back on her word and do other jobs for the agency.

"Okay," Lola began, "Harrison hasn't moved for at least ten minutes. We know they're in Bower, Georgia. Let's pull the exact location up on satellite." Her fingers moved across the keyboard. "I might be doing something wrong. Hang tight, I'm going to make a call." She picked up her cell phone. Within seconds, she was asking a woman named Rachel for advice. "Hang on, I'm going to put you on speaker." Lola set the phone on the table she'd been using as a desk. "Rachel Davis is on the line. She's CORE's computer forensic analyst. She's more familiar with this program than I'll ever be." She pressed on the phone screen. "Rachel, I have Cash, who's Mel's husband and Vlad with me."

"Ouch," Rachel said. "I bet Mel jumping in the car with Harrison isn't going over well with hubby."

"Uh, no. And you're on speaker," Lola reminded the woman.

"Right. Sorry. Okay, what you're looking at is the roof of a big ass house. If you go under file preferences, you can change your settings and be able to get the address."

Lola drummed her fingers on the table. "Can't you do that for us?"

"It'd probably be easier, huh?" Rachel's tapping echoed in the small hotel room. "I've got the address as 1113 Archer Lane, Bower, Georgia."

Cash pulled the truck keys from his pocket. "Good enough, let's go."

Lola glared at him. "We need to know who we're dealing with first."

"You might want to listen to Lola on this," Rachel said. "The recent report from the lab even had a couple of our agents here saying they wouldn't have gone undercover."

Unease crawled under his skin. He stared at Lola. "What recent report?"

"Oh, geez." Rachel sighed. "Sorry, Lola. I thought your people knew."

"How could they when I got the report the same time Madeline showed?" She smoothed a hand over her hair, then tightened her ponytail. She looked between him and Vlad. "Rachel was able to get the PET scan they did on Noah before he died. Whatever drug he'd been given damaged his brain—mainly the anterior insular cortex."

"Vlad no brain surgeon. Explain."

"I'm not a brain surgeon, either," Rachel said. "But here's how I understand it. This part of the brain is identified to be the source of a person's empathy, you know, their compassion for others. Noah's anterior insular cortex was completely black. Which is a similarity to people who have been diagnosed with autism, borderline personality disorder, schizophrenia." She cleared her throat. "Even worse, the entire frontal and temporal lobes of Noah's brain—which are linked to not only empathy, but morality and self-control—showed zero activity."

"Meaning?" Cash asked.

"Assuming Noah had normal brain function before being drugged, whatever he was given turned him into a psychopath. Whether it was temporary or not, we'll never know."

"How can you back this up?" He was a mechanic. Cars, he understood. Brains?

"There've been studies done on the brains of serial killers. In every case, they all exhibited the same brain deficiency. That being said, not every person with psychopathic tendencies is a killer."

"What would happen if a person already has these tendencies and is given this drug?" Lola asked.

"That was something I wondered, too. I made a few calls and each source told me that the drug could possibly work more quickly on those individuals than on someone with normal brain function."

Cash shook his head. "This is fucked up."

"Extremely," Rachel said. "Because if the drug is what caused the deficiency in Noah's brain, then this means whoever lives in that big ass house is creating psychopaths. Whether it's intentional or not, that's for you three to discover."

The worry in Lola's eyes heightened his own fears. Madeline—whoever the woman was—would not have the chance to scramble Mel's brain. If her intent was to create a killer, he'd gladly give her what she wanted...without the drug.

All she had to do was mess with his wife.

PART IV

*"Even psychopaths have emotions. Then
again, maybe not."*
—Richard Ramirez

CHAPTER 16

The House of Archer, Bower, Georgia
Monday, 3:29 p.m. Eastern Daylight Saving Time

S*HE'S DEAD.*
   Rodney paced the hallway in front of Adeline's bedroom. Imagined curling his hands around her throat. Watching the life drain from her eyes. Her breath leaving her body.

The door swung open. He crowded her at the threshold. She showed no intimidation. Instead, her lips tilted in a mocking smile. He didn't know whether to wipe it off her face with his fist, or his mouth.

He backhanded her, knocking her into the door. Before she could react, he took her by the arms and threw her on the bed. Her eyes wide, her hands fisted, she swung at him. He caught her by the wrist, pinned her against the mattress and kissed her. Tasted her blood, her anger, her vibrancy. He could never kill her. He couldn't live without her. He couldn't live with anyone *but* Adeline. From the moment Gramma had left for Arizona, he'd changed. Or maybe he'd been a violent bastard all along. Like his father, like his grandfather. Like all the Archer men.

He kissed her harder, gripped her breast, then pinched her nipple. Maybe he'd been suppressing his thirst for inflicting pain. Now that he and Adeline were alone in the house, and no longer under Gramma's watchful eye, he'd had the freedom to explore and act on the gratuitous, lustful and cruel thoughts in his head. Was that how it was for Adeline? Had she been wired to not give a shit about suppressing anything? Did she even give a shit about him?

He broke the kiss, then moved off of her. "Bitch," he said, wiping her blood from his mouth. "You say you love me, that you care about me, but you don't. I think you like hurting me, just like you like hurting everyone around you. And I was stupid enough to believe you could at least feel love for me." He shook his head. "I won't leave. I won't force you to leave. Instead, I'm going to chain you to your bed."

She scooted across the bed until she was seated at the edge of the mattress, and gave him another one of her sexy, mocking smiles. "Will I be naked? Will you use me whenever you want?"

The image of her naked and at his disposal filled his head, and hardened his dick. "You're a bitch."

"I heard you the first time. But this bitch brought you a present."

"Three new subjects to kill. How thoughtful." After spending all morning digging Jim's grave, he'd decided he was finished experimenting. He wasn't even sure if his drug could fix Adeline. Who the hell was he to play God and try to manipulate the warped brain she'd been given? Even if his drug worked, who would believe him? His career was tainted. He'd been compared to Nazi doctors who'd experimented on the Jews. He was ruined. The only thing he could count on at this point in his life was his love and hatred for Adeline.

"Unless you're blind, you had to notice the woman. We did agree that we should experiment on a female subject, did we not?"

"That was before our subjects started dying."

She rolled her eyes. "Only one died. You murdered the other one."

"For you."

Her eyes softened. "I know," she said quietly. "And I brought the woman for you." She held up a hand. "Yes, as one of our subjects, but I also thought you might want to experiment with someone other than me."

He shoved a hand through his hair. "You want me to have sex

with the woman? I think you've finally lost your mind." He didn't want another woman. God help him, he wanted Adeline.

"But you've only been with me."

"What does that matter?" he asked, then narrowed his eyes as jealousy burned a path along his chest. "This is about Liam. Give me the girl you brought, then maybe I'll let you have him, right?"

She tossed her hands in the air. "Forget it."

"I won't forget it. Tell me the truth. You want that man." He quickly rushed toward her and gripped her upper arms. "Admit it."

"If I wanted another man, I would have left you years ago. Instead I've humiliated myself, begging you to have sex with me." She struggled to free herself. "If you don't want to have fun with the girl, or for *us* to have fun with her, then just drug her and move on with the experiment. Gramma's going to be home before we know it, and then we'll be back to dealing with the old bag again."

A sense of urgency rushed through him. He didn't want to go back to the days before Gramma had left. The old woman knew Adeline was a murderer. She was always watching, waiting, insinuating herself in their lives and making them miserable. While they'd had heated moments since Gramma had been away, Adeline had also showed her softer side. A side he hadn't seen from her in years.

He gave her a shake. "You wouldn't be jealous if I had sex with the woman?"

"Of course I would. I love you. I love knowing no one else has experienced what I've had with you."

"I won't rape the woman. But I will drug her." He let go of her. "I've already doubled Liam's dosage for today. Tomorrow we're skipping the placebo and going straight for *my* drug. No more A-Line."

Her eyes narrowed. "That could kill him."

Good. "He's going to die anyway. I also plan on skipping the initial testing phase on the three you brought home today. Since you gave the woman a small dose, and she hasn't reacted any differently than our previous subjects, she should be fine. As for the men, I don't care how they react." He turned away and started for the door. When he stepped into the hallway, he looked back at her. "There will be no other test subjects. By the end of the week, the experiments will be through. If my drug works, fantastic. If not, you *will* help me bury them in the barn."

With concern in her eyes, she took several steps forward. "And then what? We'll still have three weeks before Gramma comes home."

He approached her, then pressed his hand between her thighs. "I'm sure we can find something to do." He moved his hand to her breast. "Are you going to stay in your room, or do you plan to help me prep the subjects?"

Her eyes glittered with defiance and desire. "I'd be happy to help, doctor. Which subject shall I prep for you?"

"Take the woman. She doesn't have a penis for you to hold."

SHE DOESN'T HAVE *a penis for you to hold.*

Rodney could kiss her ass. She didn't need a penis to have fun, just a playmate—willing or not.

Adeline reached the second floor landing. Rodney stood at the stairs leading to the attic rooms, but faced her, his arms crossed over his chest. "If you finish with the woman before I'm done in the attic, wait for me. I don't want you alone with the other man."

"Yes, doctor."

The one corner of his mouth turned up in an irresistible smirk, before he turned his back and headed up the stairs. She watched him go, and wondered how Liam was dealing with the double dosage. Based on both her and Rodney's studies of the brain, she was fully aware of what hers lacked. In theory, A-Line should take a normal brain and make it just like hers. If that were the case, what would A-Line do to a schizophrenic? People with the illness were already wired wrong. No, they weren't psycho-pathic, but they had psychotic episodes and lacked the empathy necessary to be considered *normal*. Liam was clearly schizophrenic. If she worked him the right way, she could possibly train him to be under her control, listen to only her voice. Or, he could snap and try to kill them all.

She would have to watch out for Rod. While the idea of creat-ing her very own monster to do her bidding was appealing, she would kill Liam if he dared to harm Rodney.

Pushing Liam and Rod from her mind, she opened the door to Melanie's room, the same room where Rodney had killed Troy. The pretty blonde lay flat on the bed. Since they only had the two adjustable beds in the attic rooms, and because of the way Noah had been able to escape by breaking the chair, they'd had no choice but to bind her to a regular bed. Gramma's bed.

"How are you feeling?" Adeline asked as she closed the door.

Melanie slowly rotated her head toward her. "I'm going to kill you," she said, her words more coherent than twenty minutes ago, but still slightly slurred.

"You're repeating yourself."

"I'm making my point clear."

"Still, you should come up with a new way to threaten some-one. Like: *I'm going to slit your throat.* Or, *I'm going to strangle you.* Maybe, *I'm going to bash in your skull.* I prefer the *slit your throat* line. I actually did that once. Oops, almost forgot. I bashed some-one's skull in, too."

Melanie moved her head and stared at the ceiling. "Aren't you scary."

"Sarcasm. How clever." She approached the woman, then bent close to her ear. "Just wait until you see how scary I truly am." She kissed Melanie's cheek. "Okay, sweetie, here's the deal. You're screwed. Plain and simple. If you don't remember, my name is Madeline. The strong, handsome man who carried you to this bed is Roderick. I'm trying to talk him into having sex with you, but he's not interested." She shook her head. "He has all kinds of moral standards. The good news—I don't. We'll have to save the good times for later. Rod will be down shortly to give you your dosage, and I need to have you prepped before I move on to Harry."

Tears slipped from Melanie's eyes and into her hair. "Why are you drugging us?"

She went into the closet, then took several pillows from the shelf. She had no intention of discussing the whys and hows with the woman. That was boring and, quite frankly, none of her business. Once she reached the bed again, she shoved the pillows beneath Melanie's head and upper back until the woman could have a clear view of the TV.

"Tell me why," Melanie sobbed.

"First, tell me how much you love your husband," she countered.

Melanie squeezed her eyes shut. "With every part of my mind, body and soul."

"Even though he couldn't support you and keep you from living on the street? So strange." After pulling on a pair of latex gloves, she picked up the duct tape from the nightstand. "This is going to be unpleasant," she said, slapping tape over the woman's mouth. "Very unpleasant." Adeline began wrapping the tape along the woman's forehead, and around the top pillow. Satisfied Melanie's head had been secured in place, she tore off a piece of surgical tape, captured a chunk of the woman's long eyelashes, then taped her eyelid open. Although annoyed by Melanie's muffled screams, she honestly couldn't blame the woman. How helpless she must feel. How vulnerable.

She grinned as she finished taping the other eyelid open. "Am I starting to get the teeniest bit scary?"

The woman fought against her restrains. Her eyes bulged with fear. She moaned and groaned as tears streaked down her face.

"Relax." Adeline turned on the television. "Enjoy some entertainment," she said, walking to the recording device. "Listen to this recording I made for you." When she hit PLAY, her voice filled the room.

As Melanie continued to cry, Adeline took care of her IV. Just as she checked to ensure that the proper amount of saline was going into the woman's veins, the bedroom door opened. "How's Eliot? Enjoying his first trip on the A-Line?"

"I wouldn't say that. He's understandably upset." Rodney approached the bed and looked down on Melanie. "But once he comes to terms with the drug and what it does, he'll relax. They all do. Is she ready?"

"All set." She grabbed his wrist before he reached for the syringe. "Are you sure you don't want to touch her? Aren't you curious to know what another woman's breasts feel like in your hand?"

"No. Are you?"

"I am." She rested her hand on Melanie's breast, then kneaded it. Boring. If she wanted to touch a tit or nipple, and gain any pleasure from it, she'd touch her own. "Mmm," she hummed anyway. "I can see why a woman might take pleasure in another woman's body." She removed her hand, and placed it on Rodney's erection. She grinned as she rubbed him through his jeans. "I think you liked that."

He knocked her hand away. "Enough. We still have the other subject to prep." He tapped Melanie's arm, then inserted the needle. After he removed it, he turned for the door.

"Wait, you only gave her half the dosage," she said.

"Because you gave her some earlier and she's *half* the size of our male subjects."

Since he made absolute sense, she didn't argue. After all, she didn't want Melanie a drooling basket case. For what Adeline had planned, she wanted the woman cognizant. Melanie claimed to love her husband with her mind, body and soul. She couldn't wait to test the lovebird. By the time she was through, Melanie wouldn't be thinking about her love for Harry, or even divorcing the man. She'd be thinking of ways to kill him.

TERROR TORE HER from the inside out, pierced her rapidly beating heart, scraped her brain to the point Melanie knew she was on the verge of losing her mind. Whatever drug they gave her again, it rushed through her body. The first time she'd been injected was nothing compared to what she was dealing with now. The rope around her wrists and ankles kept her immobile. The tape holding open her eyelids left her eyes burning. Being forced to watch gory videos and listen to that witch's voice was torturous. Made her stomach sick.

Poor Noah. Now she understood. Now she could see why the man had gone over the edge, far enough he'd gouged his own face. She didn't understand the point of the drug. When Madeline had shot it into her system while they'd been in the car, the drug had affected her body, her speech and had screwed with her thought process. She didn't know if the same thing wasn't happening because Roderick had only given her half of a dose, or because her body had become quickly accustomed to it. She only knew the couple scared the hell out of her.

Madeline was crazy. Certifiably so. Thank God she couldn't coerce Roderick into touching her. For now. She'd been in Madeline's presence for probably no more than two hours. Even if Lola was able to track the GPS chip implanted beneath Harrison's skin, too much could happen in the next thirty-four.

Tears stung her eyes. God, how she wanted to blink them away. How many others had suffered the same fate? How was Harrison handling what they were doing to him? How angry was Cash? When Madeline had asked how much she'd loved her husband, she'd told her the truth. She'd do anything for Cash. Right now, she wished she had quit ATL before agreeing to this case. Or, at the very least, had chosen *not* to go with the woman.

For the first time in her life, she had no hope. Not an ounce. Growing up poor was nothing in comparison to this short time in hell. Even then, she'd had hope, along with courage and strength.

At a young age she'd known that the only person who could change her course, was her. She didn't have to be swamp trash, she could be a lady. While her memories of her mom were sketchy, she'd never forget the time Mama had dressed up in a beautiful pink dress, elegant enough to be worn by a princess. She'd made it herself. Had spent months saving money for the material, then another month sewing the dress. There hadn't been enough material left to make one for Mel, but there'd been enough for Mama to create a small purse.

Tears stung her eyes. Instead of thinking about how it ached to not be able to blink them away, she focused on that tiny purse. Carefully wrapped in tissue paper, and safely stored in the closet Cash had made for her. In her mind, she unwrapped the paper, then opened the purse. There were the diamond earrings in it that had once belonged to her mother. Although the diamonds were real, they were so microscopic, she didn't know how they hadn't slipped from the prongs. She'd had them appraised once, and the jeweler about took a knife to the throat when he'd laughed at her.

She still didn't know what Daddy had paid for those earrings. Any time she'd asked him, he gave her a different number. But when she brought them up, a wistful smile would always cross his face, and he'd tell her all about the night he'd taken her mama out in the beautiful pink dress.

A sob tore through her as she remembered the second time Mama wore that dress. But she couldn't allow herself to think about her mama's funeral. She had to remind herself where she'd come from, that right now, only she could change her course. She had to maintain strength and courage.

Damn it, she had to keep hope alive in her heart. Because they were both stubborn and insecure, she and Cash had wasted two years of their lives together. Madeline and Roderick would not keep them apart. She had to believe that.

She stiffened.

The switchblade.

Oh, God. Please tell me they didn't take it.

They hadn't removed her shoes—a good sign. Had either of them frisked her while she'd been out cold? Holding her breath, she rolled her right ankle as much as the binding would allow, then half-laughed, half-cried when the small blade pressed into her lower calf. The hope she'd been searching for blossomed in her chest. She might be unable to reach the knife right now, but knowing it was there had her thoughts toppling over one another with ideas of what she could do once she had the blade in her hand.

All of those thoughts collided into one…killing Madeline.

Lola's Hotel Room, Tallahassee, Florida
Monday, 6:27 p.m. Eastern Daylight Saving Time

CASH CHECKED THE clock on the nightstand, and wished it was later. Lola had insisted that they not only find out everything they could about who occupied the Georgian plantation house, but that they wait until dark before making a rescue attempt. Instead of going after Mel like he'd wanted, he was stuck in the damned hotel room, impotent, frustrated and worried, his mind constantly straying to his wife and how she was doing. He understood why they were waiting, but he didn't have to like it. He was also glad they had Rachel helping them. Using the address they'd received from the GPS data, the CORE agent had researched the Bower County archives and had found the floor plan for the plantation home known as the House of Archer. To keep his mind somewhat occupied, he, along with Vlad and Lola, had been studying the layout of the house, along with its land, and coming up with a plan of attack for later that night.

Needing a break from the confining room, and something to drink, he stood. "I'm going to the vending machine. Want anything?" he asked Lola.

"I'm good," Lola said without looking up from the laptop.

He stepped out of the room. Vlad sat on the concrete, his back against the stucco wall, smoking a cigarette. The Russian looked up at him, then down at the pile of butts smashed into the concrete.

"Why everything bad?" Vlad asked.

"Everything isn't bad."

"Cigarette bad. Vlad like cigarette. Vodka bad. Vlad like Vodka. Food fry in oil bad. Vlad love that. Polina grow too big and kill Vlad. Vlad love gator." He looked up at him again. "Everything Vlad love is bad."

"Women aren't bad."

"Vlad love of life bad. Misty take bat to Vlad car, smash Vlad phone."

"Sounds like you just need a new woman."

The Russian pulled out another cigarette, then shoved it back in the pack. "Could Repo Man leave Mel for new woman?"

"We don't have a bad relationship. She doesn't take a bat to my truck or smash my phone."

"This true. Ice Cream Lady not violent."

Cash sat against the column across from Vlad. "Mel has a temper on her. She likes to push and shove. She's badass with a knife, but I know she'd rather throw it at targets than people."

He cocked a brow. "Vlad would hope. Vlad have knowledge of knife wound."

"You've been cut?"

The Russian chuckled. "No. Vlad have made many of cut." He shrugged. "Two have died—the rest only wound of the flesh."

"You're fucking with me, right?"

"Why Vlad lie about such things?"

"Okay, so you're telling me you've killed two people with a knife."

"That what Vlad say. Understand, Vlad a lover, not a killer." He shrugged. "But, when Russian mafia own Vlad...Vlad have no choice."

Cash had no idea what to do with this man, or what to believe.

"No choice is bad," the Russian continued.

"Yeah, back to the *everything is bad* deal—who's Polina and what does she have to do with a gator?"

"Polina *is* gator. Vlad's pet. Did not Repo Man hear Harry crybaby over Polina?"

He chuckled and shook his head. "I heard something about it, but blew it off because I thought the way you two were fighting was stupid."

Vlad narrowed his eyes. "Vlad Russian heavyweight—"

Cash held up a hand. "I'm not talking about *physically* fighting. But for the record, if I was living in the same house as you, I wouldn't crybaby about your gator, I'd get it the hell out of my house. Harrison has a lot more patience than I ever would. And, you're right. If you don't get rid of it, it'll—at the very least—rip off your arm."

The Russian hung his head. "Vlad know such things."

Cash looked to the hotel room door, willed it to open, and for Lola to tell them it was go-time. He wasn't good with heart to heart conversations. With Mel he did okay. But he loved her. He thought about the part of the brain that makes people empathetic toward others. He had it. He just didn't like to deal with other peoples' emotions. It didn't mean he didn't have sympathy for them if they were down. Like now...Vlad was down about Harrison. Instead of focusing on his fears for his friend, the Russian was lumping his troubles together. His therapist would tell Vlad this behavior was unhealthy and self-destructive. That he needed to pour his energy into what was really bothering him.

"Vlad, you're scared for your friend, not about losing your arm to a gator," he said, because he was no therapist. "Keep your mind on the real shit bothering you, and try to figure out a way to get it to *stop* bothering you."

Vlad stared at him. "Repo Man very wise. This true. Vlad fear for Harry. Vlad also wish..." He heaved a deep sigh. "Vlad say bad thing to Harry. What if Vlad never see friend again?"

"You're gonna see him. Don't think like that. When you do, end the fight between you two."

He nodded. "That mean Vlad cannot smoke." He tossed the cigarettes onto the cement. "Polina also must go. It break Vlad heart."

If the Russian started crying, he was out of there. "I get it, man. I love my dog. Maybe that's what you need. Set Polina free into the Glades where she belongs and adopt a dog."

"Vlad partial to chee-chee-wa-wa."

"Chee-chee…do you mean, Chihuahua?"

"да. Chee-chee-wa-wa. That what Vlad say."

Cash tried to picture Vlad with a tiny dog, but couldn't. A man Vlad's size needed a big dog to match. "What about a Great Dane?"

"Like Scooby-Doo?" Vlad shook his head. "Man-size dog leave man-size poopy."

The Russian knew how to take a conversation and make it uncomfortable. "I'm going to the vending machine. Need anything?"

"Vlad have made offense?"

"No, man. It's weird to hear a guy say 'poopy'."

Frowning, Vlad stood. "What that mean? Does Repo Man question Vlad's manliness? Would Vlad sound like tough guy if Vlad say shit?"

Cash held up a hand. "I am in no way questioning your manliness. I apologize."

He gave Cash a nod. "Vlad let it slip under couch."

"You let what slip under the couch."

The Russian rolled his eyes. "Repo Man insult to Vlad. Vlad let it slip under couch."

"Good," he said, still confused. "So do you want something from the vending machine?"

"Vlad have Hershey bar."

As he made his way to the vending machine, his thoughts drifted to Mel. His strange conversation with Vlad had given his mind a short break from reality. Once he had a Coke and chocolate bar in hand, and neared the hotel room, reality quickly returned.

Lola held the door open, as Vlad walked into her room. She met his gaze, and he didn't like the anxiety in her eyes. He quickened his pace. "What's wrong?"

"With Rachel's help, I found out who else is living in the plantation house."

Earlier they'd discovered Florence Archer, a seventy-eight-year-old widow, owned the home. None of them believed Florence to be Madeline. Although he still had yet to see the woman, Bobby had claimed Madeline was in her twenties or thirties. That didn't mean Florence wasn't involved, but it had led them to assume there were others working with or for her. Or, the woman was dead and someone was using her house.

He stepped into the room, and tossed Vlad the chocolate. "Who?" he asked, once she closed the door.

"Her grandson." Lola moved to the table, then turned the laptop in his and Vlad's direction. "Meet Dr. Rodney Archer."

Without opening the Coke, Cash set it on the nightstand. His stared at the *Time* magazine cover, which displayed a picture of a man who could have been posing for *GQ* or an ad for expensive clothes, and moved toward the laptop. Unease balled in the pit of his stomach as he drifted his gaze from the man's photo, to the Nazi swastika splashed along his forehead, to the caption below the man's face. *Dr. Rodney Archer: The Modern Mengele.*

"Please tell Vlad this all mistake."

"You know who Joseph Mengele is?" Lola asked.

"Vlad was not born under rock. Дед fought in war."

"English, please."

"Grandfather. Vlad дед with Soviet troops who liberate Auschwitz. Vlad have love for history. Good and bad. Mengele very bad man who experimented on prisoners." He shook his head and ripped the wrapper off the chocolate bar. "Mengele have decide fate of prisoners. Jews go into Auschwitz, none come out. Same for Poles, Gypsies, Soviet POWs. Vlad have seen many things. Vlad have done things that would make Дед sad. But Vlad never want to see what Дед did in 1945."

Cash stared at the man. Less than ten minutes ago, Vlad claimed he wanted a Chihuahua and used the term 'poopy'. Now he was giving them a history lesson.

"I'm glad your grandfather survived," Lola said. "Life wouldn't be the same without you."

The Russian's ears and face reddened.

"Did you read the magazine article?" Cash asked, keeping the focus on Archer.

"I did. About five years ago, Dr. Archer developed a drug that he claimed would target the part of the brain where psychopaths are deficient."

The unease in the pit of his stomach traveled north, lodging in his chest. "The drug used on Noah can't be a coincidence."

"Agreed. Anyway, the U.S. government had taken an interest in the drug, and allowed the pharmaceutical company Dr. Archer worked for to use federal inmates as human guinea pigs. Supposedly, the prisoners consented. Since each man who took the drug is now dead, we will never know."

"Why would government allow such thing?" Vlad asked.

Lola shrugged. "Think about it. If there were a drug out there that could remove all psychopathic tendencies from an individual, in theory, violent crimes would become nonexistent, and war and terrorism would be a thing of the past. Of course, I'm not sure how the government would go about getting the drug into our enemies' bodies, or even in the guy in the room next to mine."

"Does not government allow fluoride in water?" Vlad asked.

"I don't want to even think about our government conspiring to taint our water with a drug to control our levels of activities." Frowning, Lola rubbed her head. "Back to Archer...he went to the prison, then administered the drug to five men. After forty-eight hours, with the men showing no sign that they'd been affected by the drug, they were released from the clinic and placed back in their cells. Within twenty-four hours, each man had committed suicide, but not before killing two prison guards and seven inmates."

"Were they able to explain the delayed reaction?" Cash asked.

She shook her head. "Dr. Archer claimed that the experiments he ran from his lab had never seen these results."

"Who was he experimenting on from his lab?"

"According to the article, the pharmaceutical company posted ads in the paper and online for people who had been diagnosed with schizophrenia, since that illness causes slightly similar brain deficiency."

Infected with worry, Cash's hand trembled as he picked up the can of Coke. Before he hurled it at the wall, he cracked open the can and took a long drink. He'd allowed his wife to go into a house where a mad scientist lived. No, she *chose* to go with the woman. The woman…

"Can you explain Madeline?" he asked.

"Not yet. Maybe she's his assistant or girlfriend."

"We don't need a maybe, we need confirmation." He looked to Vlad. "We need to go to the plantation house and get Mel and Harrison out of there."

Lola's lips slid into a grim line. "Look, I'm just finding out about Rodney Archer. Rachel's looking into everything she can find on the man. Before you and Vlad storm the building, we need to know exactly who we're dealing with and if they are dangerous. Two of my people are already at risk. I won't do anything without thinking this through or having a plan."

"Vlad wonder, this drug Archer make…it same or different from drug in Noah?"

"Thank you for bringing that up," she said. "While you two were outside, Ian, Rachel and I talked about this. We all think it's interesting that Archer's original drug had been developed to stimulate the psychopath's inactive part of the brain, and yet the drug used on Noah did the exact opposite. I'm wondering why Archer would go from one extreme to the other."

"What happened to him after he'd been accused of being no better than Mengele?"

"His career was obviously ruined. Because the pharmaceutical company was held solely responsible, and Archer was merely an employee, he never faced criminal charges. Several civil suits were brought against him, but none of them made it to court."

"So he got away with murder," Cash said, then finished the Coke.

"*He* didn't murder anyone. The drug he'd administered somehow had an adverse effect."

"Well, what if Archer is a psychopath? He wants to hurt people, but doesn't want to go to prison for it. So he makes a drug that causes people to become like him, they kill—unknowingly— for him, and he still gets off on the thrill."

She stared at him for a moment before shaking her head. "That's ridiculous," she said, her tone unconvincing. "Archer isn't Frankenstein."

Although she was right, he had no other explanation. "Really? Then why dope up homeless people with a drug that can turn them into monsters?"

"Vlad have theory. Archer make drug to help psychopath, but fail. Archer laughingstock, no?" He pointed to the *Time* magazine cover. "Vlad would not want associate with Nazi doctor. What if Archer feel same? What if Archer make drug to make killer so Archer can fix him?"

"That's an awesome theory, man." Cash looked to Lola. "Vlad nailed it. *That* makes sense."

"In a very strange way." She tightened her ponytail. "If Vlad's theory is right, and I hope he's wrong, then Rodney Archer and Madeline—whoever she is—are going to try and turn Mel and Harrison into psychopaths." She picked up her cell phone. "I'm calling Ian. Thirty-six hours could be too late."

Finally. Although relieved they were going to take action, Cash couldn't shake the unease. What if they didn't stop Archer in time? Did the drug have lasting side effects? Would his wife go from being a passionate, loving woman to a cold-hearted killer?

Lola ended the call. "Do you own a gun?" she asked him.

"In a lockbox mounted under the backseat of my truck. My concealed carry permit is in the glove box."

"Good. We'll still leave at dark. By then, we'll hopefully have more information on Archer and who might be working with him."

He didn't want to wait until then. Too many things could happen to Mel. He knew where the house was located. He had a gun. He could drive there right now and take his wife out of there.

Hell, that was how he handled his repo business. He went in, took what he wanted, then hauled ass.

And he'd almost lost his life because he'd been too stupid to go in with backup. When he'd been in the Army, he'd never go on patrol without Dolly. Now that he thought about it, Dolly had been the only partner—next to Mel—he'd counted on, and his dog had lost her legs saving his life. His therapist popped in his head, and Cash remembered a session they'd had earlier this year. The man had asked him why he was afraid of depending on anyone. He'd thought the question stupid. He depended on Jude to help take care of the garage, and on Sully, Pete and Ross to do their jobs.

Later that evening, when he was helping Dolly from the pool, he'd thought about what the therapist had asked him, and about the honest answer he should have given him. He was afraid someone would be hurt or killed trying to help him. Dolly had lost her legs in war. The repo business wasn't even comparable to war, but there were plenty of dangers and unknown factors with each job. What if he took Sully with him on a job, and a frickin' nutter pulled a gun out and killed his buddy? Better him than Sully. He couldn't feel guilt if he were dead.

He glanced to Lola, then Vlad. Both were in front of the laptop, looking at the file Rachel must have just sent. They were good people, with the same goal in mind. Remove Mel and Harrison from the house, and stop Archer from killing or hurting anyone else. He could understand why Mel was loyal to them. He needed to be, too. He needed to trust them, and his gut. Trust that Mel was strong enough to handle whatever she was enduring.

Even if the not knowing was killing him inside.

CHAPTER 17

The House of Archer. Bower, Georgia
Monday, 7:21 p.m. Eastern Daylight Saving Time

ADELINE UNBUTTONED THE top four buttons of her white blouse, then spread the material aside to reveal her abundant cleavage. After giving her neck a spritz of the perfume Rodney had given her for her birthday, she used her fingers to give her thick curls added volume. She applied a small amount of lip-gloss, then stepped in front of the full-length mirror. Turning to the side, she eyed the ultra-short, denim cut-offs, and the way they exposed plenty of leg and a hint of her ass. She faced the mirror, then decided to tie the bottom of her blouse in a knot to bare her belly. The effect was perfectly sexy and slutty, especially since she wasn't wearing a bra. Rodney would love seeing her nipples poking through the material, along with all of her tanned skin.

She slid her hand between her thighs and rubbed herself. He'd promised to have sex with her after they'd finished prepping the subjects. He'd made her come with his mouth instead. While that had been fine, she'd wanted a good hard fucking—which was just another reason why the female subject didn't appeal to her. The woman was missing important parts. Unfortunately, the damned clinic where Rodney worked had called to see if he could come in for a few hours to cover for one of the doctors who'd taken ill. To keep up the ruse of the caring country doc, Rod had agreed— leaving her all by herself.

Leaving her time to play.

She left her room, then went up the stairs. When she reached the second floor landing, she debated how to handle the married couple. She could free Liam, and use him to control the woman, but Liam might not appreciate her plans for Harrison. With Liam on her mind, she climbed the steps to the attic. When she opened his door, his sole focus was on the TV. She glanced to the screen, then she let out a chuckle, drawing his attention.

"That's not a real snuff film," she said. "Even I'm not crazy enough to buy that kind of crap off the Internet." She eyed the erection straining beneath his pants. "How are you feeling?"

When he grunted, she tore the tape from his mouth. "The voices," he panted, and looked past her to the TV. "They're driving me crazy."

"I told you what to do. Think of only me. Hear only my voice. Let the drug break you free from them."

His face contorted in rage. "Don't you think I've tried? I picture you in here, on top of me, blow-ng me…damn it," he shouted. "You know what they're saying now? They're telling me I should do what I'm watching. They want me to rape. They want me to rape *you*." A tear slipped down his cheek. "I'm not a rapist. I'm better than that. Better than this and you, and Roderick the dick."

"Ssh." She picked up a hand towel from the table and wiped the sweat and tears from his face. Damn, was she good. The voices would take Liam over the edge of no return. He would be cold, heartless. There would be no more tears. Ever. He would take what he wanted with premeditation and without thought for others. While Rod's formula might fix him, and make it so he could function in society without thoughts of rape or murder, she wondered if there would be permanent damage to Liam's brain. A-Line had been designed for a normal brain, not a schizophrenic's. She supposed it didn't matter. She had no intention of allowing Rod to give Liam his drug. She had the man right where she'd wanted him. Liam relied on her, and she needed to keep it that way. Given the chance, she wanted to send her creation off into the world and see what kind of damage he could do.

She set the towel aside and gripped his erection through his pants. Hard. "You can't rape me when all I've been thinking about is having sex with you again."

He groaned. "Please. I need release. I'll do anything." His mouth twisted into a sneer. "Don't make me beg. If you do, you'd better pray to God I'm never free."

She let go of him, then widened the opening of her blouse until the air touched her nipples. "You're in no position to threaten me." She traced her areola. "I'm curious…if I brought you another woman, what would you do?"

"Take her."

"Just like that. You don't care that she could be someone's mom, sister, wife?"

"No."

"Do the voices agree?"

"Yes. I'm warning you. Stop teasing me, or I will make you pay."

God, she loved screwing with him. She also loved that the voices were no longer acting as his conscience or making him paranoid. "Again with the threats?" She shook her head. "Promises, promises," she said with a grin, and fixed her shirt. "I'm going to check up on the rest of our guests. While I'm gone I want you to think about something. I want you to give me a reason why I should talk Rod into setting you free, and how you can prove your loyalty to me. If you can tell me all of that, I'll climb on your big cock and go for a ride. If not, then I'm going to have to allow Rod to handle you the way he wants. And I'd hate for that to happen." She slapped the tape over his mouth, then left the room.

Ignoring Eliot's door, she headed back to the second level. Eliot, according to Rodney, had been the model subject thus far. He'd easily taken to A-Line, had quickly showed psychopathic signs, and had shared horrible thoughts and ideas with Rodney. Because Eliot was young and healthy, his body had been able to handle the high doses he'd been given. Too bad she wasn't attracted to him. He could have been just as fun as Liam.

Rodney's treatment of their subjects had become surprisingly erratic. He'd decided to cram as much A-Line into Eliot without causing the man to overdose—because he could, and because he'd wanted to see what would happen. Yet, he hadn't done the same to Harry. He'd given Harry more than what he would have ever given their first few subjects—two full doses on day one. As for Melanie, he'd stuck with the one dose only, explaining that he'd wanted to make sure he had treated the female right. After all, the entire point of the experiment was to come up with a way to fix her.

Adeline wondered if Rodney had a clue that in trying to fix her, he'd been slowly unraveling, revealing his inner psychopath one day at a time. With that happy thought in mind, she opened the door to Harry's room. The man was attractive, and so different from both Rodney and Liam. Darker in color than Liam, yet lighter than Rod. Fascinating hazel eyes, thick hair she could pull on while she rode him. He wasn't meaty like Liam, but still thinner than Rod. He certainly didn't have skinny noodle arms. Yes, she could see why Melanie found him attractive. But for how long?

"How are you feeling, Harry?"

He shifted his gaze from the TV and glared at her.

She walked over to the bed, then ripped the tape from his mouth. "Are you enjoying the A-Line?"

"Where's my wife?"

"Would you like to see her?"

"Now," he said with a sneer.

"Awfully demanding. Tell me how you're feeling first?"

"I hate you. I'd like to see you and Roderick die slow, painful deaths."

She chuckled. "Excellent. Now you hang tight. I'm going to give you and Melanie a chance to reunite. But you have to make me a promise. You can't tell Roderick. If you do, I will kill Melanie. Understood?"

"What will happen to you if I tell?"

She thought about it for a moment, and honestly didn't know. Rod had hurt her after she'd helped Liam urinate, and she wasn't sure how much pain he would inflict if he knew she was having sex with their subjects. "Forget about seeing Melanie. I'll allow one of our other subjects the conjugal visit."

"No," he shouted. "Don't. I won't tell."

"I thought you'd see it my way." She placed the tape over his mouth, then went to the corner of the bedroom. She picked up an old wooden chair that Gramma claimed had been in the family for generations, and set it a few feet from the side of the bed. She didn't dare move the monitor, or the IV. She didn't want to worry about too many things being out of place. Rodney was a brilliant man with a keen eye. If he noticed the monitor was off a couple of inches, he'd come after her.

Satisfied with the placement of the chair, she then went to the dresser drawer and retrieved a set of handcuffs. Before they'd brought home their first test subject, they'd placed the four sets of handcuffs they'd ordered in each room. Unsure how their subjects would react to A-Line, they'd wanted to err on the side of caution. She put the handcuffs in her back pocket, then left the room. "Good evening, Melanie," she said, as she opened the bedroom door. "I thought we'd take a field trip." The woman had her bulging eyes downcast, and not on the television. Adeline removed the tape covering Melanie's mouth, then snapped her fingers. "Hello? Anyone home?"

Melanie shifted her gaze toward her. "I'm going to kill you."

"You really need to come up with a new line," Adeline said, pulling a pair of handcuffs from the nightstand drawer. "Would you like to see your husband?"

"You're an evil bitch, so no good could come from it."

The woman was perceptive, and too damned defiant. "Fine. Then I'll give you one of two choices: come with me to Harry's room, or I'll bring one of my other subjects to see you. He's spent the majority of the evening and afternoon watching fake snuff films, but I can assure you there is nothing fake about his erection. I think he'd like having his way with you."

The woman's stoic veneer cracked. Fear dilated her pupils and had the lines on the heart rate monitor quickening. "I'll go to my husband."

"Good choice." She secured the handcuffs to Melanie's right wrist, then unfastened the bindings attached to the bed frame. "Roll to your side and cuff your other wrist." The woman did as she was told, the pillow attached to her head lifting from the mattress. "Good." She pulled the handcuffs from her back pocket, cuffed Melanie's ankle, then walked around the monitor and unfastened her other wrist. "Lean forward and finish cuffing your ankles." When the metal snapped in place, Adeline smiled. "Let's go for a walk."

With no intention of helping her, Adeline waited for the woman to scoot off the bed. Melanie lost her balance and fell to her knees. "Crawl," she ordered.

The pillow strapped to her head blocked the view to Melanie's face as she moved across the floor like an inchworm. When they finally reached Harry's room, Adeline's patience snapped.

"Let's go," she ordered, grabbing Melanie by the hair.

The woman cried out as Adeline dragged her onto the chair. Sobbing, Melanie's handcuffs tinkled when she wiped the tears from her face.

Rolling her eyes, and now questioning if the game she was about to play had been worth the effort, Adeline began wrapping duct tape around Melanie's upper body, securing her to the wooden chair. Although tempted to do the same to her legs, she didn't want to run the risk of a kick to the face.

Adeline gave her hair a little fluff with her fingers, then dabbed at the perspiration along her upper lip. "That was a pain in the ass. But I believe the reward will be worth it." She looked between the two lovebirds, who stared at each other with so much longing it made her want to be so damned bad.

She climbed onto the bed, catching both Harry's and Melanie's attention. "I imagine it's hard to have sex when you're homeless. Screwing in a rat infested alley just isn't hot." She ran her hand along the front of Harry's jeans, up his abs and chest, then removed the tape from his mouth. "When was the last time you two had sex?"

"Don't touch me," he said, his voice panicked. "I don't want this."

She kneeled between his stretched legs, and widened the top of her blouse. "Would you prefer I touch your wife on your behalf?" she asked, lightly squeezing her nipples and looking to Melanie. "I'm not into girls, but I'll make an exception for you."

Melanie's nostrils moved in and out like a plunger, but she made no sound. Instead, she kept her eyes trained on her husband.

"Please leave her alone," Harry said. "Do whatever you want to me. Just don't hurt her."

"What a prince." Adeline unfastened his jeans, then pulled his penis from his underwear. "I love that he's willing to sacrifice his dick for you," she said, then took him in her mouth. As she worked the man's penis with her lips and tongue, she kept her eyes on Melanie. Tears coated her face, mucus ran from her nose. The agony and sympathy in the woman's eyes fueled her desire to inflict pain. How could this woman love a man who'd kept her homeless? Was she crying because it made her miserable to know another woman could make her man hard? Or was the selfish twat crying because she was concerned for her own safety?

"Mmm," Adeline hummed, and rubbed Harry's erection along her lips. "I can see why you've stayed with your husband. I bet he's great in bed." She licked the length of him, then grinned at Melanie. "Go ahead and tell me how you're going to kill me. A little hard to do with tape over your mouth. But you think about the ways, while I give you another reason to plot my demise."

She took Harry's length deep in her throat, then pumped him. "I want to hear you, lover. Tell your wife how good my mouth feels."

His face and ears had turned an incredible shade of red. Veins protruded from his temples and neck. "Fuck you," he growled, breathless.

"Sorry, Harry. While I'd love to ride you, I've got another cock waiting for me. Don't worry, I'll make sure you're satisfied before I leave." She stroked him. "I better start hearing some appreciation. I'm growing bored with having to threaten you and your wife."

Adeline took Harry into her mouth again. The man's breath quickened, but the stubborn bastard refused to give her the moans she wanted his wife to hear. That was okay. A picture was worth a thousand words.

After a few minutes, her jaw began to ache. The man needed to come. Blowing him had become tiresome, and she would rather be with Liam. She'd bet he was primed and ready by now. Unless he came in his pants, which would be too bad. Then she'd have to hope Rodney was up for some fun after he came home from the clinic.

Life was good. Three weeks ago, she'd given birth to a baby she didn't want, and was living under the scrutiny of an old busybody. Now, the once empty house had nearly all of the bedrooms filled. There was activity. Games to be played. Men to seduce. Subjects to warp. She didn't want this time at the House of Archer to end. But she did want this blowjob to come to a finish.

She released his penis, then righted his jeans. "That was anti-climactic. Now I'm really questioning why you've stayed married to him," she said to Melanie as she climbed off the bed. "Party's over. Time for you to go back to your room." Adeline covered Harry's mouth with tape, then unwound the tape surrounding Melanie's upper body. "Get up."

The woman rose, then promptly fell. She curled into the fetal position and sobbed.

Adeline let out a sigh. What a disappointing mistake this had been. "Move," she ordered, then kicked the woman in the back.

Melanie let out a muffled cry, pushed to her hands and knees, then inchwormed back to her room. Once she had the woman secured in her bed, Adeline made a quick check of the room. She placed the one set of cuffs back in the drawer, then, sure everything was as it should be, left the room, closing the door behind her. She went to Harry's room, put the other handcuffs away, pulled the tape from the chair and placed it in the corner of the room. Before she left to pay Liam another visit, she stopped by Harry's bed. She smiled when she noticed the man still had an erection.

"I could have taken care of you, lover." She squeezed him. "Too late for that now." After closing the door, she checked the hallway clock. Eight-fifteen. The clinic closed at nine, giving her plenty of time. Especially since it took Rodney an additional fifteen minutes to drive home.

Adeline made her way to the attic, then into Liam's room. He shifted his gaze to her. She licked her lips, loving the primal hunger in his eyes, the promise that he planned to make her orgasm. She moved onto the bed, then straddled his legs. She kissed the tape covering his mouth.

"Would you bite me if I let you kiss me?" she asked as she removed the tape. She leaned back and showed him her nipples. "Or if I let you suck me?"

Liam drew in a deep breath. Hatred and lust slammed into him.

"Bite her," one voice said.

"Lie. Tell her you won't, then chew off the bitch's tongue," the other encouraged.

He wanted to hurt her. He wanted to mark her. To let Roderick know that she now belonged to him. She was *his* whore. If only he could free himself of his bindings. He would beat her into submission. Make her bleed. Make her understand who held the power. Show her that Roderick was no longer necessary in this world.

"Rape her," one of the voices whispered.

"Kill Roderick," the other voice echoed over the first.

He couldn't, not with his wrists and ankles bound. For now, he was a slave to her and a pincushion to Roderick. That man would pay. The moment he had one wrist free, he would rip out Roderick's throat. The prick loved to taunt him. To tell him how much he loved fucking Madeline. Earlier, he'd come into the room smelling like sex. As Roderick had shoved another syringe into his arm, he'd given Liam blow-by-blow details of how he'd brought Madeline to orgasm with his mouth and tongue. Jealousy had him wanting to tell the man how his woman liked to come to his room, but he'd remained silent, even when Roderick had removed the tape from Liam's mouth and had encouraged him to speak. He wouldn't betray Adeline. Not yet. She was the answer to his freedom. He needed her body to release his lust. Once she was of no use to him, she'd better run.

She had wanted to break him, and she'd succeeded. He could no longer remember how he'd come to this place. He knew he'd been on a bus, but couldn't recall where he'd been going or where he'd come from. He was certain he had family, but every time he tried to force the memory of them, the voices became worse, along with the mental images of exacting pain, of blood, of the sweet sound of agonizing cries. It was almost as if his previous life had been erased, and he'd been reborn—the spawn of Madeline and Roderick. He was, after all, their creation.

Hot air rushed along his penis. Startled he glanced down. Madeline grinned. "Who were you talking to?"

"Did I speak out loud?" he asked, not sure what had happened.

"No. You just got a faraway look."

"The voices were with me. They told me to bite you. One suggested I chew off your tongue."

She rubbed the head of his erection along her nipple. "It'd be a shame if you chewed off my tongue. I couldn't do this." She bent her head, then licked him.

He groaned and watched her. Moved his pelvis as much as he could to drive himself deeper.

"We need our hands."

"Rip her hair out."

The voices quieted when she moved to her knees and shoved her shorts down over her hips. He stared at the thatch of dark curls, and saw Roderick's head between her legs. "Bastard." He pulled at his restraints.

She finished removing her shorts, then straddled him. "Who's a bastard?" she asked, and guided him inside her.

"Roderick," he said on a moan. "He told me how he licked your pussy today."

She stilled. "He did? Did this make you jealous?"

"It made me want to kill him."

"Smash in his skull," a voice shouted.

"Burn him," the other said.

"What if I told you I didn't want you to kill him? He's very important to me."

"If he's so important to you, then why is *my* dick inside you?"

She narrowed her eyes. "Because I allow it." She moved over him, rode him slowly, when he wanted her hard and fast. "Don't forget your position here, Liam. I'm here to help you break free from the voices, and to give you back your life. You are not my lover. You are my toy." She lifted her rear and slammed down on him. "Given the chance, you'd kill me."

"Then why not let Roderick kill me now?"

"Because I'm not finished with you yet. You're almost ready." She ground her sex against him. "I know it. You're going to fall over that edge and never come back. It'll be wonderful," she said, rubbing her hands along his chest. "Then you'll know freedom. And you'll thank me. You might hate me now, but when this is over, you'll be on your knees thanking me for the gift I've given you."

The door moved ever so slightly. If his eyes hadn't been wide open for days, he would have missed it. Roderick. Had to be. He fought from smiling. While he didn't want the man to kill Adeline, he loved that the bastard now knew the truth. Roderick wasn't enough for the little slut.

"The gift of freedom?" Liam asked, pretending Roderick wasn't there.

"Not the kind of freedom you're thinking." She pressed her hands against his chest and moved into a catcher's stance. "Freedom of the mind, freedom from morality." She groaned as she bounced on him. "Freedom to embrace being a psychopath."

His heart suddenly thudded at a slow, heavy pace. The voices in his head laughed in unison, while the last shred of humanity exited his body.

"Listen to her," one of them encouraged.

"Oh, yes," the other concurred. *"We've needed this. You've needed this. Now we know our place in the world. No more roaming. No more hospitals."*

"No more pills."

He didn't know what they were talking about. He couldn't remember ever being in a hospital, or taking any drugs other than the ones Roderick shoved in him.

Roderick.

"Does Roderick know what you're giving me?" he asked, not caring what the man heard, or if any of this affected him. But he *did* want to know what he was up against. He might not remember being educated, but he knew he wasn't stupid, and knew that not all psychopaths were killers.

He wasn't a killer.

"But you want to be. You want to kill Adeline."

"You want to mutilate Roderick and piss on his dead body."

Damn it, he did. But there was a difference between thinking about killing and actually going through the act, he argued.

Ecstasy crossed her face as she smiled. "Rod is just like me. He'll know soon enough." She bounced faster. "Shut up and let me fuck you."

The voices quieted as his orgasm neared. "Let me come inside you this time," he said, knowing Roderick was still watching, and wishing he could twist a real knife in the man's back.

She groaned. Her sex clenched his dick, then she quickly climbed off him. "No. Only Roderick." When she took him in her mouth, he let out a deep breath. Roderick now had a nice view of her ass, of the way she continued to rub herself. He'd bet the man regretted bragging about their earlier tryst. A little cunnilingus was nothing compared to the way she'd rode him and now took him deep in her throat.

Suck on that, Roderick, while your woman sucks me.

As his orgasm hit him, he hoped the man experienced nothing but misery. The bastard deserved it.

Madeline wiped her mouth, then fixed his pants. "I'm not sure when I can come to you again."

"I thought you said the tape would come off my eyes," he reminded her. "You said that would happen today or tomorrow."

She shrugged. "That's for Rod to decide, not me."

"You talk about power, and yet you have none. You're pathetic."

She slammed the tape over his mouth, then pulled on her shorts. "I created you, didn't I? Don't bother answering. I'll also recommend that Rod continue drugging you. Clearly you're not as ready as I thought."

"She'd better hope we don't escape," one voice said, its tone menacing.

"Death is too easy for her and Roderick," the other added.

They were right. Whatever he'd once been was lost to him—for now.

CHAPTER 18

The House of Archer, Bower, Georgia
Monday, 8:28 p.m. Eastern Daylight Saving Time

RODNEY RUSHED FROM the House of Archer, damning Adeline to hell. With the image of her mounted on top of Liam seared to his brain, he pressed the heel of his hands to his eyes, then sank to the ground.

The manipulating bitch. He'd loved her so much. Everything he had worked for had all been for her. He could have done something else with his life. He could have been a neurosurgeon. Instead of living in his grandmother's house, hiding from the public eye and playing the country bumpkin doctor, he could be living in Boston, New York or Los Angeles. Working for one of the country's best hospitals, making the big bucks, screwing a different woman every night. He dropped his hands. Tears welled in his eyes as he looked to the west of the plantation house. Shades of purple, pink and burnt orange overlapped one another in a psychedelic blend, while the trees hid the dying sun.

He drew in a shaky breath and stood. Wiped his eyes, then climbed back into the Buick. He'd come home because the cheap bastards who ran the clinic had caught wind that he'd gone into work while he was still on leave. They hadn't wanted to pay him overtime, and he hadn't wanted to be there anyway. He'd wanted to be with Adeline. During the short drive home, he'd decided they needed to regroup, to remember *why* they loved each other. Lately, all they'd done was argue. There'd been nothing tender between them. Not when they'd kissed. Not when they'd made love.

He slammed his hand against the wheel. Damn it, she'd had sex with another man. And not just any man, but Liam. Their subject. The one person he'd told her to stay away from. God, why did she test him? Did she think he wouldn't make good on his threats? Did she doubt him?

"Not after tonight," he muttered, glaring at the house. At the yawning shadows devouring the rotting columns that at one time had been the grandest in all of southern Georgia. At the wood siding, missing in some places, filled with termites in others. Sickly ivy wound its way along the side of the house, reaching for the front, as well. Like spidery fingers attached to a giant hand, he imagined the ivy coming to life and ripping the house in half.

He looked to the second floor balcony, and remembered the pale lavender dress his mother had bought for Adeline. She'd been so innocent then, had yet to show the signs of her brain deficiency. He'd stood in the driveway, gazing up at her and grinning like a fool. When she'd turned her eyes on him and had given him the sexiest, sultriest smile he'd ever seen, he'd known then that no other woman would match Adeline.

Rod is just like me. He'll know soon enough…

His chin trembled as a sob tore through him. "Why?" he wailed, and hugged himself. Then he winced when he envisioned a blow from his father.

"Are you a sissy, boy?" Dean Archer hit him. Blood spurted from Rodney's nose and onto the dirt.

He quickly wiped it away and willed himself not to cry. But his face hurt, and he was terrified of his father, especially when the man had gotten into the whiskey.

"I ain't no sissy," he said, loud and proud, hoping that Mama would hear him through the opened window. He knew Gramma wouldn't do anything to stop his father from wielding another punch, but Mama would.

"And then she could take the beating for him," Rodney said,

remembering his final thoughts from when he'd been twelve years old. "Oh, my God." He covered his mouth and shut his eyes, tried his damnedest to block out the rest of the memory. He couldn't. It was as if the creeping vine infecting the house had taken on life, reached into the car and gripped his skull. The pressure on his head made him shake, made his eyes water. The vine wanted in, it wanted to show him what he didn't want to see.

"Leave that boy alone." Matilda Archer stormed onto the porch carrying a cast iron frying pan.

Rodney's heart galloped so fast, he was worried his chest might break. He looked from his mama to his father. Dean Archer let a slow smile lift his meaty jowls. "Are you sure you want to do this, woman? It's between me and the boy."

"What'd he do wrong that gives you the right to bust up his face? He's just a boy, not a grown, drunken man."

Rodney knew what would happen. He'd known all along, which had been why he'd made sure to talk loud enough for Mama to hear him. The woman would come running to protect her child. She would take the beating, leaving him slightly banged up and more wary of his drunken father. He'd known, and he'd wanted it to happen. He had wanted it to be her, not him.

Rodney pounded on the car's ceiling. What had he done? What had he known, but denied?

"He sassed his old man," Dean Archer said.

Rodney wanted to defend himself, but knew that would be asking for trouble. His father could knock his mama out with a few hits, then come after him.

Mama looked to him. "He's gotten his punishment. Take your whiskey to the barn. It's late, and Rodney needs to wash up before bedtime."

Rodney saw Gramma in the window. The old hag looked to her son, then shook her head and disappeared.

"Go on, now," Mama said to him.

He started up the back porch steps. "Boy," his father said, stopping him mid-step. "I'm gonna give you a choice. Either you take the beating you have comin' to you, or your mama gets it on your behalf."

Rodney looked to his mother. At the quick rise and fall of her chest. At the way her knuckles whitened around the handle of that cast iron frying pan. His nose and mouth hurt. He didn't want to hurt anymore.

"Why can't you just let us both alone?" he stupidly asked.

His father grinned. "'Cause someone has to pay. You pick."

Rodney looked to his mother, a woman he loved and respected. "I'm gonna go wash up for bedtime."

Mama's eyes moistened with tears. She gave him a watery smile. "You do that, son," she said, her tone quiet, disappointed.

But he didn't care if he disappointed her. He'd make up for it tomorrow by bringing her flowers to fill the vases in her bedroom, and ice to help with the swelling. Better her than him.

The moment he entered the house, he heard the crack of that cast iron pan, then his father's nasty diseased laughter. "If you're gonna hit me, you better make sure I don't get up. Now I'm comin' for you."

As his father hit Mama, Rodney walked past the old hag crocheting on the sofa, and made his way to the bedroom. Was he man enough to have handled a few more blows from his father? Yep. He put on the headphones of his Walkman, then hit PLAY. Garth Brooks drowned out his mama's cries and his thoughts about the whole thing. What he needed to do was to go through his stack of baseball cards...

Rodney wiped a hand down his face. While he'd taken a trip down memory lane, the sun had officially died. A part of him had, too. That night hadn't been the only time he'd wanted his mother to take the beating for him. Now that he thought about it, there'd been a few times he'd thought she had deserved one, so he'd provoked his father. Why had he thought that? Matilda Archer had been nothing but sweet, kind and nurturing.

Because he could. Because he could manipulate his stupid father and make him do what he'd wanted.

Just like Adeline had manipulated him. She had wanted to move in with him when they'd been in college, but Dean and Matilda Archer had considered that unorthodox. When Adeline's roommate had been murdered, they'd changed their mind. Poor Adeline shouldn't be left in an apartment alone with a murderer on the loose. She needed the protection of a man.

If they'd only known the truth. He had. He'd accepted it and hid it. Because he'd loved Adeline, accepted her for what she was and hadn't cared about the girl she'd murdered. Same went for his cousin. The kid had been a pain in the ass anyway.

The baby Adeline broke...that still pissed him off. But he'd looked past what Adeline had done and to the future. He'd been so damned excited that Adeline had wanted to help him with his experiments again, even if he'd known all along they were unethical. Even after he'd killed Troy. Even if he'd known none of the people who came into the House of Archer would leave alive.

He'd let it happen because he'd wanted it to, and because he'd wanted to be with her. And she'd played him. This whole time, she'd played him.

Now she needed to be taught a lesson. He'd been faithful to the whore. Had never once looked at or touched another woman. He could have had the blonde locked up in Gramma's bedroom any which way he'd wanted. The only reason he hadn't was because of Adeline. The promise they'd made to each other had meant something to him. Now that he knew where she stood, now that he was aware of the way she'd been conspiring behind his back—with Liam—she'd learn quickly to never disobey or betray him again.

He opened the visor and checked his reflection. After wiping his eyes and using a napkin from the glove compartment to blow his nose, he climbed out of the car. As far as she was concerned, they were good. Everything was on track. Nothing was amiss.

He entered the house. The scent of buttery popcorn filled his nostrils. He followed it to the family room. Adeline sat on the sofa, wearing nothing but a tight tank top—no bra—that bared her stomach, and a pair of panties. She tossed a piece of popcorn into her mouth. "Go get changed and come sit with me."

Despite his hatred for her, he couldn't tear his gaze off her body, especially when she spread her legs and set the bowl of popcorn between her thighs. He snagged a piece, then leaned in and grazed his mouth along hers. "I didn't get to finish fucking you. Did you take care of yourself?"

She ran her hand along her breast, then toyed with the strap of her top. "I've been waiting for you."

Lying bitch. "I need to shower."

"Don't be long," she said, running her foot along the inseam of his pants.

He forced a smile and headed for the bathroom, then quickly turned and slipped out the back door. What he needed was in the cellar. They had handcuffs, rope and duct tape, but he wanted chains. The old rusty ones that had been collecting dust for dozens of years. The one's he had in mind were thick and heavy, and would look beautiful, taut against Adeline's skin.

After grabbing the battery-powered lantern they kept on the back porch, he made his way around the corner of the house. When he reached the cellar doors, he pulled on the handle, then quietly rested the wood on the ground. Holding the lantern in front of him, he took his time taking the two-hundred-year-old steps leading into the dark, dank cool cavern. When he reached the bottom, he raised the lantern. Dust motes he'd kicked up floated on the air. He shone the light toward the right. The chains he wanted hung where he remembered. As he neared them, the oppressive stench of rotting meat rocked his senses. Keeping his nose and mouth covered, he angled the lantern toward the source. A cobweb hit him in the face. He knocked it away and edged forward.

The lantern swung, casting eerie shadows along the rock walls. Swallowing, he aimed it at the corner, then jerked back when the light touched on white hair and a gaping, toothless mouth. Rage tore through him, making him want to smash the lantern against the wall. Fighting the bile rising in his throat, he walked over and gave the decomposing body a kick. Gramma's rotting corpse fell forward. More dust motes rose in the air when her head rolled along the dirt floor. Christ, had that crazy bitch decapitated the old lady? He nudged her head with his shoe.

He didn't care that Adeline had killed Gramma—well, he did a little, because how would they explain her disappearance? What he really cared about was that Adeline had never intended to take their experiment seriously. With Gramma gone, why would she stop? Who would know? She could continue bringing back homeless people, drug them, screw with their heads, kill them, then move on to another batch of subjects. Not only had she been trying to create psychopaths—for what reason, he still wasn't sure—but she'd created a house of torture. A playground for a serial killer.

And he'd walked into it with his eyes wide open.

He kicked Gramma's head across the cellar floor, then turned his attention back to the chains. Maybe he would wrap one around her neck as if she were his animal, then parade her in front of their subjects to make it clear who was in charge.

He raised the lantern. Light drifted along an old sickle, a long saw missing teeth, the head of a broken hoe. He held the lantern near a hatchet, remembered how Dean Archer had once gone after his mother with it. The woman had outrun his father, but she'd paid dearly later. He'd heard her screams long into the night. What his father had done to her, he still didn't know. He just remembered that she couldn't walk for close to a week.

He grabbed a smaller chain—no more than four feet long and weighing next to nothing—then turned away from the wall. Those other farm tools weren't necessary to teach Adeline a lesson. Between the chain and his fists he would school her well. He'd warned her. He'd promised that if she went near Liam, he'd beat her, then kill him.

He exited the cellar, slamming the wood door behind him. Taking several backward steps, he glanced up at the house. Light glowed from the second story and attic rooms. But he was only interested in one room.

Her lover's.

Blood rushed to his head. Holding one end of the chain, he let the rest drop and dangle. As he slowly began wrapping the chain around the crease of his hand, he continued to stare at the window, noticed the creeping vine reaching for the glass, pointing, as if giving him a signal. Then the ivy, the window and house blurred into a yellow glow. In his mind, he stood in the hallway of the attic, a voyeur in his own home, holding his breath, fighting the agony and tears. Watched as his beautiful, manipulative, hateful Adeline rode another man. He ignored his numbing fingers, the way the chain pinched his skin. He only saw Adeline. Climaxing. "Taking that bastard into her mouth," he muttered.

He knew she wasn't capable of loving Liam. There were times he questioned if she even loved him. But she had a fondness for the man. Like an artist for his sculpture, she'd molded Liam's mind, manipulated it in order to create a version of herself.

She did the same to you.

No. His eyes swam with unshed tears. She had been right. He was, and had always been, just like her.

After all these years, he'd finally realized the truth.

He should be analyzing the situation, making plans to seek medical help, go to the authorities and tell them what he and Adeline had done, who Adeline had murdered in the past. For forcing him to take a long hard look at himself and making him understand exactly who and what he was, he should want her dead. He couldn't kill her. Whether he wanted her to be or not, she was his life force. The one person who had kept him going. Even before his obsession with finding a cure for her murderous ways, she'd inflicted him with something that had gone beyond love. Now he knew she hadn't inflicted him with anything. She hadn't poisoned his mind. Just like Adeline, he was born wrong.

Now it was time to find out what it was like to be her. To beat and have no remorse. To kill and not care. Tonight, there would be plenty of killing. Starting with Liam.

With murder on his mind and the urge to break bone, he ran onto the porch and tore into the house. He slammed the backdoor shut. Glass shattered.

"What happened?" Adeline called, and hurried around the corner. Her eyes widened when she saw him, and her foot slipped as she stopped herself against the corner of the wall. "Why do you have that around your hand?"

"I told you to stay away from him."

Still staring at the chain, she took several quick steps backward. "I don't know what you're talking about. I'm going to bed."

He rushed her, raced around the corner, lengthening his strides until she was a foot away. He lunged, fell on top of her, then gripped her by the hair. She screamed, the sound almost as pretty as her sensual groans.

"Shut your filthy mouth," he said, dragging her by the hair with his chain-free hand.

She clawed at him, broke skin, kicked her leg and twisted her body. When they reached the staircase, he continued to drag her by the hair. She'd smartened up, though. Used the heels of her hands and feet to help her ascent, and to likely keep her hair from coming out at the roots.

"Rod," she pleaded on a tortured cry. "Please stop. Tell me why you're doing this."

When they reached the second story landing, he let go of her hair, bent, then gripped her mouth. "Get up." He squeezed her jaw tightly. "Or I'll lift you by the throat."

Tears streaming down her face, her dark curly hair a tangled mess, she moved first to her knees, then to her bare feet. He shoved her against the wall. Her head bounced off the plaster. Her eyes dazed, her mouth slack, she started to slide down the wall and to the floor.

"Either get on your feet and walk up those attic stairs, or I'm going to wrap this chain around your ankles and drag you there." He fisted his hand and shook the rusted chain. "What I should do is free the blonde, strap you to her bed, tape open your eyes and take her right in front of you." Nodding and liking the idea, he added, "After I cover you in Liam's blood."

Narrowing her eyes and pressing her palms against the plaster, pain crossed her face as she slowly rose. "Have you been shooting the A-Line?"

He smiled. "This is all me. Just like you wanted."

She shifted her gaze to the staircase leading to the attic. "I don't know what you're talking about, but if you want to kill Liam, do it." She looked back at him. "He means nothing to me. I never wanted anything to do with him. I just wanted to make you jealous so you would come to my bed again. But I see I pushed you too far."

If he hadn't watched her have sex with the man, he would have believed her. She was a damned fine actress.

"I am going to kill him, after you say those exact words in front of him."

Her dark brow lifted slightly. "No problem." She pushed off the wall, swayed, then started for the steps.

"While I fuck you in front of him."

She paused, and glanced over her shoulder. "And you think I'm the psychopath."

MEL HELD HER breath, tuned out Madeline's recorded voice, and waited. Strained her ears, hoping to hear the creaks and groans of the stairs. In a short time, she'd grown accustomed to the sounds of the house. Although she'd been unconscious when brought to her prison, she'd seen the staircase when she'd scooted her way into Harrison's room. While she'd lain in bed, avoiding the gore on the TV, she'd heard footsteps along the stairway to the attic, to the point that she could tell the difference between Roderick and Madeline's. Right now, it sounded as if both of them were heading up the stairs. But who was residing on that level?

She assumed Eliot was there, but now wondered about another man. Liam. At least that was the name she'd thought she had heard. She'd been so shocked and scared—sickly satisfied, too—

when Madeline had been screaming and crying, she could have imagined the man's name. The rest of Madeline and Roderick's conversation had been too muffled to understand, but based on Roderick's tone, on the way the walls had rattled, it was obvious the two were arguing.

The stairs continued to creak under two sets of footsteps. She finally released the breath she'd been holding, then went back to work. Madeline had been so concerned with keeping her distance when Mel had been forced to move from her room into Harrison's, then back again, the woman hadn't noticed when Mel had pulled the switchblade free from her sock. The crying jag Mel had gone through on the floor of Harrison's room hadn't been for Madeline's benefit, it had been real, and had given her the opportunity to try for the knife. Once she'd had it in her fist, she'd crawled to her room, her heart breaking for Harrison as she'd vowed to get even with Madeline. But she couldn't think about Harrison, or how he would be once they left this place. She needed to maintain focus.

Her eyes stung. Her stomach continued to seize with the same painful cramps that had been piercing her abdomen from the moment she'd become conscious.

She wouldn't give up. Although her eyes were taped open, she worked blind and on instinct. She'd had the small switchblade since she was kid, and had always kept it—along with all of her knives—razor sharp. Dull knives were more dangerous than sharp ones. Right now, she needed this blade to cut through the rope attached to her wrist.

Madeline and Roderick had made a mistake. Although they'd made sure the rope had been tied tightly around her wrists, they'd given her enough slack to turn her arm and use the switchblade to saw the rope tethered to the bed frame. She had no idea how much of it she'd cut through. For now, her only concern was keeping the blade in her hand.

A door slammed above her. Straining her eye muscles she looked upward, then smiled when Madeline screamed...until a thought occurred to her.

What if Roderick was crazier than Madeline?

RODERICK STRUCK ADELINE again, knocking her to the floor. She didn't cry out this time. With the back of her hand, she smeared the blood trickling from her lips. "Is that all you got?" she asked, but didn't try to rise.

He glanced to Liam, who glared at him with hatred. The malevolence in the man's eyes would have meant something if he were still conducting an experiment. But his ideologies had changed. Or rather, he'd finally accepted who he and Adeline were. There was no need to fix them. There was nothing *wrong* with either of them. The years he'd spent studying the brain and how different drugs affected it, had been a waste. Maybe he and Adeline, and others like them, weren't sick or deficient, but *special?* Only the special ones had the courage to take someone else's life. The rewards? Power. Freedom.

He shook his head as he realized how right Adeline had been. "Freedom of the mind, freedom from morality," he said, repeating what Adeline had told Liam while she had been riding the bastard. He took his fist wrapped in the chain and punched Liam in the groin. "Freedom to embrace being a psychopath."

Liam's muted cries filled the room. Rodney glanced away from the prick to look at Adeline. "I wonder if I broke your toy. Do you want to pull his penis out of his pants and investigate?"

She shook her head. Instead of showing fear, her eyes held curiosity. "What do you plan to do to me?"

"Nice apology. You're not going to try and defend yourself, or offer up a valid excuse for why you cheated on me?"

"I've murdered four people, and tricked you into killing Troy. Cheating doesn't quite rank up there on my list of no-nos."

His vision swam with rage. *She'd tricked him?* "Troy beat you. He tried to rape you. When I walked into the room he was choking you."

She leaned against the wall and spread her legs. "He was mad that I wouldn't finish him off."

The chain bit into his skin as he tightened his fist.

"I knew you were just about done with Noah, and that you'd be right outside the door. So, I sucked on Troy's big cock, took him right to the edge, then stopped." A sexy smile played along her bloody lips as she touched herself. "You should have seen the look on his face. He still had A-Line humming through his veins, so I knew he wanted to kill me."

"He was on the placebo."

"Every time you gave him the placebo, I gave him A-Line. I wasn't ready to see if your drug worked." She rested her head against the wall and cupped her breast. "I could have done without being choked, but God did I love the way you stormed into the room to save me. You looked so damned sexy. When you wrapped your belt around his throat..." She slipped her hand inside her panties. "Then smashed his head."

He rushed over, then yanked her arm from her underwear. "How did he get free?" he asked, releasing her.

"I loosened the rope, silly," she said, then dipped her finger into her mouth.

"Were you planning on doing the same with Liam?" he demanded, the thought tainting his love for her, the betrayal crushing him. "Or were you going to have him help you kill me?"

She frowned. "If I wanted you dead, I would have killed you a long time ago. I might have done things you disapprove of, but I never want to see you die."

"Right. Because you love me," he said with sarcasm, yet clung to the hope that she *did* love him. Maybe he didn't know the true meaning of the word, but whatever it was he and Adeline had, he didn't want to lose it. He'd been with her for too long to know how to go on without her.

"As much as you love me." She cocked her head and looked toward Liam, who'd finally stopped moaning. "Again, what do you plan to do to me? You said something about beating me, then killing him."

"You're right, I did mention that." Except Adeline could take the beating, and he doubted she'd care if Liam died. He wanted her to show remorse. He wanted her to hurt. And not just her body. For what she'd done to him, to them, she deserved it. "Stand up."

"I can't. I'm too weak," she said, her tone bored.

Liam's muffled chuckled came from behind him.

Hatred and humiliation suddenly burned through his veins. He yanked her by the hair. She gripped his wrist, cried and struggled as he pulled her toward the bed where Liam lay. "Shut your mouth." He let go of her hair, pulled the handcuffs from the drawer near the bed, then reached for her.

She swung her arms and kicked her legs. "Don't do this," she shouted and panted. "Beat me, kill him, but don't do this."

He pinned her with his weight, loved the way she clawed at his back, and snapped a cuff around her wrist. "Why are you afraid?" he asked, pressing his hand with the chain against her throat. "Are you worried about not having control?" She wheezed and slapped his arm, just as he secured the other cuff to the bedframe.

He eased his hand off her throat and leaned back. Ran the chains along her breasts, then stood. Adeline coughed as he snagged duct tape off the table. He tore a piece. "You have no idea how many times I would have liked to shut you up," he said, sealing her mouth mid-cough." He leaned down and placed his lips to her ear. "I don't think beating you and killing Liam will hurt you enough. What will?" He nipped her ear. "What would humiliate you? You on your knees begging?"

For the first time ever, Adeline's cold exterior cracked. Her eyes dilated with fear. Her nostrils flared as she took in short, quick breaths. He smoothed her hair from her face. "Don't worry, I won't kill you. But I *will* teach you a lesson. No one cheats on me."

He stood, then left the room. The equipment he used for his experiments were in his childhood bedroom on the first floor. Adeline had been determined to create a psychopath, and he honestly believed she'd succeeded with Liam. He also believed that because she'd vested herself in the man, had risked punishment to be with him, that simply killing Liam would be too easy. The man's death would probably bother her for a split second, then she'd move on and forget about him. That had been the way she'd acted after she'd murdered her roommate and Geoff. She hadn't shown an ounce of remorse over killing their child, and he hadn't a clue that she'd decapitated Gramma. So Liam's death wouldn't be a big deal. But he knew Adeline just as much as he now knew himself. He knew what would hurt her.

He'd kill Liam, had planned to all along, but he'd *fix* him first. He would destroy what she'd created, and in the process, make one important fact crystal clear...*he* held the power.

CHAPTER 19

The House of Archer, Bower, Georgia
Monday, 9:47 p.m. Eastern Daylight Saving Time

MEL SHOVED THE knife between the mattress and box spring. She glanced to the heart rate monitor. Moving too fast. She forced herself to relax and use some of the breathing exercises she'd learned from doing Pilates. As her heart rate dropped, she kept her eyes off the TV and listened for movement from the hallway.

Two people had gone to the attic, but only one set of heavy footsteps had pounded down the staircase. Roderick's? Then where was Madeline? While she couldn't care less if the woman was dead, she was concerned what that meant for her and Harrison, along with anyone else being held there.

With no intention of becoming another one of Roderick and Madeline's victims, she used all of her energy and pulled her arm toward the bed, hoping, praying, she'd cut the rope enough it would snap. No luck. There was extra give, so she must be close.

Should she risk using the knife again, or wait for more of Roderick's footsteps? She knew he hadn't gone into Harrison's room—the hinges of his door could use oil—and assumed he'd gone to the lower level. What if he'd gone down there with the intent to come to her and Harrison, drug them again or, this time, kill them?

Deciding to risk it, she ran her hand along the side of the mattress. Her fingertips brushed on the small handle of the blade. Keeping her concentration solely on retrieving the knife and nothing else, she carefully pulled it free.

Roderick's heavy steps groaned from the hallway. She froze, squeezed the handle tightly, worried fear and an unsteady hand would make her accidentally drop the switchblade.

She let out a shaky breath when the stairs leading to the floor above her complained, creaking under his weight. Confident he wouldn't be coming for her—yet—she went back to work on the rope. She *would* free herself. She'd cut the damned rope, remove the rest of her bindings, then help Harrison.

Harrison.

He'd been in a strange state of mind when she'd crawled from his room, and rightfully so. Since returning to her prison, she'd tried to not think about him, about what had happened, but she couldn't help herself. Madeline had raped him, with the intent to humiliate, and to test what she'd thought was a married couple. They might not be married, but she'd realized how much she loved her friend. She ached for him, for what Madeline had done to him, and couldn't wait to tell him how much she admired his strength. He'd kept his cool, had endured the assault with gritted teeth, and in the end he'd won. He hadn't given Madeline any satisfaction, forcing the raunchy whore to quit.

A loud thud came from the ceiling, rattling the walls and the windowpanes.

Then Madeline screamed…

"GO AHEAD AND rape me," Adeline shouted as Rodney tossed the shirt he'd ripped from her body to the floor. "If that's what will make you feel like a man." She grinned and decided to go for the throat. "Better yet, why not make this rape interesting and force me to suck on him while you take me from behind. I *promise* not to enjoy it."

He grabbed her throat, thankfully without the hand wrapped in metal, and squeezed. "Or maybe I should cut off his dick."

That would be a waste. "You might want to cut off his tongue, too. He definitely knows how to use it," she lied, just to piss off Rodney even more. Although she could have done without the hair pulling and the punches he'd wielded, the satisfaction of knowing he'd finally snapped had been well worth the aches and pains. She finally had him where she'd always wanted him...on equal ground.

"I hate you," he said, then forced his tongue down her throat.

She could bite him, hurt him, but she loved the punishing kiss, the excitement rushing through her body and straight to her sex. Now that he'd finally understood that he was just like her, the two of them could be unstoppable. They could spend their days at the plantation house, luring the unsuspecting, torturing them, finding new ways to experiment on them, and continue to fill the barn with bodies. Or travel the country, maybe even the world leaving death in their wake. The idea thrilled her as much as Rod's kiss. She could finally be free. She would no longer have to hide behind a veil, pretending to be good, or wanting to be better. If only she could talk Rodney into keeping Liam. He could be their muscle. Plus, he was expendable.

He tore his mouth from hers, then stood. After stepping over her body, he walked to Liam, then removed the tape from his mouth. "Did you enjoy having sex with Adeline?"

She scooted upright, and craned her neck. Saw the frown scrunching Liam's face and wondered if the name game would screw with the voices still left in his head.

"You mean Madeline," Liam corrected him.

"That's not her real name, just as Roderick isn't mine. So, tell me, did you enjoy her?"

"It beat the hell out of watching TV."

Rodney chuckled and looked down at her. "That had to hurt."

It didn't. Liam was proving his loyalty to her. After the way Rod had punched him in the crotch, then had proceeded to beat her, Liam had to know that if he answered truthfully, the consequences wouldn't be good for either of them.

Rod looked back to Liam. "How do you feel?"

"My dick is sore, maybe you should let *Adeline* kiss it and make it better."

Rodney's face reddened as he let out a bark of laughter that held no humor whatsoever. "Apparently I didn't hit you hard enough, you still have balls." He opened up the small plastic box he'd returned to the room with, then pulled out a syringe. "I told you I was going to break you, fix you, then kill you. After I saw you and Adeline, I was going to just kill you, but I want to hurt her with more than my fists. So now I'm going to fix you, humiliate her, then kill you. Sound like a plan?"

"Go to hell," Liam said, as Rodney pierced his skin with the syringe, and sent the drug into the man's system.

The joke was on Rodney. She'd modified his drug, just as she'd done years ago when he'd tested it on Federal prisoners. Rod would *not* be fixing Liam. If anything, he'd make the man more violent, his thoughts darker. Based on the prison experiment, it might take a day or two for the change to occur, but those prisoners hadn't been saturated with A-Line. Liam could experience the break within hours, maybe minutes.

Rodney set the empty syringe back in the box, then walked over to her. After taking the key for the handcuffs from his pocket, he removed the cuff securing her to the bed, then shoved her onto her stomach before she had the chance to react, and cuffed her wrists together. He forced her to her feet, then pressed his mouth to her ear. "No reaction to what I've done? You're not upset that I've just destroyed the psychopath you've created?"

She grinned. "I hate to break it to you, sweetie, but I played with your drug. *Again.*"

He jerked her to his chest. "I know." He slammed her to the mattress. Pain shot across her cheek as it connected with Liam's shin. Holding her down, he unraveled the chain from his hand. "Did you really think I wouldn't check and recheck my formula after the prison experiment failed? How stupid do you think I am?"

Adeline stared at Liam, who began sweating profusely. Her heart raced. "You knew? This whole time, you knew?" Something inside her…cracked. There had to be a way to stop Rodney from destroying what she'd created. Liam was on the edge of no return, she'd been sure of it when she had left his room earlier. He'd accepted the man he had become, the psychopath she had wanted him to be. Just like his morality, anything good that had been left inside of him, had shriveled up and died, Liam had enjoyed the pleasure of her body, making him *loyal* to her. Like any animal, that hadn't meant she would trust Liam, but she'd suspected he would have done whatever she had commanded. After all, her voice would have been the dominant one in his head.

If Rodney's drug worked, Liam would go back to his schizophrenic self. For the first time in her life, she understood defeat. Rod was right…it hurt. And pissed her off. She'd been careful, calculating…

"I didn't know about Gramma," he said, taking her panties down over her hips. "When were you going to tell me?"

The chain bit into her skin, but not enough that she couldn't breathe. "After you realized you and I were alike," she answered honestly, and didn't struggle when his penis pressed against her sex. He'd won—this round. In the end he would come to realize that she'd done them both a favor. They'd move on, do other things. Not the way she'd hoped, but she could be persuasive. "The old lady was in the way. Don't deny it."

He pulled the chain tighter as his entered her. "And how will we explain her death? When you were killing her, did that occur to you?"

She sucked in a breath as he pushed himself deeper. "I didn't care. I just wanted her dead."

"Like our baby?"

"Who said she was yours?" she asked, wanting to hurt him. The baby had been his, and had needed to be destroyed. Although the child could have been molded into something greater than

Liam, she would have taken up too much of Rodney's time.

Rodney stilled. *The whore.* He glanced to Liam, who grinned. Holding the man's gaze, needing to prove he was the dominant one in the room, that he held the power, he moved over Adeline, faster, harder.

"You filthy bitch. If I'd known, I would have killed her myself." Liam's smiling, sweaty face doubled as the rage, the deceit, the utter betrayal fragmented his self-control. "Smile away motherfucker," Rodney shouted. "When I'm done with my whore, I'm going to kill you." Darkness shrouded him. He closed his eyes, took pleasure in Adeline's body while he pictured slitting the man's throat. Liam thought to laugh at him, at the way Adeline had duped him, duped them all. He'd see how much the bastard was laughing when blood spurted from his throat.

Adeline grabbed the front of his shirt with her cuffed hands. He ignored her, and instead, quickened his pace. The slut didn't need to get off tonight. This was all about him and would be for a long time. Just thinking about the many ways he would continue to punish her over the next few weeks, maybe months, had him harder than he'd ever been in his life.

"S-stop," Liam shouted.

He ignored the man. Thought only about the way he'd humiliate her, shame her, bring her to her knees. Focused on his pleasure, on showing Liam how it was done, on proving to Adeline that she belonged to him. His orgasm neared. "No stopping, this is the proper way to handle a woman." He glanced at the man. Liam had grown pale, and sweat poured from his forehead, coated his twitching upper lip. "What it's like to be the one in control," he said with a grunt, blood rushing to his head, the room becoming tinny.

He let himself go…

Breathing hard, he eased up on the chain, then slipped from her. After pulling his pants back into place, he smacked her rear. "Get up. I want you to watch me kill your creation." When she didn't move or make a sarcastic comeback, he grabbed her hair and pulled back. "Don't act…" The room went out of focus. His stomach dropped. His heart stuttered. "Addy?" He flipped her onto her back.

Mouth gaping, eyes open wide, her head lolled to the side.

"No. No. No!" He pressed his head to her chest, rested his fingers at the pulse point of her throat. *Can't be.* He'd been scaring her. Wanted to prove a point.

He began CPR. Breathed into her mouth. "Come on, Addy. Fight for me. You can't leave me. Please," he begged, then breathed into her mouth again.

"You killed her."

Never taking his eyes from Adeline's beautiful face, he ran his fingers along the marks he'd made against her neck, then grabbed the chain. "Because of you," he shouted, whipping the chain at Liam's face.

The bastard cried out as he raised the chain again and struck. Once, twice…he fell against the bed and wept. What had he done? "I didn't mean…" He quickly removed the handcuffs from her wrists, then covered her with his body and kissed her still warm lips. "I love you so much. I'm nothing without you." Tears blurred her face as he cradled her dead body. "I don't know what to do," he repeated over and over. Rocking, trying to make sense of what had just happened, of what to do next.

What would Adeline do?

"Burn it." He glanced to Liam, who had turned incredibly pale. "I'm going to burn it to the ground."

The man's forehead wrinkled. "Something's wrong. I-I can't explain what—"

Rodney stood. Wiped his face, then fell to pieces when he looked at Adeline again. He lifted her in his arms, took her from the bed, then he dropped to the floor, holding her, hugging her, wondering how the hell he was supposed to exist without his other half.

"I-I c-can't—"

Rodney glanced up, couldn't care less that Liam convulsed

against his restraints, that drool flowed from his mouth, that his drug not only hadn't worked, but that it might kill the man. He looked away. Held Adeline close, kissing her forehead, her cheek, her lips.

Rage ripped through him as he looked back to Liam. "This is your fault," he yelled, and fed off the welts rising along the bastard's face. "You're going to pay." He hugged Adeline tighter. "Slitting your throat would be too easy for what you've done."

Liam continued to convulse, even as Rodney set Adeline on the floor, even as he wept over her and kissed her one last time. He stood, wiped the snot from his nose, then approached the bed. "I pray you'll burn in hell. In case you don't, I'm going to give you a taste of it." He punched him in the face. Flexing his fist, he stepped back, looked to his beautiful Adeline, then sucked in a sob. "I'm so sorry."

He rushed from the room. There was nothing here for him anymore. There was no reason to live. He would die tonight, because one day without Adeline was too much to bear. She was his life, the other half of him. As he made his way down the steps to the second floor, then the first, his only focus was on death.

His.

He reached the first floor, ran into his childhood bedroom, then quickly used the chemicals he had to create a flammable substance. Within minutes, he left a trail from his room, to the living room, the hall, then ran out of the liquid after dousing the parlor sofa with the remains. He reached into his pocket for the lighter he'd grabbed. Another sob tore through him as he pictured Adeline, as guilt compounded and shredded his insides. He flicked the lighter, then rested it against the sofa. If burst into flames.

He stared at the blaze, saw only Adeline. After taking several backward steps, he dropped to the floor, then curled into a ball and wept.

Outside the House of Archer, Bower, Georgia
Monday, 10:18 p.m. Eastern Daylight Saving Time

CASH SCRATCHED THE back of his neck where another mosquito had taken a bite. The waiting, the worrying ate at him. Gnawed at him like thousands of mosquitos. Every second that Mel was inside that ugly, old house was a second too long. Not knowing what was happening to her scared the hell out of him. She was tough, but he didn't want her strength to be pushed to its limits. Everyone had a breaking point. Even highly trained soldiers. On the battlefield, he'd witnessed the downslide of a man's spirit, the shattering of the mind. If it hadn't been for his dog, he could've come home one of those men. Broken. Depressed. Unable to connect with civilian life.

But who'd have taken care of Dolly? His girl had saved his life, and he owed it to her to prove the loss of her legs had been worth it. Mel had saved him, too. Instead of only proving his worth to his dog, he'd had an intelligent, sassy woman who'd needed to know he was man enough for her. That he could give her the love and home she'd needed.

What they'd both needed.

He dropped the binoculars, then wiped a hand down his face. Tasted the bug spray he'd coated his skin with earlier, then checked his watch. He brought the binoculars back to his eyes. He'd been lying on his stomach in the tall grass for only twenty minutes. He didn't know if he had the patience to last another twenty. They knew who likely lived in the plantation house. Dr. Rodney Archer had once been employed by a pharmaceutical company to create drugs—specifically a drug to counteract the symptoms caused by whatever Noah had been given. The man had to be responsible for drugging Noah.

As for the woman, Madeline? All they'd need was the element of surprise. After Rachel had sent them the architectural blueprints she'd found in Bower County's archives, he, Lola and Vlad had studied the House of Archer to the point he probably knew the place better than his own home. He'd suggested attacking from the front, back and side doors—the only three points of exit and entry. While Lola had agreed, she'd thought they should wait until closer to midnight, when Rodney and the woman were likely sleeping.

He couldn't help but think about the people the couple had kidnapped, and how much he respected Mel and the agents she worked with for being willing to risk their lives to help those victims. Although he respected Mel and her position with ATL, he still didn't want her being a secret agent anymore. The both of them needed to put their dangerous lifestyles to rest and start focusing on the future. Expanding the garage, starting a family...

What would Mel be like pregnant? At the time of the miscarriage, she'd been eight weeks along. She'd still been so slim, if he hadn't seen the plus sign on the pregnancy test stick, he wouldn't have believed she was expecting. Regret bit into him just as another mosquito nabbed him on the wrist. He ignored it. Let the insect feed off his bitterness. Where would they be today if he hadn't chosen the need to experience the rush, the brush with danger? If he hadn't been worried she'd leave him for good. She sure as hell wouldn't be inside the House of fucking Archer.

Anger heated his skin, seeped into his bones. Burned in his gut. Fuck ATL, CORE and every other damned acronym out there. Screw their evidence, their protocol. They were in the frickin' sticks. The local sheriff wouldn't even know what to do if they presented him with the evidence Lola assumed they could obtain. Ian Scott thought he could eventually involve the GBI, FBI or DEA—if the sheriff was no help. A lot of good that did Mel and Harrison right now.

He let the binoculars hang around his neck and stood. The house was less than one hundred yards away. Fueled by the need to see his woman right goddamned now, he'd be there in ten seconds.

As he started to move, his cell phone vibrated. Torn between the need to find Mel and blowing their cover, he stopped, ducked, then answered his phone.

"Stay where you are," Lola said. "I'm coming to you."

The phone went dead. She was covering the side of the house, while Vlad had the back. How in the hell had she seen him on the move? He shook his head. She played him and Vlad. Took the side of the house so she could place herself in a position to keep an eye on both of them.

The grass rustled. He switched the binoculars to night vision and stilled.

"Cash," she whispered.

When he spotted Lola, he rose a head above the grass. "Here."

Within seconds, she was next to him. Panting hard, and grabbing his arm.

"What's wrong?"

"I didn't want to do this via phone."

Panic gripped him. "Mel?"

She held him tighter. "Don't know. Listen, Mel and Harrison are my people. They mean more to me than I have time to explain. But I know what you feel for Mel is different, same with Vlad, which is why I'm doing this in person to you, and only giving Vlad the go sign."

"What the hell does that mean?"

"It means that once I tell Vlad what I just learned…I don't know if I'll be able to stop him."

He grew cold and clammy. "Stop him from what?"

"Killing. Rachel just contacted me. Rodney Archer has a twin sister."

"So?"

"Her name is *Adeline*."

His skin prickled with dread. "Madeline?" Cash rubbed his hand along his mouth. "And she's *just* finding this out now?"

"Eight years ago, Adeline legally changed her last name from Archer to her mother's maiden name. *After* she was accused of killing her roommate."

"What the—?"

"I'm not finished." Lola let go of him and looked to the plantation house. "Four years ago, their fifteen-year-old cousin went missing while he was staying here for the summer. According to the grandmother, the last person to see him alive was Adeline."

He pulled his gun from its holster. "Forget your evidence. We have a doctor who was trying to find a way to cure psychopaths, and Noah who was given a drug that would—essentially—make him psychopathic. Now we have a twin who clearly *is* a psychopath. I'm not waiting."

"I'm not either, but we do this as a team, and as we'd planned. Let me get into position, then contact Vlad. I'll send you a quick text when we're set."

This was why he liked working alone. He could've already been in the house. "Contact Vlad from here."

"No, I need to cover the side door. We don't want these people escaping." She rose slightly, but kept her head below the grass line. "Remember, we are not shooting to kill," she said, then took off in a sprint.

If he recalled, when Lola had brought up that point at the hotel, neither he nor Vlad had agreed. And Lola hadn't pressed them.

He raised the binoculars again and stared at the house. Minutes ticked by. Anxiety, fear for Mel and Harrison, tightened his body, caused blood to rush to his head.

Get it together, Maddox.

He couldn't. Looking for roadside bombs...if he'd made a mistake, it would cost him *his* life. Repo jobs...again, going at it alone meant no one but him could be injured. What was happening tonight was different. This wasn't about risking his life, but about saving his woman's. He couldn't make a mistake. There wouldn't be any second chances. Once they entered the plantation house—

Dark orange glowed from the first floor of the house. He shifted the binoculars, followed the glow, watched as it grew and spread.

Instinct knocked any sense from him, tripped his heart, propelled his body. One thought remained. *Melanie.* Sheer willpower kept his knees from buckling as he ran toward the house. Terror destroyed any decency, any of his principles as his temper erupted, burning brighter than the fire engulfing the House of Archer.

Someone was going to die tonight, and it wouldn't be his wife.

CHAPTER 20

The House of Archer, Bower, Georgia
Monday, 10:29 p.m. Eastern Daylight Saving Time

M EL PUFFED OUT a series of quick short breaths. She stood in front of the dresser mirror, ignored her red, puffy eye and focused on carefully removing the last of the tape from her other eyelid. Her eyes watered as several lashes stuck to the surgical tape and ripped from her sensitive skin. Relieved, she closed her eyes for the first time in hours, rubbed them, enjoyed the simplicity of blinking. Something she would never take for granted again. Same went for her freedom.

Grabbing the switchblade from the dresser, she quickly moved to the door. Pressed her ear to the wood. Although she thought Roderick had gone to the lower level again, she couldn't be sure. As for Madeline, she suspected the woman was either bound or dead. Even if the woman, or Roderick, surprised her, the small blade could do serious damage—especially to the throat.

Confidence, the need to leave this place and make sure the couple paid for what they'd done, had her slowly turning the doorknob. She looked though the crack in the door, stared at the closed door of Harrison's room. Her chest filled with vengeance as quick images of what had happened in Harrison's room rushed through her mind. She'd thought she had known what it was like to hate, until she'd met Madeline. Determined to make good on the threats she'd made to the woman—after she freed Harrison—she quickly scanned the hallway, then hurried to Harrison's room.

She opened the door, swallowed a sob, and went to him.

"Harrison, it's me, Mel. Honey, are you in there?"

His gaze was locked on the television. She removed the tape from his mouth. A small half-smile immediately tugged at his lips as he continued to gape at the violence on the screen.

No, no, no! Fear and panic set in, buzzed through her head, numbed her fingers, as she quickly removed the ropes around his arms and ankles. He still didn't move. "Harrison. You have to get up." She cut the duct tape from the pillow, then unwound it from his head. "You have to snap out of it. We've gotta get out of here before they come back."

She couldn't leave him, couldn't carry him, but figured there was one way to snap him out of his catatonic state. He didn't protest when she quickly slapped the tape back over his mouth, but kept his focus on the screen. Hands trembling, stomach twisting, she reached for the surgical tape holding his right lid in place. "I'm so sorry," she said, then tore it off of him.

Harrison arched his neck and screamed. Even with the tape covering his mouth it pierced her ears, and she prayed to God Roderick or Madeline hadn't heard him.

Breathing hard, he finally turned his head. Narrowed his one eye, then tore the tape from his mouth.

Tears filled her eyes. "Are you with me?" she asked, and touched his cheek.

He shoved her hand away. "You stupid bitch."

She quickly jerked back, taking the knife with her.

"Harrison, get it together," she warned him. "This is *not* you. It's the drug. Remember Madeline. Remember what she did to you."

Hardening his jaw, he ripped the tape from his other eye, taking some of his lashes with it. He blinked several times and tossed the tape aside. Sliding his legs to the side of the bed, he pushed off the mattress.

"Check yourself," she said, trying desperately to keep from crying. She hated what they'd done to him. While she knew this wasn't Harrison, but the drug, the brainwashing, it terrified her to think that they could lose him, that he could never be his old self again. The tears fell anyway. "You don't want to hurt me. We're friends. Think about Polina's Paradise, Vlad, the airboat company, how I sneak you your favorite ice cream."

His forehead wrinkled. Tears filled his eyes. His face reddened as he blinked them away. "I didn't want her touching me."

Sick inside, she hurt for him, for the pain and humiliation agonizing him. "I know, honey." She approached him with caution. "Don't think about that. Just think about getting out of here." She touched his arm. When he flinched, she smoothed her palm along his bicep. "You got this, right? You're with me?"

Without meeting her gaze, he nodded. She took his hand, and led him toward the door. "There's at least one more person being held in the attic, possibly two."

"Fuck 'em. We go."

She'd been worried Roderick would continue to feed his drug to those left in the house, and was determined to take the others with them. They could end up like Noah, a fate no one deserved. After the way Harrison had reacted toward her, she decided she didn't want to risk injury to herself or Harrison. The victims didn't know them and could react violently, or call attention to them and bring Roderick running. She absolutely did not want that. After what she'd been through, she selfishly wanted to be home with Cash, and to let the police deal with Roderick and the other victims.

"Fine." She turned, then jogged to the corner of the room. She picked up the wooden chair Madeline had forced her to sit in earlier, set it on its side, then stomped on the wooden legs. After breaking off two pieces, she went back to Harrison and handed them to him. "If we run into Roderick," she explained.

"He'd better hope I don't start swinging, because I don't think I'll be able to stop."

Harrison had never been prone to violence, had never talked about hurting anyone but Vlad. Even then, she knew he wouldn't.

This Harrison was foreign to her, and she prayed to God he'd return to normal once the drug was out of his system.

She reached for the doorknob. "Ready to sprint?"

He smacked the sticks against his hand.

She turned the knob, slowly cracked open the door, then held up a hand. "Do you smell that?" she asked, swearing she detected the faint odor of smoke.

Harrison pushed open the door, and stepped into the hallway. A light-gray haze rose up the stairs, reached for the ceilings and fogged the area. Her tender eyes burned. She rubbed them as indecision and guilt messed with her conscience. "We can't leave the others," she whispered. "If the house is on fire, they'll die."

"If they've been on the drug longer than me, longer than Noah was, they're probably better off dead." He started for the downstairs. "Like I said, fuck 'em."

The old Harrison would have at least wrestled with the choice. While she'd been drugged, too, she'd only been given a small amount. Although she'd noticed a slight change in her mood after the dose Roderick had given her, most of her violent thoughts had been directed at one person: Madeline.

"You go, I'll meet you outside," she said, moving toward the attic staircase. "Watch out for Roderick."

"Whatever. Go ahead and be stupid."

Hurt, angry, she turned away before she said something she could regret later, and headed up the attic stairs. When she reached the first room, she readied the switchblade, then opened the door. A man lay bound to the bed, his eyes taped open, his gaze on the TV.

CASH KICKED IN the front door. Weapon raised, he cautiously entered. From the opposite side of the house—the kitchen—Vlad came into view through the cloud of smoke and flames. The Russian nodded to the left. The parlor, according to the architectural blueprints. As Cash eased his way toward the room, he shielded his face from the heat and followed the path of the fire. It had splintered off to the stairs leading to the second floor, and had already traveled into the living room, maybe even the bedroom off that wing. Or maybe the fire had started there. He couldn't tell and it didn't matter.

"Here," Vlad shouted, and pointed at the opened French doors of the parlor. "Corner."

A man fitting Rodney's description rocked and hugged himself. "You got this?" Cash called.

Vlad gave him a single nod, then rushed into the room. Although he wanted to make sure the Russian didn't lose his life over Rodney, his priority was finding Mel. He wished he knew if Lola had entered the house yet. She could either cover Vlad or help him. Not willing to wait, he ran back toward the entrance, then rushed through the fire's weakest point. He smacked a few flames off the forearm of his long-sleeved shirt, and kept moving.

The fire hadn't extended to the kitchen—yet. He prayed time would remain on his side and the blueprints they'd studied were correct. If so, there would be a servants' staircase near the butler's pantry. Within seconds, he found it, took out his flashlight, then made his way up the stairs. His foot caught on a hole in one of the steps. He'd need to be careful. Breaking an ankle or falling through rotting wood was not an option. Not if he was going to get Mel out of there alive.

"HEY," MEL SAID softly, and entered the room. "How you doin', honey?"

"Who are you?" he asked, terror, paranoia clear in his tone.

She studied the vicious welts along the man's face. "A victim just like you. I'm gonna get you out."

"Roderick?"

She cut the rope around his right ankle. "I don't know where he is. You're Liam, right?"

The man nodded. "He said he would break me, fix me, then kill me."

She began working on the rope around his right wrist. "You're here, aren't you?"

"He *did* fix me," he continued as if he hadn't heard her. "The voices I've been hearing for years...they're gone."

"That's good, honey," she said, trying to keep the man calm. Thank God Harrison hadn't received the same amount of drugs as Liam. With the way he was talking, Roderick and Madeline might have damaged him permanently. "Do you think you'll be able to walk?"

"But there's one voice left."

"We'll get you to the hospital," she said, trying to keep the man focused. "Just stay with me. Now, can you walk out of here?"

He dragged in a deep breath, and nodded again. "I-I think I can do it."

"Good." She shoved the rope from his right wrist, then edged around the bed. "Oh, my God," she gasped, staring at Madeline's lifeless body. Since she was in the process of freeing Liam, he couldn't have killed Madeline. Which left Roderick. She didn't care why he'd murdered her, she worried what Harrison might face when he made it to the lower level.

She turned away from Madeline, and went back to work on Liam's ropes. "Did Roderick kill her?"

"Yes," he said, wincing as he used his free hand to yank the duct tape from one of his eyes. "He choked her."

"I can't say that I'm upset. The woman was pure evil." She cut through the last of his bindings. "Come on, there's another man in the next room. Eliot. He came in with me," she said as he slid off the bed.

She hurried for the door. Hot breath suddenly coated her neck. Her legs gave as fear cut her to the core, and Liam rammed her against the door. He gripped her wrist before she could reach back and slice him.

"Guess whose voice I hear?" he murmured, his tone no longer filled with fear, but with pure malice.

"I'm here to help you," she said, hoping, praying that there was something inside this stranger that could still connect with reality.

"I don't need your help." He grabbed her by the hair, then slammed her head against the door. Pain shot through her skull. Stars burst in front of her eyes. "I need to kill," he growled, his voice tinny as her head swam. She dropped to the floor. He took the knife from her hand. "The only reason I'm letting you live is because you freed me. As for the *victim* in the next room?"

He swung open the door. Through blurred vision, she watched his shoes move across the hardwood floor. Determined to try to stop him, or at least save herself before the house was engulfed in flames, she pushed to her knees. Fell, then tried again.

She made it to her feet. Dizziness engulfed her. She stumbled to the wall, toward the opened door, then jerked back just as the man snapped Eliot's neck.

Horrified, she pressed herself against the wall. Stared at the steps leading to...what? Freedom? Fire?

Smoke filled the small alcove between the two attic rooms. She couldn't think about the man and what he'd done. Self-preservation, fighting her way back to Cash was her sole focus. They needed each other. There were others who needed her, too. Daddy, Bobby...Harrison.

Harrison.

Panic and relief swept through her as Harrison reached the top step. Worried Liam would hurt him, she held a finger to her lips, then jerked her head toward the room where Madeline lay dead. Harrison moved past her, just as Liam exited Eliot's room, cracking his knuckles. He glanced to her and held up the closed switchblade. "Thanks for the souvenir," he said, then rushed down the staircase.

"Who the hell was that?" Harrison asked, coming up beside her and wrapping her arm around his shoulder.

"I'll explain later. Go," she said, hanging onto him. "How bad is the fire?"

"Spreading." They made it to the second floor landing. "In here," he said, dragging her into a bathroom, then slamming the door behind them.

The tub faucet sprayed against several towels. Harrison pulled out one, then placed it over her head. She shivered when the cold terrycloth hit her skin, but quickly wrapped it around her, then ·helped Harrison with his. "Thank you for coming back."

He took another towel from the tub and draped it over her shoulders. "Keep this around you and cover your mouth."

She touched his face. "Thank you," she repeated, her tired eyes burning and filling with tears.

Harrison's eyes misted with tears, too. "If you were dead, I wouldn't be humiliated. But if you were dead because I didn't have your back...I can't live that way."

She hugged him close and let out a sob of relief. The drug hadn't destroyed him. They could make it. They could do this.

The door burst open, bouncing against the wall. Cash stood at the threshold, soot covering his face. His dark eyes, wild with fear, settled on her as he quickly closed the door. She never wanted to see that same fear in his eyes again. Ever. Unable to speak, to tell him what he meant to her, about the horrors they'd faced, she rushed into his arms.

Cash smoothed a hand over the cold wet towels coating her head and back, and held her tight. After tonight, boring would be their new lifestyle. His heart couldn't take this kind of danger, not when it meant he could lose Mel. "I love you," he said. "We have to go. Where's the woman, Madeline?"

"Dead," Mel said.

"Was anyone else working with her and Rodney?"

"Who?" Mel asked.

Smoke began to filter in from beneath the crack between the door and floor. "One of the people who were drugging you," he said, hoping to God they hadn't screwed up and Vlad was killing the wrong guy. "Dark hair, tall."

"You mean, Roderick," Harrison said. "He and Madeline kept us here."

Roderick and Madeline were so close to Rodney and Adeline, he didn't have to be a super-spy to figure out the twins were using fake names. "Sure, whatever. Let's talk about it later." He nodded to the tub. "Smart move with the towels. Do you have one for me?"

Harrison yanked one from the linen closet, then tossed it into the tub. "The main staircase is blocked. How'd you get up here?" he asked, soaking the towel.

"There's a servants' staircase down the hall. It's narrow and in bad shape, but the fire hasn't reached it yet. At least it hadn't when I went through." He chose to leave out that the staircase had no light and was completely made of wood. If the fire had spread, it'd burn instantly. "The stairs lead to the butler's pantry near the kitchen. There's an exit to the backyard from there."

"There's another man." Mel fisted his shirt. "A victim, I think. He's dangerous. I saw him kill a man."

He looked to Harrison. "I saw him head down the attic steps, but don't know where he is."

"I've been in all the rooms on this level looking for you two." Although he didn't like the idea of a murderer on the loose, they needed out of the burning house. "We'll worry about him later."

Harrison handed him the wet towel. "Where are Lola and Vlad?"

"Haven't seen Lola. Last I saw Vlad, it looked like he was killing Roderick." Cash tested the doorknob for heat before turning it. "We're wasting time. Cover your mouths. Mel, hang onto me. Harrison, don't let go of Mel."

He quickly wrapped the towel over his mouth and nose. After turning on the small flashlight he pulled from his pocket, he raised it, then rested his gun on his forearm. Adeline might be dead, but the man Mel and Harrison had been talking about could have doubled back.

Cash led them down the hall. Smoke surrounded them, grew thicker, darker. When they reached the panel to the servants' staircase, he thanked God for giving them a break. The narrow space held little smoke, but it didn't mean there couldn't be a fiery surprise waiting for them at the bottom.

He wanted to race down the steps, but kept his pace, and theirs, slow. The wood was old, rotted or absent in some places. "Stay to the left. There's a missing board two steps down," he said, flashing the light ahead of them. When they reached the bottom without incident, Cash lightly touched the doorknob with the tips of his fingers. Still cool. He touched the door. Again, no heat.

"Here we go," he said, then opened the door. They were met with a wall of dense gray smoke. His eyes immediately burned. Knowing the layout of the house, that they didn't have far to go before reaching the back door, he could endure. He wanted to glance back and check on Mel, but didn't want to lose his bearings in the smoke.

Heat suddenly blasted him from the right. Mel tugged his shirt when a flame shot through a wall. The fire on the other side of the wall roared as if it were a wild beast. His heart pounded. Sweat poured from his scalp. The kitchen was around the corner. Almost there…

Frustration devastated his confidence. The fire had spread to the kitchen, licked at the wooden cabinets and blocked the back door. Not willing to give up and let his wife die, he glanced to the window above the farmhouse sink.

"Stand back," he said, moving her away from him. He grabbed the coffee maker from the counter, then tossed it through the window. The glass shattered. Drawn to the fresh oxygen, the smoke and flames shifted pattern, moved along the butcher-block counter toward the sink. With no time to lose, he pulled the towel from his face, wrapped it around his hand, and knocked the remaining glass out of the way.

He lifted Mel and sat her in the sink. She held his face in her hands, kissed him, then swung her legs over the sill. "Go," he said, helping her turn to her stomach.

Through the cloud of smoke pouring from the window, he saw Vlad's outline. The Russian ran toward the house. With the way he hauled ass, he could help Mel the rest of the way. Relieved, he motioned for Harrison to follow Mel through the window. As Vlad assisted Mel to the ground, Harrison climbed into the sink.

"Get this over your face," Harrison said, throwing his towel at Cash.

As he waited for Harrison to go through the window, he covered his mouth. The flames traveled faster, growing as they moved. Sure they'd reach him before he escaped, he jumped into the sink. Once Harrison made it over the sill, Cash heaved himself out headfirst. Vlad and Harrison latched onto his arms, just as heat seared his legs. When he hit the ground he and Harrison slapped the towels around his calves and feet, snuffing the fire.

Breathing hard, tasting ash, he turned toward the field in the back. Together, he, Vlad and Harrison ran to where Lola and Mel stood, a man—with his hands behind his back—was on his knees and between the two women.

When they reached them, Harrison kicked Rodney Archer in the face. Blood flew from the man's nose, as Rodney fell backward.

Lola jerked him back to his knees. "Don't," she shouted when Harrison lifted his leg as if he were going to use Rodney's head to practice punting.

"Why not? The prick deserves to die," Harrison said, turning on Vlad. "Fucking Russian pussy. Why didn't you kill him? Cash said you were on him." Before Vlad could answer, Harrison reached for Vlad's gun holster. "I'll do it myself."

Vlad released a right hook, sending Harrison onto his ass. "Harry do not touch Vlad's gun. Ever."

Harrison rubbed his jaw, but didn't rise. "I think your gator has made you soft. Or maybe the Florida sun has fried what little you've got in your thick skull." He glared at Rodney. "I don't need a gun to kill him." He started to rise, but Mel pushed him down.

"Enough," Mel shouted, then turned to the rest of them.

"This is the drug talking. Not Harrison."

"The hell it is," Harrison said.

"Really? You called me stupid after I set you free. The Harrison I know wouldn't have."

"Wasting your time to save those two homeless guys *was* stupid. Now one of them is dead, and the other practically knocked you out cold. Oh, and do we know where he is?"

Laughter rose from Rodney's direction. They all looked at him. "Care to let us in on the joke?" Lola asked.

Harrison pulled a chunk of grass from the ground and threw it. "Should have let me kill him."

Rodney looked over at Harrison. "I wish you would."

"Death too simple." Vlad backhanded the man. "Answer question."

Rodney gave Vlad a bloody grin. "Harry was right. Melanie is stupid. She just set Adeline's creation free."

"Meaning?" Lola prompted.

"A lot of people are going to die."

"Again, why are we letting him live?" Harrison asked. "Come on, Lola. Admit it. If we were back in the Everglades, you'd already have Mel moving his dead body to her daddy's swamp."

What in the hell was Harrison talking about? The drugs, like Mel had said, were affecting the man.

"Shut up, Harrison," Mel said, and Cash recognized the warning in her tone.

Lola wipe her forehead with the sleeve of her black jacket. Now that he looked at her, the burning fire revealed a cut across her forehead, and a swollen lip. "Mel's right. You need to keep your mouth shut. If you keep it up, I will personally gag you."

"Whatever the hell."

Damn, did he want to kick Harrison's ass.

"Vlad have no problem to gag Harry."

Lola raised a hand, then rested it on Rodney's shoulder. "I'm going to fill you in on why Vlad spared your life. This way my colleagues, who you drugged and left for dead in a house you set fire to, can understand." She cracked the man in the back of the head with her knuckles. "Your twin sister, Adeline. We know about her and that she's a murderer."

"*Twin sister?*" Harrison asked. "Are you kidding me?"

"Last warning," Lola said to Harrison, who still looked dumbfounded. "You were trying to help her get better, correct? But the only way to find out if your drug worked would be to create someone as psychopathic as her. Am I right?"

When he didn't answer, Lola nodded to Vlad, who lifted the man off the ground by the throat. "Vlad will hurt, torture, but not kill." He shrugged. "Vlad have all night," he said, then dropped the man to the ground.

Rodney coughed and wheezed. "Who are you people? I want a lawyer?"

Lola knelt. "Yeah, well, we're not lawyer kinda people. No worries, we'll let the police have you. More likely GBI or the Feds, but in the meantime, we'd like you to answer a few, easy questions. I suggest you do that, or my friend here will make it look like you broke several bones as you tried to escape from the house fire. Clear?"

"Fuck you."

She nodded to Vlad again.

Rodney shrank back. "Wait."

"He killed his sister," Mel said.

Lola smiled. "All the more reason to keep you alive. I'm an only child, but I longed for a brother or a sister. To have that bond...but to have a twin? That *had* to be something special."

As the house behind them groaned and pipes burst, Cash wondered how much longer they'd have before the authorities would be alerted. And yet, he didn't want to cut Lola's questioning short. The tears in Rodney's eyes were priceless. Once the man lawyered up, he doubted they'd be able to force him to talk again.

"And you killed her," Lola continued. "Why'd you do that, Rodney?"

He shook his head, as tears streamed down his face. "I didn't mean to, I was trying to humiliate her in front of *him*." He glared at Mel. "And that dumb bitch let him go. *You* have to live with that, not me. Every person he kills is on *your* head."

Cash wanted to go to Mel, tell her the man was insane, talking shit, but knew they needed what they could get from him. He might not be part of ATL, and Mel would be exiting out of the agency once this man was turned over to the authorities, but he also wanted to understand why. Why would these people do this? And what did they do to the man, who might or might not have escaped, that would turn him into a killer?

"Why would he kill?" Lola asked, dabbing at the blood along her lip.

"Oh, my God," Mel gasped, looked to Harrison, then to Rodney. "He said you'd break him, then fix him."

"Who did?" Cash asked.

"Liam, the man I cut loose. He also said Roderick—Rodney—*did* fix him. That all the voices were gone, but one. Hers." Mel pushed her hair from her face. "He told me that the only reason he wouldn't kill me was because I set him free." She doubled over and hugged herself. "Oh, God. We need to check the house. We need to make sure he's dead."

Cash rushed to her, pulled her close. "Don't. You didn't know, you *don't* know."

When Rodney laughed again, she stiffened in his arms. "You people are so fucked."

Lola shoved him to the ground and pressed her foot against his chest. "Explain."

Rodney grinned. "I'll tell you one thing about Liam, then you can either kill me or get my attorney. Otherwise, I'm not talking. I have nothing to live for now, so it's really up to you as to how far you want to take this."

Lola drew in a breath. "What's the one thing?"

"He was schizophrenic."

"And?" When he didn't respond, she pressed the heel of her boot against his groin. "You need to give me more."

Rodney's breathing grew labored. "If he told Melanie the voices were gone, all but *Adeline's*, she'll be in his head, constantly talking to him. My drug might've gotten rid of the voices driven by his schizophrenia, but *she* dominates his mind now." His face crumpled as he let out a sob. "She was brilliant…"

"I didn't get a good look at him when I ran into him in the living room, except to say smoke was rising off his burned clothes and he had a mean punch." Lola stepped back and rubbed her swollen lip. "Mel, could you describe him?"

"Absolutely."

"Good," Lola said. "I know the side entrance was blocked by the fire, and Vlad didn't see him come out the back door. Cash, do you think he could've made it out the front?"

"With the height of the flames when I came inside, I don't see how."

Lola let out a frustrated sigh and scanned the dark fields surrounding the house. "We need to make sure he's dead." She nudged Rodney with her boot. "If not, we'll need everything you know about him."

Rodney laughed as the House of Archer—a home that had stood for two centuries—collapsed. "Then I guess you better hope Liam is dead."

CHAPTER 21

Cash and Mel's House, Tallahassee, Florida
Tuesday, 3:23 a.m. Eastern Daylight Saving Time

M EL STARED AT her reflection, wondering how long it would take for the few eyelashes she'd lost to grow back. As the ridiculously vain thought passed through her mind, the memory of the way Adeline's monster had snapped Eliot's neck replaced it.

Oh, God. What had she done? How many innocent people would die because of her mistake? Despite the hot steam lingering from her shower, she shivered as a knot grew in the pit of her stomach. Lola had called Ian while Cash had been rescuing them from the burning house. That had been before Lola had known about Adeline's monster, Liam. Even then, Ian had reached out to a contact with the Georgia Bureau of Investigation. The owner of CORE had wanted the situation contained *without* any mention of ATLs involvement. The GBI agent and his partner had made it to the plantation house before the local police and fire department, and had suggested Lola, Vlad and Cash leave. As far as anyone had been concerned, she and Harrison were victims—heroes for not only escaping, but detaining Rodney Archer.

If only they knew the truth. She doubted anyone would consider her a hero once the monster began killing.

The knot in her stomach had her doubling over as a wave of fear and guilt rushed through her. Her throat tightened, but she held back the tears. Cash was waiting for her in their bedroom, and she didn't want to add to his worry. At the hospital, he'd hovered over her, over every doctor or nurse who'd come near her. Once they were home, he hadn't wanted her out of his sight and had insisted she keep the bathroom door open. She'd closed it anyway. She had needed privacy, a moment alone to digest everything that had happened, and to think through what she dreaded telling Cash.

"I can't hear anything," Cash said from the opposite side of the bathroom door. Her guilt compounded. He'd probably been pacing the hallway, waiting for her.

She reached for her brush. "I'll be out in a second."

"Do you feel okay? Are you hungry or thirsty? I can make you something."

Tears misted her eyes. "I'm good."

"Your pain meds?"

She wasn't in any pain, but the ER doctor had written her a prescription for the discomfort she might experience around her eyes, along with a mild sedative should she have trouble sleeping. After her urine sample had come back clean, and she'd been thoroughly examined, they'd sent her home. Harrison hadn't fared as well. He'd still had trace amounts of Adeline's drug in his system, along with the symptoms. The doctors were hopeful he could be released as early as tomorrow. Even though he'd been mean and nasty toward Vlad, the Russian had remained at the hospital with him, while Lola had gone back to the hotel to confer with the GBI agents. *She* should be with Lola now, discussing what they needed to do next.

Setting the brush aside, she slipped into some underwear, then pulled one of Cash's old t-shirts over her wet head. After dragging in a deep breath, she opened the door. Cash stood in the threshold wearing nothing but a pair of athletic shorts. She was glad to see that he'd left his post outside of the bathroom long enough to use the guest bath to shower. She preferred the smell of soap to smoke, and didn't need any more reminders about their time in the plantation house.

"I don't need my meds," she said. "I just need to sleep next to you."

He pulled her into his arms and held her tight. "Every night. That's all I want. Come on, let's go to bed."

With his arm around her shoulder, he led her into their bedroom, then tucked her into bed. After he crawled in next to her, he drew her close to his chest.

Although exhausted, she couldn't keep her eyes closed. Her mind kept racing, going back to the House of Archer, to the monster, to how they were going to find him. She reached for her cell phone resting on the nightstand.

"What are you doing?" Cash asked.

"Setting my clock?"

"For what? Neither one of us has to be anywhere in the morning. Jude has the garage covered, and Lola said Shane won't be flying in to pick her up until the afternoon."

"Yeah, but I need to get home. If I'm on the road by noon, I'll be in Everglades City by seven."

He tightened his hold on her. "You *are* home."

She set the alarm for ten, then tucked the phone under her pillow. "You know what I mean."

"Actually, I don't."

To avoid an argument, she should have waited until he had fallen asleep, then set her alarm. But she'd worried she would doze off before she had the chance. "Look, it's late. We'll talk about it in the morning."

"You're not quitting, are you?" he asked, the accusation and disappointment in his tone sat on her chest like a seven-ton elephant.

"I am," she answered honestly. "After we find Adeline's creation."

He rolled away, taking his warmth and security with him. "That could take months, years. Unless Rodney starts talking, you know nothing about the man except his first name and what he looks like. And people can change their appearance."

"If CORE steps in to help us—"

"I don't care about CORE or ATL." He sat up, then threw off the comforter and sheets. "I care about having my wife home and safe, not chasing killers or dumping dead bodies in a swamp."

Dread sucker-punched her. She reached toward the nightstand, then turned on the lamp. "I can explain."

"Don't bother. Vlad filled me in on what you did." He shoved off the bed. "Imagine how happy I was to learn that my wife is the agency's *cleaner*."

"I'm not—"

"You get rid of bodies, boats, cars, weapons...what the hell else would you call yourself?"

"I'm the Ice Cream Lady." Tired, hurt and defensive, she kicked off the bedding and stood. "That's all you were ever supposed to know. I cleaned up a few messes for ATL and CORE, so what? Instead of yelling at me for things that I can't undo, admit what's really bothering you."

He narrowed his eyes. "You know exactly what it is."

"Right. You want me home—in Tallahassee. I get it. I want to be here, too. But I'm obligated to go after that man."

"No. You're *choosing* to go after him. No one is making you do anything. It's all on you."

He was right. Staying with ATL until this case was officially over would be her choice. Since Liam was free because of her, she felt duty-bound. Cash, who'd spent his Army career ensuring soldiers could safely move forward without meeting with a roadside bomb, should comprehend her reasons.

"It *is* my choice," she said, edging around the bed. "I don't want to fight about it, or disappoint you." She wanted him to hold her, to understand that this was something she needed to do to waylay the guilt. When she reached him, she ran her hands along his arms. "If you were in my position, I think you'd do the same thing."

"I spent two years without you because I was too selfish to give up my job, and too scared to admit I was worried you'd reject me even if I did." He took a step back, disengaging them. "At this point in my life, my number one priority would be you. Not getting off on the rush."

Tears filled her eyes. "I'm not staying with ATL because I *get off* on putting myself in danger. I'm doing it to clean up a mess I've made."

"Fucking up our marriage is the only mess you're making," he shouted, betrayal darkening his eyes. "Hey, but you're the *cleaner*. You'll make it all good, right? Sashay that sweet ass into town every few weeks for a weekend of sex to keep Cash happy."

"You'd know best how that works since you've been stringing me along for two years, and I was stupid enough to fall for it." She hugged herself. "This is ridiculous, *repo man*. I don't even know how you can compare stopping a murderer to your selfish need to keep the adrenaline rush going."

He shook his head in disgust. "You really don't see it, do you? You want to talk about selfish? I know now what I put you through. I get it." He wiped a hand down his face. "I'm ashamed of what I did to you. You saw me broken and beaten, nursed me back to health, and then I betrayed you by going back to the repo business. I honestly don't deserve to be with you."

Tears slipped down her cheeks and burned her sensitive eyes. "Don't talk like that."

"Let me finish. I don't know exactly what happened to you in that house today, but between what you've said, and how Harrison came out of there, my imagination has been running a horror film in my head. I don't think I've ever been so scared, not in combat, and not when a bunch of guys were beating the hell out of me." He stepped forward, gently touched her face. "But you're still willing to put yourself in a position where you could end up hurt or dead. You're doing exactly what you've accused me of doing." He dropped his hand. "Until a few days ago, I never promised to quit the repo business. Whether you stay or go, I still intend to get out of it. But the difference is *you* promised to quit ATL, now your breaking that promise."

"There's a *big* difference," she said, defensive.

"Explain it to me."

As his words sank in, she stared at her husband. While she did, the memory of Liam snapping Eliot's neck replaced Cash's face. She lightly touched the lump on her head from where the bastard had slammed her skull against the door. She couldn't explain the difference. Her job had landed her in the hospital, and if she hadn't had her switchblade, or if Cash hadn't been in the house at the right time, she might not be standing in front of him now. But she still couldn't shake the fact that *she* had let that monster go. She didn't care if her guilt for what he could do to other innocents was premature. She cared about stopping him. Cash was hurting right now. Once he thought all of this through, he'd realize the importance of the situation and that she needed to remain employed by ATL.

"I need to go to Everglades City anyway," she began, choosing her words carefully. "My things are there, and I doubt you expected me to be moved back in by the end of the week. Let me just see how things are going, what Lola has learned, if Rodney has talked." She let out a deep breath. "Just give me some time."

"We've already wasted two years."

"That's on you."

He nodded and looked away. "You're right. Is this your way of punishing me? You do enjoy the whole *tit for tat* thing."

"Not at all. Come on, Cash, why was it okay for you to keep working your job, but I can't work mine? Think about it. You were risking your life to repossess *cars*. At least I'm willing to risk mine to save lives." The shock widening his eyes had her regretting her words. She latched onto his arm when he moved past her. He shook her off. "Wait," she said, walking after him. "I don't want to fight. I spent the day fighting to come home to you."

He turned on her. "While I spent the day drinking beer and swimming in the pool. Christ." He shook his head. "Watching you get in that woman's car with Harrison was like the beginning of dying a slow death. Knowing where you were, then finding out who had you...I wanted to tell Lola to go to hell and go after you."

"Then you know exactly how I felt every single time you went on a repo job."

"Then *you* should know that staying with ATL will screw up our marriage," he shouted. When Dolly barked from the kitchen, he looked toward the bedroom door. "Get some sleep. I need to take care of Dolly."

As he left the room, her heart broke. She collapsed on the bed and finally allowed herself to let go. She cried for Harrison, for the others that Adeline and Rodney Archer had murdered. Cried for herself, for the misery she'd endured, for the terror she'd gone through. Mostly she cried for Cash. She loved him so much. Why couldn't he understand she needed to right the wrong she'd created, that she *would* come back to him? After spending two years waiting on him, the least he could do was give her a couple of weeks or months.

Exhaustion set in, and she forced her body to move under the blankets. Cash's scent was everywhere. While it wasn't the same as having him hold her in his arms, it would be enough for tonight. Maybe once he took the time to think over what they'd argued about, he'd realize he was wrong about her and them. They'd been through so much together. Their relationship could handle this.

But as she started to doze, instead of memories of the monster, the people who'd held her prisoner, the fire…only one thing filled her mind. The fear in her husband's eyes.

Cash and Mel's House, Tallahassee, Florida
Tuesday, 11:47 a.m. Eastern Daylight Saving Time

CASH SAT AT the patio table, his dog by his side. When he stopped scratching Dolly behind the ear, she nudged him with her nose. He looked down at the dog. Her big brown eyes held the same kind of worry that weighed heavily on his heart.

He'd never been good with using words to express his emotions. When his therapist had brought this subject up during one of their sessions, he'd considered telling the man to go fuck himself, but had thought better of it. After all, he'd been the one to seek out a therapist, and had done so to improve the issues he knew were keeping him and Mel apart. Honestly, until his therapist had told him that not everyone left, that his mom had been a selfishly poor excuse of a parent, that risking his life on a daily basis—whether in the Army or on a repo job—was his way of avoiding commitment, he hadn't realized he'd been sabotaging his relationship with Mel. That he'd been using the rush of adrenaline to keep from worrying about being rejected.

He'd grown up in the 'hood, had graduated from the school of hard knocks, and rejection had never been part of his vocabulary. Worrying about someone leaving him had never crossed his mind until the day Dolly had taken a hit. Because his dog had meant everything to him, his perspective on life had changed. When the two of them had returned to Tallahassee, he'd started thinking about his mom, and had even decided to pay her a visit to tell her that he'd made it home in one piece. She'd been so messed up on whatever drug she had been doing when he'd gone to Iraq, she had forgotten he was even in the Army. He had left, angry at her, angry with himself for bothering, but had gone back to her again after he'd opened his own garage, and business had started going well. Her response had been, "Good, I could use some money." Although hurt, he'd given his mom a couple hundred dollars, then washed his hands of her.

Sometimes he really hated his therapist. The man wasn't even sitting at his patio table, and he was in his head. Telling him that Mel's leaving wasn't rejection. She was trying to find her way through what she'd experienced, and trying desperately to rid herself of guilt she had no business carrying. She hadn't known that the guy she'd set free had been warped into a psychopath. After she'd cut his ropes, anything the man had done, or would do, wouldn't be on her shoulders, but Adeline and Rodney's. No one could ever fault her for caring enough that she had risked her life—when she'd known damn well the house had been on fire—

to save a total stranger.

She had faulted herself.

Now his wife would leave him again, not because of his job, but for hers. Now he knew the true meaning of having the tables turned. Only he wouldn't wait two years for her. Maybe that made him a hypocrite, but he didn't care. She didn't have to do this. The original case was closed. ATL, the GBI, FBI, or CORE could handle this new investigation. He was tired of being without her. He wanted to finally settle down, enjoy being married, start the family they'd talked about. If that made him selfish, so what? It was their turn at happiness.

He knew how stubborn his woman could be. Nothing he would say could change her mind. While he loved that about her, he didn't right now. He wanted to persuade her, but she had to stay with him on her terms. He had every intention of being honest, though. He would not wait. He might never move on, and couldn't imagine himself with another woman, but he refused to live in limbo for an undetermined amount of time. They both deserved better than that.

The glass door behind him slid smoothly on the track. Dolly turned her head and perked her ears, while the coffee he'd drank earlier soured in his stomach.

"I'm ready," Mel said.

"What about your things?"

She pulled a patio chair away from the table, then sat. "I only brought a small bag."

"I'm talking about the stuff you left in the closet, pictures on the wall, things in the kitchen cabinets I don't even know what they're supposed to be used for."

She stared at him with disappointment. "Those things haven't bothered you for two years."

"You haven't been here, so how could you know?"

She tightened her jaw, and looked away. "I know what you're doing, and it isn't fair."

"No, what's not fair is you choosing your guilt over us."

When she met his gaze, he couldn't help loving the fire in her eyes. "This isn't just about guilt." She pressed her hands against the table. "Do whatever you want with my stuff. But I want the chandelier from my closet. Just let me know how much the shipping costs." She stood, then walked over to Dolly. After hugging the dog and kissing her on the head, she stood and faced him. "Are you going to walk me to my car?"

His head and heart screamed for him to move out of the chair and find some way to convince her to stay. His pride kept him seated. "You go back to your swamp and figure out a way to get rid of your guilt."

"You're such a jerk."

"Fully aware." Unable to pretend he was okay with this, he shoved the chair back and stood. "I know all about guilt. I've lived with it since you moved out of here. I'm not about to rehash the past two years, or my reasons for keeping us apart. You know about them, I *thought* you accepted them. Maybe I thought wrong." He shook his head and decided to put himself out there one last time. "Do you feel any guilt about putting your job before me?"

Tears slipped down her cheeks. "Of course."

"Do you love your job more than me?"

"Fuck you for even asking me that. I never gave up on us, even when you chose your job over me."

"I didn't choose the job over you. I told you I—"

"Couldn't handle the rejection. I heard you the first time."

"That wasn't too bitchy."

She swiped tears from her face. "We're both in a bad place right now. You cool off, I'll do the same, and I'll call you in a couple of days."

"Don't bother," he said, hating himself for meaning it. "I can't have you coming and going in my life anymore. I love you, I want to be married to you, but not like this."

She tossed her hair over her shoulder and looked away, tears streaming down her face. "That would leave only one alternative."

He swallowed around the lump in his throat. "Right. I want a divorce."

Mel's Rental House, Everglades City, Florida
Tuesday, 8:11 p.m. Eastern Daylight Saving Time

WHEN THE DOORBELL rang, Mel glanced from the six-pack sitting next to a bag of wilted lettuce, to the microwave clock. A miniscule amount of hope fluttered in her chest. If Cash had left not too long after she had, he could be standing on her front stoop. She wouldn't kid herself though. He'd made it clear, hadn't even bothered with the ultimatum that she'd been waving in his face for the past few months. He had come right out and told her what he'd wanted.

Divorce.

Whoever was at her door needed to go away. She wasn't in the mood for company, and needed to lose herself in the garage. During the seven-hour drive home, she'd replayed every detail, practically every second that had transpired since she'd knocked on Cash's door—their door—six days ago. *Six days.* So much had happened in such a short time. How could she have reconciled her relationship with her husband, stopped a deranged couple from continuously kidnapping, drugging and murdering homeless people, nearly succumb to the same fate only to set a murderer free *and* lose her husband in the process?

If she didn't have bad luck, she wouldn't have any at all.

The doorbell rang again, and she remembered that she'd called Barney earlier, hoping to talk with him tonight. She'd wanted to tell him about Cash, the marriage she'd kept secret, then ask him for advice. Too sad and tired to do any talking, she released a frustrated sigh and berated herself for the impulsive call to Barney. She closed the refrigerator, then headed for the front door. When she opened it, she jerked back. "Harrison." She pushed open the screen door and let him inside. "You're back?" she asked, hugging him.

He stiffened and patted her back. "Obviously." He stepped away. "I'm wondering why you are."

She waved him off, and led him into the kitchen. "I didn't think you'd be home until tomorrow. When I spoke with Lola this morning, she said your last toxicology report still showed traces of the drug."

He shrugged. "I discharged myself. It's not like the doctors could have me arrested." He looked to the fridge. "I'll have a beer if you've got one."

"Not with the drug in your system. You have no idea how alcohol will react with it," she said, taking a seat at the kitchen table.

After an eye roll, he opened the refrigerator door and pulled out a beer anyway. "The only way Lola would agree to letting me on Shane's Cessna was if I went to her doctor once we landed." He popped the cap off the beer bottle and sat across from her. "Which I did, five hours ago. He took a sample of my urine, had it tested…I'm good."

"How are you and Vlad?"

He took a long drink, then set the bottle on the table. "How are you and Cash?"

"I asked you first."

"Did I ever tell you that Vlad was ordered to cut out my brother's tongue?"

Her skin prickled at the thought. "You're not serious."

"Unfortunately, I am. He didn't end up having to, but I asked him later if he would've gone through with it. He said, yes. He also told me that if he'd been ordered to, he'd do the same to me, but that 'Vlad would not like to hurt Harry'." He lifted his beer. "You don't go through that kind of sh.t with a guy, and lose it over a gator. And yes, I know our issues aren't just about me being forced to live with a wild predator who'd have no problem adding me to the food chain."

"So what's the real issue?"

He pulled at the beer label. "I've been thinking about my brother a lot lately. The anniversary of his death wasn't too long ago, and it had me wondering about the future. Don't get me wrong, I love working for ATL, but how long will this gig last? How long will I be forced to live with a giant, chain-smoking Russian?" He sighed. "As crazy as you and Cash are, you two have it going on, do you realize that? I mean, you have a nice house, the garage, it's clear you two love each other…I'd like that some day, minus the crazy part."

She forced a grin. "I suppose it's hard to date with your schedule."

"I need to…" His cheeks reddened as he looked away. "I feel like we need to talk about what happened at the House of Archer."

She touched his hand. "Only if you want to, otherwise, it's okay. You came back for me. If you hadn't, I'm not sure I could've made it down the attic steps. Cash wouldn't have found me, or—"

"I'm sorry I called you stupid, or for anything else inappropriate I said. I know you know it was the drug doing the talking, but I still owe you an apology." When he met her gaze, the shame in his eyes had her throat tightening. "I haven't been with a woman for almost as long as you and Cash have been separated. While you two were choosing to stay apart, I chose not to pay for a prostitute. I'm not exactly the best candidate for online dating, and I doubt many women are interested in a guy who lives with a Vlad and an alligator. Let's face it, on paper, I make minimum wage booking tours for an airboat company." He took another long drink from the bottle. "To have Adeline…do what she did to me, in front of you…" He chuckled and rubbed the back of his neck. "It's pretty sad that I have to be kidnapped and drugged to get a woman to touch me."

"It's not funny," she said, wiping tears from her cheeks and reliving the horrible memory.

"Never said it was." He looked at her, while the shame remained, anger was also banked in his eyes. "Last night, when I was in the hospital, I kept hearing you cry. The sound was awful. Sometimes I was awake when I heard it, other times it was just a nightmare. Vlad was in the room through every one of those episodes. He asked why I was sweating and shaking. At first I told him it was the drug leaving my system—which was the truth. But around four in the morning, I told him what happened."

He grinned and shook his head. "You know what Vlad said? 'Better to have dick sucked than cut. Harry worry too much.' But I told him I wasn't worried about me, I was worried about you, and how you'd look at me. You're this tiny, beautiful hard-ass. You don't let anything get to you. Until I saw you with Cash, I thought you possessed the emotional range of a sarcastic teenager to a knife-wielding girly-girl."

Between berating herself over leaving Cash, questioning her choice to remain with ATL and the guilt from setting a killer free, she didn't need this from Harrison. She'd take what he had to say, only because she cared about him and knew he was trying to work through what was going on in his head.

"I'd like to think I'm more than that," she said, trying to keep the hurt from her voice.

"You definitely are. I've never met anyone like you, and doubt I ever will again. When I saw you with Cash, I realized that you're still all those things, but you'd been hiding from everyone. I knew you were loyal, could be trusted, could be counted on, otherwise I would've refused to work jobs with you. But I didn't realize how sweet and thoughtful you are until I saw you with Bobby, how vulnerable you are until I saw you with Cash. How much I care about you, or how much I need our friendship. Do you know how many people have cried for me? For what I might be going through?" He raised his index finger, then pointed it at her. "Why are you crying now?"

"Because I hate what she did to us, and I can't stand the shame in your eyes." She cleared her throat, tried to gain her composure, and failed. She slammed her hand on the table, and stood. If Harrison truly wanted to see how vast of an emotional range she possessed, he'd find out if he didn't leave. "I cried for you because you're my friend, and you didn't deserve the humiliation Adeline tried to force on you. For whatever it's worth, I left that room proud of you. You'd beaten her at her own sick game. You're stronger than I think you realize." Emotionally drained, she choked back a sob. "I think you should go."

"Of course you do."

Anger shoved all of her gushy emotions aside and moved front and center. "What's that supposed to mean?"

"Before we went to meet Shane at the Tallahassee airstrip, Lola wanted to stop by and see you and Cash, and tell you about Rodney. Imagine our surprise when Cash told us you'd already left for Everglades City. He said something about you wanting to remain with ATL until we found Liam."

"I do, and there's nothing wrong with that," she said, tired of having to justify her decision. "What did Lola find out?"

"GBI found two bodies—both males—buried in a barn on the Archer property. They're still in the process of IDing them. They also found Florence Archer—the grandmother—dead in the cellar. Cause of death was multiple stabbings and eerily similar to the way Adeline had murdered her college roommate." Disgust crossed his face. "Investigators noticed a fresh grave at the family plot. Since there were no records of a recent death in the family, they dug it up and found an infant. How much do you want to bet it was Adeline and Rodney's baby?"

"I don't want to think about it," she said, hating the couple more than she already did—if that were even possible. She still couldn't believe that Rodney and Adeline were brother and sister. With the way they'd acted around each other, Mel had assumed they were a couple, not siblings carrying on twincest. Their sick relationship made her wonder what had happened to them as children. Had they turned to each other during childhood? Was their unhealthy relationship, their psychopathic ways, the result of bad parenting, or were they both just born wrong? They might never know, and she supposed it didn't matter. What did matter was stopping what Adeline and Rodney had created.

"Anyway, Rodney lawyered up, and we're betting he plans to string us and GBI along just to screw with us. If you think about it, the man tried to commit suicide. He doesn't want to live without his twin. So, what does he really have to lose?"

Nothing, which could make this investigation even more frustrating. They had nothing on Liam, no DNA, no fingerprints—all of that had gone up in flames. They couldn't even be certain Liam was his real name. "Does Lola have a problem with me staying on board?" she asked.

"I doubt it, but you'd have to ask her." He drained his beer, then rose from the chair. "I need to know something. How easy is it?"

"How easy is what?" she asked, not certain which direction he was heading. Their short conversation had been all over the place.

"For the past couple of months, I've been looking for a place to rent. There was one open at Barney's trailer park. The price was right, but I couldn't sign the contract. Vlad, his habits and his gator get under my skin, but if I left, nothing would be the same. Since you make leaving look easy, maybe you can give me some advice on how to walk out on my best friend without making him feel like hell about himself."

"You're siding with Cash?" she asked, stunned Harrison would meddle in her personal business, but even more shocked Cash would tell Harrison, who less than a week ago was a total stranger, what was going on in his head. "You know what? You *really* need to leave. I'm not sure why you came here tonight or what you expected to accomplish, but I'm through with this conversation."

"I came here to talk about what happened with Adeline."

"Great, then check it off your to-do list. Mission accomplished. And while you were sharing your shame and guilt, if you'd also come here to insult me, you've managed that, too."

"I didn't come here to insult you, and I'm not siding with Cash. I told you what he said to us. What I haven't told you is what I said to him."

"And?" she asked, taking the bait. Leaving Cash this time around had been harder than any of the other times. But if Cash couldn't understand why she needed to be here in Everglades City, then maybe he didn't know her as well as either of them had thought.

"I told him I wouldn't put up with your bullshit. Then he started with the *unicorns are magical* crap and I knew I'd better get in the car before he clocked me."

Disappointment settled on her shoulders. "Thank you for that. You're a good friend," she said, not hiding her sarcasm. "Since you care about me so much, it'll probably make you happy to know that Cash is planning to divorce me."

"Good move. I couldn't see you two lasting if you moved back to Tallahassee anyway. You're both too selfish and self-centered. And kids? You two are so bat-shit crazy, whatever rabid offspring you brought into this world would make Liam look like a helpless kitten."

She struck him. "How dare you talk about us like that?"

"Maybe I crossed the line about the bat-shit kid thing, but I'm right on you both being selfish." He rubbed his cheek. "What do you care? You're getting divorced."

"Because I don't want a divorce," she shouted, and went to slap him again.

He blocked the blow. "Then why are you here?"

"I set Liam free."

"So what? I didn't come back into a burning building to save your life so you could waste it on hunting a man you may never find, or who could kill you. I came back because I saw what you and Cash have, and I saw how much love there was between you." He jabbed his thumb to his chest. "I wasn't kidding. I want what you have. And it pisses me off that you could walk away from something not everyone gets a chance at in life."

She shoved both hands through her hair, and turned away. She'd been telling herself much of the same during the seven-hour drive home, but had kept countering herself with images of Liam, with the guilt. Pictured the coldness and anger in Cash's eyes. The hurt in his voice, his final ultimatum had played over and over in her head, drowning out whatever music she'd had blaring from the Camaro's speakers.

"I thought about turning around and going back to Tallahassee dozens of times during the drive home," she admitted, and reached for a paper towel to dry her face and blow her nose.

"Why didn't you?"

She looked away to hide her own shame. "Because I said things I didn't mean, and I knew I was wrong."

"Call him and tell him."

She shook her head. "Maybe tomorrow. I know Cash, and I know when not to push him." Plus, he could decide that their relationship was too much work, and that being alone was easier. He could look at her leaving as a green light to still do repo jobs.

The doorbell rang, and relief eased the tension in her shoulders. "That's Barney," she said, now glad she'd called him. "If you don't mind, I need to be alone with him."

He gave her a sad, half-smile. "I'm sorry I pushed you the way I did. But if I'd tried to get you to talk out your issues with Cash, I knew you'd shut down on me. You like going for the throat, so I figured I'd get your attention that way."

She looked to the handprint she'd left on his cheek. "Your plan worked. Sorry I hit you."

He offered his hand. "Friends?"

She pushed his hand away and hugged him. "You don't think it's wrong of me to choose Cash over going after Liam?"

He pulled back. "The only thing you're guilty of is caring. Nothing more." The doorbell rang again. "Talk to Barney about it. He's good at giving advice." He headed for the door. "But you might have to listen to a half dozen Vietnam stories to get it." He opened the door, then grinned. "Cash?"

Mel's heart raced. Cash in Everglades City? He'd never once set foot there, not for a vacation and certainly not to convince her to come home. She hurried toward the door to see for herself, then came to an abrupt halt.

Cash stood on the stoop, the wariness in his eyes matching her own. "What are you doing here?" she asked, then went into self-defense mode. "Let me guess. You came for your bike."

"I came for my wife."

CHAPTER 22

"**H**ARRISON, YOU NEED to go," Cash said without looking at him. He couldn't tear his gaze away from Mel. Her puffy eyes, red nose, tear-soaked face. Had she been crying because of him, or because of what she and Harrison had gone through yesterday? Either way, he was the one who should be here comforting her, not Harrison. He should have shoved aside his pride and ego, climbed in the Camaro with her and come to Everglades City to help her work through what she'd experienced inside the House of Archer.

"Yeah, I've gotten that a lot tonight," Harrison responded, then left the house.

Once Harrison's car had started, and tires crunched over gravel, Cash took a step forward. "Aren't you going to invite me in?"

She nodded and hugged herself, moving back to give him plenty of room to enter. "Why are you here?"

"I already told you. I came for my wife."

"The wife you want to divorce." The pulse point at the base of her throat beat hard, yet her face remained cool, passive. "I need a better answer, so why don't we play a game and raise the stakes," she suggested. "I ask you a question, if you answer right, I'll lose a piece of clothing. If you're wrong, you do."

"I know the rules. But I didn't drive five hundred miles to play games or for sex."

"It's exactly four hundred and eighty-two miles," she said, her voice rising. "I should know. Until today, I'm the *only* one who's bothered to drive it. And who said anything about having sex?"

"You're the one who wants to get naked."

"No, I want to strip everything standing in the way of us. Whether it's your hang-ups or mine. I want them gone." She hugged herself tighter. "I don't want a divorce, but it's not fair for either one of us to keep using it as a threat."

He instantly relaxed. She'd said what he needed to hear. He didn't want a divorce, either. "I couldn't agree more." He closed the door, then stepped into her small living room.

The ranch-style home she'd been renting was tiny, claustrophobic and not what he'd expected. Hell, he'd bet if he raised his arm, he could touch the ceiling. The walls were in need of repair, same went for the old, scuffed-up hardwood floors. Like a badass bounty hunter in hot pursuit, the regret that had been tracking him from Tallahassee, caught up with him, wrapped bands of guilt around his chest and throat, left him unsure of what to say. He'd planned his speech. He'd had it all laid out in his mind. One look at her tears, a quick glance at the house his wife had been living in, and he couldn't do anything but wallow in self-disgust.

Then he remembered the money he'd been sending her every month. "Is this the best you could do?" he asked.

"Are you referring to yourself or the house?"

God, she knew how to twist the knife. "You know damned well I'm talking about the house."

She looked to the chipped ceiling. "I can't believe *that's* the first thing you're going to ask me."

"Why's it so unbelievable? Between what I send you monthly for your portion of the garage, your jobs here…you could afford something better than this."

"What I do with my money isn't any of your business."

He took a step forward. "I'm your husband. It damned well *is* my business."

"Not when you're living four hundred and eighty-two miles away." She dropped her arms, then stabbed a finger at his chest. "You forfeited that right."

"Only according to you. You're the one who left."

"Old news. But in case you forgot, you never tried to stop me or attempted to get me to come home."

"I'm here now," he shouted, unable to contain his frustrations. "Christ, Mel, doesn't that mean something?"

Tears filled her eyes. She swiped them away, then hardened her jaw. "First question: for two years I've been hoping you'd show up here and ask me to come home. *Two years*," she repeated, her voice shaking. "Why are you here now?"

"Because we have unfinished business to discuss and I didn't want to do it over the phone." Not a lie, but not necessarily the truth.

"Wrong answer, lose the shirt."

"How do you know it's wrong?" he asked, pulling his shirt over his head. "You don't know what's going on in my head."

"Because I *know* you. During the past two years you could have come here to see me, try to talk me into moving home, but you didn't, not once. You'd call, send flowers, cute notes with my share from the garage, but you wouldn't dare get in your truck and come here. For you to do it today, it's for more than to discuss unfinished business." She glanced away and ran a hand through her hair. "I don't want to fight. I just want the truth."

When she met his gaze, he knew he couldn't deny her what she deserved. The hurt, the apology, the uncertainty in her eyes tore at his heart. He'd known fear, but not this kind. Yesterday, he'd been afraid Mel could be killed. Today, he was scared she'd finally push him out of her life for good. No more occasional weekends, no more phone calls. No more love or chance for a future.

"The truth," he repeated. "I've never loved anyone but you. I don't think anyone but you has loved me. Well, maybe Dolly, but I feed her."

Tears welled in Mel's eyes as she gave him a small, watery smile. "That's not true."

"Which part? About me loving you, or you loving me?"

"Don't ever doubt that I love you," she said, her voice strong and holding conviction.

"I never have, but I took your love for granted."

She gripped the hem of her pink tank top, then whipped it over her head. "You have no idea how long I've been waiting for you to say that," she said, tears slipping down her cheeks. "Your turn."

"I don't want to play a game." He wrapped his hands around her waist, brushed his thumb along her soft skin. "I want you in my arms. I need you to tell me you'll give me another chance to prove I can be the husband you deserve."

She reached up, and pressed her palms against his chest. "I said things I didn't mean, and I broke my promise to you."

She had, and after Mel had left, he'd told himself she was the one who now had to apologize. Then Harrison, Lola and Vlad had stopped by, and he'd been given a dose of reality. Mel was part of a team. When he'd refused to give up his job, she'd paved her own way—successfully. She wasn't just a *cleaner*. She was an important member of an organization whose mission was to give justice to those the regular authorities couldn't always help. Who was he to tell her she couldn't work for ATL? If he hadn't been such an insecure fool, she wouldn't have had to go back to Everglades City in the first place. She wouldn't have joined ATL.

"You did promise you'd quit, but I get why you want to stay on with ATL. I won't lie, I'm not happy about your decision. But I'd be miserable without you." He would and had been for years, which was why he'd make any sacrifice necessary to make their marriage work. Even the business he'd worked so damned hard to build. "How do you feel about me selling our portion of the garage to Jude and moving to Everglades City?" he asked.

"What?" she asked on a gasp, and gripped his biceps. "Are you out of your mind? You can't sell the business. The garage might've been up and running when I came on board, but I've invested sweat equity into it, too."

She had, working late hours with him, Jude and the boys. Helping with advertising, the accounting, making sure they had good suppliers. Not to mention working on cars.

"I can set up another garage here," he suggested.

"This is a fishing town and tourist spot. If you're going to have a successful garage, you'd be better off going north into the Naples area. Then you're up against other garages or big name franchises. It'd take years to get established."

"Sounds like it'd be a mistake to try to move here," he said, disappointed with her reaction, and how easily she'd dismissed his attempt to solve their long distance problem. Now he wondered if distance wasn't the real issue. "If we were still playing the game, you'd lose your shorts for your answer."

"Are you kidding me?" she asked, her forehead wrinkling in confusion. "You shouldn't have even asked the question in the first place. And it's the right answer. You can't give up the business for me."

He shrugged, tried to act as if his stomach wasn't a mess, or that worry wasn't wrapping around his throat. "It's a business. Like I said, I can start another one. But I can't lose my wife."

When she looked away, he touched her chin. "Or is this your way of telling me you don't want me here?" He prepared himself for the rejection he'd feared was finally coming. All of the years he'd been worried she would come home and live with him as his wife, only to discover he wasn't worth the effort, had just been a long period of procrastination. By continuing on with the repo business, keeping her a state's length away, he'd been prolonging the inevitable. Now he had his answer. He didn't doubt that she loved him, but she couldn't live with him. Even if it was on her turf. He wouldn't give up on her, though. He might leave here hurting, but at least he'd head back to Tallahassee knowing he'd done and said what he could to keep their marriage intact.

Tears shimmered in her eyes. "How could you think that? All I've wanted was to be with you."

"Now you can, on your terms. I was dead serious about the garage," he said, some of the worry lessening. "I don't have many examples of what makes a good marriage, but I'd like ours to be filled with compromise. You've given up too much for me, and I haven't been there enough for you. Let me make up for that. I need to prove you didn't make a mistake by marrying me."

Shock and irritation widened her eyes. She curled her arms around his neck, then tugged at his short hair. "I never once considered a single moment with you a mistake."

"Then tell me what to do." He ran his hand up her back, pressed her against his chest. "Tell me what you need."

She brushed her lips along his. "You."

"Damn it, Mel, I'm not talking about sex. I'm talking about your job, how you're coping with the guilt you're heaping on yourself. I want to be there for you. I want to make it go away, but I don't know how."

Tears fell as she blinked a few times. "Tell me I shouldn't feel guilty for wanting to be with you instead of going after Liam. Please tell me I'm not a bad person for walking out on my team." Desperation, love, and worry clouded her eyes. "I'm scared of dying, of never having those lazy Sunday afternoons swinging on the hammock with you. Since the accident, have you ever had those kinds of thoughts?"

"The only thing I've ever been scared of is losing you. That's why I'm here." He ran his hand through her silky hair. His woman was hurting, worse that he'd imagined. What had happened to her in that house would take time to overcome, and he wanted to be there for her—here or in Tallahassee. "Whatever you decide, in my eyes, you'll never be a bad person. You have no idea how much I admire you. For what you've done for me, for how you helped save Harrison's life and tried to save two other strangers—no matter that one of them wasn't what you'd thought. There's nothing wrong with being scared of dying, and you better damn well believe I think about you every single day of the week." He cupped the back of her head. "I will stand by whatever decision you make. I started out with nothing before. I can start again. As long as I have my woman and my dog...the garage, the house in Tallahassee doesn't matter."

"But they do. I've missed working at the garage, and I miss our house. Those things are *ours*. I think one of the reasons I was drawn to ATL was because I missed being part of something. You and I were a team. We ran that garage, we bought our house together and made it a home." She rose to her tiptoes and kissed him. "During the drive here, I kept wanting to turn around and go back *home* to you."

"We would've missed each other," he said, running a hand along her back. "Because I was making the four hundred and eighty mile drive to you. I'm just sorry it took me so long to show you that I can't be without you."

"Four hundred and eighty-*two*." She kissed him again.

"I know the drive here better than you think," he admitted. "Over the years, I found a few ways to shorten the trip. Not by much, but every mile counts."

She tugged his hair again, and not gently. "Are you telling me you've driven to Everglades City before, and you never once thought to stop and see me?"

"I thought about it, almost came in for an ice cream a few times, but then what? Nothing would have changed. I was still working a job you hated, and you wouldn't have come home with me. I just missed you so damned much. There were days I couldn't sit in the house, and I needed to see your face. Even from a distance." He let out a breath. "I'm sorry, maybe I shouldn't have told you that. It kind of makes me look like a cowardly stalker."

"Not to me," she said, grazing her lips along his. "I'm glad you told me. It's good to know you were hurting as much as I was."

He chuckled against her lips. "I love you."

"I love you, too," she murmured, then kissed him.

He tasted her, breathed in her sweet scent, traced his hands along her skin and knew he would do more than just move for her. He'd give up his job, money, his freedom, and even his life. Last night, he'd been prepared to kill for her. He pressed her closer, deepened the kiss. Tried to block the memories, the fear of losing Mel in the fire, the ER doctors hovering over her afterward, watching the taillights of her Camaro disappear as she'd left him.

"What's wrong?" she asked between kisses, and unfastened his jeans.

"Nothing now."

"Then why are you squeezing me like a boa?"

He relaxed his hold. "Sorry, baby," he said, and needing to be inside her, to hold her, love her, he unbuttoned her shorts. He slid his hands inside them and over her rear, then pushed them to the floor.

She shoved his jeans down over his hips, then kissed his chest. "I was scared, too." She kissed him again, and looked up at him. Her pretty blue eyes held understanding and love. "When I saw you coming out of the window, the fire behind you, then on your clothes, I swear my heart stopped. Then it happened again when you said you wanted a divorce."

His woman knew him too well. He unhooked her bra, kissed her shoulder as he slid the strap down her arm, then tossed it aside. "I'm still scared I'm going to screw up and make you un-happy." She'd wanted to strip away everything standing between them. Not just clothes, but everything that had been keeping them apart. If they had any chance of making their marriage work, he wanted to be completely honest, even if it chipped at his pride. "I thought I was doing okay before I met you, but I didn't start loving life until you turned my world on end." He ran his fingers through her hair, then cupped her head. "Any day without you is a bad one."

Her eyes shined with unshed tears. "Then I guess we better make sure we're never apart again," she said, leaning forward.

When their lips touched, he kissed her as if it were the first time. Gently, leisurely, taking pleasure in the soft contours of her mouth, the way her body curved against his. There was no need to rush, no sense of urgency like there'd been every time she'd come home for a short weekend. Because their home was with each other, it didn't matter to him where they lived, as long as his wife was happy.

She sighed against his mouth, then smiled. "That was a nice surprise. You haven't kissed me like that in years."

"I'm savoring the moment."

She grinned and reached between their bodies. "Savoring?" she asked, and began stroking him. "Does this mean you'll want to go slow tonight?"

As he kissed his way along her neck, he moved his hand between her thighs and ran his fingers along her heat. "I want to make love to my wife, is that a problem?"

"Not at all." She let out a quiet moan when he pressed his fingers deep. "But does this mean you won't be taking her against the wall."

He smiled against her throat, then gently tugged her hair and met her teasing gaze. "Against the wall." He pumped his fingers harder, faster. "Bent over the couch…" As he rubbed his thumb along her clit, her eyes darkened with desire. He pressed his mouth against her ear. "I plan on spending the night making you come."

On a groan, she kissed him. Not with the urgency he'd expected, but with the love he depended on and needed. Love he'd never take for granted again.

Cap'n Ryan's Airboat Tours, Everglades City, Florida
Wednesday, 8:45 a.m. Eastern Daylight Saving Time

MEL ENTERED THE souvenir shop, then made her way toward the back office. Cash had asked if she'd wanted him to come with her, but this was something she needed to do on her own, and without an audience. Which had been why she'd texted Lola late last night, asking her to meet before anyone else arrived.

Although confident in her decision, she wasn't ready to face the rest of the ATL team yet. She'd never been much of a crier, but lately she'd been bawling like a baby. If she took even a quick glance at any one member of their crew, she'd lose it. Barney, Shane and Ryan, they'd always been like family, and she knew their relationships wouldn't change. But she'd miss seeing them on a daily basis. As for Lola, Vlad and Harrison, until this past week, she hadn't realized how much she'd valued their friendship. She'd miss seeing them, too. Going to Polina's Paradise for cookouts, brainstorming sessions for an investigation, or just to have a few beers with her friends. She didn't even want to think about Daddy, but knew he'd be okay. He had plenty of people to check up on him, and she and Cash planned to come visit Everglades City at least once a month.

Her nervous stomach settled when she pictured Cash where she'd left him, lying in her bed, looking sexier than any man had a right to, and waiting for her. She thought back to those lazy Sundays on the hammock, to swimming or snuggling with Cash and Dolly, to long days working at the garage, to the rewarding night in Cash's arms. She imagined the future, how they could expand the garage and their family. How the poor kid from the ghetto and the girl from the swamp would continue to build a successful life together. How the repo man and the ice cream lady would become a thing of the past, leaving the happy couple, Cash and Melanie Maddox in their wake.

Loving what the future had to offer, she walked into Lola and Ryan's office with bittersweet excitement. "Morning," she greeted Lola.

"Morning. How are you feeling?"

Sore, well loved, happy. "Great. How are you?"

Lola cocked a brow. "You sent me a text at midnight asking to meet this morning—alone. I'm nervous and happy for you."

"You talked to Harrison?"

"He might've called me and mentioned Cash was in town." She nodded toward the extra office chair. Once Mel took a seat, Lola said, "I never expected you to come back to ATL, especially after the talk we had the other night."

"I didn't either, but I also didn't expect to set a killer free." Mel held up a hand. "I know. I had no clue who or what the man was, so I shouldn't feel guilty. I do, though. I also can't put my life with Cash on hold. I'm ready to go home, but I'm going to miss you guys and working for ATL."

Lola let out a breath and reached for her hand. "We're going to miss you, too. And I think you're making the right decision." She gave Mel a squeeze, then released her hand and leaned back in the chair. "Even though you won't be part of ATL, I'll be sure to let you know what happens with the investigation."

"Yes, please do. I'm praying you guys, or whoever is going after Liam, brings him in before he hurts anyone. I know I gave the GBI agents a description, but if they want me to sit down with a sketch artist, I'm available."

"You don't think Cash would mind?"

"Not at all. I'm not going back to work for you. I'm simply around if you need anything."

Lola gave her a small smile. "That's good to know. Did Harrison tell you what GBI found in the Archer's barn?"

Her stomach turned. "That, and about the infant," she said with disgust. "Why?"

"Never mind." Lola waved her hand. "You'll be busy moving and getting settled back into your routine with Cash and the garage."

Mel rolled her eyes. "You do know that tactic doesn't work on me, right?"

Lola sighed. "It doesn't seem to work on anyone. I don't know how Ian gets away with it." She shrugged. "Okay, to the point it is. Tallahassee is about forty minutes from Rodney and Adeline's hometown of Bower, Georgia. Ian wants us to continue to pursue this case and find Liam. The GBI and FBI do, too. Our GBI contact isn't sure how much longer they'll stay involved in the investigation, and Ian's FBI connections won't be able to get involved until Liam crosses state lines and does something wrong."

"What? That's ridiculous. I saw him kill Eliot."

"Mel, Eliot's body was so badly burned, there's no way to ID the man or how he was killed. We don't even have a last name for Eliot. As for Liam, the one GBI agent said a local cop suggested that you might've hallucinated the murder. You were drugged, you were injured, confused."

Her temper spiking, she shoved out of the chair. "I know what I saw."

"And I believe you. We all do. But with only you as an eyewitness, I can understand why the authorities don't want to sink men and money into pursuing Liam."

She did not like the direction this investigation, or lack thereof, was going. She knew what she saw, and still had the lump to prove it. "But Harrison saw him, too. And Liam fought you on the way out the door. Plus, Rodney admitted to Adeline's creation."

"Harrison was drugged. The man who fought me could have simply been a victim, scared and running for his life." She shook her head. "Rodney's not talking, not now. So, Ian wants us to dig into his and Adeline's background. I'm going to have Harrison research the hell out of the family. I want to find out as much as we can about the Archers, namely Rodney and Adeline. If Rodney was being honest, which I think he was, Adeline is in Liam's head."

"Liam told me her voice was the only one left," Mel said, a shiver running through her as she remembered his hot breath along her neck. "I think the main focus should be on Adeline. She could be the key to finding Liam."

"I agree, which is why I was hoping you would go to Bower. I was thinking you could go undercover as a reporter or something. I'll let you decide."

She'd promised Cash she'd quit ATL, and she would keep that promise. "The local police have seen my face, but only know me and Harrison under the fake names you gave us. Going in as a reporter wouldn't work. Doing anything undercover after I told my husband I was quitting is not something I'd consider without talking to him first."

"I understand," Lola said with a smile. "I would never want to put you in that position or be the cause of a problem between you and Cash."

"But," Mel continued, "I don't see how Cash would object to going to Bower with me, the concerned husband, hoping that his wife finds peace of mind while she learns to deal with the horrors she'd endured at the House of Archer."

Lola's smile grew into a big grin. "The locals might be more apt to talk to a victim rather than a nosey reporter who could make their small community look bad. I love it. Are you sure Cash will go along with it?"

"I know how to persuade my husband. But I'll talk to him about it while we're packing my things, and let you know."

"You can tell me later, when we're at Polina's Paradise."

Mel pulled her keys from her purse. "What's going on there?"

"Your engagement, wedding, retirement and going-away party." Lola rose. "We'll be expecting the guests of honor at seven. I know Ryan and Barney are looking forward to meeting Cash."

Touched and surprised, Mel hugged Lola. "Thank you," she said. "You're a good friend." She stepped back. Her throat tightened when she saw tears shimmering in Lola's eyes. "Are you sure you don't need me to scoop ice cream today?"

"Nope. I've got you covered."

"Already found my replacement, huh?"

A tear slipped down Lola's cheek. "No one could replace the ice cream lady."

EPILOGUE

*"When this monster entered my brain, I
will never know, but it is here to stay."*
—Dennis Rader, BTK Killer

Thomasville, Georgia
Wednesday, 9:36 a.m. Eastern Daylight Saving Time

L IAM SWEPT UP behind the dilapidated shed flanking the
heavily wooded property. A small, whitewashed farmhouse in
bad need of repair stood fifty yards away. He glanced to the gravel
driveway that had been overrun by weeds, to the rusted mailbox
where *Dougal* had been painted along the side.

"Go inside. You need to go inside," Adeline whispered. *"You're
hurt, hungry. You need food, money. You need to kill for me."*

Rodney's drug had 'fixed' him. He hadn't been lying to the
blonde who'd set him free. The voices were gone. The drug had
worked, yet one voice had remained. Even in death, Adeline
taunted him, goaded him. Suggesting violence and murder.
Tempting him with lewd thoughts, her filthy words planting
images of cruel sex, of how he'd wanted and fantasized about
taking Adeline once freed.

Murderous rage burned through him. He turned away from
the shed and started for the woods again. He wanted Rodney dead
and hoped the prick had died in the house fire. He'd wanted
Adeline dead, too. But he had wanted to be the one to kill her.
Slowly. Painfully. Rodney had robbed him of the fantasy. He'd

been stripped of the chance, deprived of the utter satisfaction of ending her life on his terms.

"*You know you want to go inside the house,*" she said. "*Something smells good, and you're hungry.*"

The aroma of bacon hung on the humid air. The hunger pangs he'd been fighting since yesterday morning had left him hollow inside.

He would not kill for food. He was better than that. Although he couldn't remember his past prior to meeting Adeline, he knew in his gut that he hadn't always thought about murder. Yet that had been all he could think about since fleeing the fire. Killing, mutilating, violence. That couldn't be him, couldn't be who he was.

"*But it's you now,*" she said, her words rolling over one another in an eerie echo. "*Remember how good it felt slamming the woman's head against the door. Remember the rush when you snapped the man's neck. The power. I gave you that power, that freedom. Admit how good it felt. Admit it, Liam.*"

God, how he'd wanted to do more to the blonde. He patted the front pocket of his jeans until his fingers ran along the outline of the small switchblade he'd taken from her. Such a tiny blade, and yet the possibilities of what he could do with it were endless.

"*Admit it, Liam. You want to go into that house. Feel the power and rush again. Feed off the fear.*"

"I want you to shut up," he said, stopping when a cramp seized his side. He leaned against a tree and looked over his shoulder. Sweat trickled into the swollen, open lacerations along his face where Rodney had hit him with the chain. He ignored the stinging pain. The scent of bacon teased his senses, made his mouth water, made him forget his head hurt. He staggered forward.

"*That's it. Take what you want, what you need,*" she encouraged.

He took another step, then several more until he reached the shed again. The blisters along his feet had been rubbed raw yesterday morning. He'd had no choice but to continue to move on and through the woods. He'd needed to distance himself as far as he could from the burning house. By now, the authorities would know what Rodney and Adeline had done. Whether Rodney survived, he didn't know. He was hopeful, though. As much as he'd gladly slit Rodney's throat with the switchblade, he wouldn't risk captivity to hunt the man down and kill him. After having been bound to a bed for days, the subject of Rodney and Adeline's experiment, he would die before ever being imprisoned again.

"No thoughts of dying," Adeline said. *"You're a survivor. A born hunter. A killer."*

She was wrong. He somehow knew he'd never killed before, but what he *did* know? When he'd twisted the man's neck, Adeline had quieted. While he'd used the woods and darkness as his shield, she'd stayed quiet for hours. But yesterday morning, she'd awoken. Hungry. Encouraging him to push forward, to reach an unknown destination and take shelter, to regain his strength and tend to his wounds.

To kill. Without reason, without mercy.

Her laughter filled his head. *"You know me so well, lover. I am hungry. And look what's on the menu."*

An old man in a pair of coveralls stepped onto the slanted porch, a pipe dangling from between his lips. "Breakfast will be done right shortly," a woman called from the house. "Don't be lightn' that pipe now."

The man waved a hand, then struck a match. "I hear ya', Ma," he replied, then lit the pipe anyway.

"Go for it, lover. Take their food, their lives, their money. I'm so hungry," she screamed, piercing his head, fracturing his mind. *"Do it. I created you. Now give me what I need. Show me. Don't stop until you're done."*

He leaned against the shed and pressed his hands to his ears. Pain shot through his skull when the heels of his hands brushed against the wounds he'd sustained from the chain. He needed her to stop. To shut up and leave him alone. Breathing hard, his head filled with her endless taunts, he dropped his hands. He shoved away from the shed, then stepped out from behind it and started for the house.

Time to feed the bitch inside him.

TO BE CONTINUED...

Look for Harrison's story January 2016...

Perfectly Tortured
Book Three of C.O.R.E. Above the Law

Perfectly Twisted
Book One of C.O.R.E. Above the Law

What do you get when you mix a snake-handling reverend, a necrophiliac, a cop and an ex-con? Something perfectly twisted...

Sound like the start of a bad joke? Not to Shane Monahan. The ex-con, former Army Night Stalker and newest recruit to the underground criminal investigation group, ATL or Above the Law, has it bad for Collier County Deputy Beth Price. But ex-cons and cops don't mix, especially when this particular ex-con is looking at going back to prison for his involvement with ATL.

All Beth wants is a fun distraction from the stress of her job and law school. She thinks she's found that when she meets Shane during an airboat tour through the Florida Everglades. But Shane's a felon, a man who could destroy her career as a deputy, and jeopardize her future as an attorney. She doesn't know what to do—until dead bodies start showing up around the county.

When three abused corpses are found with snake remains inside them, the discovery brings a murderer out of retirement. The Reverend, as he calls himself, doesn't like his kills being mimicked, especially by a man who abuses the dead—after all, the Reverend does have a reputation to uphold and a congregation to scam. Now it's time to teach his copycat a deadly lesson...

Other C.O.R.E. Titles Available (listed in order) by Kristine Mason

Shadow of Danger
Book One of the C.O.R.E. "Shadow" Trilogy

Beware of what lurks in the shadows...

Four women have been found dead in the outskirts of a small Wisconsin town. The only witness, clairvoyant Celeste Risinski, observes these brutal murders through violent nightmares and hellish visions. The local sheriff, who believes in Celeste's abilities and wants to rid their peaceful community of a killer, enlists the help of an old friend, Ian Scott, owner of a private criminal investigation agency, CORE. Because of Ian's dark history with Celeste's family, a history she knows nothing about, he sends his top criminalist, former FBI agent, John Kain, to investigate.

John doesn't believe in Celeste's mystic hocus-pocus, or in her visions of the murders. But just when he's certain they've solved the crimes with the use of science and evidence, more dead bodies are discovered. Could this somehow be the work of the same killer, or are they dealing with a copycat? To catch a vicious murderer, the skeptical criminalist reluctantly turns to the sensual psychic for help. Yet, with each step closer to finding the killer, John finds himself one step closer to losing his heart.

Shadow of Perception
Book Two of the C.O.R.E. "Shadow" Trilogy

What happens when negligent plastic surgeons receive a taste of their own medicine...?

Chicago investigative reporter, Eden Risk, receives an unmarked envelope containing a postcard ordering her to watch the enclosed DVD...or someone else dies. No Police. After Eden watches the DVD, a gruesome, horrifying surgery, she turns to the private criminal investigation agency, CORE, for help. Only she hadn't expected that help to come with a catch. Her former lover, Hudson Patterson, has been assigned to the case.

Hudson would rather have another CORE agent handle the investigation. Two years ago, he'd screwed things up with Eden...bad. And as more DVDs arrive, Eden and Hudson find themselves not only knee-deep in a twisted investigation, but forced to deal with their past, and the love they'd tried to deny.

Shadow of Vengeance
Book Three of the C.O.R.E. "Shadow" Trilogy

Welcome to Hell Week. You have seven days to find him...

At Wexman University, male students will do anything to get into a top fraternity. They'll prove their worth during Hell Week by participating in various physical, psychological and even juvenile pranks. But those shenanigans aren't so funny when pledges start disappearing. What kind of evil has stalked this small Michigan university for the past two decades? Theories range from obscene scientific experiments to grotesque satanic killings...but they're all wrong. The murdered boys serve a single purpose...the ultimate revenge.

Rachel Davis, forensic computer analyst for the private investigation agency CORE, has been itching to leave her desk behind and work in the field. When her brother Sean, a student at Wexman, is found beaten and his roommate kidnapped during Hell Week, she gets her chance. Only her boss insists former U.S. Secret Service Agent, Owen Malcolm, helps her with the investigation. Owen is the last person she wants on this assignment. She'd been secretly half in love with him for over four years, until the night he'd crushed her ego and destroyed her hopes for any kind of future with him.

For his own reasons, Owen refuses to risk becoming involved with a coworker. Now that he and Rachel are stuck working side by side to solve this perverse investigation, he's having a hard time fighting his attraction to her...an attraction he's tried to deny from the moment they met. But time is ticking. They have seven days to find the missing pledge and catch a killer. Seven days before the body count rises and the pledge ends up another victim of Hell Week.

Ultimate Kill
Book One of the Ultimate C.O.R.E. Trilogy

When the past collides with the present, the only way to ensure the future lies in the ultimate kill...

Naomi McCall is a woman of many secrets. Her family has been murdered and she's been forced into hiding. No one knows her past or her real name, not even the man she loves.

Jake Tyler, former Marine and the newest recruit to the private investigation agency, CORE, has been in love with a woman who never existed. When he learns about the lies Naomi has weaved, he's ready to leave her—until an obsessed madman begins sending her explosive messages every hour on the hour.

Innocent people are dying. With their deaths, Naomi's secrets are revealed and the truth is thrust into the open. All but one. Naomi's not sure if Jake can handle a truth that will change their lives. But she is certain of one thing—the only way to stop the killer before he takes more lives is to make herself his next victim.

Ultimate Fear
Book Two of the Ultimate C.O.R.E. Trilogy

When a deranged mother's grief drives her to replace her dead son over and over, obsession leads to murder...

Chicago detective Jessica Donavan will never stop looking for her missing daughter. Her obsession has destroyed her marriage, but the search is the only thing that helps keep her sane and her mind off of everything she's lost—her husband and her baby girl. When she uncovers a string of unsolved disappearances and reappearances of a number of baby boys, Jessica turns to her soon to be ex, Dante Russo, a former Navy SEAL turned investigator for the private agency, CORE, to help her fit together the pieces in this perplexing puzzle. But as Dante helps her, she realizes just how much she still craves his support—and his touch.

Dante is still in love with his wife and would do anything to have her back in his life again. He's been miserable since she left him to deal with the grief over their daughter's abduction, never understanding how much he grieves as well. When Jessica tells him about the case she's working, he jumps at the chance to take part in her investigation. He's hoping not only to save their marriage and ease his personal pain over the loss of their daughter, but to stop a serial kidnapper from taking another victim.

As Jessica and Dante work side by side, pregnant women begin to turn up missing or dead, and they start to uncover the consequences of another woman's unfathomable grief. The childless mother doesn't just want a baby. She wants a newborn straight from the womb.

And when forced to confront the dark and twisted perversion of a mother's obsession, can Jessica and Dante find their lives again...or merely more death?

Ultimate Prey
Book Three of the Ultimate C.O.R.E. Trilogy

When the hunter becomes the hunted...who will become the ultimate prey?

CORE agent Lola Tam has two things on her mind, quitting her job as a criminal investigator and baking a frozen pie for Thanksgiving dinner without burning it. But a midnight call forces a change of plans. Her boss and future stepfather, Ian Scott, has been kidnapped from his Florida vacation rental—along with her mother. The kidnapper's plan? Drop Ian and her mom in the Everglades and hunt them like animals. Terrified for her mom, Lola takes the bait and travels to Everglade City, Florida where she's determined to end the hunt before it begins.

Ryan Monahan, former Navy SEAL turned airboat captain is used to taking tourists through the Everglades, not guiding a sexy agent on a rescue mission. After spending years dealing with a past filled with guilt and regret, he needs a little action and adventure in his life—he needs to prove he could still be a hero. What he doesn't need? Falling for a woman he has no business wanting, especially when the hunt takes a deadly turn...

Psychic C.O.R.E. Series

Celeste Files: Unlocked
Book 1 Psychic C.O.R.E.

Some secrets should remain locked in the past...

Celeste Kain hasn't had a psychic vision in two years. After being brutally attacked while helping criminal investigation agency CORE stop a serial killer, her mind repressed her clairvoyant abilities. Married to CORE agent, John Kain, mother to their toddler, Olivia, and owner of an up-and-coming bakery, Celeste has been doing fine psychic-free. Only now the dead are using her body to tell their stories again...putting her new life and family at risk.

Haunted by a murdered woman, Celeste turns to a psychic mentor to learn how to control her gift, protect her family and bring justice to the dead. But the more she digs into the dead woman's past, the further she slips into the unknown, unlocking secrets literally worth killing for. As the body count rises, it becomes clear: someone in the dead woman's family is deeply, violently *wrong*. And Celeste needs to be careful, before she loses something more precious to her than her life.

Celeste Risinski, the heroine of Shadow of Danger (Book 1 C.O.R.E. Shadow Trilogy), is back with her own series. Join her as she learns how to deal with being a wife, mom, baker and...psychic investigator.

Celeste Files: Unjust
Book 2 Psychic C.O.R.E.

Dealing with the dead is murder...

Psychic Celeste Kain has two things on her mind, relaxing for a week in Florida with her husband, John, and making a baby. But a fishing trip turns her vacation into a nightmare when she reels in the body of a dead boat captain and accidentally unleashes an evil ghost who has one thing on his mind...revenge.

As the dead boat captain haunts Celeste, she looks deeper into his past and discovers that his murderer had done the world a favor. The ghost tormenting Celeste doesn't see it that way and will go to any length to avenge his death. If Celeste won't give him what he wants, he will take over her body and use her as a weapon...to kill her husband.

Contemporary Romances by Kristine Mason

Kiss Me

Pick Me

Love Me

About Kristine Mason

Kristine Mason is the bestselling author of the popular romantic suspense trilogies C.O.R.E. Shadow and Ultimate C.O.R.E. She is currently working on her next trilogy, C.O.R.E. Above the Law, along with a series of Psychic C.O.R.E. novellas.

Although Kristine has published a few contemporary romance novels, she focuses most of her energy on her romantic suspense stories, which she loves for their blend of dark mystery/suspense and sexy romance. She is fascinated with what makes people afraid, and is famous for her depraved villains whose crimes present massive obstacles for her heroes and heroines to overcome.

Kristine has a degree in journalism from Ohio State University and lives in Northeast Ohio with her husband, four kids, and two dogs. If she's not writing, she's chauffeuring kids, gardening, or collecting gnomes. Oh, and she makes a mean chocolate chip cookie!

Connect with Kristine on Facebook www.facebook.com/kristinemasonauthor, Twitter twitter.com/KristineMason7 or email her at authorkristinemason@gmail.com. You can also find out more about Kristine's books at www.kristinemason.net.

www.ingramcontent.com/pod-product-compliance
Lightning Source LLC
Chambersburg PA
CBHW072110250626
47159CB00007B/2382